MORE RAVE REVIEWS FOR VICTORIA ALEXANDER!

THE PRINCESS AND THE PEA

"The Princess and the Pea is an exciting update of the classic fairy tale. Another victorious triumph for Victoria Alexander!"

—*Affaire de Coeur*

"You'll believe fairy tales can come true after reading this endearing, engaging and highly entertaining love story. Victoria Alexander outdoes herself!"

—*Romantic Times*

"A dazzling, juicy romance. High praise for Ms. Alexander's clever version of The Princess and the Pea!"

—*Rendezvous*

YESTERDAY AND FOREVER

"A wonderful time-travel! Ms. Alexander's bittersweet story is truly a gem."

—*Romantic Times*

"Fascinating, irresistible, and humorous writing . . . Victoria Alexander has a writing style that leaves you wanting more."

—*Rendezvous*

"One of the best time-travel romance novels since the sub-genre first began appearing."

—*Affaire de Coeur*

"A charming, sexy, fun-filled trip through time with an engaging new writer who is bound to become a favorite."

—Barbara Bretton, bestselling author

TOO LATE

Pippa sighed up at him with a mad, undisguised longing she'd never dreamed existed. "Really."

"You are quite lovely, you know."

"Am I?" She shouldn't encourage him. It was not too late to stop.

"Indeed you are. Your hair—" he brushed an errant curl away from her face and her knees weakened at his touch, "—is the color of summer itself."

...just once.

"Are you a rake, sir?" She trembled at her bold words, shocked and excited.

He laughed. "In some circles, I suppose I have been called that. And you, my dear, are delightful."

"Then—" she swallowed hard. "Then perhaps you should wish to kiss me?" Now, it was definitely too late.

His eyes widened slightly, as if he were surprised by her innocent eagerness. Then he dipped his head toward hers. "I should like nothing better."

"Just once," she whispered.

"Just once."

Play It Again, SAM

VICTORIA ALEXANDER

LOVE SPELL BOOKS ◆ NEW YORK CITY

LOVE SPELL®

February 1998

Published by

Dorchester Publishing Co., Inc.
276 Fifth Avenue
New York, NY 10001

ISBN 0-505-52247-0

Printed in the United States of America.

*This book is dedicated to my long-distance e-mailing,
hand-holding, daily support group:
Rebecca Sinclair and all the Eclectics
Denise Dietz Wiley
Lori Handeland
Jan McDaniel
and
Mariah Stewart
Great writers and wonderful friends.*

A bug is a bug...

... is a bug.

Period.

I don't care what anybody tells ya, kid. If you were a bug in the last life, you're gonna be a bug in the next. Oh, ya might be a butterfly or ya might be a roach, but you're still gonna be a bug. It's as simple as that.

Yeah, yeah. I know all the talk about this reincarnation business. I know they say if ya were good in one life you'll come back as somethin' better. That story's been going around forever, probably started by some optimist on the bottom of the food chain. Well, take it from me, kid, it's all garbage.

Here's how it really works. I'm a dog now and I've always been a dog. Sometimes I get to be a really swell mutt or even a purebred but I've also lived out entire

11

lives in the streets. I'm telling ya, ya don't want to do that. Boy, that's tough. Scrounging for food. Fighting with rats. Grrrr. Gives me shivers just to talk about it. Nah. To live the good life ya gotta be a blue blood. A pampered pooch. Now that's livin'. I remember once I was a poodle. What a way to go. Aside from that stupid haircut . . .

Sorry, kid. What was I saying? Oh yeah. Reincarnation. You're just a pup, but think for a minute, do ya remember any other lives? No? Good for you. You're free and clear for this go round. No worries, no problems, no sweat.

What do I mean? It's kind of a quirk about this whole past lives thing. If ya don't remember nothin', it means ya don't have nothin' important to do this time around. It ain't easy to explain. There are rules, see?

Take humans, for example. They never remember other lives even though they keep running into the same people life after life. Now your animals don't remember unless they got a mission, a purpose, something they just gotta do. Cats are the exception. Damn cats always remember past lives. That's where that saying about them having nine lives comes from. They got more than nine. We all got more than nine. They just remember and they got long memories. Let me give ya a little warning about cats, kid: don't ever piss one off. They'll always get ya back. If not in this life, then in the next.

Yeah, I got a mission this time. I'd say I've been a well-behaved little mutt to come back like this. Here, I'll stand up so you can get a good look. What do ya *think? Pretty swell, eh? Not too big, not too small, great coat. Somebody in the park the other day called me a dust mop. What a jerk. I tried to give him a withering look but in this breed the best you can hope for is a less-than-enthusiastic grin. It's okay, though. I left him a little present where he'd least expect it.*

Heh heh heh.

Sheepdog? You got it all wrong, kid. I'm a Bearded Collie. They call me a Beardie. It's a good breed. Smart, quick and cute. I'm damn near irresistible. It's the same breed I was last time, back when all this started, nearly two hundred years ago. That's people years, ya know. In dog years it'd be . . . Never mind. Anyway, that's where this mission of mine began. It's a tough job but somebody's got to do it.

I don't know, it's a long story, sure ya want to hear it? Okay. Let me just get settled down here. There, that's better. Now, pass me the milkbones, kid, and keep 'em coming.

To start with, back then, they called me Samuel. But you can call me Sam.

Chapter One

Spring 1818

"Samuel! Samuel, come back here, you silly creature!" Philippa Morgan laughed and raced after the shaggy canine who cavorted amidst the rolling hills of Sussex as if he hadn't a care in the world. And no doubt the furry beast hadn't. He was not a dog given to bouts of melancholy.

"Where did the creature go?" Caroline Lyndon planted her hands on her hips and glared at her cousin. "Gracious, Pippa, the way you let that dog do exactly what he pleases, one would think you were the pet and he the master."

"Don't tell anyone, Caro." Pippa leaned closer in a confidential manner. "Samuel thinks so too."

"For goodness' sake." Caro sank down onto the grassy hillside and glared at her. "It's high time you put aside catering to that scruffy animal and concentrated on the important things in life."

"He's not scruffy."

As usual Caro ignored her, far too caught up in her own excitement to pay any heed to anyone else. Her brown eyes flashed with eagerness. "Only two days left, Pippa, just think of it."

Pippa collapsed onto the grass beside her and smiled weakly. "I am thinking of it."

"A London season. Finally. It feels as if we have waited forever for this."

"Forever." A sensation akin to illness brought on by damp weather fluttered in Pippa's stomach.

"We shall have such fun. All the parties and balls and routs." Caro stared dreamily off in the distance as if she could see the joys of London somewhere just beyond the horizon. "It will be glorious."

"Do you really think so?"

"Of course I do, you silly goose. It's our very first season and we shall simply have the best time. There's Almacks and the presentation at court and of course, our own coming out ball and . . . well, everything." Caro grinned. "I think these will be the most exciting months of our entire lives."

"I'm sure they will. Still and all . . ." Pippa wrinkled her nose. "Don't you find it a bit overwhelming?"

"Certainly not. We've had lessons in dance and deportment. We know exactly what is expected of a young lady in society, what we are permitted to do and what is forbidden." Caro nodded confidently. "We are most definitely ready."

"I suspect we are." Pippa forced all the enthusiasm she could muster into her voice.

Caro eyed her with exasperation. "I still do not understand why you are the least bit nervous about this."

"I don't either, not really." Pippa plucked at the bits of grass clinging to her skirts. "I suppose I'd much rather ease my way into society than be thrust upon it all at once. It simply seems impossible to be able to remember everything. All the rules and . . . well . . . to be completely honest, I simply cannot for the life of me remember what one is supposed to call the second son of a cousin of a duke once removed." She widened her eyes innocently.

"Why, you call him . . ." Caro glared. "Pippa, stop it right now."

"I am sorry. I couldn't resist." Pippa laughed and a reluctant smile quirked Caro's lips. "I do apologize. I shouldn't tease. To make up for it, I'll tell you my secret."

"Secret?" Caro leaned forward eagerly. "What secret?"

"Well." Pippa cast her gaze from side to side and lowered her voice to a whisper. "I must admit, somewhere, deep inside, I am looking forward to this too, at least a little."

Caro whooped in a manner no lesson in deportment ever taught. "I suspected as much." She threw her arms around Pippa and gave her a quick hug.

"I am so glad. We shall have such a marvelous time together."

Caro grinned and her dimples deepened. "And the gentlemen, Pippa, just think of the gentlemen."

Pippa shuddered. "I have no need to think of them."

"All of them looking for wives." Caro sighed in anticipation. "I want one that's handsome, of course, with a sizable income. Oh, twenty thousand a year at a minimum I should think."

"Why not thirty? Or fifty?"

Caro nodded, her dark curls bobbing around her head. "I shouldn't want to be greedy, although fifty would be nice. And a good, respectable title. At least an earl."

"Why not a marquess or a duke perhaps?"

"Indeed. A duke—" Caro slanted her an accusing glance. "You're bamming me again, aren't you?"

"Just a bit." Pippa laughed, and a moment later Caro joined in.

"Joke about it all you want, but we both know the only reason for a season at all is to find a good match."

"I daresay, you won't have any trouble. I suspect you'll be declared an incomparable, a diamond of the first water, and will have your choice of anyone."

"Oh, Pippa, don't be silly." Caro paused as if considering her cousin's words. "Do you really think so?"

"I have no doubt whatsoever." Confidence rang in Pippa's voice. Caro would indeed make her mark on society. Her looks alone would assure attention. Tall, with dark eyes and darker hair, the girl had a ripening figure that showed to full advantage in the low-cut, high-waisted fashion of the day.

"I suspect we both will," Caro said stoutly.

"Dearest, no one would possibly look at me with you around." The cousins did bear a certain resemblance in the shape of their eyes and tilt of their noses. But there the similarity ended thanks to their mothers choosing husbands at opposite ends of the spectrum in appearance, although the fathers of both girls did share a common, genial disposition.

"Nonsense. In point of fact, I believe together we will make an impact. With your fair coloring and my dark, we shall draw the attention of every man in London."

"Perhaps you will—"

"No, Pippa. *We* will." Caro studied her with an assessing eye. "Your hair is that lovely white-gold color. Your features are regular and really rather pert. And your eyes are the most remarkable shade of green."

"I think you're being kind. I know it's fashionable, but I've always felt far too pale to be truly attractive. I suspect I shall be rather more vivid as a ghost walking the halls of the manor than I am as a solid living being." Pippa heaved a heavy sigh. "Next to you, Caro, I am a watercolor faded in the sun beside a brightly painted portrait."

Caro laughed. "Don't be absurd. You're really quite charming. And I've always suspected men

19

adore women who are as dainty and petite as you are."

"I'm not dainty and petite. I'm short and thin." Pippa cast a rueful glance downward, then looked at her cousin's well-filled dress and grimaced. "Very well, petite."

Caro rolled her eyes in resignation, wrapped her arms around her knees and gazed out over the countryside. Pippa released a relieved breath. The question of appearance was an ongoing debate between the cousins, and while she truly appreciated Caro's encouraging comments she could not take them to heart. Oh, she did not believe herself to be completely unattractive, but in a very realistic sense, knew without question she could not compare with Caro. Still, it scarcely mattered anymore.

"Pippa." Caro's gaze still focused on a far-off point. Her voice was a shade too casual and Pippa's heart sank. Appearance wasn't the only continuing discussion between the two. "Have you spoken with Hugh recently?"

"A few days ago."

"Have you . . . perhaps . . . reconsidered your decision?"

"No."

Caro turned. Her gaze met and locked with Pippa's. "Why not?"

"I see no need to change my mind." Pippa clenched her jaw. "Hugh Winston will be an excellent husband."

"I'm certain he will, but—"

"His family's estate borders our own. I have

known Hugh all of my life. My parents, as well as his, have wanted this match nearly from the day I was born. They never said anything, but I believe they actually expected it. Besides, Hugh is his father's only heir. He will one day be the Earl of Winsleigh." She nudged Caro and grinned. "An earl, Caro. I shall be a countess. Isn't a respectable title one of the requirements you're looking for in a husband?"

"I want more than that and you well know it." Caro pressed her lips together in a firm line. "And you should too."

"No one is forcing me to marry Hugh. I may have been prodded a bit in his direction but this is entirely my decision. Mine and his. Caro, please listen to me. I do so want to make you understand." She cast her a pleading look. "In a very practical sense, everyone benefits from such a match. Eventually it means our properties will be merged, our wealth combined, our two families joined. It's very nearly perfect."

"But you don't love him."

"I did not notice love on the list of items you wished for in a husband. And I do love Hugh."

"As a brother perhaps. Or a friend."

"And no doubt with luck and time, it will grow to be much more." Pippa wrapped her arms around herself and stared out across the hills. "We already have a certain amount of affection between us. I was quite fond of him before he went off to school and—"

"You were a mere child."

"—even though he has lived these past years more in London than here, the sentiment remains. Many couples do not share even that much. And you must admit, he is a handsome man."

"But he doesn't make your heart race and your mouth dry and your hands tremble. He doesn't make you feel as if you could not bear to draw another breath on this earth unless he was with you. He doesn't make you want to sacrifice your very life to save his." Caro's eyes shone with the intensity of her words. "Don't you want a man who will make you feel all that?"

Pippa stared for a long moment, unable or unwilling to answer. A myriad of responses whirled in her head and an odd pain stabbed her at the thought of never knowing a love so deep you would surely die without it and gladly die for it.

She drew a steadying breath. "I want Hugh. We shall have a good life together."

Caro's voice softened. "It sounds very much as if you are not trying to convince me as much as yourself."

"No, Caro. I'm quite satisfied with my choice. This marriage is right for all concerned."

Caro looked as if she was about to say something more but thought better of it. She shrugged. "Well, at least your betrothal will not be announced until the end of the season. We shall still have London together."

Pippa smiled, relieved at the change of subject. "And we will have a wonderful time. I even promise to throw myself into the spirit of each and every festivity and enjoy myself."

"The soirees, the balls, the routs?" Caro raised a brow. "Everything?"

"Everything. You have my word on it."

"And do I also have your word that if a handsome stranger sweeps you off your feet and offers you undying love you shall not cast him aside without due consideration?"

"Caro." Annoyance pulled her brows together. "I have had quite—"

"I am sorry. I shall try not to bring it up again." She scrambled to her feet. "I suspect someone at the manor will be wondering where we are, although, between my mother and yours, there is scarcely any necessity for us."

Pippa laughed. "They do seem to be intent on packing everything we could ever possibly require during our stay in town."

"We shall no doubt need a fleet of carriages to move the household items alone." Caro shaded her eyes and scanned the countryside. "Where do you suppose that animal of yours has gotten himself to?"

"He'll be back," Pippa said with a nod. "Samuel always comes back. He really is a very good dog, you know."

Caro snorted. "He's a big, mangy beast. I simply cannot believe you're bringing him with us to London."

"Samuel will love London."

"But will London love Samuel?"

"Everyone loves Samuel." Pippa grinned. "Except you."

"I, too, would love him if he'd restrain from leaping all over me with wet, sloppy abandon."

"He adores you."

"That type of adoration I can well do without, thank you."

Pippa laughed. "Why don't you go ahead. I'll find Samuel and I shall be home soon."

"Very well." Caro turned and started toward the manor, hidden behind the rolling hills and meadows. She tossed a casual wave behind her and strode off.

"Samuel?" Pippa got to her feet, her gaze skimming the area. "Samuel?" Let's see. When last she spotted Samuel, he was headed in the opposite direction to Caro's. She nodded to herself and started off after him. Surely she would catch up to him soon.

"Samuel?" Where had the creature disappeared to? One thing she could always depend on was Samuel's return. He was a very good dog, after all, if perhaps a bit overspirited.

The same could be said for Caro as well. Pippa grinned at the thought of Caro's reaction to being compared to the dog. Still, it was an accurate comparison. Why, hadn't Pippa heard her own father say that very same thing?

". . . yes, I've no doubt Caro will make a good match," Lord Morgan, Viscount Morgan, had said. "She is a bit overspirited but marriage will settle her down."

Pippa sighed. She did so wish to have just a bit of Caro's excess spirit. Pippa could best be described as, well, good.

". . . as her father, frankly I'm quite relieved Pippa does not share her cousin's temperament," Papa had said. "Pippa is a good girl. Never a problem with that one. Why, she'll make an excellent, biddable wife."

Good. The word alone was enough to make her shudder, though she admitted it only to herself. Good girls lived pleasant but boring lives. Good girls made good matches with affectionate if rather dull husbands. Good girls did precisely what was expected of them, never once experienced the thrill of the unknown, married earls and became countesses.

Overspirited girls teased the thin edge of ruin and had all the wrong kinds of men dropping at their feet with passionate promises on their lips and desire burning in their eyes. Overspirited girls shared kisses with men they had no intention of marrying. And overspirited girls lived fast-paced lives full of slightly dangerous adventures and even a touch of scandal, and often they too became countesses. Caro would have such a life.

Pippa was a good, biddable girl and was to marry Hugh. Exactly as expected.

"Samuel!" The sharp tone in her voice surprised her and she realized it had nothing to do with the dog.

Did she indeed regret her decision? No, of course not. Hugh would make an excellent husband. Besides, the season did not come with a guarantee. There were no certainties of making a match at all, let alone one as good as hers and Hugh's. And there were no promises of love.

Still . . . wouldn't it be exciting to feel all those things for a man that Caro had talked about? The kind of man she knew only in her dreams, late into the night, when she slept a sleep so deep she shed all weight of goodness and danced beneath the stars clad in little more than a whisper, held tight in the arms of a faceless, mysterious true love. They were dreams so intense that she'd wake with her heart pounding and her flesh still warm from the heat of his body next to hers and a yearning ache so strong she marveled that she could bear the pain of it. And she'd lie for long hours in the dark wondering if she was indeed good or simply scared.

What would it be like, just once, not to be good or biddable? To be the kind of girl who teased the thin edge of ruin? To be wide awake and bold and willing to taste, if just for a moment, the sinful delights given only to those with the courage to defy convention and flirt with scandal?

Would it be so terribly wrong, just once?

Abruptly, the sound of padded paws in rustling grass jerked her from her odd reverie and she turned just in time to see a ball of fur barreling toward her.

"Samuel!" Pippa grinned at the sheer exuberance of the dog. Caro was right: he could be overwhelming. "What have you been up to?"

The dog grinned and flung himself at her.

"Samuel!" Pippa thrust out her hands to halt his forward lunge, but the animal slammed into her with an unexpected force, knocking her from her feet. Pippa's hands flailed at her sides in a desperate attempt to stop her haphazard tumble down the hill—a hill far less gentle from this position than when her feet were planted firmly on its slope. The dog yipped and gamboled around her toppling form as if this was yet another game for mistress and beast. Grass ripped through her fingers and she struggled to grab hold of anything that could halt her out-of-control spill, until finally she rolled to a shuddering stop.

Pippa lay on the ground, her heart thudding, gasping to catch her breath. She stared upward, stunned. Goodness, was she hurt? Had she suffered a serious injury?

At once Samuel's face filled her vision. Just inches from her own, the dog's expression appeared both troubled and quizzical, as if he wondered if this was play or cause for concern.

"Now see what you've done, you naughty creature." She groaned and glared at the unrepentant animal. "I suspect I shall be extremely sore for the next few days."

Samuel smiled down at her. "Are you quite certain you're not hurt?"

"Samuel?" Pippa eyes widened in disbelief and then she quickly squeezed them closed tight. Perhaps she had suffered some harm after all to believe Samuel had acquired the gift of speech. Had she smacked her head as she fell and failed to note the severity of the blow? Was she now faced with the horrible prospect of losing her faculties all together? Still, in a practical sense, a talking dog would make madness a bit easier to endure. Odd though, she'd never imagined Samuel to have a voice quite so resonant and rich.

"Do you need assistance?"

Pippa clenched her fists. No doubt the way to face insanity was head-on. She swallowed hard and cautiously opened her eyes.

Samuel's shaggy head was gone, replaced by the face of a stranger. He bent beside her, brows furrowed with concern, lips pressed together in a worried line, anxiety coloring eyes as deep and dark as the skies before a storm.

"Samuel?"

"Samuel?" The man's frown deepened. "I fear you are somewhat confused. There is no one here but you and I and this furry canine."

"You're not Samuel."

"Who is Samuel?"

"Samuel is my dog."

The stranger raised a cautious brow. "You believed your dog to be inquiring about your condition?"

She struggled to prop herself up on her elbows. Indignation colored her words. "He is an extremely thoughtful dog."

For a moment Pippa glared at this intruder who had the nerve to question the character of her animal and abruptly realized how very ridiculous the entire discussion was. She bit back a giggle and a roguish smile tugged at the corners of the man's lips.

"I did not mean to insult him. I am certain he is not only thoughtful but also good-natured and obedient." The smile grew into a grin. "And no doubt a charming conversationalist as well."

Pippa laughed. "Well, he is quite prone to discussions of a governmental nature. The current debates in Parliament, policies of the foreign ministry, that sort of thing."

"I see." His words were solemn, but a twinkle shone in his eye. "He is a political pup, then? Is he a conservative canine as well?"

"I haven't the faintest idea." She shook her head in a serious manner. "He is surprisingly reluctant to discuss his own views." She leaned toward him confidentially. "I suspect he fears offending those who might be a potential source of treats someday. Purveyors of bones and such."

The stranger laughed, a warm, wonderful sound that seemed to reach inside her to touch her soul. "What a clever creature." He rose to his feet. "And as for you"—he reached out his hand—"I cannot guarantee the same stimulating discussion as your Samuel, but may I offer you some assistance?"

"Thank you." She kept her voice prim and placed her hand in his. He pulled her upright in a smooth, swift movement.

"I daresay, you—" Without warning, Samuel leapt at her as if to welcome her back to her feet and she stumbled against her rescuer. He caught her easily in hard, strong arms.

"There, now." He smiled down at her. Goodness, the man was certainly much taller than she'd expected. Her heart skipped a beat at the proximity of his body to hers. How could she have failed to note the striking features of his handsome face? His chin was square and strong, his nose straight and noble, his lips full and firm and his stormy eyes were filled with humor and light. His hair was the color of night and cut in the first stare of fashion. His clothes too were the epitome of well dressed. He was obviously a gentleman. Abruptly she regretted the serviceable but worn day dress she had tossed on this morning. "Are you quite all right?"

She stared at him, her gaze meshing with his. She'd never been held like this by a man before. Even Hugh had not dared take such liberties. She should step out of his embrace now, immediately, at once, but somehow she couldn't seem to move. It was as if she were mesmerized by his nearness, bewitched by the subtle but heady scent of man and heat, captivated by a vague but compelling promise of something as yet unknown and trapped as well by a strange sense of comfort and peace. Had she hit her head harder than she thought? Or was this yet another dream?

He pulled his brows together as if he knew the wellspring of emotions his touch aroused. As if he too shared her confusion.

"Yes. I'm—" She swallowed hard. "I'm fine. Really."

"Really?" His gaze searched her face, settling on her lips. Her breath caught. Surely he wouldn't kiss her? They had scarcely met. She did not even know his name. It was extremely improper. Scandalous in fact. He was no doubt a scoundrel of the worst sort even to consider taking such license. And yet . . .

. . . *just once.*

A recklessness she'd never known before seized her. Was it possible, given her thoughts before his appearance, that their meeting was no mere coincidence? Could this indeed be the hand of fate? Or destiny?

. . . *just once.*

She sighed and looked up at him with a mad, undisguised longing she'd never dreamed existed. "Really."

"You are quite lovely, you know."

"Am I?" She shouldn't encourage him. It was not too late to stop.

"Indeed you are. Your hair," he said as he brushed an errant curl away from her face and her knees weakened at his touch, "is the color of summer itself."

. . . *just once*

"Are you a rake, sir?" She trembled at her bold words, shocked and excited.

He laughed. "In some circles, I suppose I have been called that. And you, my dear, are delightful."

"Then—" She swallowed hard. "Then perhaps you should wish to kiss me?" Now, it was definitely too late.

His eyes widened slightly, as if he were surprised by her innocent eagerness. Then he dipped his head toward hers. "I should like nothing better."

"Just once," she whispered.

"Just once." The words skimmed along her lips in a touch so light she wondered if she would swoon from the teasing brush of his mouth on hers. Her hands crept around his neck and he pulled her close. His kiss deepened, his breath mingling with hers and she wanted to melt against him and lose herself in his embrace. In a far corner of her mind not fogged by remarkable and newly discovered sensations, she marveled at the odd stirrings this stranger triggered within her. Stirrings at once both welcoming and forbidding. Stirrings even the touch of the man she was to wed did not arouse. Why, Hugh's polite kisses were not nearly so stimulating—

"Oh, my." She pulled back and stared wide-eyed at the man whose bemused expression no doubt matched her own. "I have never done anything like this before. It is quite improper, you know."

He heaved a deep sigh of regret. "Yes, indeed, I have known that from the beginning." He quirked a slightly lopsided smile. "I simply hoped you didn't."

"I do. I don't know what came over me. I don't know why I failed to remember . . ." A sense of intense yearning and familiarity swept through her and she struggled from the strength of it. "Perhaps—" She couldn't quite seem to catch her breath. "Perhaps, since we are both agreed as to the impropriety of, well, this, you should, um, release me."

"Of course. Thoughtless of me not to have realized that myself." Did he hesitate before opening his arms? For just the barest second, did he appear reluctant to let her go? Was there a light of regret in his eyes? No, of course not. And surely she did not experience a strange sense of abandonment when he unwrapped his arms from around her.

She stepped back, at once at a loss for words. What did one say to a handsome stranger who had literally swept you into his arms and kissed you as you had never been kissed before? And at your invitation, no less. Heat crept up her face. How could she have been so . . . so . . . overspirited?

"Beautiful day, is it not?" she blurted out. *Beautiful day?* Surely she did not comment on the weather?

"Indeed." He nodded firmly, as if the weather was of extreme interest. "It is a fine spring day."

"Oh, yes. Springtime in England is always, quite, um, fine." She groaned to herself. *Springtime is fine?* What a goose he'd think her. And not just any goose but a wanton goose. With any luck, a huge fissure would open up beneath her feet and she would sink far out of sight of spring in England and all its glories.

"Oh, especially in England." Teasing laughter sparked in his eye. Chagrin turned to irritation. What a vexing man he was. Here she was struggling to overcome mortification brought on by her scandalous behavior, and he thought it amusing.

"Yes, well, indeed." Why couldn't she get even one intelligent word out? There were scores of things she could ask him. Indeed, things she should ask him. Who was he? Where was he from? Was he staying at a nearby estate or had he moved to the neighborhood? Did they share mutual acquaintances? Friends? Interests? Did he have a dog? Once again, heat flushed her cheeks at the thought of one interest she already suspected they shared.

"The dog seems to like it." He nodded toward Samuel, who studied them from a distance. The animal appeared pensive, as if trying to decide if he did indeed like what he saw or not. Well, it was certainly too late for that, since it was clearly his fault that anything had occurred in the first place.

"Likes what?"

"The day. The fine, English spring day." He pressed his lips together tight as if fighting to hold back a chuckle at her expense.

At once her senses cleared. She did not appreciate being the subject of a joke, even if she did deserve it. "Of course he does. He's a dog. Dogs always enjoy a good romp on a nice day. Especially on a fine, English spring day. Now, if you will excuse us."

She pursed her lips and let out a strong, shrill whistle. Samuel's ears perked up and he bounded toward her.

"Excellent." The stranger grinned in appreciation. "I haven't heard such an outstanding whistle since my boyhood."

"Thank you." She raised her chin. "I spent long days as a child perfecting it. "It's a skill I cherish."

"As well you should."

"Samuel. Come on, boy." The dog loped up beside

her. She cast the stranger her best, aloof gaze, the very one she'd been practicing for London, and smiled in the condescending manner she assumed the most fashionable ladies of society used. "If you will excuse me."

Again, the man looked as if he was barely stifling a laugh.

"My lady." He took a deep bow, then straightened and clasped her hand, pulling it to his lips. His gaze caught and trapped hers. His eyes smoldered with amusement—and something more. He turned her hand palm up and placed a kiss as light as a breath in the center. His gaze never broke from hers. She wondered why, at this very moment, she didn't simply melt into a small puddle and trickle away down the grassy hill. "If you ever need my assistance again, even for so simple a matter as pulling you to your feet, I shall be at your service. Like your faithful Samuel. You need do little more"—he grinned and she thought her knees would buckle—"than whistle."

He dropped her hand, nodded and then turned and strode off in the direction of a neighboring estate. Her wits left with him. She could only stare in bemusement.

Samuel nuzzled her hand and absently she stroked his head. Goodness, she certainly was not at all used to such adventures. Especially such improper adventures. Was this what was to be expected if one was overspirited? Is this what London would be like? Full of rakes and rogues? There was no question this man was both. Why, men who weren't simply could not have shoulders that broad, or a stride that long, or a kiss that polished. It would, no doubt, be best not to mention this particular encounter to either her parents or Hugh. No, most definitely not to Hugh. Hugh would never understand the deep longings of a girl good and proper and biddable. A girl expected to make an excellent wife.

She watched the stranger's figure grow smaller in the distance. Who was he? Not that it mattered of course. She would never see him again. No indeed. She turned and started toward home. She'd only wanted to know what it would be like to be something she wasn't in the first place. Something she would never be. Why, he was almost incidental to the entire incident. An afterthought. Nothing more.

Even so, she glanced back over her shoulder, and a tiny part of her ached when she found him completely out of sight. What an intriguing man. The kind of man a girl's dreams were made of. Her dreams. The thought drew her up short and her stride faltered. No, not her dreams, of course. Never hers. Not even dreams late in the night when the burden of goodness vanished into the dark and lovers danced together as one with only the stars to bear witness. Even in her own mind the denial had a vague ring of falsehood about it.

"Come along, Samuel, let's go home." The dog trotted by her side and she kept up a brisk pace, all in an effort to stop the thoughts and emotions she did not particularly wish to examine. Thoughts and a lingering memory of a slightly lopsided smile, eyes the color of stormy skies and a forbidden kiss that must last her a lifetime. A kiss she would only know . . .

   . . . just once.

Chapter Two

"Samuel, get down at once, you naughty dog!"

"Bloody beast," Hugh said under his breath, hoping Pippa would not hear his inadvertent comment. For reasons he simply could not fathom, she adored the despicable creature. Hugh couldn't abide him. And judging by the gleam in the brute's eye, the feeling was mutual.

"Oh, dear, Hugh, I am sorry." Pippa grabbed the dog's collar and pulled him back. "I suspect he's simply glad to see you." She flashed Hugh a quick smile and at once his irritation vanished. "As am I. Come along, Samuel." She half-dragged, half-pulled the animal to the door of the parlor. "Collins? There you are. Would you take Samuel, please?"

The butler's words were indistinguishable from

the recesses of the hallway in the London mansion Pippa's family shared with Caroline's. It was too much to hope that Pippa would ask the servant to dispose of the damnable animal permanently. No matter. Once they were wed, Samuel could well become the victim of a tragic accident or simply disappear without a trace. Hugh smiled to himself. The dog would not be an irritant to him in the future.

"There now." Pippa turned from the door and brushed a tendril of white-gold hair away from her finely boned face. "I do apologize for Samuel, Hugh. I don't know what gets into him around you. It's quite odd. Samuel likes everyone."

"No doubt."

Pippa stepped closer and Hugh's throat clenched. Lord, the girl was beautiful. Her skin glowed like fine porcelain, her green eyes pools of color in the purity of her face. Small in stature, she was as ethereal as a dream, as delicate as a wish, as exquisite as desire. His desire.

He picked up her hand and brushed his lips against it. "I have missed you, my dear."

"And I, you." She smiled up at him with an innocence that tightened his stomach. He stifled the impulse to pull her into his arms and ravish her right here, right now. No, he had waited years to claim her as his wife. He could wait a few months more.

Still, he held her hand a moment longer and gazed into the green eyes that had haunted his nights since the moment he realized Pippa the child had become Miss Philippa Morgan and very much a woman. "I thought to wait until you had settled in here in London before I called on you but I must admit the delay to see you again was interminable."

"Really, Hugh." She laughed, the sound akin to bells shivering through his veins. "You are such a tease. But I do so appreciate your thoughtfulness." Gently, she withdrew her hand. "And your timing is excellent. We arrived two days hence and, while we were quite at odds and ends in the beginning, we do seem to be rather nicely organized now.

"It's really quite amazing to watch my mother and my aunt, you know. Together they are simply whirlwinds of efficiency." Pippa sighed and shook her head in a show of regret. "I daresay I shall never be as good a household manager as either of them."

Hugh drew his brows together in mock concern. "Oh dear, Pippa, that will not do. Not at all. There is but one solution to this." Abruptly he grinned. "We shall have to have a great number of very efficient servants."

"Do you think there are that many servants in the entire world?"

"I have no idea," he said solemnly. "We will simply have to look into it."

"We will indeed." Pippa laughed and Hugh joined her. She turned to perch on the edge of a silk-covered settee. "And how do you find London this year?"

"London is London. I once thought it was the center of the universe until I realized my responsibilities lie primarily with the family estate. Now"—

41

he settled beside her—"very little seems to change here from visit to visit. Except, of course, for this year. This season London has a totally new charm all its own."

"Does it really?"

"Indeed it does." His gaze trapped hers. "This year you are here and all the other treasures of London pale in comparison."

"Hugh!" Pippa's eyes widened in surprise. "You must stop saying such things. You shall quite turn my head."

"Ah, my dear, but I wish to turn your head."

"Goodness, why?" She tilted her face in that unique way she had that reminded him of a rare bird studying a flower. "You have never resorted to such extreme flattery before."

"Before, we were in the country and I had nothing to fear from other suitors for your hand."

"But you have my hand, Hugh. We have agreed to wed after the season."

"Agreed, yes, but nothing is as yet official. An announcement has not been made publicly. You could in fact change your mind." He leaned toward her in a confidential manner. "London is full of rakes and scoundrels who would like nothing better than a flirtation with a young woman of beauty and good character and fine family. I am merely trying to beat them to the mark."

Pippa waved his words away. "What utter nonsense you're spouting today. I would never have thought it of you."

"What can I say?" He heaved an overly dramatic

sigh. "You have stolen my heart and I live in fear that another man—"

"One of those rakes or scoundrels, no doubt."

"Exactly. One of those rakes or scoundrels could steal your affection and then I would surely die of despair."

"Do not be absurd." Pippa laughed. "We are to be married."

"But not for months. Pippa—" He slid closer and took her hand, catching her gaze with his. "Let us not wait. Let me talk to your father again. Today. We could announce our plans immediately. Better still, let us wed. At once."

Pippa's green eyes widened. "Hugh, I—"

"I can procure a special license. Or we could be in Scotland by this evening." Urgency gripped him and he tightened his hold on her hand. "I adore you, Pippa. The very thought that I could lose you—"

"You won't—"

"I could not bear it, my dear. I cannot imagine my life without you in it." Restraint, built up over years of wanting her, cracked within him. Desire, stark and absolute, swept through his blood and he pulled her into his arms. She stared at him, astonishment flushing her cheeks pink. "I need you, Pippa. I want you as my wife. Now and always."

He crushed his lips to hers, smothering the small gasp of surprise that left her mouth slightly open, soft and yielding beneath his. He pressed her closer, so close he could feel her exquisite breasts heave against him with every breath. He hardened at her nearness, passion vanquishing any rational thought, leaving only the mindless insanity of need too long denied.

"Hugh!" She wrenched her lips from his, her hands pushing hard against his chest. He ignored her, caught fast in the haze of unrelenting desire that gripped his flesh and his mind. Lord in heaven, he wanted her. Wanted her naked and thrashing beneath him. Wanted her to weep with aching for him the way he ached for her until she begged and pleaded with him to take her. Take her innocence and her body and her soul. And make her finally and irrevocably his and his alone.

"Hugh!" Her voice rang on the sharp edge of panic and he stilled, desperately struggling for control. Damnation, how close had he come to taking her right here? How could he be such a fool? He released her and drew a deep breath.

Confusion shone in her eyes. "Gracious, Hugh, I scarce—"

"Forgive me." He plowed a shaky hand through his hair. "I don't know what possessed me."

Pippa stared, eyes wide with . . . what? Fear perhaps? Disbelief? Disgust? "I daresay, I—"

"No, Pippa, please." He pulled himself to his feet and turned away, stepping quickly to a table bearing a convenient decanter of brandy, and poured a glass with an unsteady hand. He pulled a long, deep swallow. The bite of the liquor burned off the last vestiges of his irrational behavior and restored his composure. It would not do to scare her. She was so fragile, so pure, so naive. "Please accept my heartfelt apologies. I have no excuse for my behavior. I am merely a man entranced by the presence of his future wife."

"Entranced?" Pippa's crystal laugh echoed around him and he swiveled toward her in surprise. Her eyes twinkled and amusement colored her voice. "I never dreamed you were entranced. How could you keep such a thing from me?"

Relief brought a smile to his face. She was neither afraid nor offended at his foolish actions. He exhaled a breath he didn't know he held and muttered more to himself than to her, "It has not been easy."

Her eyes widened. "Why, Hugh, you are serious, aren't you?"

"Indeed I am, my dear," he said, forcing a casual note to his voice. "But who would not be? I suspect you shall make quite an impression on even the most jaded of society's members this season."

"Now I know you're not serious. I never dreamed you were such a tease."

"Yes, well . . ." Hugh took another sip of the quelling liquor.

"I daresay it will be Caro who is declared incomparable this season. She is far prettier than I and far more dashing as well."

"Dashing is not at all what society expects of a proper young lady of good breeding."

"My goodness, Hugh." Surprise colored Pippa's voice. "You needn't sound so stuffy."

"You may call my views stuffy if you wish, but Caro has always struck me as the type of chit prone to scandal. I daresay with all the temptations of a

45

London season, Caro's parents had best keep an eye on their offspring until she can be suitably married and settled."

A frown creased Pippa's forehead. "She is a bit overspirited."

"Overspirited?" Hugh snorted. "You are far too kind to her, Pippa. I would term her behavior as quite often beyond the bounds of propriety."

"I wouldn't say—"

"No my dear, you wouldn't. And your loyalty to your cousin is admirable. Nonetheless"—Hugh shrugged in disdain—"overspirited is not a desired quality in a young lady or a wife."

"She does seem to have a great deal of fun." A wistful note underlay her words.

He narrowed his eyes. Surely Pippa did not admire her exuberant cousin? That would not do. Not at all. Thank God the chit and her family lived a good two days' travel from Pippa and visited only once or twice a year. While he had not spent much time in Caro's company, he had the distinct impression she did not care for him or his match with her cousin. Her influence on Pippa would have to be watched and watched closely.

He chose his words with care. "I do not wish you to take what I am about to say in the wrong way. My only concern is for you and you alone."

Pippa stared. "What on earth do you mean?"

"London during the season, especially a young lady's first season, is an extremely exciting place."

"Yes?"

"But it can be fraught with hazards for those inexperienced in the nuances and undercurrents of society."

She nodded knowingly. "Oh, we are back to the rakes and scoundrels again."

"Indeed, among other perils. I simply think," he said, pinning her with his sternest gaze, "it would be wise if you distanced yourself somewhat from your cousin. If perhaps you and she went your own separate ways in as much as it is possible."

Pippa rose to her feet. "Hugh, how could you say such a thing?"

"I am simply thinking of your best interests." He noted the imperious tone in his voice but dismissed it as necessary. It was not too soon to impress upon his future wife the importance of acknowledging his counsel and acquiescing to his wishes. "I have no desire to see the woman I intend to marry touched with even the faintest brush of scandal."

A spark flared in her emerald eyes. "Caro has done nothing scandalous."

"Not yet, my dear." He shrugged. "But the possibility, the very real possibility, is ever present with a girl like your cousin."

"You cannot be certain of that."

"Oh, but I can. I have seen countless others precisely like Caro in their first season. Green girls straight from the schoolroom, whose exuberant natures have led them quickly down the path to scandal and ruin. I do not want to see you dragged along with her."

"I have no intention of being dragged anywhere." An attractive flush colored her cheeks.

"Excellent. Then you understand the wisdom of following my guidance in this matter."

"I most certainly do not!"

"Pippa." Hugh glared. "You are to be my wife and I expect you to behave as such. That behavior includes following my wishes regarding the company of your cousin."

"I am not your wife yet, Hugh!" Pippa raised her chin, anger etched into the stiff lines of her body. "And I resent being treated as if I haven't a brain in my head."

Hugh heaved a heavy sigh. "I do not think I was—"

"You most certainly were. And I will not stand for it!"

Hugh stared with disbelief. Rebellion? From Pippa? "I scarcely feel—"

"I think you have made your feelings all too clear. Now, perhaps, you should listen to mine." Pippa's voice rang with an ire he never dreamed possible. "I am not a fool, Hugh—"

"I never—"

"Nor am I so feebleminded as to blindly stumble into disgrace like an unwitting lamb being led to the slaughter."

"I didn't—"

"But you did." Fire he'd never seen before shown in her eyes. "You have assumed that I am a ninny who can be easily led astray. I am made of far sterner stuff than that."

"So I see." Unease gripped his gut.

"Furthermore, I quite disagree with your assessment of my cousin and I think you do her a grave disservice. She is a bit more enthusiastic than perhaps is ideal, but she is not foolish. Caro well understands the rules of behavior and I do not believe she will come to a ruinous end. Beyond that—" Pippa squared her shoulders and glared. "She is not merely my cousin but my dearest friend as well. And I shall not abandon her nor shall I deny myself the pleasure of her company."

Hugh stared, speechless. Apparently he had made a significant error in broaching the subject of Caro. Pippa had never shown such pique. Perhaps her cousin's influence had already done irreparable damage. Or perhaps he did not know his beloved as well as he thought.

Very well. He drew a long, steadying breath. It was no doubt time for a graceful retreat.

"I did not mean to overset you, my dear. I am concerned for your reputation, nothing more. Perhaps I was too hasty in my assessment of Caro's temperament. It appears another apology is called for." He cast her a hopeful smile. "Do you forgive me?"

Pippa studied him for a moment, then nodded, the anger easing out of her with a dispelled breath. "Of course I do. You simply do not know her as well as I. And I admit I can see where you might draw the wrong conclusions as to her character." She stepped toward him and placed her hand on his arm.

"She may surprise you, you know. Why, here in London, Caro could well be the model of decorum." A slight smile lifted the corners of her mouth and the teasing light returned to her eyes.

"As you said, I do not know her as you do. Is there a chance of that?"

"Certainly." Her smile broadened. "Slim, no doubt, but a chance."

He laughed with relief.

"You needn't worry about her. Or about me." Sincerity shone in her eyes. "I am, after all, to be your wife. I have as little desire for scandal as you do."

"Very well." He nodded. "I shall consider the matter closed. And I shall learn to trust both the wisdom and the virtue of my future bride." He took her hand and feathered his lips across it. "Now then. It is nearing the hour when all of London takes it into their heads to ride through the park in a quite impressive parade of carriages and distinguished persons. Would you care to accompany me?"

"Oh, Hugh." Excitement rang in her voice. "I should love to go."

"Go where?" Caro swept into the room in a flurry of silken skirts and a flutter of annoying enthusiasm. "Where are we going?"

Hugh clenched his teeth. "Miss Lyndon."

Caro flicked him a dismissive glance. "Lord Winsleigh."

"Gracious, the two of you needn't be so formal with each other." Pippa crossed her arms and glared. "Why, we are all to be members of the same family soon enough."

"Pity," Caro said, so softly Hugh was certain it slipped by Pippa altogether.

"So I should think it's past time for you both to get to know each other better. Hugh?"

"Quite." He forced a tight smile and nodded at the irritating chit. "Caro."

"Hugh." She cast him a disdainful look then turned to her cousin. "Now then, where are we going?"

"*We* are going for a ride in the park." Hugh said. *Alone.*

Caro's eyes lit up. "What fun. I should like nothing better than a ride in the park. It sounds quite delightful."

"Then you must accompany us." Pippa's gaze sought his, a slight warning note in her voice. "She is welcome to join us, isn't she, Hugh?"

"Of course." Hugh struggled to keep his tone cool.

Triumph gleamed in Caro's eye. She fluttered her lashes at him. "If you are certain I shan't be in the way?"

Lord, he wanted to slap the victorious smirk from her face. This bit of baggage needed someone to take her in hand and put her firmly in her place. With force if necessary. A satisfying image of the lovely Caro whimpering at his feet, submissive and terrified, flashed through his mind. He smiled slowly. "Quite certain."

His thoughts must have shown on his face. Caro's eyes widened with what? A touch of fear perhaps? Excellent. Fear would keep her in check and temper her influence on Pippa.

"Very well." Pippa's eyes sparkled with anticipation and she led the way out of the room. "I'm confident we shall all have a grand time."

"As am I," he murmured, too low to catch Pippa's attention, but Caro threw him a sharp glance.

"Collins, would you—oh dear!" Pippa tottered backward, jostled by the flea-bitten bag of fur she called a dog. The vile creature cavorted about her skirts with the unbridled enthusiasm of a small child or a lunatic. "Samuel!"

Pippa's laughter filled the hall. Hugh managed a stiff smile. Blasted beast. When they were wed . . .

"I daresay Samuel would enjoy an outing as much as the rest of us. Poor dear has been cooped up for far too long." Caro's voice carried a suspicious innocence. "I should think a ride in the park would do him a world of good."

"What a wonderful idea, Caro." Delight simmered in Pippa's voice. "Samuel would love it. Could we bring him along, Hugh?"

A muscle clenched at the back of his jaw, but he kept his voice light. "I don't think a dog as, shall we say, energetic as Samuel quite belongs in a carriage."

Pippa's expression fell. "Dear, I hadn't thought—"

"But once we get to the park, he can always run alongside us." Caro shot him a flash of triumph. She obviously knew how much he disliked Pippa's pet.

"Of course." Pippa clapped her hands together. "It will be perfect. Oh, Hugh, do say we can bring him? Please?"

Could he deny her anything? One glance into the

deep forest of her eyes and he was lost. "As you wish."

A whirlwind of chaos erupted in the front entryway between laughing girls and cavorting dogs and the odd, scurrying servant assisting with wraps and bonnets and cloaks. Hugh bit back a disapproving frown and reminded himself of the need for patience. Pippa would be his soon enough and then there would be little, if any, contact with her impudent cousin and no possibility of any detrimental effects on his wife's behavior.

He escorted the girls through the massive front doorway and out into a typical London spring afternoon, with a touch of chill in the air and just enough sunshine to make one believe in the promise of warmer days to come. Hugh glanced at Pippa's shining face and his heart turned over in his chest. He gripped her hand, tiny and warm through the fabric of their gloves, and helped her into his elegant barouche, the top folded back in honor of the fine weather. At once he regretted the odd stroke of bad luck that had led him to select this carriage instead of the smaller gig he normally would have chosen for an outing in the park. With the gig accommodating only two people, he could have legitimately left Caro and the beast behind.

Pippa smiled up at him and squeezed his hand, and his annoyance vanished. Soon she would be his. Her smile, her touch, her presence, would be reserved for him and him alone. He'd make certain of it.

"Hugh?" Caro's bright tone interrupted his

thoughts and reluctantly he released Pippa and turned to the other girl. Caro extended her hand and he assisted her into the carriage. A hint of smugness teased the smile on her lovely face. No doubt she knew full well she had intruded on his plans. Once more a vision of her cowering before him brought a smile to his face. Caro jerked her hand from his, as if the image in his head had somehow heated his flesh and singed her own. She cast him a quick glare, then perched next to Pippa, leaving Hugh the opposite seat facing the girls. Not at all what he'd had in mind.

"Samuel." Pippa patted her lap and the creature leapt into the carriage, pushing past Hugh in a most unruly manner and plopping onto the seat across from the girls. The dog stared at Hugh with what could only be described as a satisfied grin, as if the animal knew the last thing in the world Hugh wanted was to be anywhere near the mangy beast.

Hugh clenched his teeth and climbed into the carriage, taking the only spot available: beside Pippa's loathsome pet. The dog stood on the seat and turned around, as if seeking the perfect position before settling down, shifting his weight to press closer to Hugh. It was all the man could do to keep from throwing the animal out of the vehicle.

"Samuel," Pippa said sharply, "be still."

"Are you comfortable, Hugh?" Caro smiled pleasantly, but the gleam in her eye told him his comfort was scarcely her concern.

Soon. Very soon. Pippa would be his and Caro

would be firmly out of their lives. Caro and . . . Samuel.

"Why yes, Caro, I daresay I am comfortable." He smiled, a slow, steady, satisfied smile fueled by thoughts of the not-too-distant future and leaned back in the seat. Caro's own smile faltered. "I am quite comfortable indeed."

"Goodness." Caro stared wide-eyed at the activity bustling all around them.

Carriages and horses packed the long, narrow park drive in an impressive display of English aristocracy. It was a sight quite beyond the expectations of either girl, and Pippa couldn't suppress a flutter of excitement.

"It's quite amazing, Hugh, isn't it?" she said.

Even Hugh seemed to relish the spectacle. "Welcome to London, my dear."

"I daresay, I never imagined a simple afternoon drive to be quite such an event." Pippa's gaze darted from vehicles packed with ladies in their finery to strollers far more concerned with their appearance than physical exertion to gentlemen attired in the latest stare of fashion upon the finest horseflesh available.

"Everyone who is anyone in London seems to take it upon himself to parade through the park at this time of day. It is practically de rigueur." He chuckled. "I have always thought it a bit tiresome myself but today I find it rather amusing. No doubt it's the company I am in."

Pippa glanced at Caro, who looked uncharacteristically awed by their surroundings. Hugh appeared more relaxed than he'd been since setting out on their drive. Even Samuel seemed to enjoy the scene, wagging his tail with enthusiasm.

"Will we meet all these people, do you think?" Pippa leaned forward eagerly. "There are rather a lot of them."

"They are the very cream of society. And yes, I believe you will be introduced to many of them as the season progresses." Amusement colored his face, no doubt at the unsophisticated nature of her question. Not that she minded. Pippa was well aware of her naïveté and could scarcely resent Hugh's acknowledgment of her lack of experience. A newfound excitement at the prospect of the season ahead surged through her.

"Goodness," Caro murmured again, and Pippa laughed. Who would have imagined her thoroughly confident cousin would be subdued by the sight of what looked like all of London milling about the lanes of Hyde Park?

Curiosity filled her. "Who are they all, Hugh?"

"I don't know them all, of course, but I have met a fair number. Over there is Lady Wentworth and her daughters. Not an especially attractive group, and quite prone to gossip, but well respected for their breeding and income nonetheless. And in that particular carriage . . ."

Hugh's words washed over her and she gave herself up to the sheer enjoyment of his running commentary, her gaze drifting to the various personages he discussed. He'd been far too modest.

Hugh seemed to know not only who was whom but what was what as well. Which young women were expected to make good matches. Which gentlemen were considered a good catch. Which family would no doubt increase a daughter's dowry to insure a successful season for a less-than-attractive offspring. There was obviously much more to a London season than she had ever suspected.

Hugh's awareness was a revelation as well. She'd always admired his intelligence but his knowledge of the ins and outs of society was impressive and, coupled with his cutting sense of the absurd, drew a laugh to her lips more often than not. A warm feeling of belonging flowed through her. Hugh might not make her head swim but he would indeed make a fine husband. They would have a nice life together. Their families would be pleased and they would take their expected place in English society. Why, what more could a good, biddable girl ask in this day and age?

". . . and I suspect the—damnation!" Hugh's voice cracked and Pippa's gaze jerked back to her betrothed.

Hugh struggled in the seat with Samuel, who was trying his best to escape from the moving carriage.

"Hugh, what are you doing?" Pippa stared at the jumbled bodies of dog and man.

"What does it look like I'm doing? I'm trying to control your bloody beast!" Hugh couldn't seem to get a firm grasp on the squirming creature. It would have been quite humorous had Pippa not noticed the furious look in Hugh's eye.

"Samuel!" Pippa snapped. "Stop it at once."

Immediately the dog stilled and cast her a baleful stare. Hugh straightened in his seat, brushing imagined dog hairs off his coat with a look of disgust. Pippa sighed. Samuel did not shed.

"You shall have to do something about that creature." Hugh flicked an invisible hair off his sleeve. "I will not permit that animal in my house."

"Hugh!" Indignation raised her tone. "Samuel is my dog. My pet. Why, he's practically a member of the family."

"Not my family." His tone was hard and firm.

"He will be." Pippa raised her chin. "Samuel goes where I go."

Hugh clenched his teeth. "The nasty brute does not like me and I am not fond of him."

"Nonsense, Hugh. Everyone loves Samuel," Caro said, a wicked gleam in her eye. "And Samuel loves everyone."

As if to confirm Caro's declaration, Samuel leaned toward Hugh and slapped a long, wet, pink tongue across the man's cheek.

"What the—" Hugh clapped his hand to his face, his eyes wide with disgust.

Caro laughed.

Pippa groaned to herself, quickly pulled a lace kerchief from her reticule and thrust it at her outraged fiancé.

"I told you. He likes everyone." Caro shrugged. "The dog simply has no taste."

"Caro," Pippa said sharply. "Hugh, I am quite sorry. Samuel was simply trying to be friendly."

"I have no desire to be his friend." Hugh ground out the words.

Samuel cocked his head and studied the irate human with an expression that could only be described as thoughtful.

"Samuel?" Pippa held out her hand. "Come here, boy."

Samuel turned, cast her his canine version of a grin, then performed a four-legged pirouette and leapt from the carriage, fully stretched from front paw to rear, sailing a good six feet through the air before landing with a light spring as if he were as much dancer as dog.

"Damnable creature!" Hugh snapped.

"I didn't know he could do that." Caro stared in astonishment.

"Neither did I." A tiny part of Pippa wanted to applaud. Samuel's leap had been quite impressive. But one look at the dark wrath on Hugh's face stifled that impulse and she muttered instead. "Bad dog."

"I suspect you wish me to go after the animal?" Hugh glared as if this was somehow her fault.

"I should think someone should and quickly." Caro's gaze followed the sprinting dog. "Samuel's moving at a surprisingly rapid pace."

"Bloody hell." Hugh stepped out of the carriage, Pippa right behind. He swiveled toward her and she had to catch herself from stumbling into him. "You stay here."

"But Hugh, I—"

"Do not argue with me, Pippa." Hugh's words

59

rang clipped and sharp. "Stay in the carriage. I do not wish my betrothed running about the parks of London chasing after fleeing dogs."

Of course he expected her to obey without question. And of course a good, proper, biddable girl would do just that. Unless, of course, a girl's dog was concerned.

Pippa squared her shoulders and glared at him. "I most certainly will not. Samuel will come to me whereas I do not know if he'll come to you."

"The dog has better taste than I thought," Caro said under her breath.

Pippa ignored her. "Please, Hugh, let me come."

"It is not necessary." His teeth clenched and a muscle ticked at the jawline. "I am certainly capable of rounding up one wretched beast."

"Samuel likes everyone," Caro murmured.

"Hugh." Pippa clutched his sleeve. "I have no doubt of that. But with my help, we shall simply find him that much sooner."

Hugh heaved an irritated sigh. "As you wish." He raised a brow in Caroline's direction. "Are you planning on joining this escapade as well?"

"I wouldn't miss it." Caro flounced past him, stepping lightly from the carriage.

"I believe he headed this way." Pippa nodded in the direction she'd last seen Samuel.

"Not at all," Caro said. "While you two were arguing, I distinctly saw him run toward that side of the park."

Hugh narrowed his eyes as if he did not quite

believe her. Caro returned his gaze with unflinching innocence. "Very well," he said. "We shall search in this—"

"Don't you think it would be best if we separated?" Caro said.

Suspicion underlay Hugh's response. "Why?"

"What if I'm mistaken? If we separate we have a much better chance of finding the dog." Caro shrugged. "It simply makes sense."

Hugh's hands fisted at his sides. "I do not think—"

"She's right, Hugh." Concern for her pet and annoyance with Hugh's attitude pushed Pippa's words faster. "We have already wasted far too much time debating the method of looking for Samuel. This is London and if we do not find him soon he shall surely be lost forever. Caro and I will look in this area, you search in that direction." Hugh's stormy expression was anything but agreeable. "Please, Hugh, let us go."

"Very well." He leaned closer, his words for her ears alone. "But I warn you, my dear, keep a tighter rein on that cousin of yours than you did on the dog. Remember where you are. This is not the country. You may not behave here as you would at home. You have a position to maintain in London and a reputation. All eyes are upon you at all times—"

"I scarcely think searching for a dog in a park is the stuff of scandal," Pippa said.

"Scandal strikes when one least expects it." His gaze narrowed. "I have said it once today already:

61

I do not wish you to be tarnished with even the hint of impropriety."

She pulled a deep breath and drew her brows together in annoyance. "I am quite capable of finding Samuel without bringing disgrace upon myself and your good name."

"See that you don't." He nodded sharply, turned and strode off, muttering all the while, no doubt about the stupidity of dogs and the lax behavior of their mistresses. Pippa stared after him. Who was this terse, unyielding man? Was it London that made him seem so very different from the easygoing Hugh she'd grown up with? Or was it the strain and stress of adulthood that weighed heavily upon him now? Whatever the cause, unease settled in the pit of her stomach like an overcooked pudding.

"I thought we'd never get rid of him." Caro stepped up to stand beside her.

"He is concerned that somehow our search for Samuel will lead to impropriety." Pippa studied Hugh's stiff figure growing smaller in the distance.

"What a prig."

"Caro!"

"Well, he is." Caro's lips pressed together in a stubborn line.

"He is not. He's simply very proper. Hugh is . . . um . . . a high stickler." Pippa nodded with an enthusiasm she didn't feel. "That's it. He's a high stickler."

Caro snorted. "He's a prig. What did he think we could possibly do here that would bring ruin toppling about our heads?"

"I have no idea," Pippa snapped. "Perhaps he thought we'd throw our skirts over our heads and run screaming through the lanes!"

Caro's eyes widened and she stared for a long shocked second. Pippa returned her gaze with a newfound defiance.

"My," Caro said slowly, "that would be scandalous." A smile twitched the corner of her mouth. "One wonders what dear Hugh would make of it."

"I suspect he wouldn't like it." Pippa bit back a grin at the thought of the two girls racing through the park with their bottoms exposed to all of society. "No, Hugh would not be at all pleased."

"Might turn him an interesting shade of red though," Caro said.

"Caro, how can you say that?" Pippa shook her head. "I should think purple is more his color."

Caro nodded somberly. "Apoplexic purple."

"Exactly. Sort of a plum." Pippa's gaze caught Caro's and they burst into laughter at the intriguing range of shades that could color Hugh's fair skin.

Caro linked her arm through Pippa's. "Come along. Let's find that beast of yours."

The two girls started off in the opposite direction from Hugh. Pippa's gaze skimmed the scene around them. Concern for Samuel was uppermost in her thoughts, although he'd always been an extremely responsible dog and he'd always returned to her. But the previously unsuspected side of Hugh revealed today nagged in her mind with an unrepentant persistence.

"Are you really going to marry him?" Caro's voice was quiet.

"I said I would."

"Aren't you afraid he'll make you dreadfully unhappy?"

"What a goose you are, Caro." Pippa refused to admit she'd been thinking just that. "Of course, I'm not worried. What nonsense."

Silence fell between them, but Pippa knew Caro was merely choosing her words with care.

"He doesn't like me, you know," Caro blurted.

"Don't be silly, Caro. He . . ." Pippa's gaze caught her cousin's and she sighed. Of all the people in the world, she could never lie to her dearest friend. "He thinks you're a bad influence on me."

Caro drew up short and stared. "A bad influence?"

Pippa nodded. "He believes you'll come to nothing but ruin."

"Ruin?" Caro's eyes widened.

"Indeed." The absurdity of the conversation struck Pippa with an insane desire to laugh although the stricken expression on Caro's face dampened her mirth. "He thinks you're headed toward scandal."

"Scandal?" Caro fairly choked on the word.

"He thinks the temptations of London will prove too great for a girl of your exuberant nature."

"He does, does he?" Sparks shot from Caro's eyes. "Well, I have some thoughts of my own about his temperament I should be more than willing to share with him!"

"Now that would indeed be scandalous." Pippa grinned and Caro joined her with obvious reluctance. "Don't worry about Hugh, Caro. I shall not let him dictate to me where you are concerned."

"He's a prig," Caro muttered.

Pippa sighed. "If you and Hugh are to be at each other's throats, the season won't be nearly as much fun as we'd hoped." Pippa linked her arm once again with the taller girl's and urged them forward. "Now, forget about Hugh for a moment and tell me all about our first ball. It is tomorrow, is it not?"

Caro studied her for a moment with an expression that proclaimed she was not through with the subject of Hugh. With obvious reluctance she took the bait Pippa offered. "Very well." She sighed. "The ball is to be given by Lady Farnsworth, and from what Mother has said it should be very grand, with . . ."

Pippa breathed a mental sigh of relief. Whatever had possessed her to tell Caro of Hugh's concerns? Her cousin had already made her feelings on Pippa's impending nuptials known. This new information would surely only serve to fan the flames of her opposition to the marriage. Hugh's stiff behavior had already given Pippa pause as to the wisdom of the match.

"We are not going to find him." Caro crossed her arms over her chest and glared. "I do not see that animal of yours anywhere."

"He's got to be here." This was not at all like Samuel. Perhaps, here in London, she could not count on his reappearance. Perhaps something had happened to him. All thoughts of Hugh and his admonishments fled in the face of her growing anxiety. "You were right, Caro, we will cover more ground if we go our separate ways."

Caro started. "I certainly did not mean you and I should separate. Why, we have no chaperones. Mother says a young woman alone—"

"Caro, I am quite certain your mother would appreciate your concern with propriety but at this moment I do not care in the slightest."

"Perhaps Hugh is correct." Caro glared. "Perhaps I am a bad influence on you. I am the one who is far more likely to urge us to part than you. This is not at all like the proper Philippa Morgan I know."

Pippa clenched her jaw. "I only wish to retrieve my pet. Besides, look around. The park is scarcely a dangerous place. Why, it's simply littered with the very best people society has to offer. We are as safe here as in our own homes."

Caro's forehead furrowed with a considering frown. "Do you think so?"

"I do indeed. Now." Pippa gave her a tiny shove. "You head that way and I shall go this way and with luck one of us will find him. We can meet back here—"

"I really don't know—"

"—and I do promise not to throw my skirts over my head and scream."

Caro shrugged. "Very well. Let's hope one of us finds him, and soon." She leaned closer to Pippa. "As much as I am not overly fond of Hugh, somehow I suspect crossing him would not be wise."

"No doubt." Pippa was surprised to realize just how much she agreed with her cousin. "Go on now. The sooner we get going the sooner we shall surely find him."

Caro nodded and each cousin headed in her own direction. Pippa's gaze skimmed the area, darting from shade to shadow and face to figure. She held her chin high, desperately trying to ignore the vaguely curious stares directed at a young woman obviously unescorted.

Long minutes passed and despair crept upon her. "Samuel!" Her voice rose. Where was the blasted beast? "Come here, boy!"

She did so love him and to lose him here in London was more than she could bear. She'd had him for six years, a full third of her lifetime, and even though she was an adult now with a proper future as a wife and countess and mother laid before her, he was still her dearest companion and closest friend. She could not, would not give up. And Samuel always came back. It was the one sure thing in her life. All she ever had to do was call for him or whistle.

Whistle?

Lord, she couldn't possibly whistle. Not here. Not now. Certainly it would not be as scandalous as running partially clothed through the park but it would surely be frowned upon. But perhaps no one would pay her any notice. No. She had such a wonderfully shrill, piercing sort of whistle, one would have to be deaf not to pay it some heed. Still, if it was a choice between retrieving Samuel and a momentary flouting of society's rules—so be it. After all, Samuel was her dog.

Pippa glanced around, grateful that she was in a section of the park not quite as crowded as the drives closer to the entrance. Hugh would not like this. He would not like this at all. Fortunately, Hugh was not in the immediate vicinity. At least she hoped not.

She drew a deep breath and released a long, high-pitched whistle that cut through the air like the scream of a bird of prey and resonated in the dark, green recess of the trees and shrubs. In the back of her mind, she noted with pride what a truly fine whistle it was.

Park goers, on the other hand, froze in place, as if her whistle had plunged them into sudden frigid temperatures. Her heart sank as well, but she struggled to plaster an innocent expression on her face in hopes that no one actually saw her do the impressive deed. She glanced about, pretending to be as shocked as the rest of them.

A woof sounded behind her and she whirled to see Samuel bouncing toward her as if he hadn't a care and had, in fact, just completed a wonderful adventure.

"Samuel!" Laughter and relief swelled within her. She dropped to her knees and the dog leapt into her arms, licking at her face with rapt abandon. "You naughty dog." She laughed and dodged his lapping tongue. "I was quite beside myself with worry." She scrambled to her feet and planted her hands on her hips. "Where have you been?"

"He's been having a rather pleasant day of it, I should think."

Her heart stilled. She stared straight down at Samuel, clenching her fists tightly as if to grasp her own leaping emotions, afraid to look up at the owner of the rich resonant voice she'd known only once awake, but time and again in her dreams.

Slowly she raised her gaze upward to a chin square and strong, lips full and firm, and gray, stormy eyes. Eyes that lit with delight when his gaze met hers. Time seemed to stretch and slow. Her breath refused to come and her pulse pounded in her ears.

A lopsided smile stretched across his face.

"I believe, my lady, you whistled."

I tell ya, kid, I never fail to be amazed . . .

. . . by how plain stupid humans can be. Ya can talk about bigger brains or opposable thumbs or just a simple matter of bein' able to open a can of dog food by yourself, but none of it really matters 'cuz when it comes right down to it, they don't have the smarts God gave a beagle.

Any animal within a hundred miles of those two could have told you what was gonna happen next. I didn't see it the first time they met, but ya gotta admit the circumstances were a little strange. But this time . . . well, there were sparks. Lots and lots of sparks. It was fate, destiny, inevitable. It was like Romeo and Juliet, Lady and the Tramp, Bogie and Bacall.

What?

Play It Again, Sam

Oh, yeah, thanks, kid. You ain't the first one to say I sound like him, ya know. I picked it up back in the forties. I was a schnoodle. Mom was a real classy poodle. She said Dad was a schnauzer. I never knew him. Hey, don't give me that look. I don't need your pity. Face it kid, it's the way dogs are.

Anyway, where was I? Oh yeah. My human was a projectionist at a movie house. He used to bring me with him. I must have sat through hundreds of screenings of Bogie's movies. He held me up occasionally to see the screen, I was kind of small, but most of the time I just listened. And I heard 'em all. All the greats. The Maltese Falcon, The Big Sleep, Casablanca, *they don't make movies like that anymore. And there ain't nobody like Bogie. I thought he was swell. And the voice? Well, I just kind of started talkin' like this and it stuck with me. What do ya think? Yeah, I think it suits me too.*

Now somebody like Sam Spade or Philip Marlowe would have picked up on the electricity around those two. Great characters, Spade and Marlowe. Really smart. Almost canine. But they weren't real and it would still be more than a hundred years before somebody invented them anyway.

As it was, nobody but me really seemed to notice what was goin' on between Pippa and Spencer. Yeah, his name was Spencer. Not as good as Rick or Steve or even Humphrey but better than Hugh. Ugh. I still get shivers when I think about that guy. To give him his due, though, Hugh really loved Pippa in his own way. He just didn't know the difference between love and obsession.

As for Pippa, it was plain from the moment she and Spencer met in the park that she'd lost her heart. There was probably nothin' anybody could do, but I could kick myself every time I think about it.

I never even dreamed, before all was said and done, what else she'd lose.

Chapter Three

Her heart leapt with a shocking sense of joy and for the barest moment, mirrored the pleasure in his eyes. But the sensation vanished as quickly as it appeared, leaving only a sick, heavy panic in her stomach and her soul.

No, no, it simply can't be! Not him! Never him!

She stared in stark disbelief. She'd convinced herself he was a dream, a vision brought on by her fall down the hill. Philippa Morgan would never, ever allow, let alone invite, a strange man to kiss her. No, he was a dream, nothing more. He simply had to be. Why, this entire day was no doubt a nightmare induced by the excitement of at long last being in London.

She squeezed her eyes closed and willed him to disappear and herself to wake.

"I say, are you quite all right?"

She snapped her eyes open. He was still there.

"I . . . I . . ."

"You haven't fallen again, have you?" A frown of concern creased his forehead.

"I . . . I . . ." Words refused to come. Her tongue seemed tied in knots. She could do nothing more than stare wide-eyed and speechless.

"You certainly appear well enough. Quite lovely, in point of fact." A smile caught at his lips as if she were a matter of great amusement. "I do not recall you having this much difficulty with speech when last we met. Although, I was pleased to note, that exceptional whistle of yours is still quite impressive."

"You remember," she whispered, the tiniest hope that perhaps he would not recall their first meeting snuffed out at his words.

"I remember"—he quirked a dark brow—"everything."

She groaned. "Everything?"

He nodded. "Everything."

"Thank goodness you've found—oh!" Caro stepped to Philippa's side and pulled up short at the sight of the stranger. She stared with a frank, appreciative look and a dimpled smile. "Why, I didn't know you knew anyone in London."

"I don't," Pippa said quickly, and threw him a silent plea. *Please, please be so kind as to be quiet.* "He was simply . . . that is to say, what I mean is—"

"What she means," he said smoothly, "is that I

found her dog cavorting through the park and am now returning him to her."

Pippa breathed a sigh of relief. She could never explain knowing this tall, striking gentleman to Caro. Although, judging by Caro's rapt expression, Pippa could have said virtually anything and the other girl would have believed it. Caro was far too intent on staring at the stranger's handsome face to pay attention to anything else. A sharp twinge of annoyance stabbed through Pippa.

"There you are." Hugh's piercing tone rang behind her and she whirled to face his oncoming figure. "Well, I couldn't find the beast and I can't say I'm terribly unhappy about it. I daresay we shall—"

Samuel stepped out from behind Pippa's skirts, grinned and wagged his tail.

"Oh." Hugh threw the dog a withering glance. "You did find him. How . . . fortunate."

Samuel settled down at Pippa's feet and gazed up at Hugh with a remarkably innocent expression.

"Very well then." Hugh's lips compressed in a tight line and he glared down at the dog. "I suppose we shall have to make the best of it." He pinned her with a cool look that matched the tone of his voice. "Although you will have to do something about the creature's—" his gaze slid past her to the stranger beyond and her breath caught. What would he think of her speaking to a man she did not know, let alone—she shuddered at the thought—a kiss shared with a stranger? Would Samuel's rescuer reveal her secret?

"St. Gregory?" Hugh said.

St. Gregory?

"Winsleigh." Her stranger nodded.

A grin broke on Hugh's face. "It is you. How delightful. I was confident I'd see you here in London but did not expect an encounter quite so soon."

St. Gregory chuckled. "A happy circumstance, my friend."

"My friend?" Caro said.

"Indeed. St. Gregory and I have been friends since our school days. In fact, he paid me a visit in the country just a few weeks ago."

"Did he?" Pippa's voice was oddly strangled, the words barely understandable. Dear Lord. Her stranger, the man she kissed, was not merely an acquaintance of her fiancé's but a friend no less! And judging by the remarkable change in Hugh's demeanor, a friend he thought quite highly of.

"Lovely county, Sussex." A twinkle shone in St. Gregory's eye. "So many unexpected charms. One never knows what one will encounter during a simple walk in the countryside."

Heat flushed up her face. He was teasing her now. Would he also expose her?

"Hugh." Impatience colored Caro's voice. "You're being dreadfully impolite. Aren't you going to introduce us?"

"Of course. Ladies, may I present Spencer St. Gregory, the Viscount St. Gregory. This"—Hugh nodded at Caro—"is Miss Caroline Lyndon. And this is her cousin, Miss Philippa Morgan. My soon-to-be betrothed."

Surprise flickered in St. Gregory's gray eyes. "This is Pippa?"

A hint of pride in ownership touched Hugh's voice. "Indeed. Is she not just as lovely as I've described?"

"Quite." St. Gregory grasped her hand and raised it to his lips. His gaze locked with hers and she trembled at his touch. The rest of the world faded away and for a moment—or an eternity—only she and he existed, one for the other. "She is everything you said. And more."

Fear at the excitement his words triggered shot through her. She snatched her hand away and willed herself to stay calm. "And what have you been saying about me, Hugh?"

Hugh laughed. "Only that you are the most exquisite creature in the world and I the most fortunate man to be able to claim you as my own."

"Nonsense," she said, far more sharply than she intended. "You embarrass me. I am the fortunate one."

Caro cleared her throat and broke the awkward moment. She extended her hand to the newcomer. "I believe we're all fortunate to have met today."

Amusement glimmered in St. Gregory's eye. He politely clasped Caro's fingers and brushed his lips across the back of her glove. "We are indeed. Especially on a day like today." He released Caro's hand and turned his attention back to Pippa. "Don't you think so, Miss Morgan?"

"It's a lovely day," she said. What was he doing now?

"Actually," he said, his manner thoughtful, "one would even call it beautiful."

"Yes, yes," she said quickly, "it's a beautiful day."

"Isn't it, though." St Gregory glanced around as if to confirm his comments. "There's something unique about springtime in England. It's so, oh, what is the word?" His voice was light but laughter twinkled in his eye.

She gritted her teeth. He was toying with her with all his talk about the weather, obviously to let her know he could reveal her scandalous secret at any time. She was well aware of the power he wielded over her. The scoundrel. "Fine. The word is fine. Springtime in England is fine."

"We are agreed, then." A puzzled note shaded Hugh's voice. "I daresay, I never expected the weather to be quite so fascinating."

"Neither did I," Caro murmured, and cast Pippa a speculative glance.

"It's not at all fascinating." Pippa struggled to keep her voice light. "It's simply convenient, that's all."

"Convenient?" St. Gregory said. "I hadn't thought of it like that."

"Perhaps now we could move on to more scintillating topics such as the condition of the roads," Caro said under her breath.

Pippa turned toward Hugh. "Don't you think we should be going?"

"Of course, my dear." He nodded at Samuel. "I gather you helped recapture this recalcitrant brute?"

St. Gregory chuckled. "He seems a rather intelligent animal to me."

Pippa's heart softened with gratitude. Whatever else this man was—and she was confident he was indeed a rake and a rogue—he was obviously a dog lover as well. A most redeeming quality.

Hugh snorted. "He's an undisciplined, ill-mannered lout disguised as a canine. The best thing for all concerned is to—"

"Hugh!" Pippa's eyes widened with shock, Caro looked uneasy and even St. Gregory raised a brow. Pippa had no idea Hugh's dislike of Samuel was so extreme. This did not bode well for the future. Again, apprehension as to Hugh's true nature and their life together nipped at the edges of her mind.

"Sorry, my dear." Hugh offered her his arm, and she linked hers through his. "It was good to see you again, St Gregory. I suspect we shall run into you often during the season."

"No doubt." St. Gregory directed his comments to Hugh but his gaze lingered on Pippa. "I find I am rather looking forward to the festivities now. I believe the season will be a bit brighter this year."

A thrill ran through her at his words, and at once heat burned in her cheeks at the sheer disloyalty of her reaction. She was to wed Hugh and no matter how often this Spencer St. Gregory visited her dreams he was not now, and never would be, part of her life. She lifted her chin and stared into his eyes.

"I do appreciate your help in finding my dog, however we really must be—"

"Will you be at Lady Farnsworth's ball tomorrow, my lord?" Caro tilted her head in the flirtatious manner she'd spent long hours practicing before a mirror for just such an occasion.

"I had not yet decided but if you and your charming cousin are to attend . . ." St Gregory smiled. "I would be a fool not to put in an appearance."

"How wonderful." Caro beamed.

"Very nice," Pippa murmured.

"Excellent." Hugh nodded. "We shall see you then."

"You will save me a dance, won't you, Miss Lyndon?" St. Gregory favored Caro with his attention and Pippa's heart twisted.

"Why, of course." Goodness, Caro was practically falling at the man's feet. Did she have no shame? No pride? Perhaps Hugh was right about her all along.

"And you, Miss Morgan?"

Pippa snapped her gaze to his and knew without question he was asking for much more than a mere dance. "I really do not think—"

"Nonsense, Pippa," Hugh said. "St. Gregory is a very old and trusted friend. You certainly have my blessing if you wish to dance with him."

"She doesn't need your blessing." Caro smiled sweetly. "Not yet anyway."

"Miss Morgan?" There was that curiously endearing lopsided smile again.

"Very well." Her voice sounded helpless to her own ears, as if she had surrendered to a persuasive enemy, to a will greater than her own, to a force she could never fight. And perhaps, did not want to fight. *Is this how a drowning man feels?* Her throat constricted in a tight swallow. "But just once."

"My dear lady, what more can I ask but the opportunity to share a dance even if it's only"—his gaze burned into hers and she thought surely she would swoon at the intensity that shot between them—"just once."

Who was this girl, really? Spencer narrowed his eyes and watched her retreating figure, posture erect, one hand linked about Winsleigh's elbow, the other resting gently on her dog's head. Today she was the consummate picture of propriety, a far cry from their first meeting. At a distance, he'd watched her romp with her dog and tumble down the hill. Then he had thought her far too bold and undisciplined for her own good. A chit destined for ruin, he'd suspected. Now, he wondered.

Hugh too had changed. He was no longer the fun-loving friend Spencer remembered from their school days. Granted, it had been a good year or so since they'd last met, but Spencer found the difference in his old chum quite remarkable. With maturity and the increased responsibility of a man destined for an earldom, Hugh had become rather pretentious and somewhat pompous. It was not difficult to determine the reason behind Hugh's transformation. His father, the current earl, was a model of haughty self-importance.

Spencer turned and strode toward the fashionable, high-perched phaeton he had abandoned upon spotting the dog frolicking on the lawns. What was his name? Ah yes: Samuel. Spencer shook his head. A rather noble name for such a high-spirited creature. Odd. He had believed the girl high-spirited at first as well. But now she was, for the most part, quite reserved, eminently proper, the perfect, biddable, well-bred young lady. Exactly as Hugh had described.

Spencer snorted a short laugh and vaulted into his carriage. He had always detested perfect, biddable, well-bred young ladies, much preferring women like Lady Felicia Dusault. Felicia was no more than a year or two older than the respectable Miss Morgan but already the widow of an elderly lord who, no doubt, expired upon learning first-hand the unbridled enthusiasm of his young wife.

Spencer should have been escorting Felicia at this very moment except that when he'd arrived at her townhouse her butler informed him the lady had tired of waiting and had gone without him. Spencer shook his head. He was a scant ten minutes late, no more. Felicia was simply trying to make a point. Regardless of the rumors linking the two of them together, and in spite of how well they seemed to suit each other by day and by night, Felicia wanted him to know she had no intention of shackling herself to any man. Especially not a viscount of substantial, but by no means extraordinary, wealth.

Spencer grinned at the memory of Felicia's many and varied talents and picked up the reins. She suited his needs right now for both female companionship and as a way to ward off the interests of this season's crop of marriageable young misses and their matrimony-minded mothers. Spencer had as little desire to be wed as Felicia, and the two made an altogether splendid couple. Yet . . .

There was something about Miss Philippa Morgan—Pippa, Hugh called her—that lingered in his mind and surfaced in his dreams. Ridiculous of course, and annoying. Obviously, their first meeting had been an aberration, no doubt brought on by her topple down the hill. It was clear she was not at all the type of woman that he typically found attractive.

Then why couldn't he get her out of his head? Why did she seem to fit into his arms so perfectly, as if she belonged there and always had? What was there about her that tugged at him and kept her in the back of his mind and hovering at the edge of sleep?

He snapped the reins in a manner much sharper than usual and furrowed his brow. Oh, she was lovely in a very pale, delicate sort of way. He could well see how those enormous green eyes would induce a man to do nearly anything. And her blonde—nearly white—hair was distinctly angelic. But he was not partial to angels and much preferred women cut from a more vivid cloth. Robust dark-haired beauties like that cousin of hers or fiery red-heads like Felicia were more to his taste. No doubt the chit was a virgin in the bargain.

An unmarried man eminently desirable for his income and title, Spencer had long ago learned to be wary of virgins. Until, of course, the inevitable day dawned when he would be called upon to choose a bride and sire an heir. Then he would insist his bride untouched. No, virgins were strictly for marriage and he was not at all prepared for that questionable state. Why, he was only four and twenty: far too young to wed.

The unbidden thought popped into his head: Hugh was four-and-twenty as well and apparently more than willing to give up his bachelorhood. Nonetheless, while he and Hugh were once close, they had chosen different paths, and given Hugh's change of temperament, Spence could only thank God they had.

Still . . .

He had received an invitation to the Farnsworth ball but had not planned on attending. He'd never been fond of the overly crowded, overly boring, overly predictable events society was so partial to. Now, however . . . What would be the harm? It would no doubt be wise to see the girl once more if only to determine why she'd made such an impression on him. Perhaps there was much more to her than even Hugh suspected. She had kissed him after all. And he was confident he'd seen a spark of something in the depths of her emerald eyes. Desire? Surely not.

He smiled slowly. It would obviously be in his best interest to find out for himself. Not that anything would come of it. No, she was to be betrothed to Hugh and as much as he found the man boorish and stuffy, honor forbade his doing more than polite society decreed in such circumstances.

He nodded absently at a passing carriage and considered the situation. Finding the truth hidden beneath the public persona of Pippa Morgan might well be an exercise in futility. Or it could be the most intriguing activity he'd attempted in a long time. He always did enjoy a mystery. At any rate, he needed to satisfy his own curiosity as to why the young lady's kiss had seemed not merely pleasant but familiar—indeed, right—as if she were somehow meant for him. A bothersome matter, of course, but he did wish to discover why she appeared more and more often in his waking thoughts and in his dreams.

Very well then. He'd go to the ball and he'd dance with the lovely creature if only to satisfy himself that their single kiss, and its persistent memory, was a peculiarity brought on by the impact of a fine spring day and nothing more.

What harm could it do? It would be only . . . just once.

"If you would slow down a moment, Hugh." Caro scrambled to catch up with them. "I want to hear all about the dashing Viscount St. Gregory."

"Dashing?" Hugh cast Caro a look of disdain. "My dear, he is precisely the type of man you should avoid."

"Why?" Caro said.

"He seemed pleasant enough," Pippa murmured.

"Oh, he's very pleasant. Especially where ladies

are concerned." Hugh snorted. "And that, my dears, is why he should be avoided at all costs."

"But if he's pleasant . . ." A stubborn note sounded in Caro's voice.

Hugh continued his brisk pace toward the carriage. "I realize your question comes from your unfamiliarity with the ways of the world and the ways of men in particular. Therefore it behooves me to be patient with ridiculous—"

"She simply asked for an explanation, Hugh," Pippa said sharply. Hugh shot her an annoyed glance and even Caro looked startled at the abrupt tone of her comment.

"Very well." Hugh rolled his eyes toward the heavens and heaved a forbearing sigh. "The man is a known rake. He has made something of a name for himself among the ladies of the ton. His is not—"

"I thought he was your friend." Caro blurted out.

Hugh cast her a withering glance. "He is."

Pippa shook her head. "I'm afraid I do not understand."

"It's really very simple." Hugh's gaze softened as if he were trying to interpret a complicated concept for a very small child. Unaccustomed resentment swept through her. "What a man does with women has no bearing on his relationships with other men. St. Gregory has an excellent hand with the reins and belongs to the finest clubs. His honor is unblemished. I have no difficulty maintaining a friendship with someone of his reputation with women. It is a different matter entirely for a young lady. Why, even to be in the company of such a man would compromise one's reputation."

"I cannot believe he's that bad, Hugh." Pippa struggled to stifle a growing irritation at Hugh's pompous comments. "Why then is he invited to balls and such like Lady Farnsworth's?"

"My dear Pippa." Hugh smiled as if she were simple minded. "In spite of his scandalous behavior, St. Gregory is considered quite a prize on the marriage mart. His title is distinguished. His income respectable. All in all his future is assured as is the future of any young miss who catches his eye. That in itself is more than enough for a family eager for an excellent match to overlook any questionable demeanor. Besides"—Hugh shrugged—"men are held to quite different standards than women."

"Not at all fair, I'd say." Caro glared.

Pippa nodded in quiet agreement.

"Well, men value different qualities than do women." His tone was lofty. "For example, men put great store in honor and the sanctity of their word. Women have no such scruples."

"I cannot agree with you on that, Hugh," Pippa said coolly. "I, for one, do not give my word lightly. And I do not break it without just and proper cause."

"Neither do I," Caro added.

Hugh ignored them. "Nonetheless . . ." They reached the carriage and Hugh assisted Pippa into the vehicle, Samuel brushing past the man to settle next to his mistress. Hugh narrowed his eyes. "It is the way of the world, and as this is the world we live in we shall all have to abide by its rules. Women, more so than men, are judged by the company they keep and to whom they extend their favors."

He offered a hand to Caro, his gaze firm, his voice unyielding. "I do hope you understand that, Caro. After all, your behavior reflects on the rest of the family."

"It will, no doubt, be difficult, but I shall try to behave myself." Caro's voice dripped with a honeyed sweetness. She squeezed into the seat beside Samuel. Hugh nodded, apparently convinced of Caro's sincerity.

Hugh turned to signal the driver and Caro stuck out her tongue and wrinkled her nose at his fashionably attired back. Pippa snorted in an effort to suppress a laugh and Hugh threw her a disapproving frown. Caro bent to pet Samuel and caught Pippa's gaze over the dog's back. She winked and Pippa shook her head slightly in discouragement. Oh dear, what was Caro going to do now?

"You know, Hugh," Caro's voice was innocent, "I have heard it said that reformed rakes make the best husbands."

He smiled in that newly condescending manner he had and something inside Pippa clenched. Why hadn't she noticed these traits in Hugh before now? "I daresay, I would not count on that were I you."

"No?" She widened her eyes and Pippa groaned to herself. "I assume you would advise against seeking out a rake for marriage then?"

"Indeed I would." He gazed at her with a pompous, self-important look.

"What would you recommend?" Caro gazed up at him with an expression akin to adoration on her face. Pippa squirmed uncomfortably. Couldn't Hugh see what her cousin was doing? Or was he too blinded by the flattering way in which she asked his advice to notice she was making a fool of him?

Hugh settled back in his seat as if ready to impart some great nugget of wisdom, and studied Caro for a moment. She returned his gaze with a trusting stare. "It's really not at all complicated. I should advise you simply to follow your cousin's example."

"Me?" Pippa squeaked.

"Yes, my dear." Hugh cast her a beneficent smile. "You have agreed to a match both suitable and respectable. A match befitting your station that will benefit your family as well as yourself, and, no doubt, generations to come. In addition, you have selected a man who cares for you deeply."

"I have, haven't I?" Pippa said quietly, an odd dismay settling in her stomach at her acknowledgement of his words.

Hugh aimed a gloved finger at Caro. "You would be fortunate to do as well."

"Dear, Hugh." Caro laughed lightly, "Fortunate pales in comparison to the word I would use to describe the match Pippa has made." Hugh's gaze sharpened as if he were seeking to uncover a hidden meaning beneath her words, but Caro's guileless stare remained unflinching.

Apparently satisfied with her response, Hugh

swiveled in his seat to have a word with the driver.

Caro leaned toward Pippa and said under her breath, "Perhaps I was wrong when I called him a prig."

"Caro, I am ever so pleased to hear—"

"I think he's a twit instead." Caro smirked.

"How can you say that?" Pippa whispered urgently.

"You're right, Pippa. I was wrong." A wicked gleam twinkled in Caro's eye. "He's a twit and a prig."

"Caro! He is neither a twit nor a prig!"

"Did you say something, my dear?" Hugh raised a brow in mild curiosity.

"Yes, Cousin." Caro effected a pleasant smile. "Did you say something?"

"No." Pippa clenched her teeth.

"I could have sworn I heard you say something." Caro's brows drew together and she tapped her chin with her finger. "Something about the trees, was it? Or a twig perhaps?"

Pippa clasped her hands tightly together in her lap and ground out the words, struggling to hide her annoyance. "I didn't say anything."

"Odd, I could have sworn . . ." Caro shrugged.

Hugh considered Pippa for a long, uncomfortable moment. "I say, Pippa, you do not look at all well. Have you a headache?"

"Yes, that's it." Pippa grabbed at his words gratefully. "I have a horrible headache. Quite painful." She touched her forehead and winced as if the slightest pressure hurt.

"Brought on by the thought of her impending marriage, no doubt," Caro murmured for Pippa's ears alone.

"I thought so." Hugh bobbed his head in a knowing manner. "My mother suffers from headaches constantly."

"What a surprise," Caro muttered.

Pippa ignored her. "If I could just close my eyes . . ."

"Of course, my dear. We shall be home shortly."

Grateful, Pippa let her head fall back against the seat and closed her eyes. Samuel nudged his wet nose beneath her hand and she stroked his furry head.

What would she do about Samuel? There was no question Hugh did not like the dog. No. Dislike was too mild a term. Hugh detested Samuel. She shuddered to think what would happen with the two of them under one roof. Surely Hugh would not ask her to give up her dog? As quickly as the idea struck she knew the answer: of course Hugh would want her to get rid of Samuel. And Hugh would brook no protest, of that she was sure. Not once they were wed. Poor Samuel.

Poor Pippa. The unexpected thought hit Pippa with an almost physical force and reverberated deep within her. The knot in her stomach tightened. A fist seemed to grip her heart. The back of her eyes burned. And her head did indeed now ache.

How could she marry such a man? She opened her eyes a slit and studied him. He was as blond and handsome as ever. Except for a subtle hardness in his eyes and a vague tight set of his lips he appeared the same as always. Yet his manner was so different than she remembered. So different from his youth. The years away from home and the mantle of responsibility brought on by adulthood had shaped him into someone she no longer recognized and, perhaps, no longer liked.

Still, she had given her word and while men may not think honor meant as much to a woman as to a man, it meant a great deal to her. It was, after all, the only thing anyone had that they could truly call theirs and theirs alone.

Unless, of course, one had a dog.

St. Gregory likes dogs.

It said something about a man's character that St. Gregory would like a dog like Samuel. Not that she was concerned about his character. No, indeed. The man was a rake and she was practically an engaged woman. St. Gregory's character was of no concern whatsoever to her. She would dance with him at tomorrow's ball of course. Why, it would be impolite to refuse him. She had promised and, just like a man, her word was her bond.

What harm would it do to dance with him, just once, and exchange meaningless pleasantries and possibly even allow him to fetch her a glass of whatever was served as liquid refreshment? One dance, perhaps a trivial conversation and possibly a glass of punch. But no more.

She would not allow herself to look too deeply into the dark gray of his eyes or remember the warm feel of his lips on hers or even dwell on the startling similarities between the flesh-and-blood man and the love who danced with her beneath the stars in her dreams.

A tremor of anticipation trickled through her and she firmly pushed it away. It was a single dance at a single ball with a single man who meant nothing to her. Not now. Not ever.

Even if it was a man who liked dogs.

Chapter Four

"Whomever are you looking for?" Caro fluttered her fan in a vain attempt to cool the flushed tones of her face, and cast her gaze across the crowded ballroom.

"No one in particular," Pippa said in a nonchalant manner. "I am merely fascinated by the crowd."

Perhaps her tone was a touch too indifferent. Caro slanted her a curious look. "It is a rather impressive crush."

"You seem to enjoy it. Why, this is the first moment we've had alone together all evening. One could barely see you past the bevy of eager gentlemen surrounding you, each one vying for your attention. Not unlike puppies begging for a bone."

"Thank goodness I have managed to shoo them

all off for a moment." Caro rested the back of her hand against her forehead in feigned weariness. "I am quite done in."

"Oh?"

"Very well, not quite." Caro grinned. "It is delightful isn't it?"

Pippa laughed. "Indeed. You are quite the belle of the ball. Eligible young men are practically falling at your feet."

"At our feet," Caro corrected. "They seem just as taken with you as with me."

"I doubt that, Caro. They are simply being polite."

"Polite." Caro snorted. "The look in their eye when they gaze at you is not at all polite. It is most definitely interested. If Hugh wouldn't hover over you so possessively you might—"

"He does not hover," Pippa said.

"He most certainly does. The only way we've been able to get rid of him is to send him for refreshments. And I'm not certain I can drink much more of that horrendous punch."

Pippa sighed. "He is simply looking after my well-being. He cares for me, you know. He is to be my husband after all."

"If he'd leave you alone you might well find someone you like better."

"I like Hugh," Pippa snapped.

Caro scoffed. "I know. I simply cannot see why. Oh he's handsome enough, but he's also dull and stuffy and way too proper even for propriety's sake. The man is quite frankly boring."

"Caro, stop that at once." Pippa pulled her brows

together in irritation at her cousin—and at herself. Hadn't she been thinking the very same thing? "I do not want to discuss this again."

Caro waved her fan in a casual manner. "As you wish, but we will discuss it again. I shall bring it up every chance I get."

Pippa groaned. "Caro, you promised."

"And it's a promise I shall break." Caro leaned closer, a determined glint in her eye. "Now that we have entered the social whirl of the ton I can see quite clearly that Hugh is not the man for you. Your life with him will be nothing short of miserable. Why, the man doesn't even like your dog."

Pippa raised a brow. "You don't like my dog."

"I have changed my mind," Caro said in a lofty tone. "I now find him quite enjoyable in a furry, disreputable sort of way."

"Disreputable?" Pippa laughed with relief. As long as they were discussing Samuel, her cousin would not voice her objections to Hugh. Objections Pippa very much feared she might well share.

"My yes." Caro nodded vigorously. "The dog is quite disreputable and really rather charming."

"Oh, now you find him charming?"

"I think disreputable is very charming." Caro paused thoughtfully. "Rather like St. Gregory."

Pippa's heart leapt at the name. "St. Gregory?"

"He is both disreputable and charming. Don't you think so?"

"He's definitely disreputable, but charming?" Pippa raised a shoulder as if to dismiss the idea completely. "Really, cousin, I think you've been reading far too many novels."

"The man is fascinating, Pippa, admit it." Caro narrowed her eyes. "And he seemed quite taken with you."

"I don't think—"

"And I suspect you like him as well."

"Caro, I—"

"Don't bother to deny it." Caro considered her carefully. "Every time I have brought up St. Gregory's name you have avoided any discussion of him and have, in fact, maneuvered to change the subject."

"I simply don't find the man of interest," Pippa said firmly. "Therefore, I have no desire to talk about him."

Caro studied her cousin for a long moment. Pippa shifted uncomfortably, fighting to keep her expression serene and unconcerned. Abruptly, Caro's eyes widened and she smacked her fan against the palm of her hand. "You like him!"

"I do not!"

"You do too! I can see it in your eyes! You always look like that when you wish to evade the truth."

"I am not evading anything. And you cannot see anything in my eyes because there is nothing there to see."

Caro stared in silent surprise. Pippa clenched her jaw. The two girls had always been close. When together, they shared the tiniest details of their relatively quiet lives. When apart, they committed their thoughts to paper and exchanged long letters, pouring out their most secret longings and desires. Pippa had always confided everything to Caro. Except the secret love in her dreams. And St. Gregory.

Awareness dawned on Caro's face and she paled. "Dear Lord."

"Caro?" Helplessness washed through her. "Caro?"

"You've met him before, haven't you?" The question carried a note of redundance. Pippa could see Caro already knew the answer.

"Caro?" A plea echoed in her words.

"How well do you know him?" Caro's voice was uncharacteristically anxious, as if the reality of her proper cousin's suspected indiscretion snatched the confidence from her manner and replaced it with a child like trepidation.

Pippa shook her head. "I don't. Well, not really. I just . . . I mean we . . . that is to say . . ."

"What?" Caro could barely choke out the word.

Pippa's shoulders slumped in misery. "*I* kissed *him.*"

"You mean he kissed you."

"No." Misery colored Pippa's voice. "*I* kissed *him.*"

Caro sucked in a hard breath. "*You* kissed *him*?"

"Yes. More or less. It's the same thing anyway." Pippa sighed with the relief of revealing her secret and the utter horror of what she'd done. "If I am to be completely honest—"

"There's more?" Stunned disbelief shone in Caro's eyes.

Pippa nodded. "In reality it was a mutual kiss.

What I mean to say is we both kissed each other. But, well, I asked him to kiss me."

"You *asked* him to kiss you? Lord, Pippa, how could you?"

"I don't know. One minute he had his arms around me and the next—"

"He had his arms around you?"

Something in Caro's shocked tone snapped Pippa's patience. "You needn't look so horrified. Surely a man has put his arms around you before and kissed you?"

"No." Caro shook her head. "Never."

"Never?"

"Not once."

"But you're so . . . so . . ."

"It's not that I'm not willing. Even eager but . . ." Caro's voice was weak. "Never."

"Oh my." It was Pippa's turn for surprise. "But your carefree manner. And your high spirits. The way you speak and act I had always assumed—"

"And I had always assumed that when the time came for kissing rakes and rogues I would be the first of us to do so and that you . . . Why, Pippa, you've always been so well behaved and proper and—"

"Good?" Pippa fairly spat the word.

Caro raised a brow. "Yes. That's it exactly. You're so good."

Silence fell between them. Pippa's thoughts whirled at the revelation of her cousin's real nature. In spite of all appearances it may very well be Pippa who was truly overspirited and Caro truly good.

"I must say, Pippa, I'm—"

"Shocked? Disappointed?" What would Caro think of her?

"Shocked, yes," Caro said, her words measured. "But not disappointed." Caro clasped her hand, giving her fingers a reassuring squeeze. "You are my dear, sweet cousin and my closest friend. I could never be disappointed in you."

Pippa caught her gaze. "What then—"

"No, not disappointed. Rather . . ." A pure, sweet, smile blossomed on her face. "Proud."

Pippa gasped. "Proud?"

"Proud." Caro's smile widened. "Quite, quite proud."

Pippa snatched her hand away. "There's nothing to be proud of."

"Indeed there is." Delight danced on Caro's face. "Why you kissed a man, a stranger I presume, although you haven't given me the details. He was a stranger at the time, was he not?"

"Yes, but—"

"Your first kiss! And it was with a man you'd never met who turns out to a be a rather well-known rake and eminently eligible bachelor and—"

"It wasn't precisely my first."

"You have done this more than once? With the dashing St. Gregory?"

Pippa pulled a deep breath. "Well, no—"

"Then who . . ." Caro rolled her gaze toward the ceiling and groaned. "Hugh? You've kissed Hugh? Hugh the prig?"

"*He* has kissed *me*. Several times." She squared her shoulders. "It's not as if *he* was a stranger. We are to be wed."

"But Hugh?" Caro shook her head. "I cannot imagine kissing Hugh—"

"*He* has kissed *me*."

"It must have been like kissing a poached fish left to cool too long on the sideboard."

"Caro! It wasn't like that at all." Pippa glared in defense of her intended.

"But it wasn't as exciting as St. Gregory, I'd wager." A challenge shone in Caro's eye. "Was it?"

She'd never in her life lied to Caro. And she'd never been able to keep anything from her. "Not exactly."

Caro fairly crowed with delight. "I knew it. He made your toes curl, didn't he?"

"Well, he—"

"And your flesh tingle?"

"Perhaps, it—"

"And your heart leap in your breast?"

"Possibly, I—"

"And that's why you didn't want to talk about him." Caro aimed her fan at Pippa in the manner of an accusation or a declaration. "You liked it. No, wait, you like him. I knew it. I was right all along."

"No, of course not. I don't—"

"Don't you dare deny it. I know you as well as I know myself. You do like him." Caro gasped. "Good Lord, you've fallen in love with him!"

"I have not!" Even to her own ears, her denial rang hollow.

"That's why you've been looking for him tonight."

"That's ridiculous! I've neither fallen in love nor looked for him."

"It's so romantic."

"I don't even know him!"

"You know he likes dogs."

"That's scarcely enough to fall in love over." Pippa glared at her cousin. "Besides, I don't care if I never set eyes on the beastly man again."

"Hah. Then why did you agree to dance with him tonight?" Caro said smugly.

Pippa lifted her chin. "It would have been rude not to. Besides, it was Hugh's idea."

Caro leaned closer in a confidential manner. "Hugh doesn't know, does he?"

Pippa's breath caught. "Dear Lord, no! And you must not ever tell him. Or anyone. Promise me."

"I will not breathe a word. Besides, he is not the type of man to take this sort of thing lightly. He'd no doubt call St. Gregory out in defense of your honor."

"A duel!" Pippa buried her face in her hands. "Lord, what have I done?"

Caro's voice was steady and firm. "You haven't done anything. Not really. Hugh is simply a jealous fool and while I hesitate to tell you this, I sense he is a dangerous one as well."

Pippa's head snapped up and she met her cousin's gaze. "What do you mean?"

"I am not exactly certain." Unease creased Caro's brow. "It is something in the way he looks at you that I find—I don't know how to say it. Frightening is the only word that comes to mind."

"That's silly." Pippa pushed the disquieting thought away. "Hugh would never hurt me."

"Of course not." Caro's tone belied her words. Was Caro right? Did she have to fear Hugh's possessive, jealous nature? Surely not. "Even so, you can't possibly marry him now."

Pippa steeled herself for the inevitable. "Of course I can."

"Pippa." Caro grabbed her arm. "It was different before. Now you're in love."

Pippa shook free of Caro's grasp. "I am not in love."

"Perhaps not. But you deserve the chance to find out if what you feel with St. Gregory is love." Caro glared. "I suspect it's already more than what you feel for Hugh."

"I shall not tell you again. I've given my word and I will marry—"

"Ladies." Hugh strode up with a delicate punch cup in each hand and a disgruntled expression on his face. "I do hope this satisfies the rather remarkable thirst you've both evidenced this evening. The wait for this drivel was trying, to say the least."

"Thank you, Hugh." Pippa took the cup with a gratitude that went beyond mere thirst. Hugh stepped into place beside her, his air of proprietorship irritating. Without thinking, she edged a step away.

"However, on my foray for refreshment I did chance upon St. Gregory."

"St. Gregory?" Caro flashed an overbright smile. "Why we were just speaking of him, weren't we?"

"Were we?" Pippa took a quick sip of punch. "I scarcely remember."

"Really? Why, Pippa, do you not recall how we were discussing the remarkable coincidence of running into him in the park?"

Pippa choked back a cough.

Hugh frowned. "Coincidence? What on earth are you talking about? What coincidence?"

"Oh, just his being your friend and all." Caro gazed up at Hugh in a highly flirtatious manner. Pippa gripped her glass tightly.

"I have any number of friends," Hugh said.

"But seeing him again after he'd so recently been to your home in the country, I'd say it was a remarkable coincidence." Pippa narrowed her eyes in a silent threat. Caro fluttered her lashes and her gaze strayed to Hugh and beyond. "Don't you think so?"

Hugh shrugged. "I daresay—"

"Indeed, I think it's far more than coincidence." St. Gregory's voice sounded behind them. "I think it may well be fate."

Pippa turned slowly. Her heart hammered in her chest. St. Gregory stood smiling down at her.

"Miss Morgan. Miss Lyndon. Delightful to see you both again."

"Isn't it though, my lord?" Caro extended her hand. St. Gregory accepted it and raised it to his lips. "I very much feared you were not coming."

St. Gregory chuckled. "Oh, I could not stay away.

Not when two such charming ladies have promised me a dance." He dropped Caro's hand and turned to Pippa. "Miss Morgan, may I have the pleasure?"

"No, thank you," Pippa said. "It's a country dance and I rather think I'd prefer to wait for something else."

"A waltz then." St. Gregory raised a brow.

"I have not yet been given permission to waltz," she said primly.

"In that case—"

"For goodness' sake, Pippa." Impatience colored Caro's voice. "Dance with the man."

Hugh smiled benignly, confident in his own position. "Indeed, Pippa. I know you enjoy such things and we have already had the two dances allowed by society's rules."

"Hugh." Caro nodded toward the other side of the ballroom. "Isn't that your father over there?"

Hugh's gaze followed hers. The Earl waved a hand in an imperious gesture. Hugh frowned. "It seems he wishes to speak with me."

"Oh, do let us go talk to him." Caro linked her arm through Hugh's, ignoring the annoyed expression that crossed his face. "I'm certain St. Gregory can look after Pippa."

"Very well." Hugh cast a glance at St. Gregory then Pippa, as if deciding if his intended would be safe with the other man. Apparently satisfied, he nodded. "We shall not be long, my dear."

"Of course," Pippa murmured, and watched the couple walk off. Caro was obviously sacrificing herself so Pippa could share a private moment with St.

Gregory. And indeed, in this ballroom packed with people she was curiously alone with the one man she neither wanted to be with nor, perhaps, be without.

"Now then." St. Gregory's voice was as intense as the light in his eye. "May I have the honor of this dance?"

"Thank you but no."

"Or would you prefer simply to talk? Here or on the terrace perhaps?"

"Let us dance," she said quickly.

"As you wish." He grinned his lopsided smile. She struggled to keep her breathing steady and allowed him to lead her to the floor, the touch of his hand on her arm a hot spark that spread warmth through her body and her soul.

His presence surrounded her and muddled her head. She could barely keep her mind on the intricate steps of the dance. Each time they came together he studied her in a way at once exciting and terrifying. Pippa did not know what to say and was very much afraid to say anything at all. St. Gregory didn't so much as utter a word, he simply studied her in a manner both proper and considering. Her head swam with a million thoughts and questions and fears. Vaguely, in the back of her mind, a dim note reached her ears over the music. It sounded very much like . . .

She stumbled and stared at him. "Are you whistling?"

"Am I?" Feigned surprise crossed his face. "Why I believe I am."

"Stop it at once," she said in a fierce whisper.

"I thought you appreciated a good whistle."

"Not here!" Lord, would the man scandalize them all with his childish behavior?

"Then where?" His expression was innocent.

"I do not know, but not here!"

"Well." He sighed. "If you do not wish me to whistle then perhaps we can talk now."

"I do not wish to talk," she said through clenched teeth.

"I do." His voice was soft but insistent. "You are an enigma to me and I wish to know more about you."

She barely noticed the end of the music and the dance. He took her elbow and steered her off the floor. "Why?"

"Why what?"

She stared up at him, he looked straight ahead, the corners of his mouth quirked upward. "Why do you wish to know more about me?"

"You are a puzzle. I enjoy puzzles, riddles, mysteries, that sort of thing."

She shook her head. "I am no mystery."

"Indeed you are, Miss Morgan. You are not who or what I was led to expect." He stopped and gazed down at her. "You have aroused my curiosity and I do not arouse lightly."

The oddly serious tone of his voice shivered through her and she stepped back, at once realizing he had led her through the French doors and onto the terrace.

She glared at him. "I told you I did not wish to go outdoors."

He shrugged and leaned against a stone baluster. "Yet you are here."

"You tricked me!"

"I did not. I merely distracted you."

"It is the same thing."

"Is it?"

"Yes." She glanced around the terrace. Here and there a couple lingered, but for all intents and purposes they were quite alone. She stiffened her spine and stared at him. "Well, now that you have me here, what do you wish to know?"

"I must admit I already know a great deal. Yet it seems quite at odds with my own experience."

Unease settled in her stomach. "What do you mean?"

He seemed to choose his words with care. "Hugh told me all about the chit he plans to marry. He said she was lovely and quite charming in a quiet, restrained sort of way. That she is the very essence of virtue and propriety. That she is in short, perfectly suited to be a countess. His countess."

"If Hugh has told you all that then I do not understand—"

"Yet it seems during my recent stay with him, I had a need to escape from the somewhat stifling, even pompous, atmosphere of his country home and found myself on a long walk. There I ran into a rather rambunctious canine and his mistress."

"Go on." She should stop him here and now but

109

his words and his manner mesmerized her. What harm could it do to listen?

"She was as free in spirit as a nymph. As light-hearted and joyous as the dog who romped beside her. As if she did not merely delight in the nature that surrounded her but was as one with it."

"Was she?" she said softly.

"Indeed." He nodded solemnly. "She was captivating and she captivated me. She kissed me, you know."

"Are you certain you didn't kiss her?"

"She asked me to."

"That was not at all proper." She shivered at the distinctly improper memory of his lips on hers.

"Not at all."

"But you did kiss her?"

He shrugged. "How could I not? A beautiful wood sprite asks me to kiss her—"

"You thought she was beautiful?" Wonder sounded in her voice.

"She is beautiful." His deep eyes burned.

She tried to shake off the impact of his gaze. "But surely you have kissed beautiful women before. You do have a certain reputation for such things."

He chuckled. "I do and I have. But there was something about this girl."

"What?" She stared up at him with a yearning she could no longer hide.

"I don't know." A strange confusion shone in his eyes. At once she knew this was not a man who was normally confused about anything. "The memory of her has stayed in my mind, popping up at the most inconvenient moments. She's even appeared in my sleep."

"Has she?" Her heart seemed to stop. He dreamed of her? Of good, proper Pippa Morgan?

"She has. It's very disquieting. I've been trying to puzzle it out ever since."

"You, you said you liked mysteries."

"I do but there doesn't seem to be a solution to this mystery. Unless . . ." He drew a deep breath as if this eminently confident man, this rake, this rogue, was unsure how to proceed. "Unless I could kiss her again."

Panic gripped her and she whirled about in an instinctive need to flee but he grabbed her arm and pulled her back. He stared at her with a yearning she recognized. A yearning she shared. "Could I? Could I kiss her again?"

She shook her head. "No. It would prove nothing."

"Are you confident of that?"

"Yes!"

"Why?" His voice was low and hard with urgency.

"Because it would do no good. Because she has pledged herself to another." She gazed up at him, struggling against the emotion sweeping through her. "How could you bear it? How could she bear it? What if she too felt as you do? What if you too dwelt on the fringes of her mind like a refrain playing over and over again in her head? What if she danced with you in her dreams not just after you kissed her but well before, as if she had known you always and the meeting was merely—"

111

"Fate?" The word hung between them like a curse or a promise.

"Yes." It was a sigh of surrender.

"If all that were true, I should think we owe it to each other to know without question that these odd feelings were only a one-time occurrence and nothing more." He pulled her tighter to him.

"It was supposed to be just once." She gazed at him with a sure and certain knowledge that just once would never again be enough.

"Then once more."

He bent his head and his lips touched hers with a gentleness that melted her very bones and a recognition that surged through her blood and stilled her heart. She could no more resist his touch than she could resist the very air she breathed. His lips pressed against hers harder and her mouth opened beneath his, his breath joining with hers and giving her life. She responded with an eager, natural joy that swept away any thought of proper behavior. All she knew, all she'd ever known or ever wanted to know, was the feel of his lips on hers, his body against hers, his arms around her. There was no longer a question, no longer a doubt: she and this stranger, this rake, this rogue, were indeed destined one for the other. Nothing in her life, in her world, was as right as this single moment. As right as the stars and the moon. As right as forever.

He pulled away and she gasped with a sense of abandonment at the loss of his lips on hers. Bemusement danced in his eyes. "I fear that brings more questions than answers."

"Questions?"

"Indeed." He tightened his hold on her. "Why do you fit into my arms as if you were made to be there? Why does your kiss seem at once new yet familiar as if we have kissed not once but many times before? Why does it seem as if my heart quickens to match pace with your own?"

"I don't know, my lord," she whispered. How could this be? How could he say the very things she had wondered all along?

"Not 'my lord'." He bent and brushed his lips along the curve of her jaw. "Spencer."

She wanted to collapse into his arms at the delightful sensation. "Spencer."

"I must see you again," he murmured, his voice tickling against her neck.

"Again?" She barely noted his words, the touch of his mouth on her sensitive flesh wiping away any rational response or concern.

"Yes."

"Yes." She sighed.

"When then, Pippa?" He pulled away and gazed into her eyes. "Tell me when."

"When?" What was he talking about?

"When can I see you?"

"Oh dear." At once her head cleared. "Why, you can't."

His brows drew together in an irate frown. "What do you mean I can't?"

She pulled out of his embrace. "Simply that. I cannot see you again."

"Why not?" He stepped closer.

She stepped back. "Perhaps you have forgotten, but I have promised to marry Hugh."

"You did not seem too concerned with that fact a moment ago." Again, he stepped toward her.

She backed away. "Nor did you."

"Therefore I—"

She flattened her hand against his chest. "There is no therefore. We agreed to kiss just once. We have and that is that."

"Is it?" His dark eyes simmered with more than the question on his lips.

She could feel the beat of his heart throbbing beneath her fingers. She vaguely noted the intimacy of her touch and knew she should withdraw her hand but somehow couldn't seem to move. Her voice was weak. "It is."

"Your hand is trembling." He placed his hand over hers still flat against his chest. "Does it tremble as well for Hugh?"

"I don't think that's at all your concern." She tried to pull away but his hand held her fast.

"I think it is. I think it's very much my concern when the woman who haunts my dreams will not give me the opportunity to discover what it is between us that pulls us toward one another."

"There is nothing between us."

"Nothing?" He quirked a brow.

"Nothing," she said softly.

"I disagree, my dear Miss Morgan, and furthermore so do you." He shook his head. "There has been something between us from the moment we met. You may deny it all you wish with words but your eyes reveal your true thoughts. You are as intrigued as I by this strange bond that ties us one to the other."

"There is no—"

"There is." He released her hand and she snatched it back against her, as if to protect it from the heat of his body and the truth of his argument. "You know it as well as I. And you further know you cannot marry Hugh until you resolve what you feel for me."

She glared with all the disdain she could muster. "You are an arrogant rake! I feel nothing for you."

"Nothing?" His eyes gleamed, his voice was soft. "You may well lie to me, Pippa, but can you lie as easily to yourself?"

She stepped away, turning her back to him, and clenched her fists against the falsehood. "I am not lying."

"Then it can do you no harm to meet me again." His voice rang firm. "If I mean nothing to you, you run no risk by seeing me."

"I run the risk of scandal."

She heard the shrug in his voice. "That is easily taken care of. I am nothing if not discreet."

"I shall see you again at the balls and routs that make up the season." She couldn't help the note of rising panic in her voice. "Is that not enough for you?"

"No. I wish to see you alone."

She shook her head. "I do not think—"

"Don't think, Pippa." His voice was right beside her ear, so close she could feel the warmth of his breath on her neck. "Not about scandal or propriety or even future betrothals. Think only about the questions you cannot deny. You want the answers as much as I, do you not?"

"Yes." She fairly sobbed the word.

His hands gripped her shoulders and she resisted the urge to lean back against the hard warmth of his body.

"I ride in the park every morning at the first light of dawn. No one is ever about. Meet me. Tomorrow."

"No." She shook out of his grasp and stepped away. "I cannot."

"Then the next day."

"No!" She whirled to face him. "I am to marry Hugh. I cannot meet you tomorrow or the next day or ever."

"I will wait for you."

"I will not come, I tell you."

His gaze trapped hers. "Nonetheless, I shall wait for you."

"You will have to wait forever!"

"As you wish." He shrugged. "Forever it is, then."

She stared helplessly, a hundred emotions battling within her. Finally, she squared her shoulders and stared up into eyes as gray and stormy as a gale at sea. "I wish you well then, my lord. It seems to me forever is a very long time."

She nodded sharply, turned on her heel and started back toward the ballroom. Her steps didn't falter once. Not even when she heard him mutter behind her.

"Curious thing though. I feel as if I've already waited forever."

Chapter Five

"She's not coming today, is she, old man?"

The dark gray stallion beneath Spencer snorted and pawed the ground. Plumes of steam curled from the beast's nostrils. Springtime in England did indeed have its fine days, but in the misty hour of sunrise there was as likely as not to be a strong nip in the air.

Spencer patted the horse's neck and turned him down the path toward the park entrance. Three mornings now he'd waited for Pippa to appear. Three mornings filled with anticipation, buoyed by hope, that faded reluctantly with the first rays of the sun. Still, he would not give up.

It defied explanation: why this innocent country girl stayed in his thoughts. He'd convinced himself that she'd simply struck some unknown chord deep

117

in his mind or his soul and that purging her was a mere matter of seeing her again, getting to know her better and, inevitably, growing bored with her. His only salvation from the chit lay in what he fully expected to be the outcome of being in her company: an unavoidable weariness at the companionship of a good, proper, biddable young lady. He had no doubt that familiarity with any such woman would indeed breed contempt or at least tedium. It always had during his brief encounters with such creatures in the past.

Still, there was something vaguely dishonorable about pursuing the intended of another man. Even a man as priggish as Winsleigh had become. It bothered him a bit. He had always considered himself an honorable man. He was consoled by knowing that he had no intention of ruining her. Why, their involvement would no doubt be short-lived. Winsleigh would not see it that way but Winsleigh would not know. Still, Spencer knew and the question of honorable behavior nagged at the back of his mind.

He stopped at the park gate, turned and studied the tranquil scene behind him. It was only at this hour that the park was a sanctuary for forest dwellers and those needing a peaceful respite for their spirit and not the bustling society arena it would be by day's end. Come late afternoon there would be dozens of young ladies in their first season riding in carriages or on horseback, clogging the lanes in a parade designed to show all to their best advantage. He had no interest in any of them, save one.

"She will come," he said softly, more to himself than to the horse who pranced in place impatiently as if eager to leave the serenity of the park far behind.

She would come. He knew it as surely as he knew his own name. As surely as he knew sleep every night brought dreams of her. As surely as he knew the sun would rise again tomorrow and he would be here to greet it.

He would get to know Pippa Morgan and, in the knowing, put whatever it was about her that haunted him to rest permanently. It was a good plan for a rake and a rogue. An excellent plan for a man who had no interest in virgins. An outstanding plan for a lord who was not yet ready for shackling in marriage to any woman. It would most certainly work and free his thoughts and his energy for the pursit of women more to his sophisticated tastes.

What if it didn't?

He pulled his brows together sharply at the disquieting thought. Of course it would succeed. After all, she was to marry Winsleigh and all Spencer really desired was to satisfy his own curiosity about the appeal of the charming bit of baggage. Why, he wasn't even interested in seduction. He simply wanted a solution to a peculiar mystery.

His horse snorted an odd note of disbelief. Almost as if the beast knew his thoughts and found them ludicrous. Spencer shook off the fanciful notion. Certainly, he had already expended more effort on the girl's behalf than he could remember exerting with any other woman. But that was simply the nature of circumstance. She was an innocent and he had to tread lightly. He only wanted answers.

That and nothing more.

The skyline of London stood silhouetted in the soft midmorning light. Absently, Pippa traced the outlines of gables and spires and chimney pots on her chamber window. Her finger followed the contours of the rooftops she'd studied yesterday and the day before and the day before that.

The morning after the Farnsworth ball, she'd risen before dawn to watch the start of a new day. Satisfaction had filled her at having resisted the insane impulse to sneak off to meet St. Gregory. The arrogant man was probably in the park even then. He could wait until the end of time for all she cared. There was no doubt about it: the man was a scoundrel and she was well rid of him.

Furthermore, her attraction to him, the very way she felt in his arms, could be attributed to nothing more than a childish infatuation. It was a coincidence and a momentary aberration on her part that had led her to this awkward situation. Nothing more. And definitely not anything as absurd as fate. Or love.

Her destiny was to marry Hugh and there was nothing more to say.

On the second morning, she'd again awakened before dawn. Her night had been restless, filled with dreams and desires, with fear and excitement.

She'd stared out at the city and wondered what it was about him, about this virtual stranger, that seemed to reach inside her to touch emotions she'd never known before.

On the third morning, she had alternately stared out the window and paced the width of her room. Did he still wait for her? He'd said he'd wait forever. But surely those were the treacherous words of a man well used to seduction. No doubt he'd found it all something of a diversion, a game for his amusement. He was very likely back to his pursuit of women far more experienced than she.

On this, the fourth morning, she traced the skyline over and over again until the sun was well up in the sky.

What if she did slip away to the park to meet him? And what if he waited still? What would happen then? Would he kiss her once again? Would she want to be kissed? Would she want more? Had she indeed fallen in love with a man she'd met but three times? Would she throw away a proper future with Hugh for a liaison with a rogue who would doubtless offer her little more than dishonor and scandal? Would she break her word to Hugh for the magic of Spencer's embrace? And would she regret it?

It was nonsense of course. Every bit of it. Still, didn't she owe it to herself to set this man from her mind once and for all? If she were to meet him, not that she had any intention of doing so, she could determine if indeed this was simply a green girl's first taste of romance and, in the process, free her dreams from his relentless presence. When one approached it from that route, it certainly seemed to make a great deal of sense.

Very well. She wrapped her arms around herself and stared out the window. It was too late to go today. But tomorrow she would go. Yes, tomorrow it would be. She'd don a disguise to avoid any prying early-morning eyes. Perhaps clothing from one of the stable boys? And her cloak with the deep hood? That would do nicely.

She bit back a smile. No one would ever expect good, proper Pippa Morgan to dress like a boy and steal off alone to meet a gentleman of questionable reputation. No indeed. That's something Caro would do. Although it seemed more and more these days that Caro was quite a bit less than anyone had ever suspected. And Pippa quite a bit more.

At any rate, she would not be at all surprised if St. Gregory had given up his vigil days ago if, in fact, he'd ever really waited for her in the first place. As long as she could remain undetected, it would do no real harm to indulge in an early-morning adventure. Of course Hugh would not see it that way. She shuddered at the thought. No, Hugh would definitely be quite overset by the very idea. Fortunately for them all, Hugh would never know.

And knowledge was, after all, the purpose of this venture. She simply had to know what the emotions St. Gregory triggered in her truly signified. Yes, indeed. This was a quest for wisdom.

That and nothing more.

* * *

The clip clop of her horse's hooves on the cobblestones echoed in the pre-dawn stillness of London's all-but-abandoned streets. Even the occasional peddler or beggar she glimpsed through the heavy curtain of fog seemed to ignore her presence. And why not? Who would pay any notice to a cloaked figure, accompanied by a shaggy, panting dog, guiding his horse through the empty lanes of the silent city?

She was grateful for the fog, of course. It would make detection that much more difficult. But it cast the quality of a dream or a nightmare over the city and made Pippa's heart lodge firmly in her throat. If sheer terror was the stuff of overspirited adventures then she would be eternally grateful for her own proper nature. She entered the park and slowed her steed to an even walk, Samuel trotting alongside. If St. Gregory was here, where exactly would *here* be?

She directed her horse down one of the park's main lanes and vowed to search for a few moments and no more. She would give him until the count of one hundred and if he had not appeared—she shrugged—so be it. One hundred and she would abandon this ill-advised quest. One hundred and no more.

"One . . . two . . ." The sound of her own barely audible voice was a scant comfort in the still of the mist-shrouded empty gardens.

". . . twelve . . . thirteen . . ." This was, no doubt, not an especially safe place for a girl to be, alone and unescorted. Of course, she had Samuel for protection, but the fog that shielded them could well hide its own secrets. Who knew what kinds of horrible people might be about in this hushed hour before sunrise?

". . . twenty-seven . . . twenty-eight . . ." Why, there could be cutthroats and thieves and pirates—well, perhaps not pirates, but definitely cutthroats and thieves.

". . . thirty-five . . . thirty-six . . ." Lord, she didn't have the stamina to be overspirited. Every rustle of a leaf, every creak of a branch terrified her. Even Samuel seemed ill at ease and a low growl sounded deep in his throat

". . . forty . . . forty-one . . ." She should go. Now. Turn and spur her horse for home. And if she left St. Gregory behind to cope with the fiends of the early-morning forest on his own, well it was nothing more than the man deserved.

". . . fifty-three . . . fifty-four . . ." Imagine. He expected her to come alone to the park at this hour of the day. Had he no thought at all as to the consequences of such a rash act? It seemed to her even the adventures of the overspirited should carry with them some semblance of responsibility, or at the very least a footman, for the sake of safety if for no other reason.

"That's quite enough." She turned the horse. "We're going, Samuel."

"I knew you'd come." St. Gregory appeared out of the mist astride a huge, gray beast. To someone far more frivolous than she, she suspected he resembled nothing less than a legendary knight upon a destrier. "Hello, boy." Samuel greeted him with a few friendly "woofs" and a madly wagging tail.

"Did you?" She lifted her chin to meet his gaze with a boldness she didn't know she possessed. "And to what do you attribute this unrelenting confidence?"

He stared for a moment, then laughed, the rich, mellow tone echoing through the trees. At once the sinister threat of the fog retreated. "You are a continuing surprise to me."

She couldn't resist a slight, smug smile. "Am I?"

"Indeed you are." He steered his horse beside hers and she urged her mount to follow his lead, Samuel trotting obediently right behind.

"In what way?"

"Well, for one, I have heard a great deal about the well-bred, well-behaved paragon: Miss Philippa Morgan. Yet I have not heard even the merest whisper about Pippa Morgan, the carefree country hoyden who invites the kiss of a stranger—"

A hot blush swept up her face.

"—or slips away to a private rendezvous with a disreputable gentleman, dressed as—" His eyes widened and he pulled his horse to a stop. "Are those britches?"

She snatched the edges of her cloak and pulled it tighter around her.

"Bloody hell, they *are* britches." St. Gregory's laughter rang through the park for what seemed forever.

"What did you expect?" Pippa glared at him. "I had no desire for anyone to know what I was about.

Therefore it was only sensible to wear a disguise."

"A disguise?" He sputtered and wiped a tear from his eye. "And what precisely are you trying to be?"

"Vague and unnoticed," she snapped.

"My dear, in that costume, you are anything but."

"Regardless, aside from my need to escape detection, this is not the most prudent time of day to be out and about on one's own."

St. Gregory sobered. "I am sorry about that. I didn't recognize the potential danger. It wasn't until the first morning I waited for you that I realized the harm that could befall a young woman alone. After that, I positioned myself beside the gate closest to your home."

"You weren't there today."

"Oh, but I was. You simply did not notice me. I believe you were too busy"—he bit back a smile—"counting."

She glanced at him. "You are quite a tease, aren't you?"

"I have sisters."

His impudent smile caught at her and she couldn't help but laugh. Their horses walked side by side for long, quiet moments filled with an odd mix of peace and excitement.

"I find it difficult to believe that you've waited for me every morning." She slanted him a curious glance. "Why didn't you give up?"

"I told you I'd wait forever."

She shook her head. "That's a lovely thing to say, but forever is an extremely long time."

"Well worth it." A bemused smile played across his lips. "To solve a mystery, that is."

"I already have my own solution, thank you very much."

"Do you?"

"I do." She nodded. "At first I believed you were an illusion and my own subsequent unforgivable behavior—"

He raised a brow. "Unforgivable?"

"—was brought on by my fall down the hill. But, of course, when I met you here I realized that was not at all likely."

A rueful frown creased his forehead. "You sound rather disappointed."

"I was rather. Meeting you again, with Hugh right there—" She blanched at the memory.

"I can see where that would be upsetting."

She shook her finger in his direction. "And you have the most amazing effect on me."

He clasped his hand to his chest in mock surprise. "Have I?"

"Yes, you most certainly have." She tilted her head and studied him. "Do you realize I have never in my life talked this freely with a man?"

"No doubt, that's for the best," he murmured.

Pippa ignored him. "I feel as if I have known you forever. It's quite disconcerting, you know."

"I know."

"I have also never in my life been the least bit overspirited. Now—" She held out her arms. "Just look at me."

"Quite lovely, I think."

"Quite scandalous you mean. You are not at all a good influence."

He choked back a laugh. "I believe you said you had a solution?"

"Indeed." She leaned toward him. "I strongly suspect you are nothing more than the foolish infatuation of a green girl."

"The foolish infatuation of a green girl?"

The crestfallen expression on his face twisted her heart. "See here, do not take it that way."

"And in what way should I take it?"

"You should be flattered."

"Flattered? Why it's practically"—he stiffened his spine—"insulting."

"Insulting?" She laughed. "Why?"

"One prefers to think he appeals to a more discriminating type of woman."

She arched a brow. "And green girls are not quite as particular, I imagine?"

"I imagine." He glared. "So you think this is a mere infatuation on your part?"

She straightened in her saddle. "I simply cannot imagine what else it could be."

"Infatuation," he said under his breath, and urged his horse to a slight canter.

"Well," she called after him. "What's your answer then?"

He wheeled his horse around to face her. "I have no idea. All I know is you are in my mind day and night. You haunt my thoughts and my dreams." He pointed at her. "*You* have the most amazing effect on *me*."

"Have I?" She widened her eyes in an innocent manner. "How delightful."

"It is not delightful at all. It is most annoying." He glared at her in a thoroughly endearing way. "I had thought if I saw more of you I would grow bored."

"Now should I be flattered or insulted?"

"Neither." He clenched his jaw. "It's simply my nature. I am not interested in a woman of your type."

"A woman of my type?"

"Yes. You know. You're the kind of woman who does exactly what is expected of her. Who follows the rules of—"

"Who would never secretly meet a man of your reputation when she's very nearly betrothed to someone else?" she said lightly.

"Who is generally good and biddable and proper." He raked his fingers through his dark hair. "There is only one thing to do with women like that."

"Oh?"

"Marriage." He grimaced as if the word left a bad taste in his mouth.

"I see." She stifled a giggle.

"I have no desire to be wed." He glared a warning. "Do you understand?"

"Completely." She paused and considered her words. "I gather, then, my honor should not be in jeopardy if I were to continue to meet you?"

He started. "Your honor?"

"If you wish to avoid marriage then it would be

best to avoid seduction. You said it yourself." She shrugged. "I am a good, proper biddable girl. Should our names be linked together in any semblance of scandal . . . well . . . salvaging my honor, as well as your own, would require marriage."

"I had not planned on seducing you," he muttered.

"What had you planned?"

His gaze meshed with hers, the look in his eyes abruptly serious. "Would you meet me again?"

"So that you may determine how quickly you will grow bored with me and get any thought of me out of your dreams?"

He smiled slowly. "So that you may decide if this is indeed a green girl's infatuation."

"And what if you don't grow bored?"

"What if you discover this is not infatuation?"

"I think," she said, her words slow and cautious, "the only sensible thing is to meet again. Only in the search for knowledge, of course, to resolve our questions."

"Of course." He leaned toward her and tucked a curl that had escaped her hood behind her ear. "I should hate for you to marry Winsleigh with such issues as yet undecided."

"I should hate that as well," she said quietly.

He cupped her chin and gazed into her eyes. "This may be the most idiotic thing I have ever done."

"I have done rather a lot of those things myself in recent days." She laughed weakly. His gaze searched her face as if to find the answers he needed there.

"Still"—his voice was low and intense—"nothing has ever seemed so right."

"It seemed very right when you kissed me." She swallowed hard. "Do you think perhaps, to further our quest for knowledge and for no other reason, you should, that is to say, what I mean is—"

He slid from his horse and pulled her off hers and into his arms. She melted against him and his lips claimed hers as if he'd been waiting just for this. Her head spun with the sheer emotion of being in his embrace. She molded her body to the heat of his. Dear Lord, what was she doing? She was honor bound to marry Hugh, but how could she stay away from Spencer? And how futile it would be to even try.

He pulled his lips from hers and gathered her tight against him as if desperate to hold her close. Her head rested against his chest and his warmth enveloped her. All banter between them vanished and a strange sadness filled her heart.

This might well be the love of her dreams, and here in the privacy of a fog-shrouded dawn, she could pretend there was little if anything of consequence in the world beyond the two of them. In his arms nothing else mattered. Not Hugh or the future or even the risk involved in this overspirited adventure. It was not an adventure at all but an urgent need that could not be denied.

She could call it foolish to his face but she couldn't hide the truth from her heart. This was emotion so deep it gripped her soul and stole her sanity and left her filled with wonder and awe. This was ruled by the fates and governed by destiny and as inevitable as the sunrise. She knew it now and perhaps had known it from the moment he pulled her to her feet in Sussex, the moment he kissed her.

This was love.

That and nothing more.

Let me tell ya . . .

. . . *there was a hell of a lot more. Ya see, she wasn't that kind of girl. No sir. Pippa really was good and the secret meetings with Spence, all the sneakin' around, took a toll on her. Poor kid. Ya could see it in her eyes. Haunted, I'd call it. She only seemed to come alive when she was with him. And she was with him a lot. Every morning she and I would go to the park. They could only be together for maybe half an hour or so but they packed a lot a livin' in that thirty minutes.*

You ever hear your human laugh? Not yet? Well, ya will. It's a swell sound. Pippa laughed all the time with him. She was happy and that's all I cared about. As for Spence, I liked him. Liked him a lot. He was good dog people, ya know what I mean? Always had a little somethin' in his pocket for me. Man, what a guy.

Talked a good line too. Heh heh heh. All that nonsense he spouted about only wanting to be with her to get her out of his system. What a bunch of malarkey. He was as smitten as she was. He looked at her the way you or I look at a T-bone sizzling on a grill. He was caught: hook, line and sinker, and all she had to do was reel him in.

It would have been damn near perfect if Pippa hadn't been so, well, good, I guess. Spence too I suppose. It bothered her: her feelings for Spence and her promise to marry Hugh. Yeah, I know Hugh was a jerk. I'm pretty sure she knew it too. But, weird as it sounds, Hugh didn't really have much to do with it. It was all about her keeping her word. She said she'd marry him and that was that. Especially since Hugh seemed to worship her, the creep.

If only Pippa and Spence had just run off together. Sure, there would have been one hell of a scandal but the dust would have settled sooner or later and they would have lived a long and happy life together. Kids, puppies, the whole ball of wax.

Sometimes humans are just plain stupid. Huh? Oh, I said that already? Well, kid, it bears repeatin'. Here ya got two nice people who are destined to be with each other but they end up blowin' it. And for what? Lip service to an ideal, plain and simple.

But it ate at her more and more until finally, she decided she had to do somethin', had to set things right. What a disaster.

Play It Again, Sam

Now, don't get me wrong, I believe all that stuff about a man's—or a woman's—word being his bond. It's a pretty noble sentiment even for a canine. But there are some things bigger than a promise.

Things like love.

Chapter Six

Where was he?

Pippa's anxious gaze skipped across the empty terrace so very much like every other terrace at every other palatial London home at which she'd been to a ball or a soiree or a rout these past weeks. Were they perhaps designed less for the enjoyment of a garden setting and more for the express purpose of providing a moment of privacy for clandestine lovers? They had certainly performed that function for Pippa and Spence.

Absently, she fingered a blossom blooming in a tall stone urn. Terraces, unoccupied libraries, vacant parlors, all had served as a meeting place for a few brief words and a quick embrace. Morning rendezvous in the park were never enough, and she and Spencer would slip away from whatever gathering they were at for a few blessed moments together.

Even with Hugh's constant presence it was far easier than she had ever imagined. He was not at tonight's soiree and she noted the sense of freedom his absence gave her, a feeling she did her best to ignore. She was fairly confident Hugh suspected nothing and was, in point of fact, quite secure in his belief that she very much belonged to him.

As indeed she soon would.

"Pippa."

She turned to fall into Spencer's open arms. He picked her up and twirled her around and laughter bubbled through her lips in spite of the heaviness in her heart. "Spencer, put me down! Someone will surely see us."

"Let them, I don't care." He grinned. "I have come to a decision."

"Indeed," she said softly. "As have I."

"It's not nearly as good as mine, I'd wager. And while the proper thing to do would be to allow you to go first, I should like to abandon the rules of etiquette"—his dark eyes twinkled—"just this once."

"Just this once," she echoed.

Without warning his gaze and his voice were serious. "Pippa, I do not wish to continue meeting in the park or slipping out of social occasions to catch a quick moment alone. It has become extremely distasteful."

"I see." Her heart clenched and it was all she could do to keep from doubling over with the pain. It was over, then, between them. He had reached the point of boredom he'd anticipated. Perhaps it was for the best. At least she was spared having to say what she'd agonized over for the last week and rehearsed all day. She squared her shoulders and nodded. "Very well."

Pippa turned to leave, but he caught her arm and spun her around. A puzzled frown creased his brow. "Where are you going?"

"I am going indoors." She drew a deep breath. "There is obviously nothing more to say."

He stared at her for a long moment; then his expression cleared and he laughed. "You think I mean I don't want to see you anymore."

She narrowed her eyes. "Well, don't you?"

"No, no, my darling Pippa." He drew her into his arms. "Quite the opposite, my love."

My love?

"Then what do you mean?"

"I mean I'm tired of furtive trysts and secretive moments snatched only when the opportunity presented itself. I feel like the worst kind of scoundrel."

She smiled. "I thought you were."

He quirked a brow. "Even we scoundrels have standards, my dear."

She shook her head and laughed.

"I love the way you laugh." He brushed his lips across hers. "I wish to hear you laugh always."

Her breath seemed to catch. "Always?"

"Indeed." His gray eyes simmered with an intensity that tore at her soul. "I want to hear your laughter echo across the hills in the countryside. I want to be in a ballroom and hear a laugh across a crowded floor and know, without looking, that it's yours. And know furthermore that when I turn, your eyes will meet mine and your laughter will be only for me.

"I wish your laugh to be the first thing I hear in the morning and the last thing I hear at night." His grip tightened. "I want you with me for all the mornings and nights for the rest of our lives."

"Spencer, I—"

"I want each and every one of those at tonight's festivity—no, I want each and every person in London, in all of England, to know precisely how I feel about you." His gaze bored into hers. "I wish all to know that I want you for my wife. I love you, Pippa."

"Oh, Spencer." Joy shot through her and her knees trembled with the weight of it. He loved her and, Lord help her, she loved him back. And for just a moment she could see in her mind's eye a life filled with love and laughter and long happy years and the delighted giggles of children with over-enthusiastic puppies romping at their sides.

As quickly as it appeared, the vision of a future with the man she loved vanished, replaced by the condemning face of Hugh: the man she was to marry. A sob broke from her throat and she pulled out of Spencer's embrace. "Oh, Spencer."

He reached out and brushed away a tear that hovered on the tips of her lashes. "I daresay, I hadn't expected quite this reaction." He smiled uncertainly. "I thought you would be happy. I have suspected for a while now the manner of our meeting was upsetting to you. It has taken me far too long to realize how important you've become to me." He grasped her hands. "How very much I love you."

"Stop it, please! Stop it at once!" She snatched her hands from his and stepped back. "This is a lovely sentiment but you know as well as I, there can never really be anything between us."

"I believe," he said, his words slow and precise, "there already is."

"Regardless, it doesn't matter! I am promised to Hugh."

"Cry off. Nothing of your intentions has been made public. No one knows of your arrangement—"

"Everyone knows!" Frustration sharpened her tone. "This is London and if I have learned nothing else here, I have learned that London society is far worse than the smallest hamlet. Everyone knows everything about everyone."

"Even so—"

"Even so, it still does not signify. I know. No one else has to. I know what I have agreed to, what promises I have made." She shook her head. "I cannot go back on my word."

"Why not?" His tone rang firm and hard.

How could she make him understand? "Would you?"

"No, of course not. A man's word is his bond. It's a matter of honor."

Her voice was soft. "Is my word then, my honor, less important than your own?"

"Of course not." He shook his head. "Still, you are

141

a woman. It's not the same thing at all."

"Is it not? I am a person, first and foremost, and my gender is irrelevant." A pleading note underlay her words. "Do you think so little of me that you would expect me to do what you would never do yourself? What you would condemn any man for?"

"And what of my honor, Pippa, what of that?"

"I—I do not understand."

"Is it an honorable circumstance to become involved with a woman practically betrothed to another man? I doubt it. I admit when we first began meeting I saw it as an insignificant lark. But now— now I am willing to sacrifice all for you."

"I . . . I don't—"

"I love you!" Anger shadowed his words. Disbelief shone in his eyes. "Does that not count for something?"

Pippa couldn't bear to look at the shock and hurt on his face. She turned away and gripped her hands together. "It makes no difference."

"It makes all the difference in the world. I have never loved a woman before."

"There will, no doubt, be other women." Her voice was faint and she struggled for control.

"I do not want other women. I want you. I love you." Outrage exploded in his voice and she cringed at the obvious pain in his anger. He grabbed her shoulders and spun her to face him. "Does that not matter to you?"

"It matters a great deal." *It's all that matters. And I shall treasure the knowledge of it until the end of my days.*

His fingers tightened on her shoulders and she welcomed the minor pain that distracted her from the ache in her heart.

"Then come away with me. We can get a special license or go to Scotland and be married by this time to—"

"No! I cannot. I have given my word to marry Hugh and I cannot, I shall not, go back on it!"

"But I love you and I know you love me." His anguished gaze meshed with hers. "You do love me, don't you? I'm not wrong in that, am I?"

She wrenched her gaze from his. Dear Lord, what could she say? Tell him the truth? Or lie in hopes that the falsehood would make their parting a bit easier for him to bear? Or perhaps say nothing at all and let him make his own assumptions.

"Pippa?" He shook her gently and still she would not meet his eyes. Long moments stretched to forever. Finally he released her. "I see.

"What was it all then, Pippa? Merely an opportunity for an overspirited adventure before shackling yourself to the pompous boredom of Winsleigh?" His voice was cold and her gaze snapped to his.

"Oh no, nothing like that. It was . . ." She shrugged helplessly.

He stared at her for an endless moment and she wondered that he couldn't hear the breaking of her heart. His voice was quiet. "I do not believe that you do not love me."

Believe me! Surely it will make it easier. For you if not for me.

She pulled a steadying breath. "Believe what you wish."

She turned to leave. If she did not escape from his presence at once she would throw herself into his arms and confess the truth without regard to the consequences.

"I will."

She stepped toward the house.

"I believe that you love me."

She stopped.

"I believe that you and I are as fated to be together as are the moon and the stars."

A cold hand squeezed her heart.

"I believe that nothing, not my honor, not anything in my life, has meaning without you in it."

She clenched her fists and choked back a sob.

"I will always love you, Pippa. Till time itself runs dry I will love you."

She couldn't bear another second of the torment in his voice, of the unyielding promise in his words. She again started toward the side door, hoping to reach sanctuary before she broke down and wept for the loss of him.

"And I will be at your service should you ever need me. You simply need . . ."

She reached the entryway and slipped inside, leaning back against the frame. The door led to a small corridor rather than directly to the main ballroom where guests were gathered, so she was blessedly alone. She closed her eyes and struggled against the emotions churning within her.

How could she let him go? He was everything

she'd ever dreamed of deep in the night. Her heart leapt when she so much as heard his name and when he touched her—she shivered at the memory—she could barely breathe for the bliss of it.

It was her own fault, of course, all of it. Impatiently she swiped at the tear that trickled down her face. She should never have agreed to wed a man she did not love, even one preferred by her family, even one she had known all her life. She should have been true, above all, to herself.

A bitter taste lingered in the back of her throat. She was doing just that with her insistence on keeping her word, her honor. But what did it matter now?

She straightened and sniffed back tears. She hoped she was presentable. No one at this party could know what had just transpired. She started toward the gathering.

Yes, indeed, she would keep her word and her honor.

It was all she had left.

". . . to whistle." Pippa disappeared into the building. Spencer's voice drifted away in the silence. He had never been much of a man for crowds and had always enjoyed a certain amount of solitude, but he had never been so alone in his life.

Forsaken. Abandoned. Alone.

How could she leave him? A hard ache settled in his gut. How could he let her go? He raked shaky fingers through his hair.

Yet how could he argue with her? She was right,

of course. Why, he would lose all respect for a man, any man, who broke his word. He would treat such a creature with disdain and disgust.

"Bloody hell, she's a woman," he muttered to himself. "No one expects a woman to meet the standards set for men."

Pippa does.

The thought struck him like a physical blow. Hadn't he already glimpsed a strength of character just beneath the surface of Pippa Morgan? Wasn't that aspect of her nature one of the things he loved?

Hot self-loathing burned his face. He had done her a grave disservice. How could he expect less of her than he did of any man? How could he be so idiotic? In all conscience, could he really demand she abandon her principles and lower the standards she lived by? Certainly he would not think any less of her.

But would she think less of herself?

And wouldn't that destroy the spirit of the woman he loved?

"Damnation." What was he to do? He shook his head and started toward the door. He was a fool and it might well have cost him the love of his life.

No. He stopped, turned on his heel and strode toward the terrace steps that led into the garden. He wouldn't confront her tonight. It would probably do no good at any rate. But this was not the end. He would not permit it.

He had not finally found the odd emotion rhapsodized in word and song since the dawn of time only to lose it now. There was no conceivable way he would allow Pippa to marry Winsleigh. Winsleigh did not deserve her. Spencer would move heaven and earth if need be but he would not lose her.

He stalked unseeing through the formal gardens lit with paper lanterns like so many fireflies on a summer eve, passed through the gate leading to the drive and glanced over the assembled carriages for his own vehicle. He needed a plan of some sort. He needed to think. But first, he needed a brandy. Perhaps even a fine Scotch whiskey.

His club would be far too crowded tonight and he did not wish for company. Home was the place then. To consider how to claim Pippa's hand without any loss of her self-respect. To sit before the fire and let the burn of whiskey dull the ache that ate at his heart. And let the whiskey, as well, sodden his senses until he drifted into a sleep bereft of dreams.

Tonight, he could not bear to dream of her.

The whirl of the dance, the bright colors of the guests' finery, the din of the music all blended into a kaleidoscope of dull sensation. Pippa moved as one asleep, without thought, without effort, without emotion.

Soon, very soon now, it will be over.

She smiled pleasantly and engaged in cordial conversation and counted the minutes until she could escape to the sanctity of home and her own bed to weep away all the pain in her heart. As if she could ever diminish the sense of loss she would no doubt carry forever.

Thank goodness Hugh was not here. He had been called away to the country yesterday and was not expected back for several days. How fortunate. His constant hovering would have inhibited anyone else from asking her to dance. As it was, she was never without partners, never given a moment to herself, never allowed time to succumb to the knot that burned with an unimaginable grief deep inside her.

"Oh, Pippa, isn't it all wonderful?" Caro's face glowed with the happy excitement of an incomparable in high demand. "Aren't *they* all wonderful."

"Indeed." Pippa managed a polite smile.

"Especially him." Caro nodded across the floor to a young man who grinned in a devilish manner and lifted his glass in a toast. Caro giggled and bobbed a quick curtsy.

"Who is he?" Pippa said, trying to put a note of interest in her voice.

"He's the one." A smug tone shaded Caro's words.

"The one what?"

"The one I shall marry."

Pippa raised a brow. "This week."

"No, Pippa, I am quite serious this time."

"You were serious about the Scottish earl and the attractive son of a Northcumberland squire and that lord who was looking for his second wife and—"

"Minor flirtations, nothing more." Caro waved a dismissive hand. "This is completely different."

148

"How?"

"This is serious."

Pippa couldn't resist a slight smile. "Do tell me more."

"He's top of the trees, Pippa." Caro's eyes sparkled. "He's all I ever wanted and more. He's handsome and dashing and—"

"And does this embodiment of your dreams come true have a name?"

"Of course he has a name. He has a truly wonderful name. It's Farleigh Bartholomew. He's the Marquess of Dunston." Caro smirked. "And the son of a duke."

"Dunston?" The name sounded vaguely familiar. "Where have I heard that name before?"

"No doubt everywhere. He's very well received."

"Is he?" Pippa stared across the room at the charming marquess and at once realized exactly who he was. She chose her words with caution. "Isn't he the one who was involved in that duel last month? Over the wife of some lord?"

"Oh, he's always involved in something or another. It's of no importance. Dunny is—" Caro leaned toward her confidentially. "—everyone calls him Dunny, you know. Why, he's—"

"He's a legend." Pippa glared at her cousin. "A legendary cad, that is. The man is the worst type of scoundrel. You may well call him Dunny but his true name is Scandal. How could you let yourself be misled by such an accomplished seducer of young women!"

Caro studied the fan in her hand. "I love him

and"—she stared straight into Pippa's eyes, daring a challenge—"he loves me."

Pippa snorted. "The man doesn't know the meaning of the word love. He's an infamous rake. No doubt he has told dozens of women he loved them."

"Perhaps." Caro shrugged. "But he wishes to marry me."

"What makes you think such a thing?"

"He told me."

"And you believed him?"

"Indeed I do." Caro flicked her fan open and waved it lazily in front of her face. "He loves me and I love him. Someday he will be a duke and I will be a duchess. I shall have everything I have ever dreamed of."

Pippa shook her head in disbelief. "I doubt that."

"I don't. Everything and love as well. It's all quite perfect. We have even talked about going to Gretna Green to be wed as soon as possible."

Pippa gasped. "You wouldn't!"

"Oh indeed I would." Caro sighed. "Just think of it, Pippa. He and I will have a simply magnificent life together. And haven't we always heard that reformed rakes make the best husbands?"

"Reformed, yes."

"Well, perhaps he is not reformed yet but he soon will be, once we're wed." Caro nodded with satisfaction. "I should think you'd do best to look for a rake ripe for reforming yourself."

Pippa's throat tightened and she fought back tears. "I have no need of a rake. I am to marry—"

"Yes, yes, I know. Even so . . ." Caro's voice grew

thoughtful. "I still think the handsome St. Gregory likes you, quite a bit. Although you do not spend any time at all with him, I have noted he dances with you at every function we attend. Has he kissed you again?"

"Caro!" *Yes, yes! Over and over until I thought I'd die from the joy of it.*

Caro's gaze skimmed across the ballroom. "I was certain I had seen him here earlier."

"I do not care if he's here or not." *I care more than words can say. And I shall care for him until my last breath on earth.*

"I certainly don't know why. I think he's a far better match than Hugh and you've as much as admitted to me that you were not unaffected by—"

"Caro, that's quite enough! I do not wish to discuss St. Gregory." Her hands trembled and she clasped them together. "Not tonight and never again."

I cannot speak of him. Not even to you. Not now, not ever. He is my secret and he shall always remain my secret. But the memory of his kiss and his smile and his stormy gray eyes will live with me forever.

Caro narrowed her eyes. "Whatever is the matter with you this evening?"

"The matter?" *I have allowed my heart to break for the love of what I can never have.*

"Yes. You don't look at all well. I don't believe I've ever seen you quite so pale. Lord, you're not developing the same headaches Hugh's mother seems to be constantly stricken with? I'm quite certain there's nothing truly wrong with the woman. It's probably the effect of living with the earl and Hugh." Caro eyed her sharply. "Are you ill?"

"I think perhaps I am." At once the emotion she'd held back swept through her and she swayed on her feet.

Caro grabbed her arm and led her to a chair. Pippa sank into it gratefully. "You are ill. I'll send someone for our parents and call for the carriage." Concern shone in Caro's eyes. "Will you be all right here for a moment?"

"I'll be fine." Pippa breathed deeply. "Really."

"Very well. I'll return as soon as I can." Caro hurried off in the manner of one who had an important job to do and would brook no interference.

Pippa leaned her head back and closed her eyes. At once a dozen images filled her mind.

Of a man appearing out of the mist and fog on a huge, noble steed. Of a dream partner with a beloved face and a dance beneath the moon and the stars. And of a lopsided grin that tore at the heart of a girl and burned its way into her dreams . . . and her soul.

Chapter Seven

Starlight filtered in through the window just enough to outline the crack in the ceiling of the bed chamber. When one studied it for any length of time, especially by the capricious glow of starlight, it looked surprisingly like the west coast of India as portrayed on the map hanging on the wall of Lord Fitzpatrick's library. The coast she had traced with her finger while waiting for Spencer to slip away from a rout and join her.

Over and over, the tip of her finger had outlined the landscape past Karachi and Bombay until his hand had fallen on hers and guided her invisible work. And he had teased her of long voyages to adventurous places and whispered against her ear and feathered kisses along her neck. Now, she couldn't pull her gaze away from that crack. Sleep would not come and Pippa was at once grateful and annoyed. Awake, she could think of nothing but him. But asleep, she faced the dreams she could not endure.

She watched and the coast disappeared, the starlight strangled by the clouds. A vast emptiness washed over her.

I am such a fool.

She slid out of bed and picked up her wrapper that lay in a heap on the floor. She tossed it on, then paced from the window to the bed.

How could she have cast away this wonderful man who made her soul sing and her body tremble? And for what? For her word? Her honor? Was it really that important?

Yes.

She sank down on the bed. It was important, at least to her. It made no sense to her whatsoever that only a man was expected to keep his word and not a woman. Why didn't other people understand that? And why wasn't there some way to salvage her honor and marry Spencer as well?

Would he even want me now?

She cringed at the memory of the pain and anger in his eyes. A crack of thunder sounded outside as if in response to her turmoil. She couldn't imagine what on earth she was to do now.

Caro would know.

In spite of learning her cousin wasn't quite as overspirited as she had thought when it came to illicit kisses, Caro still remained adventurous and mischievous. Pippa jumped off the bed and stepped swiftly through her door to the other girl's room, directly across the hall.

"Caro." She knocked softly, then opened the door and slipped inside. "Caro." She drew closer to the bed. "Wake up. I must . . ."

The bed was empty. Neatly turned down but definitely empty.

"We have even talked about going to Gretna Green to be wed as soon as possible."

Surely not! She wouldn't! Would she?

Of course she would. Why, it was just the sort of insane thing her cousin would do. Pippa flew to the huge mahogany wardrobe and threw open the doors, searching for Caro's small traveling valise.

It was nowhere in sight.

Good Lord. Pippa brushed her hair away from her face. Dunston will never marry her. The man's reputation made that clear. This will ruin Caro. Even she will not be able to live down a scandal of this magnitude.

Pippa crossed her arms over her chest and stalked back to her own chamber. She had to do something. She could not allow her dearest friend to destroy her life. Someone had to stop her. Pippa could do nothing alone but—

"I will be at your service should you ever need me."

Spencer! Of course. In spite of everything, he would help her. And maybe in the rescue of Caro they could save their own happiness as well. Her heart swelled with hope. With any luck it was not too late to save Caro.

Or themselves.

*   *   *

The hiss of water hitting hot coals sounded from the fireplace.

"Bloody hell. Rain." Spencer stared at the flames and pulled another long swallow of his brandy. He'd decided against the Scotch whiskey. As much as he would have enjoyed sliding into the oblivion offered by the potent drink, he needed to think above all tonight. Brandy mellowed his soul but still allowed his mind to function.

There had to be a way to resolve this. Why couldn't he think of something? Anything? He supposed he could always kidnap her and spirit her to Scotland for a forced wedding. That would certainly absolve her of any dishonor publicly. Why, with his reputation, Pippa would have the sympathy of everyone in the ton. However, her perception of the situation would be entirely different.

And that was the rub. He sighed heavily and swirled the liquor in the snifter in his hand. The battle here wasn't so much with what others would think of her but what she would think of herself. After all, no one expected a woman's word to be worth anything. No one but Pippa.

"Milord?" His butler's voice sounded from the doorway behind him.

"Go away, Randolph."

"But, milord—"

"I said go away." He tossed off the rest of the brandy. "I do not wish to be disturbed. Unless you care to come over here and refill my glass," he said, dangling his glass over the side of the armrest, "get out."

A slight shuffling sounded behind him and he heard the door close. Damnation. He should have been more specific. *First, refill my glass, then get out.* Now he'd have to get up and cross the room to the desk where he'd so inconveniently left the decanter.

The glass lifted out of his grasp. Excellent. Randolph hadn't withdrawn after all. The manservant knew his job all right and Spencer was lucky to have him. The now heavy snifter was placed back in his grip. "Thank you."

"You're quite welcome."

He froze and stared at the delicate hand that lingered beside his on the crystal. "Have I had far more brandy than I thought or is it really you?"

She released the snifter and circled the chair to stand before him. "It's really me."

He could do little more than stare. A slight smile turned up the corners of her mouth. Apprehension shone in the green of her eyes. Water dripped off her cloak and puddled on the floor at her feet.

"What do you want?" The words came out harsher than he'd intended, and she cringed at his tone. "Sorry. I'm simply rather confused to see you here."

"I'm rather confused myself." She laughed in a shaky manner. "I—I need your help."

"My help?" His stomach knotted. So she did not come to throw herself into his arms and proclaim her love and damn the consequences. He sipped his drink. "I see."

"You said if I ever needed you—"

"—to whistle. Yes, yes. I remember." He waved at her sodden appearance. "And this, I gather, is the proverbial whistle. The call for assistance."

She lifted her chin. "If you do not wish to help me, I will certainly understand."

"I will help you." He lifted his shoulder in a lazy shrug. "Whatever it is, I'll help you. And may God have mercy on me."

"Thank you." The stiff stance of her body relaxed with gratitude.

"Do not thank me yet. What do you want?"

She wrung her hands together and searched for the words. Whatever it was, she was obviously over-wrought by it. Fear stabbed him. "Is it Winsleigh?"

"Hugh?" Her eyes widened.

"If he's hurt you, I—"

"No, no," she waved impatiently, "this has nothing to do with Hugh. This is about Caro."

Relief surged through him. "Oh, the beautiful Miss Lyndon. I daresay, she strikes me as the kind of chit who can well take care of herself."

"She certainly cannot." An irritated frown creased Pippa's forehead. What would she do if he kissed it away?

"Spencer." She perched on the edge of the otto-man in front of his chair. "She's run off. To Gretna Green. To be married."

"Good for her." What would she do if he pulled her into his arms? "I do hope she'll be very happy."

"With the Marquess of Dunston."

"Dunny?" Spencer snorted. "Now he really is a scoundrel."

"I know." Frustration darkened her eyes. How would they look in the throes of passion? "He'll never marry her and she'll be ruined. We have to save her."

"We?"

"You said you would be at my service."

"I did not realize that meant a jaunt to Scotland in the middle of the night, and in the rain no less, to save the cousin of the woman I love from her own foolishness."

"Spencer, I—"

He rose from the chair and stared down at her. "I will help you, of course, but you knew I would, didn't you?"

She nodded. "Always."

"Not quite." He shook his head. "I will have my swiftest team hitched to my fastest rig and go after Miss Lyndon, but only on one condition."

She stood to face him. "Anything."

He tilted up her chin with his finger and stared into her eyes. "You must allow me to attempt to find a solution to the problem of reconciling your pledge with our love. Do you agree?"

Her troubled green gaze searched his face. She swallowed hard. "I agree."

He studied her silently. "So you do love me?"

She shook off his hand. "I did not say that."

"You did not deny it either."

"If we're to catch Caro we must go. At once." Urgency rang in her voice. "Please."

"Very well." He nodded. "But afterwards—"

"Afterwards"—she smiled and his heart melted—"we shall see."

He quirked a brow. "We shall indeed."

"This blasted rain is making the roads damn near impassable." Spencer yelled above the din of the storm and glared at the muddy mess just beyond his horses' ears.

"We have to keep going," Pippa shouted, and pressed her lips together stubbornly. "We've barely been on the road for an hour."

"It is pouring down rain. This my lightest and fastest rig, yet the horses are struggling and not making any progress whatsoever." Spencer shook his head. "It is useless to attempt to continue. We have to turn back."

"No! We must stop them!"

"Pippa." A muscle ticked at the corner of his jaw. "I understand your concern for your cousin and indeed I share it. But this is absurd. If we do not turn back now, Caro will not be the only one with a ruined reputation." He heaved a frustrated sigh. "I love you and I want you to be my wife, but to be embroiled in scandal is perhaps not the best way to achieve that end. At least, not yet."

"But Spencer—"

"No, Pippa. I'm turning the carriage around and we are heading back to London." He snapped the reins. "We have hours still until dawn and I can safely return you home with no one the wiser."

"Very well." Her shoulders slumped in defeat. "There seems to be little choice."

"Indeed, my love, there is no choice at all." Spencer's eyes narrowed and he concentrated on maneuvering the high-strung horses on the narrow, slippery highway.

She clutched the seat with the sway and bounce of the curricle. The road north was not an especially good one under the best conditions. Tonight it was nothing less than horrible.

"Poor Caro," she murmured.

Spencer kept his gaze fixed on the horses and the road. "He may well actually marry her, you know."

"I suppose. Although he does not have that type of reputation. Caro is lovely but"—she shook her head in dismay—"I doubt that she is what a future duke is looking for in a bride."

"You never know what will appeal to a man. Caro's heritage is impeccable. I assume her dowry is respectable and she is a beauty to boot. It may well be love." He slanted her a pointed glance. "One never knows where that fickle emotion will strike."

Heat rose in her face and she bit back a smile.

"Bloody hell." Spencer cursed under his breath. The curricle seemed to glide across the road in a sideways manner. Pippa slid across the seat and smashed into Spencer's solid form. The careening carriage stopped abruptly, lurched and tilted precariously. A sickening sensation gripped her and terror kept her still, too afraid to move for fear of upsetting the leaning vehicle.

"Are you all right?" Spencer said sharply.

The concern in his voice eased the panic that threatened to overtake her. "Yes, quite. I think."

"Good." His side of the carriage was lower than hers and he slipped carefully out of the vehicle. "Give me your hand." She grasped his fingers and in a moment he had pulled her to safety on the muddy road.

Flashes of lightning illuminated the disastrous scene. The horses still stood on the road but one of the curricle's wheels had slid off into a deep rut and was mired in the mud. The fashionable rig tiled at an odd and thoroughly depressing angle.

"Perhaps this would not have happened if you had taken a more substantial vehicle," she murmured.

"A more substantial vehicle?" His brows drew together and the exasperation of a man who has had a long, trying day sounded in his voice. "You wanted speed. You insisted on the fastest carriage I had. You—"

"I had no idea you would actually listen to me." She tried to stamp her foot but the effort was wasted in the mud.

"Of course I listen to you." He stared in angry disbelief. "Didn't I listen to you when you told me you could not marry me because of some ridiculous idea as to the precious sanctity of your word?"

Rain fell on her upturned face and she wiped her cheeks impatiently with the back of her hand. "We've said all this before. The importance of my word to me is not any more ridiculous than yours is to you."

"It's all ridiculous, Pippa, if it means sacrificing what we have found with each other!" Lightening flashed and reflected in his eyes. "I don't care about honor or anything else if the result is losing you!"

"Well you should care," she shouted.

"Why?"

"Because without honor what is there in life?"

"Love!"

"But—"

He grabbed her and jerked her into his arms. "Love, Pippa. What honor is there in marrying one man when you so clearly love another? What has happened between us has taught me that. Love is the only thing worthwhile in life and I cannot live mine without yours. And furthermore you feel the same."

"I do not!"

"You do and you cannot deny it!"

"But I do deny it."

He gripped her tighter. "You love me! Admit it."

"No!"

"Say it, Pippa, say you love me."

"I—" She glared up at him and at once realized the futility of her protest. All the emotion of the night welled up inside her and vanquished any concern over honor and promises and her word. He was right: nothing mattered beyond this. "—love you."

He crushed his lips to hers and all lingering denials washed away with the rain and the passion in his kiss. He drew back and gazed down at her. "My life was scarcely worth living until I met you."

"And I . . . I was born when you kissed me." She sighed in surrender and stared into his eyes. "So, what shall we do now?"

He brushed his lips across her forehead. "I could spirit you off to Scotland, you know, against your will, and solve this question of your promises altogether."

"No." She shook her head. "I must tell Hugh myself that I will not marry him. It's the least I can do."

"You will inform him of your decision as soon as he returns to London?"

"I promise."

He raised a brow. "And how do I know you will keep your promise?"

She gasped and pushed against him. "Spencer!"

"Well." He shook his head solemnly. "Your word does not seem to mean very much these days. Although I daresay one can scarcely expect more from a mere woman."

Shock strangled her words and she could do little more than sputter. She twisted out of his arms. "You—you—beast!"

"Ah, yes. But I am completely and thoroughly your beast." His eyes twinkled and she realized he was teasing.

"Stop it at once!"

"As you wish, Miss Morgan." He scooped her into his arms and started off down the road, carrying her like so much excess baggage.

"Whatever are you doing?" she snapped.

"It appears I am carrying you."

"I am certain I can walk." Although the sensation of being in his arms, held tight against his chest, was delightful and perhaps only a fool would protest. Still, his teasing of a moment ago was not forgotten.

"I am certain you can too. But your shoes are certainly not up to trudging through the muck and your clothes are already soaked through. I should not want my future wife to catch her death of cold."

My future wife.

She smiled and snuggled against him. What a lovely sound that phrase had. It had never sounded so delightful when Hugh said it. She pushed the thought of Hugh out of her mind.

"Where are we going?"

"We passed an inn quite some time ago but I would prefer not to head there anyway. The possibility of scandal at a public facility is far too great."

"Then where?"

"I seem to recall a cottage a short distance back. We can seek shelter for a few hours, until the rain lets up and I can get the carriage back on the road." He cast her a rueful smile. "It will be nip and tuck to get you home before anyone knows you're missing, but I think we can make it."

"Excellent." She could almost hear his heartbeat in his chest. "I should very much hate for my family to face two scandals at the same time."

Of course there would be a certain amount of upheaval when she told her parents she would not be marrying Hugh after all. But they could scarcely object to Spencer. His title was not quite as grand, his fortune not quite as extensive, but he was a catch nonetheless.

Best of all, she loved him and he loved her. And she would allow no one to argue with that.

"I say, is anyone home?" Spencer pounded on the door of the cottage.

"Perhaps they're asleep." Pippa stood behind him under the scant protection of the eaves, eager to get inside. Her wet, chilled garments clung to her and she couldn't stop shivering.

"Well, we've made enough noise out here to raise the dead." He stepped back and perused the small house. "It doesn't look abandoned but I am not at all certain anyone is home."

She shook and her teeth chattered in response.

Spencer glanced at her with concern. "Blast it all, they'll just have to shoot us for tresspassing, I expect." He braced his shoulder against the door and pushed. It sprang open with a resounding creak. "Is anyone in there?" Only silence answered. He turned to her and bowed in a dramatic manner. "My lady, your castle."

She bobbed a curtsy and stepped over the threshold. It was black as pitch inside and the room held the closed, deep chill of disuse, but it was clean and dry if not terribly cozy. She pulled her cloak tighter about her and smiled. "And a lovely castle it is too."

Spencer moved further into the room, his form all but swallowed by the shadows. She could hear his progress through the chamber and the distinct noise of his blundering into a heavy object.

His muffled oath drifted through the door and she bit back a giggle. "Do be careful."

Sounds of scraping were followed by a series of sparks, and a tiny flame blossomed to cast the handsome planes of his face in a soft light. The man must have the eyes of a cat to perform such an intricte task in the dark.

Hand cupped around the flame, he stepped around the room, searching for candles, and lit the only two to be found.

"I'm not certain about lovely but at least the roof does not leak. However, I must do something about the horses. I cannot leave them unattended on the road but I shall only be a moment." He cast her a worried glance. "Will you be all right?"

"I am fine now that we're out of the rain." She nodded toward the door. "See to the horses and hurry back."

For a moment he hesitated as if uncertain about leaving her. She laughed. "Go on now and do take care to close the door behind you."

"Very well." He sliped through the door and into the night, a sharp gust of wind slamming the door sharply behind him.

Pippa glanced about her rustic surroundings. Modestly furnished with a rough wooden table, two chairs, a cupboard and a narrow bed with blankets neatly folded at its foot. A pile of kindling and a stack of wood sat beside a fireplace as if the owner of this shelter expected to return at any minute. She hoped not. How awkward it would be to explain their circumstances.

Perhaps she could start a fire and have it well lit by the time Spencer returned? She had never actually built a fire but it did not seem especially difficult. She stared at the fireplace and a wave of exhaustion washed over her. It had been a very long day. And weariness took precedence over warmth. The fire could well wait.

She dropped into a chair, leaned her elbows on the table and propped her head in her hands. Cold, fatigue and anxiety all at once took their toll. Goodness, rescuing overspirited cousins certainly was difficult work. If she could just close her eyes for a moment, she would surely be refreshed and then she would make the fire and do something about her wet clothes and decide what to do about Caro and . . .

"The rain has let up."

Pippa opened her eyes and lifted her head. The room glowed in the orange light of the fire. Spencer sat beside her. How long had she been asleep?

"I should be able to right the carriage as soon as it stops." Spencer's voice was gentle and he brushed a strand of hair away from her face. "You should perhaps take off that wet clothing."

She jerked upright, at once fully awake. "Take off my clothing?"

"I think it would be best."

Pippa glared. "Best for what?"

"You need not look so indignant." The corners of his mouth quirked upward. "I told you once I did not plan on seducing you."

She sniffed. "That was before."

"Before what?"

Before I loved you. Before you loved me.

"Perhaps I will take off my cloak." She stood and stripped off the still-sodden garment, spreading it over the back of the chair to dry. Without the weight of the outergarment, even as wet as it was, she was freezing. She stepped toward the fire and held out her hands to the warmth. "I see you built a fire. I was planning on doing it myself before you returned but, well, I must have fallen asleep."

"I noticed." His voice sounded oddly muffled behind her.

"I seemed to have been rather—" She turned toward him and gasped. "Whatever are you doing?"

He stood with his shirt in his hand and a puzzled expression on his face. He glanced down then back at her. "It appears as if I am disrobing."

She whirled back to the fire. "Why?"

"Why? Because I am not nearly as foolish as you are."

"In what possible way am I foolish?" Lord, was he still taking off his clothing?

"Well, I have no intention of catching a chill, a very distinct possibility if I stayed soaking wet. No indeed." His voice sounded as if he was moving as he spoke. "I wish my clothes to be dry when I return to deal with the carriage and I have no desire to drive back to town in a thoroughly drenched condition. The best way to avoid that is to take my clothing off and hang it before the fire."

"But—" Her heart thudded in her chest. "Exactly

how many articles of clothing did you plan on drying?"

"All of them." She could hear the amusement in his voice.

"All of them?"

"Indeed."

"Are you . . . um . . . er . . ." Was he entirely undressed now?

A chair scraped on the floor. She didn't move but out of the corner of her eye watched it edge closer to the fire. She couldn't see him push it and preferred not to anyway. His clothes, all of his clothes, from his shirt to his stockings, hung from the chair like wilted blossoms from a vine. She groaned. "Oh dear."

"Oh dear?"

"Have you taken everything off?" she said faintly.

"Let me see." His teasing voice would have annoyed her at any other time. At this moment, it simply added to her growing distress. "Why yes, I believe I have."

She could hear him him moving across the room behind her to the vicinity of the bed. "It seemed the only sensible thing to do."

"Sensible?" Her voice squeaked.

"I believe so."

There was a distinct rustling near the bed. "What are you doing now?"

"I thought it would be much warmer if I wrapped myself in one of these blankets." A note of feigned innocence sounded in his voice. "Perhaps, if I wrapped both of us—"

He touched her shoulders. She jumped, a yelp leaping from her throat, and spun to face him.

He stood with a blanket stretched between his hands and another wrapped around him, looking for all the world like a classic Greek statue. Goodness, his shoulders certainly owed nothing to his tailor. She clapped her hands over her eyes. "Go away."

"Where would you suggest I go? I am scarcely dressed for an outing."

"You are scarcely dressed at all!"

"Pippa, my love." Amusement sounded in his voice. He pulled her hands from her face. She squeezed her eyes shut tight. "I suggest, if you are not willing to properly dry your clothes—"

She shook her head vigorously. "Not if it requires me to take them off!"

"—then at least let me put this blanket around you." The blanket settled on her shoulders.

"Very well." She refused to open her eyes. She heard him move off and a slight movement brushed past. Then again he touched her shoulders.

"If you would allow yourself to trust me for a moment." His voice was gentle.

"Of course I trust you."

"Not enough to open your eyes." He chuckled. "I wonder though, if your concern is more for me than for yourself?" He sighed. "After all, the sight of a partially clothed—"

"Partially clothed?"

"—man such as myself may well be the undoing of a innocent—"

She snapped her eyes open. "I daresay I can stand the temptation."

"Temptation?" He raised a brow. "I hadn't thought of it quite as temptation."

"It's not," she said quickly.

"Excellent." He smiled and took her hand. "I took the feather bed off the frame and placed it here before the fire." He sat on the mattress and pulled her down beside him.

"Spencer, I do not—"

"It will help warm us both," he said firmly.

"I daresay you're probably right." She sat straight and stiff beside him.

He chuckled, twisted around then presented her with a pottery mug and a bottle of spirits. "I found these in the cupboard."

"Oh, I could never—"

"Yes, indeed you can." He filled the cup and handed it to her. "And you will. It will help—"

"I know, I know." She sighed. "It will warm us. Very well." She took a sip and gasped. "What is this?"

He held the bottle up to the firelight. "I'm not entirely certain. But it is—" He took a swig from the bottle and choked. "—palatable. Although just barely."

"It burns." She took a cautious sip. "But it is not entirely unpleasant."

"Not entirely. Although I daresay you wouldn't find it served at the finest clubs."

She giggled and drank again. Warmth spread through her and she leaned against him. "It does seem to be working, though, doesn't it?"

He wrapped his arm around her and she snuggled closer. Long, contented moments slipped by. "Could we stay here forever do you think?"

He chuckled. "I doubt that the legitimate owner of this cottage would appreciate that."

"I would appreciate that."

"As would I."

A comfortable silence settled between them. She sipped from the mug and nestled against the heat of his body.

"Pippa?"

"Yes?"

Spencer seemed to choose his words with care. "We do not have to go back to London. We could continue on to Scotland ourselves and be married."

"I do not wish to steal away in the night to marry you."

"It would, perhaps, make everything a bit easier."

She shook her head. "Perhaps it would, but I must bear the consequences of my actions."

"Why don't you let me tell Winsleigh of your decision?"

"No. I have to tell Hugh myself and in person that I will not marry him. I would not want him to hear of our marriage after it is already accomplished. I believe I owe him that courtesy." She slanted him a curious glance. "I daresay there is at least one woman you should inform in person as to our intentions."

"Who do you mean?" Caution edged his voice.

She laughed. "My dearest love, London is the center of the world and all its gossip. You cannot possibly imagine I have not heard of your liaisons."

"Felicia?" he said as if hoping he was wrong.

"Lady Dusault."

"You are no doubt right." He sighed. "Felicia is something of a friend as well as, well, closer."

"Did you love her?"

"How do I explain what Felicia and I have shared?" He thought for a moment. "It was more of a convenience for her and for me." He paused. "I have never loved anyone but you."

Pippa smiled and relaxed against him. Contentment filled her. She watched the flames dance and drank more of the pungent spirits. How wonderful it was to be here with the warmth of the fire in front of her and the deeper heat of the man she loved by her side.

"Spencer?"

"Yes?"

"Did you mean it when you said you were not planning on seducing me?" How even more wonderful it would be in his arms.

He drew back and stared at her, his brows furrowed in puzzlement. "I did at the time."

"I see." And how perfect it would be to have his lips on hers.

"Do you still?" She ran her finger down the line of his jaw. In the back of her mind she noted the boldness of her action but dismissed it as insignificant. This was the man she planned on spending the rest of her days with.

He sucked in a deep breath and trapped her hand

against his face. "I do. At least I think I do."

"Does a kiss count as seduction?" Where had the sultry tone in her voice come from?

His dark eyes smoldered like the embers in the fireplace. "A single kiss?"

She nodded. "Just one."

He pulled her hand to his lips and kissed the palm. "I suspect a single kiss between us is no longer possible."

"No?"

"No."

She pulled her gaze from his and stared at the flames. "Do you remember the first time you kissed me?"

"Ah, the hoyden on the hill with the dog. The one who asked me to kiss her. How could I forget?"

"Would you then," she said as she turned toward him and brought her gaze to mesh with his, "kiss me now?"

"Pippa, I do not—"

She leaned forward and brushed her lips across his. Once. Twice. Three times.

He groaned. "Pippa."

She kissed one corner of his mouth, gently, then the other. "Yes?"

"What are you doing?" His voice sounded strangled as if he struggled with some dire problem.

"Kissing you, I believe." She slipped her hands beneath his blanket to rest on the hot planes of his chest and the smattering of coarse hair she'd glimpsed before. She fought to keep her breath even. Touching him was a delight she'd never expected.

"Pippa." He caught her hands and stared into her eyes. "I have never felt about any woman the way I feel about you. It supersedes my own sense of honor or anything else. I wish you to be my wife. And I can wait to make you truly mine but not if you continue to . . ."

"Continue to . . . what?" She gazed at him with a need she hadn't known she possessed.

A look akin to pain passed over his face. "To do that."

"I see," she said softly, and rose to her feet.

"What . . . what are you doing now?"

"It seems you were right all along." She stared down at him. This was the man she loved. The love of her dreams, of her life. How better to begin the rest of their days together then by giving him all she had to give? "My clothes are not drying properly. I believe," she drew a calming breath and whispered, "I shall have to remove them after all."

He scrambled to stand before her, clutching the blanket around him. "Do you know what you're saying? What you are offering me?"

She swallowed past the lump in her throat. "I do."

His gaze searched her face. "There is no turning back."

"I have no wish to turn back." She smiled up at him.

"Is this truly what you want? It's not necessary, you know. I wish to wed as soon as possible. We can well wait."

"Can we?"

His skin glowed in the light of the fire and she reached up to kiss his shoulder. His muscles clenched beneath her touch and he groaned. "No."

He bent and kissed the curve of her neck, trailing his lips lower to the sleeve of her dress. He eased the garment off her shoulder and brushed his lips across the exposed flesh. Shivers of delight and fear coursed through her.

She laughed weakly. "I'm really rather frightened, you know."

"Odd." He drew her close against him and rested his chin on her head. "So am I." He held her still for a long moment and she sensed a struggle inside him. "Pippa, it is not too late."

She pulled back and gazed into his eyes with all the love in her heart. "Oh, but my darling, it is."

He stared and she could see her own love reflected in his eyes. He lowered his mouth to hers and kissed her. Softly his lips caressed hers over and over until an ache welled up inside her and she slid her arms up around his neck and clung to him for support and more. She pressed her mouth tighter to his and he met her pressure with his own. Her mouth opened and his tongue traced the rim of her lips and dipped inside. Shocking need coursed through her and she greeted his tongue with her own.

He wrenched his mouth from hers to trail his lips across her face, to rain kisses on her closed eyes and her cheeks and lower. Her head fell back and his lips explored her neck to the pulsebeat at the base of her throat. And lower still to the line of her bodice and the swell of her bosom. Slowly, as if she were fragile piece of porcelain, he nudged her dress down and exposed her breasts. Her breath caught. He cupped the tender flesh in his hands and kissed one, then the other, until she thought she would swoon from the exquisite sensation. He drew a nipple into his mouth and suckled and her hands clenched at his shoulders.

"Spencer, oh Lord, please." Her voice came in strange little breaths.

He stopped. "I am not hurting you, am I, my love? There is still time to stop."

"No, no, please, do not stop." She grasped at him with an urgency that swelled and would not be denied.

He must have known, he must have sensed it, he must have shared all that she was experiencing. At once the gentleness between them vanished. Roughly, he pushed her dress and her undergarments down the length of her body until her clothes were a pool at her feet. He pulled her tight to him and she realized his blanket too must have fallen by the wayside to join her discarded garments. He was hard and hot and strong against her and she couldn't seem to get too close to him. He dropped to his knees and ran his tongue between her breasts and down to the flat of her stomach. She gripped his shoulders and reveled in the pulsing sensation that flooded over her again and again until her knees buckled and she sank down before him.

His lips claimed hers and his arms imprisoned

her in an embrace so tight she wondered where he left off and she began. Together they fell to lay on the mattress in an odd lingering manner and time itself slowed to prolong the joy to be found in each other's arms.

The hair on his chest scraped against her breasts as if to remind her of the vast differences between his glorious body and her own. Every inch of her flesh was alive with the press of his body to hers. And still she wanted more.

His hands and his mouth caressed her breasts and her stomach as if he too could not do enough. Boldly she traced the muscles of his chest with her palms and followed the arrow of the tangle of rough hair downward until she lost all sense of her own actions in the skill of his touch. He ran his fingers along the length of her leg and higher to the juncture of her thighs and fear clasped her limbs together. Gently he stroked her until she could bear no more and all she wanted was the touch of his hand. She moaned and her legs fell open.

His hand caressed her and his fingers slipped inside to touch her where she had never known, and never imagined, the touch of a man. She gasped and arched her back up and then sank back. She throbbed beneath his hand and wondered dimly if he could feel her body pulse. He bent and took her breast in his mouth. His fingers circled and stroked. She clutched and clawed at his back in a desperate, mindless effort to reach some unknown point until she thought she would surely die from the sheer bliss of it all. Without warning her body seemed to explode and she jerked in an uncontrollable spasm that spiraled from the point of his touch to every inch of her and he held her tight against him until she collapsed and thought she had indeed died or at least melted to a small puddle of joy.

"Spencer, my love." She reached her hand to the back of his neck and threaded her fingers in his hair, pulling his lips to hers. "My life."

And at once his body was over hers. He nudged her legs wider apart and she welcomed him. Slowly, he slipped into her in a not-unpleasant sensation until it seemed he could go no further.

He hesitated and she knew he feared hurting her. She had heard this act of love was painful for a woman, at least at first. But she wanted nothing to keep from him the elation he had brought to her.

She arched upward, embedding him deeper into her. Pain shot through her body and she had to bite her lip to keep from crying out. He gasped and slipped further inside her. She throbbed around him and wondered how an act so delicious one moment could hurt so the next. Slowly, he shifted within her and she clenched her teeth against the pain. He moved with a careful rhythm and an obvious concern for her comfort. Soon the pain receded and a heady pleasure drifted through her. She lifted her hips to meet his and urge him on.

He thrust into her faster and she met him stroke for stroke. He plunged and she arched and nothing in the world mattered save the feel of his body in hers and the excitement building between them. Her thoughts were incoherent, her mind filled only with the undreamed-of exhilaration and aching need of their passion. And just when she knew she could not survive another moment of such potent sensation, her body seemed to shatter and she screamed with the unyielding intensity of it all. Spencer held her tight to him and a scant second later moaned and shuddered and lay still. Finally, he rolled over, taking her with him to lie exhausted on his chest.

His heart thudded beneath her ear. He breathed in long deep gasps as if trying to regain his strength. She smiled against his chest. She could not move if she had to. A sudden thought struck her and she giggled.

He pushed her up and stared, a bemused look on his face. "For future reference, you should perhaps know, laughter is not the response a man particularly likes to receive at a moment such as this."

"I was just thinking." She laughed. "How perfectly delightful impropriety can be."

He grinned up at her. "Delightful."

She laid her head back onto his chest, warm in the comfort and safety of his arms. They lay together for long, happy moments.

"Do you know you have changed my world?" Spencer's voice carried a serious note.

"As you have changed mine."

"We will have a wonderful life together, Pippa, I promise you that. I love you."

"I know." She snuggled against him. "And I love you." Had she ever been so happy? How could she have considered marrying a man she did not love?

How had she changed so much in such a short time?

She was no longer the good, proper, biddable girl expected to make Hugh such a perfect countess. No, she was a far cry from that green girl. She'd discovered the passionate side of her nature. And she'd found love.

And nothing in her world would ever be the same.

Chapter Eight

Pippa slipped into the house by the first light of dawn. Her early-morning rides with Spencer had prepared her well. She knew the routines of the servants and how to avoid detection.

She was in her room within moments, closing the door quietly behind her. She stepped toward the bed, peeling off her rain-damaged dress.

"Where have you been?"

Pippa froze.

"I have been waiting for you all night." Caro rose from the bed like a vengeful wraith. Disapproval rang in her voice.

"You have been waiting for me?" Pippa glared in shock. "And where have you been?"

Caro snorted. "I have been precisely where I was supposed to be. Right here."

"You weren't here earlier!"

"Oh, yes, that, well . . ."

Pippa aimed an accusing finger. "You ran off with Dunston, didn't you?"

"Well." Caro plopped back on the bed. "Yes, I did."

"You were going to Gretna Green."

"We were. At first."

"Obviously you didn't." Pippa perched on the bed beside her cousin and considered her thoughtfully. "Oh dear. He has ended it, hasn't he?"

"Oh no, nothing like that." Caro shook her head. "We did start off last night with every intention of driving to Scotland but—"

"What?"

"It was raining, you know."

Pippa scoffed. "I was aware of that, yes."

"And the roads are simply terrible, especially in the rain."

"Indeed they are," Pippa murmured.

"So we returned. We decided—in point of fact, Dunny decided . . ." Caro studied her hands as if they were of intense interest. "He did not wish to run off and be wed. He said he'd much prefer to make a great fuss about it and that running off on some dreary night would not be at all proper." Her gaze caught Pippa's. "So he will talk to Papa tomorrow and put an announcement in the *Times* and marry me in the manner a future duchess should be wed."

Pippa gasped and embraced her in a heartfelt

hug. "Oh, Caro, how wonderful! I am thrilled for you."

Caro shook her head, amazement shining on her face. "I am to be a duchess, Pippa, and marry the man I love. I am still quite unable to truly believe my good fortune."

"It will be the match of the season."

Caro giggled. "I know. I can scarcely wait to—" She drew back and frowned. "But you have not explained your absence last night."

"We went after you."

Caro arched a brow. "We?"

Pippa nodded. "Spencer and I."

"Spencer?" Caro's eyes widened. "St. Gregory? You spent the entire night with St. Gregory? Goodness, Pippa, how could you?"

The memory of last night in his arms brought a slight smile to her lips. "I—"

Caro leapt from the bed and paced the room. "Lord, the impropriety of it all! Have you any idea what you've done?"

Pippa stifled her smile. "I have a certain suspicion."

"And the scandal!" Caro squared her shoulders in an imperious manner. "Have you considered the scandal this could cause? Why you will be ruined!"

"I'm fairly certain no one knows."

"No one saw you? Are you sure?"

"I believe so."

"Well that's something, at any rate."

Pippa stared at the indignant figure before her. "I

never would have suspected you of all people would be quite so concerned with scandal."

Caro stiffened her spine and looked down her nose. "When one is to be a duchess one must give due consideration to the standards of proper behavior set down by society."

Pippa tried desperately to restrain herself but could not. She fell back on to the bed and laughed for a full minute.

"I do not see anything humorous about this," Caro said. "What is it you find so extremely funny?"

Pippa giggled. "You. You who never cared about rules or propriety." She propped herself up on her elbows and grinned. "It's amazing what a betrothal can do."

"There is nothing to laugh about."

"Very well." Pippa studied her irate cousin. "Perhaps I can soothe your outraged soul somewhat."

"I doubt that." Caro crossed her arms over her chest. "How?"

"I have made a decision."

Caro eyed her suspiciously. "What kind of decision?"

"I have decided . . ." She paused, enjoying the other girl's curiosity. ". . . not to marry Hugh."

"Not marry Hugh?" Shock colored Caro's face, quickly followed by delight. She shouted and launched herself at the bed, throwing her arms around her cousin. "How perfectly delightful! I never dreamed you would come to your senses. It is far and away the best—" She drew back and a frown creased her forehead. "Why aren't you going to marry Hugh?"

"I don't love him."

Caro waved away the comment. "I knew that. But lack of love certainly did not seem to be an obstacle up to this point. You were determined to marry him in spite of that. I don't understand whatever could have happened . . ." She sat up straight. "It's St. Gregory, isn't it?"

Pippa nodded. "It's St. Gregory.

Caro grabbed her hand. "Are you going to marry him? Oh do please say you're going to marry him? He's so handsome and really rather nice I thought and I daresay he'll—"

"Stop, stop." Pippa laughed. "Yes. I am going to marry him."

"What about the prig? Have you told the prig?"

"Caro." Pippa pinned her with a serious glance. "Hugh is not a prig."

"That's right. I nearly forgot." Caro tapped her bottom lip thoughtfully. "I decided he was more of a twit, didn't I?"

"Caro!"

"Very well." Caro said, her manner gracious. "I suppose I no longer care if he's a twit or a prig as long as he's not going to be a member of our family. So have you told him?"

Pippa sighed. "Not yet, and I daresay I am not looking forward to it."

Caro leaned toward her, a wicked gleam in her eyes. "May I be there when you tell him? Oh I should thoroughly enjoy being there when you tell him."

"No, you most definitely may not. It will be difficult enough without you smirking at him."

"Pity." Caro sighed. "It would be such fun to smirk openly at the twi—Hugh."

"Well it will not be at all pleasant to present him with this news."

"No, I suppose not." Caro hesitated. "Do be careful with him, Pippa. I have never quite trusted the man."

"You just do not like him because he thought you were a bad influence on me," Pippa teased. "And that you would lead me astray."

"Hah." Caro cast her a pointed look. "He did have the two of us confused on that score, didn't he?"

Pippa laughed. "I should hate to even imagine Hugh's face if he knew."

"So would I," Caro muttered. "When are you planning on telling him?"

"As soon as he returns to London. He should be back from the country within a few days." Pippa nodded firmly. "And I shall get it over with and tell him at once. The very moment I see him."

"Why don't you simply write to him? I know he writes to you. And he's been gone so long."

"I have to do this in person," Pippa said sharply.

"But isn't Hugh pressing you for an official announcement?" Caro raised a brow. "Don't you think you have already aroused his suspicions by your continued delay?"

"No." Pippa drew a deep breath. She was so irritable lately and her stomach was upset as often as not. She blamed it all on overwrought emotions. "It is bad enough that I am crying off but to do so in a letter would be unforgivable."

Caro shook her head. "Well I, for one, disagree. And I suspect St. Gregory does as well."

"Spencer understands completely."

"Does he? I doubt Dunny would be quite so understanding in his place."

"Then I am quite fortunate that I am not to wed Dunny!"

Still, Pippa's failure to tell Hugh of her decision not to marry him was a constant irritant to Spencer. He grew more and more annoyed at the need for clandestine meetings and concealment of their intentions. It had been more than a month since their night together and problem after problem had delayed Hugh's return to London. Now, the families of both girls planned on returning to Pippa's home at the end of next week to prepare for Caro's wedding and the trip to the ancestral home of the Dukes of Dunston.

"We shall be home soon and I can tell him then." She smiled weakly. "Spencer has promised to follow us and ask father for my hand the moment I tell Hugh."

"Well, it certainly can't be too soon," Caro muttered.

"No." Pippa absently placed her hand on her stomach in a futile effort to calm her nausea and her concern. "It cannot be too soon at all."

*   *   *

"Spencer!"

Spencer shut the double doors of the parlor firmly behind him and attempted to reach Pippa. Not an easy task with an exuberant Samuel barking and dancing about his feet. He maneuvered past the excited canine to Pippa's side, swept her into his arms and kissed her. A kiss long and hard and urgent.

He drew back and smiled down at her. "So nice to see you again, Miss Morgan. You are well, I take it?"

She gazed up at him and sighed. "Quite. And you, my lord?"

"Me? I am undone." He sighed in an overly dramatic manner. "You see, I have been abandoned by the woman I love."

"Spencer! It has been but three days since we last saw each other."

He pulled her hand to his lips. "It seems a lifetime."

"You are such a tease," she murmured.

"Am I?" He gazed at her with such desire her heart hammered against her ribs. *Please, Lord, let him look at me always like this.* "Have you talked to Winsleigh?"

She stepped out of his embrace and shook her head. "I have not had the opportunity."

"Pippa." His brows drew together in annoyance. "You must tell him. And if you cannot, I shall."

"No, no. It is up to me and I shall talk to Hugh.

But we only arrived home yesterday and I have not seen him as yet."

"Send for him," Spencer said firmly.

"I do not—"

"Now, today. Every minute you delay is another minute we must wait to start our lives together." Spencer glared. "I wish to announce our intentions and marry as soon as possible. I do not appreciate the entire world believing that you are to marry Winsleigh." He paced before the fireplace. "I want everyone to know the truth: that I love you and you love me." He stopped and narrowed his eyes. "You do still love me, don't you?"

She laughed. "Of course I still love you."

Relief crossed his face. "Good."

"Surely you did not doubt my feelings?"

"Well, when a woman takes as much time as you have to break it off with another man," he shrugged in a sheepish manner, "one wonders. Especially when one knows he cannot live without her."

Warmth spread through her. "And do you know that?"

"Indeed, I do. I suspect I have known from the moment I saw you," he nodded at Samuel, "and your beast. You must tell Winsleigh. It's past time to do so, my love."

"Time has become rather important," she said softly.

"What do you mean?"

"I'm not quite sure exactly how to say this." She clasped her hands together and stared at them.

191

"What is it?" Concern sounded in his voice and he rushed to her side. "Are you ill?"

"Not exactly. I . . ." she pulled a ragged breath, "I am. . . ." She lifted her chin and summoned all her courage. ". . . increasing."

"Increasing what?"

"Increasing . . . our family."

"Our . . ." Stunned disbelief stamped Spencer's face. "You are with child?"

She nodded anxiously. "So it appears."

He ran his fingers through his dark hair. "How could this have happened?"

She arched a brow. "Perhaps you have forgotten a cold, rainy night. A carriage accident. An empty cottage, strong spirits and a need to stay warm?"

"Of course I have not forgotten that. I have not forgotten anything," he said impatiently. "It's simply that I was not expecting this."

"Are you—" She hesitated. "—angry?"

"Angry?" He shook his head. "No, not angry. Surprised, that's all. This does indeed change everything."

"Well, then are you pleased?"

He snorted. "Pleased is perhaps not the right word either."

She feared the question that must be asked and dreaded the answer. "Do you still wish to marry me?"

"Of course, Pippa. This changes nothing." His words were measured as if his mind was elsewhere and a heavy weight settled in her stomach. He stepped to her and wrapped his arms around her in a gentle embrace, his chin resting on the top of her head. "However, it does require me to return to town today. I should be back no later than tomorrow."

"Don't go," she whispered.

"I must. And as quickly as possible." He released her and started toward the door.

"Spencer."

"Yes?" His hand rested on the doorknob.

"I love you."

"And I love you." He nodded and stepped through the doorway, snapping the doors behind him.

Pippa stared at the spot where Spencer had stood a scant moment ago. He was so brisk, so hurried, so impersonal. Fear gnawed at the back of her mind. In spite of his words, was he indeed angry at her condition? When Pippa had realized she carried a child, his child, joy had swept through her. Why didn't Spencer share that joy?

She sank down onto a nearby chair and folded her hands in her lap. She loved him and she had to remember that he loved her. She simply had to trust in that love.

And in him.

Spencer leaned back against the doors and closed his eyes, struggling to sort out his raging thoughts.

A child? My child?

An heir to carry on his family name? Or a girl with hair like summer just like her mother?

A slow, giddy grin grew on his face. Bloody hell, he was going to be a father. In the shock of the news, Spencer had thought of little more than returning to London to procure a special license. There was no time to lose. He wanted to marry Pippa the moment he returned. He would not allow the world to consider any child of his baseborn. He'd never been especially fond of children but this was different. This was his child. And, no doubt, the first of many.

"St. Gregory? Is that you?" Winsleigh stepped out of the shadows by the front door and handed his coat and cane to the butler. "What on earth are you doing here?"

"Winsleigh." Spencer nodded and straightened upright. He well understood Pippa's need to be the one to tell Hugh of their plans. However, now all had changed. "I came to see Miss Morgan."

A puzzled frown furrowed Hugh's forehead. "Why would you come all this way to see Pippa?"

"She wished to be the one to tell you this, Winsleigh, but"—Spencer shrugged—"at this point it cannot be helped."

"Tell me what?" Winsleigh's tone was cautious.

"We plan to marry." There, it was said.

Winsleigh's eyes narrowed. "But she is to marry me. It is all arranged."

"I am sorry, old man, but these things happened. It is not something either she or I planned or expected. But there you have it." Guilt at the stunned look on Winsleigh's face softened his tone. "I suspect it would not make a difference to you to know that I love her and she loves me as well?"

"She loves you." Winsleigh repeated the words as if he could not comprehend them.

"She does." Spencer nodded briskly and turned toward the door. "I must run an errand in town but—"

"To announce your good fortune, no doubt?" A slight sneer sounded in Winsleigh's voice. No matter. The man was obviously overwrought.

"Not exactly."

"Tell me something, St. Gregory." Winsleigh crossed his arms and leaned against a door frame. "How long do you expect an innocent like Pippa to keep you amused when you are used to women of a more experienced nature? Women such as Lady Dusault?"

"Felicia! Blast it." He had almost forgotten about Felicia. He would have to inform her of his plans. "I'll speak with Felicia when I'm in town."

He turned to leave, then turned back to Winsleigh. "It may help you to know that even when we realized our feelings for each other, Pippa still planned to abide by her promise to marry you. It was not until—" He paused, then shrugged. "—until later that she understood loving one man and marrying another could well destroy us all. She was loyal to you for a very long time."

"Oh, I shall take great comfort in that." Sarcasm dripped off the hard, cold words.

Spencer narrowed his eyes. "I truly love her, you know, and she loves me."

"That's all anyone can ask for then, isn't it?"

"I believe that now, yes." He nodded sharply and

turned toward the door. He had far too many things on his mind to concern himself with Winsleigh, although he could not help but feel sorry for the man. But perhaps it was easier hearing such news from him instead of Pippa. He dismissed Winsleigh from his thoughts and hurried from the house, barely noting the man's parting words.

"We shall see, St. Gregory, we shall see."

"I truly love her, you know, and she loves me."
Love? What did that rake, that scoundrel, know of love? Hugh had loved Pippa for as long as he could remember. How dare St. Gregory presume to call his no doubt lecherous feelings for Pippa love?

As for Pippa, she was confused, nothing more. She knew nothing of love beyond the dreams of a girl fresh out of the schoolroom. St. Gregory was a handsome man, there was no question of that. Handsome enough to turn the head of a girl as naive as Pippa.

His Pippa. She was always, always to be his. Why, didn't he already think of her as his? Their families wanted it and he wanted it. He wanted her with a fire that burned in his stomach when he so much as heard her name. He wanted her, body and soul, and he would not give her up. Not ever.

He would find some method to get St. Gregory out of the way. The blasted man was never supposed to be a part of their lives in the first place.

Pippa would indeed marry Hugh. There was no question of that. Fury raged within him. He would not permit otherwise. Reagrdless of the cost—dishonor or disgrace—he would do whatever was necessary. Even if he had to go so far as to arrange for St. Gregory's death to make certain, so be it. As for Pippa's disloyalty—he clenched his fists—he would deal with her once they were wed.

He pulled a deep, cleansing breath. He could not let her see his anger. And he could not allow his rage to effect his mind. He needed all his wits about him to deal with this turn of events.

To deal with his bethrothed and her lover.

"Hugh!" Pippa rose from her chair. Samuel growled. "I did not expect you today."

Hugh cast the dog a nasty look of dismissal and crossed the room to take her hands in his. "You did not expect your betrothed to rush to your side the instant he knew you were here?"

She tried to free her hands but his grip only tightened. "We are not truly betrothed yet, Hugh."

"Still, you gave me your promise."

"Yes, but . . ." Words failed her and she pulled her gaze from his. "I cannot marry you, Hugh."

"I do not understand."

She met his gaze head-on. "I plan to wed someone else.

"Someone else? Who?" Hugh stared in confusion; then his eyes widened. "Not St. Gregory? I met him on the way in. Pippa, the man is a scoundrel."

She raised her chin. "He most certainly is not. Furthermore, I love him and he loves me."

"I see." Pity washed across his face. "My dear, perhaps you should sit down."

"I do not need to—"

"Please, Pippa.

"Very well." She sighed and perched on the edge of a small settee. "Now then, Hugh, what is it?"

"St. Gregory will not be coming back."

"Nonsense," she said stoutly. "Of course he will be back."

"Did he tell you exactly where he was going and why?"

"He said he needed to go to London. As to why—" Spencer's odd demeanor sprang to mind. He was in such a great hurry to leave. Unease gripped her heart. She shrugged it away. "He didn't say."

"My poor, dear, Pippa." Hugh shook his head sympathetically.

Fear teased the back of her mind. "Whatever do you mean?"

Hugh sighed and stepped to a table with a decanter and glassware. "I find this extremely difficult." He pulled the stopper from the bottle. "Especially now after your admission."

"What are you trying to say, Hugh?" She couldn't seem to catch her breath.

He poured a glass with slow care, as if he had all the time in the world. "When I saw St. Gregory outside he congratulated me on my upcoming marriage."

"What?" She gasped.

"Indeed he did." He popped the stopper back in the bottle. "And he said he had pressing business in town and winked. You know, Pippa, the sort of wink one man gives another when the topic of a particular type of woman arises." He drew a long swallow of the liquor. She rose to unsteady feet. "Then he mentioned Lady Dusault's name and laughed."

"No," she whispered. "I don't believe you."

"It is true." Hugh's eyes shone with concern. "St. Gregory has left you and gone to meet his mistress."

His words pulsed in her mind.

St. Gregory has left you.

As if in a dream the room seemed to wave and sway around her. The roar of her own blood pounded in her ears. Tears misted her eyes.

She shook her head. "He would not do that to me."

"He already has."

Pain shot through her with an intensity so fierce she thought she would surely die. And then she wanted to. Blindly, she reached out a hand to steady herself and grasped the back of the settee.

"But he loves me."

"My dear Pippa, men like St. Gregory use the word love as freely as water."

She collapsed onto the seat and buried her head in her hands. How could he? Was it all a lie then? Was she merely an amusement for him? Someone to toy with for this season and this season only? How could she have been so wrong about him? She was such a fool.

She could feel Hugh settle beside her. "There, there, my dear. You are not the first innocent to have been taken in by a rogue the likes of St. Gregory. We shall simply put this unpleasant incident behind us and proceed with our own plans."

Pippa raised her head and meet his gaze with hers. "I carry his child, Hugh."

His expression crumbled as if he'd been struck hard and fast with a blow too painful to bear and her heart went out to him. He was not the man she loved but he'd always been good to her. He'd always been her friend.

He pulled a deep breath as if to suck courage from the very air he breathed. His voice was soft but firm. "No, Pippa, you carry our child."

Confusion coursed through her. "I don't understand. What do you—"

Hugh grasped her hands in his, his grip tight and firm, and she winced at the strength of it. His blue eyes simmered with anger and burned with determination.

"Listen to me, Pippa. I do not care who fathered this child. I am willing—no—I wish with all my heart to bring him up as my own. As my heir. As my child."

"Hugh." She choked back tears. "Why?"

"Why?" An odd smile quirked his lips. "My darling Pippa, how can you not know? I have loved you always. I loved when you were a golden-haired child tagging at my heels. I loved you when you were an impish hoyden climbing trees and making the fields your private playgrounds. And I loved you every day that I watched you growing into a fine young woman and a beauty. I bided my time until the moment was right to declare myself and claim you as my wife."

"Oh, Hugh." She sobbed. "I never realized."

He smoothed her hair away from her face. "I had always hoped that you loved me as well."

"I do. You are as dear to me as—"

"As a brother?" He smiled wryly. "I know, my dear. It was not what I wanted, but I believed that in time, with our marriage, your feelings for me would deepen."

She pulled herself to her feet and stepped to the window. She stared sightlessly at the rolling hills, rich with the promise of the season. "What you must think of me."

He came up behind her and placed his hands on her shoulders. "I think you are my love, my life. I want only your happiness."

She shuddered and leaned wearily against him. "I do not deserve such kindness."

"Perhaps not," he said quietly. His hands tightened on her shoulders. "But the past is of no consequence. We will put it out of our minds and go on."

"How can we?"

"We will be married at once."

Pippa turned and stared. Resolve stamped his face. She placed her hand on his cheek. "Dear, dear, Hugh. How can I allow you to throw away your life on me?"

"Enough." Hugh's eyes burned with anger. He jerked her into his arms and glared with a fury that stopped her heart. "Don't you understand yet, you little fool? You and I are fated to be together. I've known it all my life. This sordid interlude of yours with St. Gregory was a ghastly mistake but it changes nothing. You were always, always meant to be mine. By God, Pippa, you are mine and child or no child, I shall never let you go."

He crushed his lips to hers with a brutal, shocking vengeance that left her stunned and helpless. One hand grasped the nape of her neck, the other splayed across the small of her back, then slid lower to cup her buttocks. He pulled her tight to him until heat and passion radiated from his hard, demanding body into hers and she could feel his need urgent and insistent against her. Terror spiraled through her blood. Who was this man who grasped her with an unyielding desire? Surely this wasn't her own Hugh? What had she done to him?

"Hugh! Please!" She gasped, struggling to pull her lips from his, pushing with growing desperation against his chest. "Stop! You're hurting me."

He stilled as if her words had doused his passion like water upon a flame. Slowly, he released his iron grip. She stepped back and stared.

"My dear." Hugh ran a shaky hand through his hair. "Please accept my apology, once again. I fear I have little control when I am with you."

Remorse and regret swept away her fear. "I am so very sorry."

He looked at her and laughed shortly, a harsh sound without mirth, without life. "No, Pippa, I am sorry. You spur the passion within me I suspect you never knew existed. I truly love you, you know."

"I know." Her voice was barely a whisper.

"And I know you love him."

"And he swore he loved me." She paused for a long moment, searching for the words that might make sense for him and for her. "Love is a very odd thing, isn't it? I gave him my heart and all that went with it. In return, he has abandoned me to an unimaginable fate. To scandal and disgrace." She shook her head. "It seems a very high price to pay for such a fickle emotion."

"You do not have to pay it."

Despair washed through her. "How can you possibly still want me as your wife?"

"I love you." The simple truth shone in his eyes. How had she failed to see it before? How had she let the years go by without once suspecting the awesome depth of his feelings? How could she be so lucky to have a man as honorable and generous as this man want her in spite of everything.

She drew a long breath and smiled weakly. "Very well. If you will still have me, I should consider myself the most fortunate person on earth."

He opened his arms and she stepped into his embrace. "No, my dear, I am the most fortunate person on earth. I shall do all in my power to ensure your happiness."

She closed her eyes, enveloped by his warmth and caring. "Will it ever stop, do you think?"

"Will what stop, Pippa?"

"The pain."

He sighed and at once she regretted her question. "I hope so, my dear, I truly hope so."

She nodded silently and tried to push away all thoughts of Spencer. Of the strength of his arms around her. Of the fire of his passion. Of the love smoldering in his gaze. Lies, all lies. How could she have been such a fool?

"I have a special license, Pippa. We can drive to London, marry and return before nightfall."

She pulled back and stared. "Today? Don't you think it would be best—"

"I think time is of the essence." He gaze bored into hers. "Besides, the longer we delay, the more likely there is to be talk when the child is born."

"Of course." Her voice was faint. How could she have forgotten? "But Mama and Papa—"

"Your parents have long wanted this match as have mine. While I doubt they will have any objections, they may wish to delay and, given the circumstances, that will not do." His voice softened. "It is for the best, Pippa. The sooner we are wed, the sooner we can begin our lives anew and leave the past behind."

"Hugh, I do not . . ." Pippa bit her lip and closed her eyes. Why couldn't she think clearly? Why did it seem as if she were at the center of a mad whirlwind of anguish and words and nothing whatsoever made sense? It was all so difficult to comprehend. The only thing solid and real was Hugh. "It is perhaps for the best."

"You will not regret this, Pippa."

Tears clouded her eyes but she managed a slight smile. "No, dearest Hugh, this is one thing I shall never regret."

But already she did.

Chapter Nine

"Oh, Samuel." Pippa sat in the parlor, her faithful dog resting his head on her lap. "What are we to do? I have made such a terrible mess of things."

She and Hugh had returned late in the night and agreed not to reveal their marriage to their families at once. Hugh said if they waited a few weeks, they could lie about the exact date of their marriage and claim they'd been wed far longer than they had, thus insuring the baby's birth would not trigger unwanted gossip. Pippa was grateful for his thoughtfulness and relieved at not having to immediately assume all the duties of his wife. She knew as surely as she'd ever known anything in her life, marrying Hugh was a horrible mistake. But she'd had little choice.

She barely slept at all and when she did she

dreamed. Dreams that left her gasping with a need beyond words, only to awake to an emptiness she could scarcely face. Her mind and her body were exhausted. Still, the joy she'd known at the knowledge of her condition lingered deep in a secret part of her heart. This child was Spencer's and no one could ever convince her it had not been conceived in love.

She rubbed behind Samuel's ears and he looked up at her with adoration. She smiled back. "You are my one true love, aren't you, Samuel?"

But Hugh was now her husband and she could not ignore his feelings about the dog. Samuel would have to go. Tears filled her eyes. She rested her head on his back. "Oh, Samuel, Samuel, what shall we do?"

"I should think a wedding first will do nicely."

Pippa jerked upright and stared in silent shock.

A smiling Spencer strode toward her from the doorway. Samuel leapt off the settee and lunged for the man, jumping and gamboling about him in spasms of doggy delight. Spencer laughed and patted the beast.

"I daresay it's good to know someone is pleased to see me. Down, Samuel." He bent to pat the dog then straightened. "Pippa? Is something the matter?"

"I am surprised to see you." Slowly, she rose to her feet. He cast her his lopsided grin and her heart stopped. "Where have you been?"

"I told you I needed to go to town." He took her

hands. "I have procured a special license. We can be married at once."

"Married," she said softly.

He wrapped his arms around her. "Isn't that what you want? What we both want?"

"Oh yes." Joy surged through her. It was all a mistake, then. A ghastly mistake. Awe colored her words. "You do love me."

"Of course I love you." He brushed his lips across hers. "I will love you always."

"And I will thank you to unhand my wife." Hugh stood in the doorway.

Spencer's eyes widened. He looked from Pippa to Hugh and back. "Your wife?"

Hugh sauntered into the parlor, pausing by the table bearing the brandy. "We were married yesterday."

"Yesterday?" Spencer shook his head. "I don't believe you."

Hugh poured a glass. "Ask my wife then."

Spencer studied her closely. "Pippa?"

"I . . ." She couldn't bring herself to say the words.

His voice was strained. "Tell me. Is this true?"

"Yes." She sobbed with the realization of the consequences of her mistake.

"Why?" The word rang with anger and agony. Whatever was left of her heart, whatever hadn't broken when she thought he'd abandoned her, now shattered at the look on his face. "I don't understand this. Any of it. When I left—"

"I thought you were gone forever." She fought

back tears. "You acted so strangely when I talked to you—"

"Why in the name of all that's holy didn't you think I was coming back?" Spencer's voice rose with rage.

"I—" She glanced at Hugh.

Spencer's gaze followed hers. His eyes narrowed. Hugh lifted his glass in a triumphant toast. "What did you tell her, Winsleigh?"

"I really can't recall specifically, old chap." Hugh shrugged. "I may have mentioned a certain dark-haired—"

Spencer grabbed Pippa by the shoulders. "How could you have listened to him?"

Pippa shook her head, tears pouring down her face. Hysteria threatened to engulf her. "I don't know! I don't know! You were so odd when you left and Hugh went on and on about what a scoundrel you were and Felicia and oh, dear Lord, what have I done? What have I done?"

The enormity of her actions and Hugh's treachery overwhelmed her. The room spun and her legs weakened and she swayed against Spencer. He steadied her in his arms and held her tight against him. His voice was grim. "This marriage of yours, this farce, will have to be annulled. At once."

"Annulled?" Hope trickled through her and she lifted her face to his. "Is that possible?"

"It is, my love." Spencer nodded. "It is not especially easy but it is possible."

Hugh swirled the brandy in his glass. "I think not."

"What!" Fire flashed in Spencer's eyes.

Pippa pushed out of his embrace and faced Hugh. She had not just tasted salvation only to have it ripped from her like a starving man denied sustenance. She squared her shoulders. "Hugh, you know I do not love you."

"Indeed I do," Hugh said coolly.

"And you further know, Spencer is the man I love."

"I know that as well."

"Yet you would keep me tied to you?" Dismay rang in her voice. "Why?"

"Because"—Hugh's words were precise and hard, and a chill ran through her at the sound—"you are mine. You were always supposed to be mine. And now, legally, you are. St. Gregory is the interloper here. You belong to me."

She stepped toward him. "You shall never have my heart."

"Your heart?" He snorted with disdain. "My dear, I do not care about your heart. I have never particularly wished to have an unwilling wife, but so be it. And perhaps, as the years go by, your feelings for me will change. Regardless," he said with a shrug, "you will still be mine. To do with exactly as I wish."

The threat hung in the air and she shuddered at the venom it carried.

Spencer moved to her side and placed a protective arm around her shoulders. "You have always been overly concerned with scandal and appearances, have you not, Winsleigh?"

"One has to consider one's reputation in this world," Hugh said, nodding.

"Know this then." Spencer's jaw clenched and his gray eyes hardened. "If you do not release her from this sham of a marriage I shall ruin her reputation publicly. I shall tell the world of the time we spent together and whose child she carries. You will be a laughing stock, Winsleigh."

Pippa's eyes widened. "Spencer."

He gazed down at her with a desperate expression. "I do not like this any more than you but I see no other choice to force him to release you." He tilted her chin up and trapped her gaze with his. "We will go away, Pippa. America perhaps. And I will keep you safe from Winsleigh or anyone else always."

"How sweet. How loving. How futile. Don't you understand yet, St. Gregory?" Hugh's pale face reddened and he flung his glass at the door. It shattered into a million tiny fragments of light. "She is mine! I don't give a bloody fig about her reputation or scandal or anything else. She belongs to me! Like my cattle and my land and houses! And that bastard of hers is mine too!"

Pippa's breath caught in her throat. Terror spiraled through her.

"I cannot allow this, Winsleigh." Spencer's voice was calm, emotionless. His gray eyes were dark and cold, steel forged by fury.

"Well, I wondered if it would come to this. I suspected a man who would steal another man's betrothed did not have much of a sense of honor.

However, I had hoped." Hugh sneered. "There is a set of pistols in her father's desk in the library."

Pippa gasped. "Hugh! No!"

Spencer didn't so much as flick an eyelash. "When?"

"In the city we would meet at dawn, with seconds of course. But here in the country we are not as formal." A slow, wicked smile creased Hugh's face. "The meadow behind the stables. One hour."

Hugh stepped to Pippa and took her hand. She wrenched it out of his grasp.

"I am sorry my touch is so distasteful to you today, Pippa. We shall have to work on that. St. Gregory." He nodded and walked to the door. "One hour." Hugh opened the door, stepped through, and closed it carefully behind him in an odd parody of normality.

"I must speak to him." Pippa started toward the door.

Spencer grabbed her arm and yanked her toward him. "I do not want you anywhere near him."

"Let me go." Pippa wrenched out of his grasp. "You do not understand. Hugh does nothing he does not do well. If he's willing to face you in a duel, he truly believes he will be the victor. I do not want you killed."

"I can take care of myself. I am not unskilled myself. Winsleigh may well have met his match."

"I cannot take that chance."

"I will not permit you to speak to him alone."

"This is my doing, Spencer. I will not allow you to protect me from the consequences of my own actions. If you love me you will stay here." She turned on her heel and stalked from the room.

"Pippa!" Frustration and anger sounded in his voice and echoed after her. She ignored him. She had to stop this. In whatever way she could.

She stepped into the library. Hugh sat behind the mahogany desk. The pistols lay in front of him.

"I want you to stop this, Hugh."

Hugh picked up one of the weapons and examined it. "Why should I?"

She raised her chin. "Because I ask it of you."

"This man has impugned the honor of myself and"—he fairly spat the words—"my wife. And I shall kill him for it." He gazed up at her and smiled. "And I shall quite enjoy it."

"You cannot do this!"

"Oh, but I can, my dear, and I shall." He leaned back in the chair and eyed her, his manner considering. "However, if you were to agree . . ."

She stared for a long moment. There was no need for him to say a word. She knew from the satisfied look on his face exactly what it would take for him to call off the duel. "Very well."

She drew a deep breath. "I will do whatever you wish."

"You'll give up St. Gregory?"

She nodded.

"You will be the thoroughly proper and biddable wife I had always expected you to be?"

"I will."

"And you will never, never mention the true parentage of the child." His gaze filled with such malice her hands shot to rest protectively on her stomach. He laughed. "You needn't fear for the brat. I will treat it as my own. I have no desire for anyone, ever, to know how you betrayed me."

"I agree."

"And furthermore"—he leaned forward and rested his arms on the desk—"you'll get rid of that blasted beast of yours."

"So," her voice trembled, "you are to leave me with nothing?"

He laughed, an odd humorless noise that shuddered through her. "I leave you with St. Gregory's life."

"Thank you." She swallowed hard, her throat aching, and turned to leave.

"I will allow you to tell him of his good fortune and send him on his way." She could feel his gaze burning into her back. "And then you and I shall talk." Her shoulders slumped, "about our future together."

She nodded and hurried from the room. She couldn't think about that now. About a life without Spencer, without love. About the horror of a life with Hugh. She had no doubts he would not let her escape her past unscathed.

It was a small price to pay.

Hugh stared unseeing at the pistols before him. Pippa was indeed an innocent if she thought he'd let St. Gregory live. The man had taken what should have been Hugh's, indeed, what Hugh had always considered his own. For that he must pay.

Hugh picked up one of the weapons and examined it thoroughly. Pippa's father had said this pistol was faulty and would not fire. It was a minor matter, really, and unnoticeable to a quick inspection. Only an expert would discover the problem. Regardless, Hugh had no doubt Pippa would provide a sufficient distraction. St. Gregory would never know his pistol was defective.

Until it was too late.

"Are you insane?" Spencer raked his hand through his hair. "How can you possibly imagine I would allow such a thing?"

"It is my choice." Pippa stood quietly in front of him. Now that she had made her decision, she planned to live up to it. Even if it broke her heart.

"But it is not your life alone." Spencer glared. "What of the child? Our child?"

"Hugh promised to treat him as his own."

"But he is not Winsleigh's! He is mine. Ours." He dragged her into his arms. "Does that not mean anything to you?"

"It means everything to me. You mean everything to me!" A sob rose in her voice. "I cannot allow you to risk your life."

He quirked a rueful grin. "I am really quite good with a pistol."

"I don't care. You must leave." She fought back a growing desperation. "At once."

"Not without you," he said softly. "I love you."

"And I love you! But please, please, promise me you'll go."

"How can I leave you?" He caressed her cheek and smoothed her hair away. "Your hair has always reminded me of summer. Did I ever tell you that?"

"No," she whispered. "Please go."

He didn't say a word and her heart sank. If Hugh came in and found her in his arms . . . she shuddered and he held her tighter. "I will be with you always."

She pulled away from him and clasped her hands together. "If only in my heart."

"No. I—"

"No. Mark my words, Spencer." She pinned him with an unyielding stare. "If you go through with this ridiculous duel, even if you survive, I will not marry you. I will take this child and you will never see me again. I promise you, Spencer."

Spencer shook his head slowly. "Are you that certain I will lose?"

"No." She balled her hands into tight fists. "I am that scared."

He clenched his jaw, whether in anger or frustration or resignation, she did not know. "Again, it seems I have little choice. Very well, then, I will go." His gaze trapped hers and her heart leapt just a bit at the determination she read there. "This is not the end, Pippa. I shall retreat for the moment. But I will never give up."

"Before you go . . ." Her gaze skimmed the room and she spotted Samuel sleeping peacefully unaware in a far corner of the room. "Samuel. Come here, boy!" The dog's eyes snapped open as if he

215

were merely feigning sleep and he trotted to her side. "Hugh hates Samuel."

Spencer raised a brow. "That comes as no surprise."

"Would you keep him for me? I should feel much better knowing he was"—her voice broke—"with you."

"Only until such time as we can all be together."

She swiped at the tears in her eyes. "You will take proper care of him, won't you?" She reached to pat the dog, then dropped her hand. "He's really quite a good dog."

"He and I already have a lot in common, you know." Spencer brought his gaze to lock with Pippa's. "We both love you."

She placed her hand on the side of his cheek and stared into his eyes, his wonderful gray eyes, like the sky during a storm, and remembered the first time she'd seen him. And all the times since.

"I told you once I was born when I kissed you." She swallowed against the lump in the back of her throat. "I never had the chance to tell you I died when I thought you'd left me."

"And I—" He drew her hand to his lips and brushed the palm. Tears fogged her eyes. "I lived only the days when you loved me."

His gaze burned into hers and she knew for all the rest of her life she would remember the pain in his eyes and how very much she loved him.

"Touching. Really, quite, quite touching." Hugh's sarcastic tone rang from the doorway. "If you two can pull yourselves away from one another, I know it has not been an hour yet, but I am ready if you are, St. Gregory."

Spencer slanted her a glance of surprise. "I am sorry, my love. It appears for the third time today, I have few options." A slight smile played across his lips. "I am indeed ready."

Pippa gasped. "Hugh, what are you doing? You promised!"

"My dear girl. My sweet, naive wife. You of all people should know." Hugh cast her a contemptuous smile. "Promises are not worth the breath it takes to make them."

Pippa sent every servant she could find scrambling in a desperate search for her father or Caro or her uncle or anyone who could stop this debacle. Where were they all? It was as if the world and everyone in it had abandoned her and Spencer and Hugh to play out this macabre story to its bitter end.

Pippa ran to the meadow with Samuel at her heels. Spencer already faced Hugh from a distance of twenty paces. Servants handed them their weapons and a small crowd of others stood nearby.

"Spencer!" she cried, and lunged for him. A stablehand held her back.

"Do not come any closer, Pippa." Spencer did not take his gaze from Hugh.

"Spencer! Please! Stop! Now! Leave!" Desperation gripped her soul.

"That he simply cannot do, my dear," Hugh called, and laughed. "It appears he is far more honorable than I thought after all."

"Pippa, stay back." Spencer's voice was calm. He shifted the pistol in his hand. "I do not—" He stopped and stared at the firearm. Astonishment washed across his face. And anger. "Winsleigh, this weapon is worthless!"

"Really?" Hugh smiled. "What a shame." He raised his pistol. "How fortunate for me that this one is not."

He will kill him! It's what he planned all along! How could I have been so blind? This is my doing! All of it!

Pippa wrenched herself free and flew toward Spencer. "Spencer!"

He turned toward her, an expression of horror on his face.

I cannot let him die!

Hugh fired. The crack of the pistol reverberated in the meadow. A gust of wind smacked against her with a sharp pain and thrust her forward into Spencer's arms.

"Pippa!" he cried.

She grabbed his face in her hands. "Dear Lord, you're all right. You're . . ." She struggled for words. "You . . ." Her mouth didn't seem to want to work and an odd weakness spread through her limbs and sapped her strength. Her hands fell from his face. What was happening to her?

She heard the screams of her parents and Caro off in the distance. Good. They would stop Hugh from trying this again.

"Pippa!" Agony etched Spencer's face. What on earth was wrong with him? Hugh hadn't killed him.

218

The duel was ended. They could be together. "Pippa, don't leave me!"

Of course she wouldn't leave him. She would be with him always. Why, they were fated for each other. They knew it even in their dreams. She tried to lift her hand to touch his face but couldn't. Tears glistened in his eyes. How very strange. Her rogue, her rake, her scoundrel had tears in his eyes. Tears of joy. Surely they would be together forever now.

"Pippa," he sobbed, and held her tighter. Odd. The light was going. But it was barely midday, wasn't it? Maybe a storm was coming? Of course. The sky would turn gray, just like his eyes. She gazed into them. They were filled with sorrow.

Why are you so sad, my love?

She was so very tired. If she could but close her eyes for a moment . . .

"Pippa!" Was that anguish in his voice? She fought to open her eyes and struggled to smile. Then he'd know how very much she loved him. He smiled back, his wonderful lopsided grin that would live forever in her heart.

She sighed with contentment and her eyes drifted closed. From far, far away she heard him cry her name once more but knew there was no need to answer. She was in his arms. He was in her soul.

And they would dance together forever in her dreams beneath the moon and the stars where good girls and roguish men find each other. And find as well one true love to last forever. A love their souls were fated to find. If only . . .

. . . just once.

I get choked up just thinkin' about it . . .

. . . and it don't matter how many lives I live or how many humans I have, that kind of thing stays with ya. I'll never forget that day. It broke my heart, losin' her like that. It broke everybody's heart.

It's still in my head. Spencer sittin' there, holdin' Pippa in his arms, like he thought she'd wake up or somethin'. No doubt about it: the man was in shock and the anguish on his face . . . there just aren't enough words to describe it. He was never the same. Nobody was ever the same.

What happened to Hugh? He got what he deserved. The day they buried her he killed himself. Put the same pistol he shot her with to his head and pulled the trigger. He was a weasel and I never liked him and I knew he hated me, but ya still had to feel sorry for the guy. He really loved her. Oh sure, it was an obsession and out of control in my book, but he did love her in his own weird way. And he killed her. Who could live with that?

I went to live with Spencer and he treated me pretty good. Probably 'cause I was all he had left of her. He was made of sterner stuff than Hugh but he couldn't live without her either.

Guys like Spencer don't off themselves. That's the coward's way out. But he did kill himself all the same. He drank himself into a stupor nearly every night and took up with all kinds of women. Blondes mostly. There was a funny sort of frantic edge to everything he did. Kind of like he had to keep moving to stay one step ahead of the pain.

Rain was the worst. Whenever it rained, he'd be gone all night. I think he just rode through the country. I don't know. Maybe he was lookin' for her. It was after one of those rides that he got real sick. But there wasn't any fight left in him, ya know what I mean? He didn't seem to care about life if she wasn't in it. He was too young to die that way. That was back in 1820.

What? Yeah, you're right, kid. She was too young to die too.

Well, enough of that. This is a whole new lifetime. Pippa's my human again. Of course, she doesn't remember nothin', not consciously anyway. But her heart remembers. I'm countin' on that. Ya see, there's a Hugh this time around too. Nah, I don't think he's quite as nasty but I sure as hell don't trust him.

Victoria Alexander

Spencer? Nope. She hasn't met him yet. She will. And I'll know him when I see him. The same souls are entwined from life to life, destined to meet over and over again. It's how this stuff works. But Pippa and Spencer were cheated the last time. Now they get another chance. And I got a mission. It's all up to me.

You mean you haven't figured it out by now?

I got to get these two souls together.

Chapter Ten

"I swear, in as long as I've known you, this is the first time I can remember you doing two really stupid things in the same week."

"Wow." Morgan Phillips slanted a grin at her administrative assistant and oldest friend. "Must be a new record."

"Unless you take men into account," Lindy Carroll said under her breath. "Although you've set a couple of records there too."

Morgan let the statement pass without comment. What could she say anyway? Lindy was right.

"Why don't we start with the lesser of two evils?"

Morgan groaned to herself. She'd seen this lecture coming when Lindy appeared to join her on her early-morning run. Lindy hated mornings. But Morgan had actively avoided talking to her privately ever since she'd told her old college roommate her decision.

Lindy nodded at the puppy tagging at the heels of the bearded collie trotting in front of them, their leashes bouncing along behind. "Why in the world did you agree to take in another dog?"

"I like dogs."

"Everybody likes dogs but not everybody runs a kennel."

"Well, I like them a lot."

"That's no—"

"Her name appealed to me."

"Cindy Lou Dog?" Lindy scoffed. "What kind of a name is that for a respectable animal? It sounds like a cartoon character."

"I think it's cute. Anyway, it's not forever. I'm just keeping her for a few months while my neighbor is out of town." Morgan smiled at the puppy struggling to keep up with the bigger dog. "Sam likes her."

"That dog is spoiled rotten."

"Yep." Morgan upped her pace. She knew what was coming.

"Hey, slow down!" Lindy called. "I want to talk to you."

Morgan sighed. "Okay, I give up."

She plopped down on a park bench and waited.

Lindy collapsed beside her, laboring to catch her breath. "I can't believe you do this every morning. It's so—"

"Healthy?"

"Masochistic."

"I like running. And I like the park. Especially in the morning. There's hardly anybody here. I can let Sam run without hanging on to his leash."

Lindy raised a brow. "Isn't that illegal?"

Morgan laughed. "Technically, the law says you have to have him on a leash. I don't think it says anything about holding on to it. Besides, at this time of day nobody seems to care."

"Okay, enough with the dog stuff. Now, tell me about this major, life-destroying act of stupidity you've gotten yourself into. Tell me about Win."

"What about Win?"

Lindy glared. "I can't believe you're going to marry him."

Morgan tucked her hands in the pockets of her sweatshirt, leaned her head back on the bench and gazed up at the sky. "Looks like it's going to be another beautiful spring day."

"Don't change the subject," Lindy snapped. "You're really good at that but not this time. The Final *Jeopardy!* category is marriage. The answer is: momentary insanity. What's the question?"

Morgan laughed. "I have no idea."

"The question is: how can you seriously consider marrying that guy?"

Morgan shrugged. "Win's okay."

"Winston Hughes the fourth is a weasel."

"He is not."

"Sure he is. And he's a snob."

"He's a great-looking snob."

Lindy snorted. "And he knows it too."

Morgan smiled.

"I just don't see—"

"Look, Lindy." Morgan sat upright and pinned her friend with a firm gaze. "Think about it. Win and I have known each other forever. There are no surprises with Win. We've been running the company together for the last six months. The company our fathers built. They've always wanted us to get together. We're partners in business we might as well be partners in life."

"But you don't love him."

"If you'll recall, love hasn't exactly worked out for me. How many times have I fallen in love? Dozens? Maybe even hundreds? Better yet, how many times have I been engaged?"

"Are we counting since college," Lindy said, "or before?"

"All together."

"Let's see." Lindy ticked off the list on her fingers. "There was that really cute medical student—"

"He's a surgeon now."

"And that musician—"

"Works as a bartender, I think."

"And the stock broker, and the journalist and the—"

"How many, Lindy?"

"Who can keep track?" Lindy glared. "Okay, what is it? Five?"

"Six." Morgan shook her head in disgust. "I'm twenty-eight years old. I've been engaged six times." She paused. "Seven if you want to count the Italian with the long title and the great body."

Lindy narrowed her eyes curiously. "Why don't you count him?"

"It only lasted a couple of days. Kind of like a virus. It's hardly worth the effort. Anyway"—she blew out a long breath—"without Giovanni—"

"The virus who doesn't count."

Morgan nodded. "—who doesn't count, I've averaged one fiancé every eighteen months. And it never worked out. I didn't really love any of them. I thought I did, but I was wrong."

"Ah-hah! Got ya there!" Lindy smirked in satisfaction. "You don't love Win either."

"That's different."

"How is it different?"

"For one thing, I already know I don't love Win. I don't expect love and I'm not looking for love."

"Sounds like a business merger."

"Maybe it is in a way. I mean, I know exactly what I'm getting with Win. No surprises. Period."

"You said that already." Lindy shook her head. "I don't get it. I always thought you liked surprises."

"No, I like adventures. It's an entirely different thing."

"Hah! How do you expect me to believe that a woman who has bungee jumped off a bridge into a gorge in West Virginia—"

"I only did it once."

"—and joined in a hot-air-balloon race in France—"

"Again, a one-time thing."

"—and rafted the rapids in some forsaken South American jungle—"

"A lot of fun but never again."

"—would be happy with a marriage that involves no surprises to a man as boring and pompous as Win?"

"I wouldn't call him pompous," Morgan said under her breath.

"Well, everyone else does." Lindy crossed her arms over her chest and studied her friend. "I just don't get it. When your dad put you in charge of research and development—"

"And new products."

"—and new products, and you asked me to come work for you, I thought it was great. I thought you had finally gotten all that dangerous stuff you're so attracted to out of your system."

Morgan grinned. "I'll try anything—"

"I know." Lindy sighed with exasperation. "Just once. But you really turned out to be good in the wonderful world of business. I know it's not as exciting as a shark roundup off the Great Barrier Reef—"

"It wasn't a roundup. According to the grant proposal it was a scientific survey."

"Whatever! I thought you liked what you're doing now."

"I do. And I'm not planning on quitting. This company is half mine and I have no intention of giving that up."

"So why are you so hot and bothered to get married at all?"

"I'm not hot and bothered. But with Dad and Mr. Hughes retiring, this marriage will make the company strong. Anyway, my biological clock is ticking. I want to have kids and I want them to have a father."

"Hey, my clock's ticking just as fast as yours but you don't see me getting married."

"Listen to me for a minute and I'll see if I can explain." Morgan paused and tried to find the right words. She had never told anyone, not even Lindy, her overwhelming desire for a baby that seemed to come from deep within her soul. "I've always wanted to have a child. I think that's why I've been engaged so many times. It's really weird, but there's this feeling inside me, this need to have a baby that's so strong it hurts. It's like an aching emptiness and every year it gets more intense."

"Morgan, it's almost the twenty-first century." Lindy set her lips in a stubborn line. "In case nobody's mentioned it, you don't have to have a husband these days just to have a kid."

Morgan's voice was firm. "I do."

"But marriage to Win. Yuck." Lindy shuddered. "I think artificial insemination would be more affectionate."

"Win and I will be fine together."

"Yeah, yeah, I know: no surprises."

"Nope. Not in life. Not in business." Morgan paused. "But speaking of surprises, when do I get to meet this mystery man you've been dating?"

"There's no mystery about him. I just haven't had the chance to get you two together. It's no big secret." Lindy stretched and pulled herself to her feet. "Well, I have to get home and change if I'm going to be to work on time. I have a real bitch of a boss."

"Yeah, she's a slave driver." Morgan grinned with relief. "Get going."

Lindy studied her for a second. "I'm not giving up on this one, pal. I've been your friend for too long to see you throw your life away on a man whose not anybody's version of Mr. Right."

"He'll be right for me," Morgan said confidently.

"I'll take that bet." Lindy glanced around. "Hey, where did the dogs go?"

"Damn." Morgan sprang to her feet and scanned the park. "I don't see them anywhere."

"Do you want me to help you look?"

"Don't worry about it. Sam's done this before. He always comes back. And we take the same route every day. I usually find him in that direction." Morgan started off. "I'll see you at the office."

"Okay," Lindy called after her. "But I'm not through with this yet!"

Morgan picked up her pace, her gaze skimming the park for Sam and Cindy Lou. Lindy didn't say anything Morgan hadn't thought of herself over and over again. But Lindy didn't know Win as well as she did. Morgan and Win had always been friends and if you couldn't have love, friendship was the next best thing.

So what if Win wasn't Mr. Right? There was no Mr. Right. Not in real life anyway. As a child she was convinced there would be one true love in her life. One man destined to be with her forever. She even dreamed about him: a faceless lover who waltzed with her under the moon and stars and held her in his arms as if they were made for each other. Once, when her father had insisted she see a shrink out of concern for her adventurous nature and the failure of her fourth engagement, she'd talked about the dream. She didn't remember what the shrink had said but she wasn't impressed and didn't go back. Morgan was smart enough to suspect her willingness to agree to marry one man after another had a lot to do with that mystical quest for the man of her dreams.

She didn't believe in Mr. Right anymore. If he existed at all it was only while she slept, in the dim recesses of her mind and her heart. And even the dream had faded in recent years.

"Sam!" She spotted the furry canine and his pint-sized sidekick up ahead, on the side of a slight rise. Sam barked and leapt around a tall, dark-haired man as if he'd just found a long-lost friend. Morgan couldn't resist an exasperated laugh: Sam made friends very easily. She let loose a long low whistle. The dog wheeled to a halt and stared at her. "Come here, boy."

Sam didn't so much as twitch. Stubborn beast. What was wrong with him today? She trudged up the hill.

"Sam!" The dog wagged his tail and wiggled in excitement. Morgan made a grab for the dangling leash. The Beardie danced out of her way, Cindy Lou following him step by step. "Knock it off, Sam. This is not a game." She scrambled after the leashes that slithered through the grass as if endowed with some reptilian mind of their own.

"Let me help."

She glanced at the stranger. Nice-looking guy. Kind of a hunk actually. Expensive suit too. "Thanks. If we can just grab their leashes—"

She lunged for the handle of one of the leads. The hunk dove for the other. The dogs' exuberance seemed to increase in direct proportion to the efforts of their pursuers. Damn creatures were playing with her. Great. At least someone was having fun.

Her legs tangled in the leashes and she was pushed against the helpful stranger. Sam and Cindy Lou barked their excitement and bounded around the couple in a canine game of Ring Around the Rosy. Dogs and leads and legs and arms all entwined together in a fast-motion dance.

"Hey, guys!" she cried.

"Watch it!" he called.

Without warning, Sam threw himself against her. She tottered, struggling to keep her balance, and clawed at the stranger's jacket to keep upright.

It didn't work. They tumbled to the grass together. The dogs yelped. The leashes snapped and she and the hunk rolled down the slight slope, his arms around her, she clinging to him.

They came to rest at the bottom of the hill. Morgan lay on top of him and panted for breath.

"Well, that was straight out of *101 Dalmatians*."

"He's only seen it twice," she muttered.

"Um . . . are you all okay?"

"I don't know." She groaned. "I feel like I've just been beat up."

"Feel free to lie here for a minute." A grin sounded in his voice.

She lifted her head and stared at him. He was grinning all right. A funny kind of lopsided grin. Very nice. So was the solid body beneath her. Heat rose in her face.

" 'I forgot for a moment I was a priest,' " he said under his breath.

Her eyes widened. "What did you say?"

"Nothing." The grin was sheepish. "It's just a quote that came to mind."

"You're not a priest, are you?" Damn, she wasn't lying on a priest, was she?

"Nope."

"Good." Relief surged through her.

He raised a curious brow. "Good?"

"I just mean this would be even more embarrassing if you can't do this kind of thing professionally."

"Professionally?" His eyes narrowed in suspicion. "Do you do this kind of thing professionally?"

"No!" She glared down at him. "I just mean my profession doesn't prohibit it."

He laughed and she bounced against him. Wow. He obviously worked out.

"Stop that!" She widened her eyes, groaned and buried her face on his shoulder. "I've got it. 1955. *The Left Hand of God*. You're a fan. A Bogie fan."

"You don't like Bogart." Surprise sounded in his voice.

"Oh, I love him. I watch him all the time. In fact the, um, male, I live with—"

233

"Oh. Your husband likes him too." Was that disappointment in his voice?

"No." It was her turn to grin. "I'm not married."

"Boyfriend?"

She pushed away any thought of Win. He was more a fiancé than a boyfriend anyway. And not even officially yet. "I was talking about him."

"The Beardie?"

"Yeah." She laughed. "He loves Bogart. If I'm channel surfing, it must be something about the voice, but he can pick it out as it goes by. Then he insists on watching. Blocks the view of the TV if I don't leave the movie on. It's pretty amazing."

"Let me get this straight. This is the dog we're talking about, right?"

"That's what I said." Why was she lying on this stranger talking about the idiosyncrasies of her dog? And why did she have no desire to move?

"But you're the person?"

"When it suits me."

"And you, the person, allow him, the dog—"

"Sam. His name is Sam."

"You let Sam watch what he wants?"

"Pretty much."

"What most men wouldn't give to have a woman that would let them have that much control over the TV." He sighed in an exaggerated manner.

She laughed. "I wouldn't do it for a man."

His gaze raked her face lingering for a moment on her lips. "I don't usually meet women this way."

"What a coincidence. I can't remember the last

time I've fallen on top of a strange man and rolled down a hill with him."

He laughed again and the sound was rich and warm and seemed to wrap around her.

"Um . . . we should probably . . ." She struggled to move off him. The leashes were still tangled around them. He moved with her and his lips brushed across hers. She froze. "What are you doing?"

He lifted a brow. "I'm trying to get us out of this mess."

"Oh yeah right." He hadn't even noticed the kiss. Of course, it really didn't count as a kiss. It was inadvertent. An accident. Then why did it feel suspiciously like a kiss?

"Here." He rolled her to her side and fumbled with the leashes and after a moment, they were free. He scrambled to his feet and extended his hand. She grabbed it and he pulled her upright.

"Thanks." She tried to release his hand but he held it firm. His gaze caught hers, his brows pulled together.

"This is going to sound stupid, but have we met somewhere before?"

She laughed self-consciously. "It's a good line but . . ." She paused and stared at him. He was handsome all right, his features were strong and masculine, his hair very dark, almost black, and he was tall. She only came up to his shoulder. She was sure she'd never seen him before but there was the vaguest, well, something, about him. An uneasy tremor darted threw her and she pulled her hand away. "No. No, I don't think so."

"I didn't either." He shook his head as if trying to clear his mind. "It's strange though. Must be déjà vu or something."

"Yeah." She smiled weakly. "Or something." She stepped back and stared at his clothes. "Damn. Your suit is ruined. You'll have to let me pay for it."

"Don't worry about it." He glanced down ruefully. "I should have known better than to come to a park in the morning in a business suit. Usually I run in the morning but I have a meeting"—he looked at his watch—"in about an hour and I wanted to get my mind geared up for it. Starting the day in a green space like this before it's overrun with humanity always helps me get my head on straight."

"Me too," she murmured.

"I'll just go back to my place and change."

"Yeah, I have to go home and get ready for work too. Come here, guys." She bent down and tied the ruined leases to Cindy Lou's collar, then to Sam's. The dog looked up at her and grinned. That was the joy of his breed: he always had a smile for her. She patted his head and straightened. An awkward silence settled between her and the hunk. "Well, thanks for the help with my beasts."

"No problem. If you ever need to corral those animals of yours again," he said, humor coloring his voice, "all you have to do is whistle. 'You know how to whistle—' "

" '—don't ya, Steve?' " Morgan laughed. "*To Have and Have Not*. Nineteen-forty—"

"Four."

"Right. Only she said it to him. Lauren Bacall, or rather, Marie Something said it to Steve." Morgan leaned toward him and gazed into his eyes. " 'You just put your lips together' "—she lowered her voice—" 'and blow.' "

A slow smile spread across his face.

"See ya, Steve." She turned and started off, the dogs right behind her. Nothing like a good flirtation and a bit of one-upmanship to start the day off right. And with a genuine hunk, no less. A genuine intelligent hunk with a sense of humor.

And the most amazing gray eyes she'd ever seen.

Chapter Eleven

She wasn't here. Unless he'd missed her. Damn. He sure hoped not.

He jogged through the park at his usual steady pace. He'd gotten the distinct impression she ran here every day. She and those crazy dogs of hers. But he'd run here for two mornings now and still no sign of her.

He scanned the park looking for a short blonde with a ponytail and a lilt in her step. She intrigued him and he wanted to see her again. Talk to her. Maybe get to know her. She was just his type. He'd always been attracted to pretty, petite blondes. Especially if they had green eyes. She was smart too, and funny. He liked that. Liked the challenge of trading quips with her. And she liked Bogie and dogs. What more could you want in a woman?

Where the hell was she? She should be here. She obviously kept in shape. Their roll down the hill had told him that. He kept thinking of her as Marie but that was just the Lauren Bacall character in *To Have and Have Not*. Why hadn't he asked her real name? Or where she lived? Or where she worked? All he knew was the big dog's name: Sam. There could be a million shaggy dogs named Sam in this city.

He had no idea how to find someone here. He'd just arrived in town himself the day before he met her. He slowed to a walk, his gaze searching the park. Nothing. Well, he wasn't about to give up. Nope. Gregory Spencer did not give up easily. Not in business. Not in life.

He checked his watch. If he hurried he'd have just enough time to get back to the apartment he'd sublet, shower and get ready for another round of meetings. It probably didn't matter anyway. If she'd been here today he must have missed her.

Greg strode toward the street and tried to shift his mind off those eyes and on to the day ahead but he couldn't get her out of his head; exactly where she'd stayed since the moment he met her. The moment he kissed her. He smiled to himself. Not that it was a real kiss of course. It was completely accidental but it caught at something inside him. Lust? Maybe. Hell, he'd lusted after women before. Plenty of women. This was different. He had no idea why or how, but one way or another he was determined to find out.

He dodged the oncoming traffic and headed for

what passed as home right now. It wasn't bad enough that his waking thoughts drifted back to her: his dreams were filled with her too. Surrealistic fragments of holding her in his arms, her body yielding and pliant against his, and an overwhelming need to be with her. Weird though. He'd wake from what anyone would describe as fairly erotic images to a gut-wrenching sorrow and a heart-pounding sense of loss so intense he'd grope his way into the kitchen for a shot of Jack Daniels. That was strange too. He could never remember feeling the urge for a drink in the middle of the night.

Nope, this woman had a grip on his senses and his soul and he wanted—no, he needed to figure out why.

"What is going on here?"

Morgan stared at the computer screen in the unused bedroom she'd turned into an office. None of these figures made sense. Maybe she was just too tired. She sighed, saved what she'd done and turned off the computer. The disk popped out and she set it on the keyboard. Tomorrow, at the office, she and Lindy would go over this. It was probably something trivial and relatively unimportant.

She stood up and stretched. Usually, she liked working at home late at night. She certainly didn't have anything better to do, and she sure wasn't getting any sleep. For the last four nights she'd tossed and turned until exhaustion finally brought on sleep. She'd even been too groggy in the morning to run. The dream was back. But now it came with a mind-numbing force and a heartfelt ache and she'd wake with tears on her cheeks and a sorrow so deep she'd cry into her pillow from the sheer desolation of it. And the lover who danced with her had a face now and a voice and a lopsided smile that made her breath catch.

Steve.

Sure, his name wasn't Steve but it was better than 'the hunk in the park.' Why hadn't she asked him his name? Not that it really mattered. She was no longer in the market for hunks. Nope, she was going to marry Win. And that was that. Besides, she'd never see the guy in the park again.

Except in my dreams.

She shoved the annoying thought away and wandered into the living room, sprawled on the sofa and picked up the remote control. She'd already told Win she'd marry him. And they'd told their parents. It was as much a business merger as a marriage really. They ran the company together and ran it well. Their own fathers had enough confidence in them to bow out of the day-to-day activities and simply keep their positions on the board.

She turned the clicker over and over idly in her hand. What was marriage anyway but a partnership? So what if she didn't love him. She liked him. She knew lots of couples whose marriages were based on far less. And there were no rose-colored glasses here. She was heading into this relationship with her eyes wide open. There would be no broken hearts in this deal.

She sighed and turned on the TV. Win wanted to announce their engagement at the big retirement party they were throwing for their fathers. What could be more perfect? It's what both families had always hoped for. It would be the start of the dynasty her dad had always wanted and his company would be firmly in the hands of his family.

She clicked through the channels, barely noticing the flickering images. She'd given Win her word and she had to stand behind it. Not that she hadn't broken off engagements in the past. Morgan had always firmly believed that when it came to matters of the heart, a promise wasn't worth the breath it took to make it. Emotions were too fickle to be bound by mere words. She wondered if she'd feel the same if she'd ever really been in love. Maybe that would be different. She'd never know. But your word when it came to business was your bond. Win was as much business as personal.

A soft thunk sounded from the bedroom followed by the hushed sound of eight paws padding across the carpet.

"Hi guys." Cindy Lou jumped on the sofa and collapsed against her. Sam sat down directly between her and the TV and thumped his tail on the rug. "So what's up?"

Sam looked as if he definitely had something to say.

"We're not settling in for a movie tonight if that's what you're thinking, so don't get excited." She glanced at the digital clock on the VCR. "It's past midnight and one of us has to go to work in the morning. I'm just kind of restless, that's all."

Sam cocked his head as if he was trying to decide if she meant it.

"I'm serious. No movies."

Sam rose to his feet with all the dignity of his breed and ambled out of the room. She patted Cindy Lou's head and smiled. Sam was a great dog and probably the only real love of her life. Of course, Win didn't seem to like him. Win was definitely not a dog person. Tough. Sam was her dog and would be her dog forever.

She surfed the channels for a minute and Sam returned to stand in front of her. "What do you want, boy?"

He looked at her as if trying to gauge her mood, then dropped his head and laid something at her feet.

"What have you got?" She bent to peer at it. "What is that? A driver's license?" Gingerly, she picked it up with two fingers. "Yuck, Sam, you really did a number on this."

The license was gnawed around the edges and nearly destroyed. It was definitely an out-of-state license, though, but she couldn't make out the location or the owner's name. However, the picture was intact. "Sam!" she glared at the unrepentant beast who thumped his tail in return. "Bad dog."

Sam grinned with an annoying air of a job well done. Morgan carried the disgusting identification into the kitchen and laid it on a paper towel. The man probably didn't know it was missing. How on earth would she get it back to him? She couldn't even read his name. But she recognized his picture.

She stared at the ruined license and an all-too-familiar lopsided grin.

"Okay, Sam, you got me into this, you're going to get me out of it." Morgan perched on the edge of the bench and shook her finger at the incorrigible canine, ignoring the curious stares of the few early risers in the park. At least she had the sense to leave Cindy Lou at home. Trying to get one dog to do what she wanted was hard enough. "I know you're not trained for this but you are a dog and there has to be some innate benefit to that. See this guy?"

She showed him the license. Sam sniffed it with an air of mild curiosity. She unhooked his leash. "Go find him, Sam. Go get him, boy."

Sam yawned.

"Fetch the hunk, Sam. You can do it."

Sam scratched behind his ear.

"Come on, Sam, you're a dog. Just do what dogs do."

Obediently he padded to a nearby trash can and lifted his leg.

"No, Sam!" Morgan groaned. "Not now."

Sam trotted back and gazed up at her, tail wagging expectantly.

"Sam, listen to me, pal." She cupped his face in her hands and bent close to him. "I know you've never done anything like this before. And let's face it, you weren't exactly the valedictorian at obedience school. In fact, and I've tried to keep this from you, they didn't even give you one of those cute little

245

certificates with the paw print on it." Sam sighed. "But that's all behind us. It's a new day and now's the time to live up to your heritage. What do ya say, boy?"

Sam stared as if he were giving her request serious consideration. Then his long, wet tongue flicked across the tip of her nose.

"Thanks." She pulled a tissue out of her pocket and wiped away the evidence of the Beardie's affection. "Maybe you just need someone to show you how to do it. Here's how it works. I say: go get him, Sam! And you go running off to find"—she waved the license—"the hunk." She didn't want to call their quarry Steve; it might just confuse the dog. Although Sam looked more amused than confused.

"Like this. Watch." Morgan ran a few feet and turned and waved. Sam plopped his haunches firmly on the ground. "Come on, Sam. Let's go now! Atta boy!"

Sam didn't move.

Morgan stalked back and planted her hands on her hips. "What is wrong with you? You're a dog, Sam, a d-o-g! You're supposed to do stuff like fetching and carrying my slippers—"

Sam settled his head on his paws.

"—if I had slippers that is. Dogs are not supposed to steal drivers' licenses and watch old movies. I need you to at least pretend to be a real dog right now. You know, you've seen them on TV. Four legs, fur, a tail and they bark. Not talk, bark." She snapped her fingers. "That's it! I've got it.

"Sam." She gave him a smile of encouragement. "What would Lassie do?"

Sam cocked his head.

"Benji?"

Sam tilted his head in the other direction.

"Rin Tin Tin?" Desperation sounded in her voice.

Sam rolled on his back and waved his paws in the air.

"I don't think so, pal. Rin Tin Tin was a real dog. A tough dog. A macho dog. Man's best friend and all that stuff. He was always . . ." Morgan widened her eyes and stared at Sam. She had a crazy idea but it just might work.

She sat back down on the bench. "Sam, come here."

Sam leisurely got to his feet and strolled over to her. She bent down to whisper in his ear. "Sam, what would Bogie do?"

Sam's ears pricked up. He leapt to his feet. And he was off and running.

"All right, Sam!" Morgan whooped. "Way to go, boy! Hey! Wait for me!"

Morgan raced after Sam. The dog sped through the park, a magnificent blur of doggy determination. Pride surged through her. What a dog!

Sam retraced their path from earlier in the week, stopping now and then for a quick sniff; then he was off. Still no sign of Steve or whatever his name was. What if he wasn't here? What if she couldn't find him? Ever? A surprising pang of regret twinged through her at the thought.

Sam approached the boundaries of the park with

breakneck speed. Straight ahead was the street. And there he was. Waiting to cross. Or at least she thought it was him. The suit was gone and he had on running shorts and some kind of team T-shirt. Wow, his broad shoulders owed nothing to his business clothes. Damn! If she didn't catch him now she never would.

Sam was still yards away. If they didn't act fast she'd lose him.

"Steve!" She yelled. He didn't respond. Of course not! That wasn't his name! How could she get his attention?

He stepped into the street.

"All you have to do is whistle."

She pulled up short, stuck two fingers in her mouth and let loose the kind of whistle she'd practiced for hours as a kid. The piercing sound shrilled through the park. He hesitated and she blew again. He turned.

"Hey!" She flagged her arms in the air and loped toward him. He waved and started for her. Sam reached him first, bouncing around in a canine dance of joy.

"Hi ya, Sam. How ya doing, boy?" Steve patted the exuberant animal.

Morgan pulled up short right in front of him. Now that she'd found him, what on earth was she going to say?

He grinned with obvious pleasure and her stomach flopped. "I've been looking all over for you!"

Delight washed through her. "You have?"

"I sure have." A serious note sounded in his voice.

"I need to talk to you. No, I need to get to know you."

"Oh yeah?" *Be cool, Morgan.* She had an uncontrollable urge to giggle.

"Yeah, I do. I really do. But I can't right now." He shook his head. "I've got to go or I'm going to be late. Can I see you again? Soon?"

"Uh." Why not? She couldn't resist a grin. "Sure."

"Great. Damn, I wish I had more time. How about tomorrow? Here. Early. Just after sunrise?"

"Okay." Her smile was probably pretty goofy but she didn't care. He wanted to see her again. "Tomorrow."

"Terrific." He nodded and turned to go, took a step, then swiveled back to her.

"What—"

He grabbed her and pulled her to him tight, crushing his lips to hers in a kiss hard and fast and full of promise.

He drew back and stared into her eyes. "I've been dreaming about you and it's driving me crazy. It's going to be tough to wait until tomorrow." He released her and took off, sprinting toward the street. He stopped and threw her a quick wave, then dashed through the traffic to disappear.

Morgan stared after him. Her heart thudded in her chest. *He was dreaming of me too?* How bizarre. And how wonderful.

Sam's cold nose nudged her hand. She bent and threw her arms around him. "What a great dog you are, Sam! I'm so proud of you!"

Sam wiggled in response.

"Let's go home, boy." She clipped the leash back on his collar and they walked side by side. "You can tell Cindy Lou all about your triumphant mission."

Sam halted abruptly and stared at her. "What is it, boy?"

The dog gazed at her for a minute as if deciding whether or not to confide in her. She crouched down and met his black-eyed gaze. Sam was smart, there was no doubt about that, and at moments like this he seemed almost human. "What's going on, pal? You can tell me."

Once again he licked her nose. Morgan laughed and hugged the animal. "I love you too, Sam. Come on."

They started for home, Sam ambling along beside her with a distinct air of accomplishment. An air Morgan shared.

She couldn't seem to wipe the silly grin off her face. Oh sure, she hadn't given him his license. And okay, she hadn't gotten his name. But she was going to see him again. And he was dreaming of her.

And she had the craziest desire to whistle.

Chapter Twelve

Morgan sat staring at her computer, a puzzled expression on her face. Even behind the Regency-era desk she preferred, here, in the office that was a mirror image of Win's, she looked every inch the consummate executive.

Yeah, right.

Win leaned against the doorjamb and studied her. As much as he hated to admit it, she'd taken to the business with a flair no one ever expected. Who would have thought, when her father put her in this office at Phillips and Hughes, Inc., less than a year ago, she'd not only be able to actually handle the position but excel at it? The only reason her father had forced her to take the job in the first place was to save her life. Victor Phillips was convinced the apple of his eye would end up dead if she continued her frenetic pace of adventure hunting and risk taking. Even as a child, Morgan was fearless.

Win distinctly remembered overhearing a conversation about three years ago between his father and Phillips on that very topic, triggered by Morgan's latest escapade. He couldn't recall all the details but it had something to do with a skydiving incident somewhere out West. Morgan had escaped with nothing more than a sprained ankle and a few bruises.

"The girl will end up dead one of these days if I don't do something," Phillips had said. "I keep hoping marriage will settle her down but she goes through men like she goes through money. She has too damn much spirit, that's her problem. I sure as hell don't want to break her, just calm her down."

"Good luck with that one." Win's father, Winston Hughes III, heaved a sigh. "I just wish Win had half her spirit."

Win clenched his jaw at the memory. No spirit? If his father only knew. But in many ways, he had to thank Morgan for her previous lifestyle. That episode, and the old men's response, had put Win in the position to get everything he'd ever wanted.

Morgan glanced up from her computer. "Hi, Win. What's up?"

"Nothing really." He strolled into the office and settled in one of the reproduction antique wing chairs in front of her desk. "Just thought I'd take a break and come in and say hello to my very favorite soon-to-be-fiancée."

Morgan laughed. "I'm your only fiancée, aren't I?"

"Well, I certainly haven't had the track record you have with engagements but even if I did you'd still be my favorite." The reminder of all her past intendeds, and probably lovers as well, rankled him and he struggled to keep his smile pleasant.

"You always know the right thing to say, Win."

"I do work on it," he murmured.

"Right now, I'm trying to work on the final figures of that little computer company we bought a couple of months before I started." She pulled her brows together. "You were in on that, weren't you?"

"Sure." He kept his voice light. "You've probably heard all this before—"

"Actually, I haven't. That's why I'm trying to learn as much as I can now. It's been in the hands of our lawyers and"—she glanced at the screen—"Casablanca Computers's lawyers and it's taken nine full months to get to this point. What a pain in the butt."

"Well worth it though. It's a nice little company. We already have a worldwide reputation for software development and production. Casablanca will give us the means to branch out with our own line of hardware."

"No question of that. It's a good move for us. But some of these numbers—" She shook her head. "I don't know."

Annoyance nipped at the back of his mind. "I wouldn't worry about it. It's not really your concern anyway."

"You bet it is. I'm in charge of research and development and new products. This is definitely new for us. And now that the deal is set and we're ready to kick into high gear I need to know what's going on."

"It's probably no big deal," he said smoothly. "Don't let it bother you."

"I guess." She sighed. "Anyway, the guy from Casablanca is supposed to be in town today and I think—" She paged through a calendar on her desk. "Here it is, he's coming in this afternoon."

"Nice guy. I knew him in college a little."

"Oh, is he a friend of yours?"

"Not really." Win shook his head. "We didn't run in the same circles. I knew him, that's all."

"Hopefully he can give me a hand with this."

"I'm sure he can." *Not if I can help it.* "But I didn't come in here to talk about business."

"No?"

"No. I want to talk about us."

"Okay." She leaned back in her chair expectantly.

"You know I want to announce our plans at the party next week."

"That sounds perfect."

"It's what the old men have always wanted."

Morgan frowned. "I hate it when you call them that."

"Sorry." Win shrugged. "That's how I think of them."

"Both of them are barely past sixty-five. They deserve to relax but I'm still surprised they're calling it quits."

"I think they're happy to leave it all in our hands, now that you've come on board and become the superwoman of the company." He couldn't suppress a slight note of sarcasm.

Morgan narrowed her eyes. "Do you have a problem with that?"

"A problem? Me?" Win scoffed. "Why would I have a problem?"

I've worked my butt off here from the day I graduated from college while you flitted around the world spending your father's money in your asinine search for a good time. Then you waltz in with a natural gift for business and all of a sudden it's Morgan Phillips: prodigal daughter. And you'll get half the company that should be mine. All mine.

He plastered a smile on his face and forced a note of sincerity to his voice. "I'm just as proud of what you've done here as everyone else, Morgan. And prouder yet that you've agreed to be my wife."

"Good." Morgan breathed a sigh of relief. "For a moment there, I thought . . . Never mind."

"And speaking of becoming my wife." Win pulled a small wrapped package from his inside jacket pocket. "I hope you like it." He leaned forward and placed the gift on the desk.

"Win! How sweet." She tore off the wrapping to reveal a ring box. Her gaze met his.

"Open it."

She flipped open the lid and gasped. Satisfaction surged through him. *I'll bet none of the rest of her legion of fiancés ever topped that.*

"My God, Win, it's gorgeous!" Morgan plucked the ring from the box and stared at it. Of course it was gorgeous. It was, in fact, magnificent. A five-carat emerald surrounded by diamonds. All of the highest quality.

"It matches your eyes."

"Win," she shook her head. "I don't know what to say. It must have cost a fortune."

"It did," he said wryly. "But well worth it for the future Mrs. Hughes."

"The future Mrs. Hughes," she murmured. Carefully she placed it back in the box and snapped the lid closed.

He frowned. "Aren't you going to wear it?"

"Not until we make the official announcement." She raised a brow. "Is that okay?"

No! "Whatever you want. We've already told our folks. I'm just eager for the rest of the world to know how I feel about you. You know, I have more in common with our parents than you realize."

Morgan smiled skeptically. "Oh yeah, right."

"No, really. They've always hoped that we'd get married someday." He trapped her gaze with his. "And so have I."

"Oh." Her eyes widened with surprise. "You never said anything."

"My mistake. I think even as kids I always knew we belonged together. In college, I realized you were who I wanted but you were younger and I thought I should wait. Then I started working here and you went through school and immediately took off for parts unknown."

"I was never hard to find."

"No, but you moved pretty fast."

She laughed. "It always seemed like there was

something more to do. Something I hadn't tried at least once. It's kind of strange. All my life I've felt like I had to push the limits and live on the edge of excitement. Like I'd miss something wonderful if I didn't overcome my fears and sample whatever came along."

"Fears? You?" Win leaned back in his chair and narrowed his eyes. "I find that hard to believe."

"It's true."

"So have you done everything there is to do?"

"I don't know." She toyed with the ring box, running her finger along its velvet edge. Abruptly she grinned and looked at him. "Everything but marriage."

"We'll take care of that as soon as possible," he said firmly.

"How soon?" Surprise flickered through her green eyes.

"No time like the present. The old—our fathers' official retirement date is two weeks from now. I'll settle for that."

"Two weeks?"

"Think of the symbolism, Morgan. We get married on the same day they hand over the company to us. They'll love it."

She shook her head. "Two weeks is way too soon. I mean if we're going to have a big wedding."

"I don't want a big wedding."

"But even a small wedding takes months and months of planning and I just don't see—"

"Morgan." He stood, leaned forward and planted his hands on her desk. "You run the biggest single division in a multi-million-dollar company. Add to that the fact that through the years you've already planned, how many weddings is it? Seven?"

"Six," she said quickly. "The Italian doesn't count."

"Six." He pinned her with a steady stare. "You can't tell me a woman who has already put together six weddings—"

"Most of those engagements didn't get that far."

He rolled his eyes toward the ceiling. "Still, I'm willing to bet you picked up some experience along the way. You can do it. I have confidence in you."

"But two weeks," she murmured.

"Now that we've made the decision, Morgan, I want to do it. I want to marry you as fast as we can work it out. What I don't want is to be dumped fiancé number eight."

"Seven. The Italian—"

"I know he doesn't count. Poor guy." He reached forward and cupped her chin in his hands. Damn, she was cute. Not the type he usually went for but he couldn't wait to have that pert, well-built little body squirming beneath him. "Believe it or not, sweetheart, I've always wanted you as my wife. I've always loved you."

"Oh, Win, I didn't know," she said softly.

"It's okay." He dropped his hand. "You know now. Two weeks?"

She blew out a long breath. "Sure, why not? Let's go for it."

"Morgan, here are those files you asked for." Lindy breezed into the office and set a stack of folders and a handful of computer disks on Morgan's desk. "I didn't know if you wanted the hard copy or the disks so I dug up everything."

Lindy glanced at Win. "Whoops. I didn't realize you were in here." A note of innocence sounded in her voice. "I hope I wasn't interrupting anything?"

Win raised a brow. "I'll bet."

Lindy smirked in that overly sweet, sarcastic way she had. He wanted to slap the smile off her face. From the time she started working with Morgan she'd made it perfectly clear she didn't like him. It was a pity, really. Tall and dark-haired, she was just his type. Of course, she was way too smart for her own good. And he could do without that mouth of hers. A gag would work nicely. And rope. A smile quirked his lips at the thought of the lovely Lindy bound and gagged and at his mercy.

"No problem." Morgan smiled at Win. "I have to get back to work anyway."

"So do I. I'll see you later." Win turned and headed for the door.

Morgan wasn't nearly as smart as she and everybody else thought. She'd actually bought that load of crap he'd dished out. Sure, he wanted her as his wife. Who wouldn't? She was the heir to millions. And that so-called spirit of hers would be great fun to break. In bed and in life. Marriage to Morgan would give him everything he wanted and far more than she suspected.

This was his company, damn it, and he would have it all.

Win strode past Lindy's office. Revenge would be sweet, especially when it came to that bitch. She'd be the first to go and there would be nothing Morgan could do about it.

Right now, though, he had more immediate problems. He couldn't let Morgan, or anyone else, look too closely at the Casablanca figures. She wasn't stupid. But with any luck, the old men's retirement and preparations for a wedding, even a small one, would take her mind off business. He'd make sure of it. Timing was crucial. He needed to keep her in line long enough for their fathers to officially step aside and sign over the bulk of their stock. And for their nuptials of course.

Win couldn't resist a smug, private smile. Morgan would be signed, sealed and delivered before she knew it. Just like a good business deal. Then she'd be out of the company and he'd have it all.

Oh yeah, he'd get rid of that damn dog of hers too.

"This is everything I could find about Casablanca. I've got duplicate copies on my desk," Lindy said. "Is there a problem?"

"I hope not." Morgan shook her head. "I've really been out of the loop on this deal and I'm trying to gear up for it. But I have a funny feeling about this. I just can't put my finger on it."

"You'll figure it out. You're probably so excited about your engagement you can't think straight." Sarcasm edged Lindy's voice. "You just can't get Win out of your head."

Win isn't the one I can't get out of my head. Where did that thought come from? Firmly she pushed it away.

"Take a look at this." She handed Lindy the ring box.

Lindy flipped it open and let out a long, low whistle. "Whoa. What a rock. I'll say this for Win: he knows how to do things right."

"Doesn't he though." Morgan accepted the box from Lindy, opened a desk drawer and dropped it inside.

Lindy raised a brow. "Why aren't you wearing it?"

Because I don't want to. Because I'm not ready. Because you're right and this is probably a major-league mistake. "I want to wait until we make the official announcement."

"Oh yeah, that makes sense. Any woman with an emerald the size of a boulder wants to wait until the last possible minute before committing herself publicly." Lindy sank down in the chair Win had vacated. "Don't you think—"

"He says he wants to get married right away."

"And what did you say?"

"I said sure."

Lindy groaned. "Damn, Morgan, you are so stupid sometimes. Win might be the right man for some woman, although short of Cruella Deville no one comes to mind, but he sure isn't right for you."

"It'll be fine," Morgan murmured.

"Fine? It'll be a disaster." Lindy leaned back and crossed her arms over her chest. "Well, all I can say is thank God for divorce. Make sure you get a good prenuptial agreement. I'd hate to see him get everything when you split."

"I'm not going into this marriage as a short-term proposition," Morgan snapped. "And I know what I'm doing."

"You don't love him."

"Love bites." Morgan leaned forward. "We've been all through this. I like Win and he likes me. This marriage works out great for everyone. The company will be firmly in family hands and our fathers will get the union of our families they've always wanted."

"That's a merger, not a marriage."

"Maybe. But it will work out." Morgan sighed. "I'm really tired of this whole conversation."

"I don't care." Lindy narrowed her eyes. "You're my best friend in the world and I'm not giving up until the moment you say, and I shudder at the thought, I do." Her voice softened. "I care about you and I hate to see you ruin your life."

"Thanks, I love you too. But I'm not ruining my life and I don't want to discuss this anymore." Morgan's gaze dropped to the stack of files. "I really want to get a good handle on Casablanca before that meeting this afternoon."

"Okay." Lindy stood and pawed through the paperwork. "This should give you just about everything."

"I don't get it." Morgan pulled her brows together. "If this deal was set nearly a year ago, why has it taken so long to get to this point?"

"I don't know. Since it was worked out before we

started I'm as unfamiliar with it as you are. I get the impression though . . ." Lindy hesitated.

"What?"

Lindy's words came in a rush. "I think Win's been dragging his feet."

"Why would he do that?"

"I don't know. I just know anything about Casablanca that comes to my desk or yours gets funnelled right back to Win's office. Maybe the weasel just wants all the credit."

"He's not a weasel," Morgan said absently, and sifted through the files. She looked up. "So how'd we get these then?"

Lindy studied her fingernails with an air of satisfaction. "Oh, I have my evil ways." She grinned. "Don't forget: before you decided you couldn't live without me I worked on an assignment desk at a TV station. I know how to get information. Shoot, I used to do my best investigative work right in the building. You ever want to get into a locked office, you just let me know."

Morgan laughed. "I knew you were good for something."

"It's part of my charm." Lindy stood up. "If you need anything else, I'll be in my office."

"Okay, thanks." Morgan turned to her computer. "Wait. The Casablanca guy is supposed to be here at three, I think."

"So what's the deal with that anyway? He sold us his company and now we're going to hire him?"

"He's basically coming on board as a consultant. And only for as long as we need him. Even with his setup, we don't know the first thing about hardware. It shouldn't take too long to integrate his operation into ours, but who knows."

"Oooo!" Lindy widened her eyes. "Gives me shivers just to think about it. Phillips and Hughes, mega-giant, eats another little guy."

"Knock it off. We didn't force anybody out. He wanted to sell. We wanted to buy. That's life in the big time. And nobody's hurt in this deal. We've kept all of his employees; not one person lost their job. They're getting much better benefits and we let them keep their seniority."

"P and H. The good guys of big business."

"Yeah." Morgan grinned. "We would have done it anyway, of course. It's stupid to get rid of people who know what they're doing. But keeping them on was part of the agreement." Morgan tapped her finger on a file. "The owner felt a great deal of loyalty to his employees. I think that's neat. He built Casablanca out of nothing. Started in his living room I think."

"Another computer nerd I'll bet."

"Probably. They're unavoidable. But this one seems fairly together. At least the deal he made with us was."

"I'll let you know when the nerd gets here." Lindy nodded and left the office.

Morgan's attention returned to the paperwork in front of her. She shuffled through the files. Damn. Where was that folder? She picked up the phone and punched out Lindy's number. "I know I have it here somewhere and I'll probably find it as soon as I hang up."

Lindy laughed. "I've heard that before."

"What's the guy's name?"

"The guy from Casablanca?"

"Yeah."

"Let me see." Lindy paused. "Here it is. His name is Spencer. Greg Spencer."

Lindy flew into the office, slammed the door behind her and barricaded it with her back. "He's not a nerd!"

Morgan pulled her gaze from the computer screen and frowned. "Who?"

"Spencer. Greg Spencer." Lindy heaved a heartfelt, overly dramatic sigh. "He's a god."

"A god?" Morgan laughed. "Get real."

"Okay, maybe not a god. But definitely a hunk. A genuine, bona fide, card-carrying hunk. And if you don't want him, I'll take him."

"I don't want him."

"Wait until you see him."

"It doesn't matter. I have Win and he's a hunk."

Lindy snorted. "Sure if you like 'em tall, blonde and weaselly."

"He's not a weasel."

Lindy shrugged. "Whatever."

"Lindy?" Morgan narrowed her eyes. "Is Spencer waiting to see me?"

"Whoops." Lindy grimaced. "Sorry about that." She turned to the door. "Brace yourself."

"Lindy!"

Lindy opened the door, her best administrative assistant voice firmly in place. "Mr. Spencer? Ms. Phillips will see you now."

Morgan set a polite smile on her face and rose to her feet.

"Ms. Phillips, I'm—"

Her heart stopped. Her breath caught. Her eyes widened. "Steve?"

He strode toward her: a tall, dark-haired hunk with a lopsided smile she would have known anywhere. "Marie!"

She extended a none-too-steady hand. "Actually it's Morgan. Morgan Phillips."

He took her hand. "Greg Spencer."

"I know." His gaze meshed with hers and she couldn't seem to do anything but stare into his wonderful storm-colored eyes. A warm current radiated from his hand to hers.

"You know him?" Lindy said in a not-so-subtle stage whisper.

She dropped her hand and a vague sense of loss trickled through her. "We've met."

"Actually," he said in a confidential manner, "I'm a friend of Sam's."

"Aren't we all," Lindy muttered. She stared at Morgan, then Greg, then back to Morgan. "I'm a little confused. I know who Sam is, but who is Steve? And Marie?"

Morgan's gaze met Greg's and they both burst into laughter.

"She's Marie."

"He's Steve."

"Actually," he said, "his name was really Harry."

"I don't get it. Steve, Harry, Marie?" Lindy shook her head.

Greg lifted a brow. " 'Another screwy dame.' "

"What?" Confusion stamped Lindy's face.

Morgan laughed again. "It's from *To Have and Have Not*. Lauren Bacall, Humphrey Bogart. So's the bit about Steve or Harry and Marie."

Lindy groaned. "No wonder he's a friend of Sam's. I'm getting out of here. Call me if you need anything." Lindy strode out of the room, muttering to herself. "Steve, Marie, Harry, Sam . . ." The door snapped shut behind her.

"Have a seat." Morgan sank down in the chair behind her desk. For the first time in this job, possibly in her life, she didn't know what to say. He settled in the wing chair directly in front of her and crossed one long leg over the other. She had a sudden vision of him dressed in clothes matching the era of the reproduction chair. Wow, he would have been a hunk then too. A chill shivered down her spine. "Well . . . um . . . Mr. Spencer—"

"Greg."

"Greg—"

"Or you can call me Steve."

"Greg—"

"Or Harry."

"Greg—"

"Or you can just whistle." Suppressed laughter danced in his eyes.

"Greg," she said firmly and drew a deep breath. *Business, Morgan, keep your mind on business.* "We have an office for you to use right down the hall and—"

"You're exactly as I remember you."

She smiled weakly. "You just saw me this morning."

"Nope." He shook his head. "That's not it."

"No? Then when we first met? On Monday?"

"Nope." He leaned forward, rested his elbow on her desk and propped his chin in his hand, a shade too close for comfort. "At night."

"I've never seen you—"

"In my dreams." He stared at her with an uncomfortable intensity. "Do you believe in dreams?"

"No." *Not even my own. At least, I never did before now.*

"You have taken over my head and my dreams, Ms. Phillips."

"Morgan," she murmured.

"Morgan." It sounded more like a caress than a name and something inside her melted. "Morgan Phillips. I like it. It suits you."

"Thanks." *Business. Focus on business.* "Now, then, Steve—er, Greg—I was thinking—"

"Why don't we get out of here?" He stood and smiled down at her.

"I can't. I have way too much work to do." Why was she standing up?

"Work can wait. I'll be here for months, one afternoon won't make any difference." He held out his hand and without thinking she took it. Why was she letting him lead her to the door? "Besides, I can't think about anything but you."

"This is ridiculous. I can't leave," she said under her breath. Why did it seem as if she had no control over her own movements, almost as if she were in a dream?

"Of course you can leave. You're the boss, right?"

"Well, yes, certainly, but—" And why did it seem as if she'd done all this before?

Greg pulled opened the door. Lindy stood there, her fist ready to knock.

"Oh, whoops, sorry. I just had—" Her gaze traveled from Greg to Morgan to their entwined hands. Lindy's eyes widened. "I hope I'm not interrupting."

Morgan snatched her hand from his and stepped back to her desk. "No, of course not."

"We were just on our way out." Greg nodded at Lindy.

"No, we weren't," Morgan said quickly. She drew a long, steadying breath. Sanity was back in full force. "I can't. I have a four o'clock appointment."

Lindy shook her head. "I don't remember any four o'clock—"

"Well, I do. *Read my mind, Lindy. Help me out here.* "In fact, he just called a few minutes ago and moved it up to three-thirty, so there's no way I can go anywhere. Sorry."

"Okay." He nodded. "Then have dinner with me."

"Nope, sorry, can't do it." She shook her head. "I have a previous engagement. A date actually, that's it, a date. Yep, I have a date."

Lindy frowned. "You didn't say anything about a date."

Morgan clenched her teeth. *Work with me, Lindy.*

"I have a date." Lindy and Greg exchanged glances. Obviously neither of them believed her. "I do."

She sat down at her desk. "Lindy would you have somebody show Mr. Spencer—"

"Greg," he said.

"Greg—to his office." Morgan picked up a report and stared at it in hopes they'd get the hint and leave.

"But I will still see you tomorrow morning?"

"Sure. Definitely."

Lindy muttered something to Greg. Morgan heard the door close behind them. She dropped the report on the desk, heaved a heavy sigh and collapsed back in her chair.

What in the hell was wrong with her? She'd never, never, never acted like such an idiot before. Yeah, he was good looking but each and every one of her six—seven if you count the Italian—fiancés had been hunks. Even Win was good looking by anybody's standards.

So what was it about him? Was it the dreams? Sure, that was weird but easily explained. Any amateur shrink with a self-help book in one hand could figure it out. Her decision to marry Win had prompted the return of her fantasy lover. Her subconscious had taken Greg's face and planted it on the up-to-now faceless form of said lover, probably because he'd made a distinct impression on her. That made sense completely. Why, even the legitimate, although idiotic, psychiatrist she'd seen years ago would agree.

Of course her theory didn't explain why the feeling of déjà vu around him grew stronger every time they met. And when they touched . . . She shivered with the memory.

"What is going on here?" Lindy stormed into the office.

Morgan snatched up a handful of papers and studied them carefully. She kept her voice vague. "Where?"

"Don't give me that." Lindy's voice rang with indignation. "You know what I mean."

"I haven't the faintest idea."

"Morgan. The report you're reading so carefully is upside down."

"Oh. Damn." Morgan dropped it on her desk and looked up in surrender. "What do you want to know?"

"Where did you meet him?"

"In the park."

"Are you really going to see him tomorrow?"

"Probably."

"Do you like him?"

"I don't really—"

"Are you going to dump the weasel for him?"

"He's not a weasel!" Morgan glared. "I don't even know this guy—Spencer. Greg. Whatever. We've met twice. That's it. That's all there is to it." *Unless you count my dreams. And his.*

"Bull." Lindy snorted. "From what I can see, he must have made one hell of a meeting. You can deny it up one side and down the other but when I walked in this room there was an electricity that damn near knocked me over. And you had this look

271

on your face like Cinderella at the ball."

"I did not!"

"You most certainly did. And he looked like he was in pretty deep too. So don't expect me to believe there's nothing going on between the two of you."

"There isn't anything going on." *Except for a couple of insignificant kisses.* Her cheeks warmed at the memory.

Lindy narrowed her eyes. "Maybe there should be."

"Don't be silly. I'm going to marry Win. And that's that."

Lindy shook her head. "What you need—"

"What I need," Morgan said in her best I-am-the-boss voice, "is for you to drop this and let me get some work done."

"That's not exactly what I was going to say." Lindy stalked out of the office and shut the door sharply.

Damn. Lindy was right. There was something between her and Greg. Something immediate and profound. Exciting and terrifying. A disaster waiting to happened or unimagined bliss. She'd never had feelings like this about any man, ever.

And it scared the hell out of her.

Chapter Thirteen

"You're late."

Morgan strode past Lindy's office, her assistant's reproach trailing after her. "Don't push it, Lindy. I had dinner with Win last night and got in late. I didn't hear the alarm this morning and I'm in a really, really bad mood."

"Hey, wait. I need to tell you something."

She shoved open the door of her office, stepped inside and slammed it behind her. Whatever Lindy had to say, it could wait.

"You stood me up." Greg sat at her desk, his gray eyes simmering with annoyance.

She tossed her briefcase on the sofa and glared at him. "What are you doing in my office?"

"Waiting for you." He raised a brow. "I thought we had a date."

"I wouldn't call it a date."

"Call it what you want. I waited for you in the park but you didn't come."

"Sorry. I didn't realize it was such a big deal."

"Sure you did." His voice was level. "I think you were scared."

"I was not." An overly sharp note rang in her denial.

"I think you feel the same way I do."

"Oh? And what way is that?" Sarcasm dripped off her words.

"I don't know exactly." He shrugged. "But I've always liked a good mystery and I'm going to find out."

"And just how do you plan on doing that?"

"I'd planned on starting this morning, but you didn't show." He narrowed his eyes as if he were trying to see inside her. His voice softened. "Why did you stand me up, Morgan?"

"I didn't stand you up! I overslept. That's all there is to it. I haven't been sleeping well and I just slept through the alarm. That's it. Period. No ulterior motive here. No fear of any kind."

"Not sleeping well?" A smile played at the corners of his lips and his words carried a slight edge of satisfaction.

Something inside her snapped. "No, damn it! I haven't been sleeping well. I've been very restless and when I finally get to sleep . . ." She released a long, angry breath. "I have this dream! All night! Every night! Ever since—"

"We met." It was a statement of fact as if he already knew the answer.

"Yes! It started again—"

"Again?"

"Again. I had it growing up. The same dream. It finally disappeared a few years ago."

"And now it's back," he said slowly.

"It's back."

"Tell me about it." He rose to his feet.

Abruptly her irritation vanished, replaced by unease and the tiniest touch of anticipation. "I don't want to."

"Why not?" He circled the desk.

She shook her head. "I don't think it's a good idea."

"Oh, come on, Morgan." He stepped toward her. "You tell me yours I'll tell you mine."

"Yours?" Her voice squeaked. "You mean the one about me?"

"Um-hmm." He moved closer. She willed her feet to step back. Nothing happened.

She swallowed hard. "Okay. So tell me."

"It's night, always night." He was close enough to touch now.

"Under the stars." She stared up at him.

"And the moon." His eyes darkened with the memory. She could lose herself in those eyes. "And I'm dancing—"

"Waltzing."

"Um-hmm. Waltzing to music so faint—"

"You don't hear it so much as feel it," she said softly.

"And the woman in my arms has hair the color of, I don't know." He smoothed a strand of her hair away from her face. "It reminds me of summer. And her eyes are so green . . ."

"And she fits in your arms like you were made for each other."

"Like this." He pulled her into his arms. Why didn't she resist? Why didn't she want to resist? "Like fate."

"Fate," she whispered.

He leaned closer and brushed his lips back and forth across hers. "Do you believe in fate, Morgan?"

"I don't know." She could barely breathe.

"Tell me about your dream."

"I—" She shuddered. "It's a lot like yours." The heat of his body against hers seemed to sap her strength and her will. "I'm dancing with him—"

"Who?" His voice was soft and intense.

"I never saw his face until . . ."

"Until when, Morgan?"

"Until . . ." She gazed into his eyes and realized words weren't necessary. He already knew. Maybe he'd always known. "Is this when you kiss me?"

He whispered against her lips. "I think I should, don't you?"

"Oh, yes," she sighed the words. "I think you'd better."

His lips pressed against hers, warm and firm and demanding. Her arms snaked around his neck and her body molded to his. She closed her eyes and tangled her fingers in the silky hair at the back of his neck, pulling him closer. He tightened his grip, drawing her hard against him. His kiss deepened. Her lips opened. Restraint shattered.

His mouth moved against hers with a raw hunger she greeted and recognized and shared. He ripped his lips from hers to plunder the line of her jaw and ravage the length of her throat. She ran her hands along his shoulders and his arms, reveling in the solid muscles beneath the expensive suit and the strength of the body that pressed so intimately against her own.

He pushed her jacket off her shoulders. What was he doing?

She fumbled with his tie. What was she doing?

He popped open the snap at the top of her blouse. Why didn't she stop him?

She tugged his tie free and flung it to the floor. Why didn't she want to?

He yanked her jacket off and ran his hands under the back of her blouse. Was he going to make love to her right here in her office?

She groped at the buttons on his shirt until they pulled free and slid her hand beneath the starched fabric and over the hot, smooth flesh of his chest. Why couldn't they get these damn clothes off?

Blind desire and relentless need such as she'd never known before swept aside any thought of control or reason or judgement. Her heart thudded against her ribs, her blood surged through her veins and roared in her ears like the buzz of an insect or the ring—

"Morgan," he gasped, his words tickling her neck. "Is that the phone?"

She sagged against him, desperately trying to catch her breath. "I sure hope not."

"I think it is."

"Should I answer it?"

"Is the door locked?"

"No."

"Then answer it."

"Good idea." She staggered to the desk and fumbled for the phone. "Yeah?"

"Morgan, did you want—"

He stared at her from across the room and she stared back.

"Lindy? Can this wait?"

A shrug sounded in Lindy's voice. "Sure, I guess but—"

"Great. Thanks." She snapped the phone back in its cradle and leaned on the desk for support.

"Wow." He tunneled his long, tanned fingers through his dark hair. "What the hell was that all about?"

She released a shaky laugh. "Don't you know?"

"Maybe"—abruptly a serious note sounded in his voice—"I do."

His eyes seemed to bore into hers. Her heart stilled. She couldn't pull her gaze from his. Time slowed around them. It was a second, maybe less, or an eternity, possibly more, but in his eyes she saw joy and love and anguish and despair. Life and death. Always and never. And the part of her dream she hadn't told him came back to her with a force that stole her breath away. And yanked her firmly back to reality.

She wrenched her gaze from his and sank into her chair, folding her trembling hands primly on her desk. "So, Greg." She gave him a courteous smile. "How do you like your office?"

He narrowed his eyes suspiciously. "How do I like—" A grin broke across his face and he laughed. "Oh, I get it. You don't want to talk about this, right?"

"How perceptive. Do you know what else I want?"

"You want me to leave."

"You are good." She pointed at the door. "Now, go away."

He bent over, scooped up his tie and dangled it from two fingers. "Should I put this on here or just carry it with me? Down that long corridor? Past your assistant's office? And all those secretaries? Not to mention—"

"Put it on," she snapped.

He buttoned his shirt and nodded at her. "I know you've probably already thought of this but . . ."

Morgan glanced down and groaned. She scrambled to her feet, ran to her personal powder room and stared in the mirror. A shocking image stared back. Her shoulder-length hair was disheveled. Her blouse was pulled halfway out of her skirt. Her face was flushed, her lips slightly swollen and her eyes a deep, intense green. She looked exactly like what she almost was: a woman who'd been made mad, passionate love to.

She straightened her clothes and a pulled a comb through her hair with hands that wouldn't stop shaking. *Maybe he'll leave while I'm in here.* She

279

drew a deep breath and turned back to the office. Greg lounged in one of the wing chairs.

"Why are you still here?" She stalked to her chair and sat down, pretending a great interest in the memos on her desk. "Don't you have work you need to do?"

"I just wanted to make sure you don't need anything."

"I don't need anything." *Just get out before this happens again.* "Thanks for asking. Feel free to go now."

"Okay." He pulled himself to his feet in a decidedly laid-back manner. *Why wouldn't he just go away?* He sauntered toward the door. "So, I guess this means you do dream about me."

"Yes. All right. I admit it!" She slapped her hands on the desk. "I dream about you. Every night. Every single time I close my eyes, there you are. But it doesn't mean a thing. Nothing. Nada. It's some sort of weird psychological quirk. That's all." She glared. "There. Are you happy now?"

"For the moment." A smug note sounded in his voice. "It's just nice to know that I am the, uh, 'stuff that dreams are made of.'"

She narrowed her eyes. "Sounds like Shakespeare?"

"He may have said it first but he didn't say it best."

She couldn't resist a smile. "Sam Spade. *Maltese Falcon.*"

"Very good. I'm impressed."

"Thanks. Now bye." She waved him toward the door.

He pulled it open and glanced back at her. "By the way, I like your desk. Is it real?"

Her gaze fell to the well-preserved piece. "Genuine antique. I bought it in England at an estate auction. It dates to the early 1800s." She ran a loving hand along the polished mahogany surface. "I paid way too much but the moment I saw it I had to have it. It seemed to call out to me."

"It's like your name, you know, it suits you."

"I love this piece. Now—"

"I know. Go away." He stepped over the threshold. "You'll miss me when I'm gone."

"Get out!"

The door shut and she was alone.

She leaned back in her chair and closed her eyes. What was happening to her? She'd never wanted to rip a man's clothes off like that before. At least not until she'd gotten to know him. Even then, she'd never known anything like this overwhelming attraction he held for her. When she was with this near stranger the passion that gripped her was stunning in its power. And worse, it seemed so right.

It was the dream, obviously, it had to be. The sensual—almost erotic—atmosphere that haunted her nights had geared her up for this crazy encounter in her office. That was all there was to it.

Win's never made me feel like that.

Of course not. She didn't expect it anyway. No surprises, remember? Win was safe and secure and she was going to marry him and make everybody happy.

Greg Spencer would be out of her life in a few months and back to wherever he'd come from and that would be that. With any luck, the dream would go with him.

In the meantime, the guy was dangerous. She wasn't sure why, but she knew with every fiber of her being that any relationship with him would end in disaster. The uncontrollable desire she'd given into a few minutes ago would have to be kept leashed. She'd have to keep their involvement on a business level. Sure. She could do that. Easy.

As long as she didn't gaze too often into his stormy eyes.

Or inadvertently brush against his hard, toned body.

Or let her glance linger too long on his lopsided smile.

Oh yeah. No problem. Right.

She opened her eyes and straightened in her chair. The man liked her desk though. And he liked her dog. She trailed her finger along the edge of the desk. And he must like her.

But this whole thing petrified her. Since she'd met him the dream always ended the same way. Not that she believed in dreams or omens or any of that stuff. At least, she didn't used to. But she had to believe in her feelings and the devastating misery that surrounded her heart when she woke was too real to ignore.

No doubt about it. Greg Spencer would bring nothing but heartache.

It was weird though. Somewhere along the line she'd realized she wasn't scared only for herself.

She was terrified for him.

"Damn." Morgan struggled to find her keys in the briefcase that had way too much junk in it. She shifted the bag of groceries and waited for the elevator to reach her floor. Win had asked her to dinner again tonight but she'd begged off. He'd been charming and really quite wonderful last night as if he was making a real effort to, well, court her. It wasn't necessary. They'd known each other forever. It was flattering and very thoughtful of course, but it also made her just a tad uneasy. A feeling she tried to ignore. She wasn't in the mood to deal with him tonight. Not after this morning with Greg.

Why did the damn phone have to ring?

That was another thought she was determined to ignore even though it popped up over and over through the day. She hadn't seen him after their encounter in her office. She did casually ask Lindy if he was settling in okay. It was no more than any considerate, thoughtful employer would do for a new employee. Lindy didn't say anything but Morgan knew she wasn't buying her act.

The elevator door opened and Morgan started for her apartment.

"Where is it? Ah hah!" She plucked the over-burdened key chain free and looked up.

"Hi." Greg leaned against her door with a large

pizza box and a couple of plastic bags. A sharp thrill of anticipation shot through her. "Your apartment, right?"

"Right." She stabbed the key in the lock and opened the door. Sam and Cindy Lou barked a greeting and gamboled about their feet. "Look out, guys. Let me get rid of this stuff." She glanced back at him. "I live here. What are you doing here?"

He followed her in and slammed the door shut with his foot. "I come bearing gifts. In case you didn't notice."

"Yeah, I noticed." She set the groceries on the table, dropped her bag and bent to hug the dogs. "How'd you guys do today? You get walked?" A note left on the table by the college student who came twice a day to take the dogs out answered her question. She skimmed it, then turned toward Greg. "Why?"

"I thought you might be hungry. Look." He opened the box and waved it under her nose. "Deep dish. Tomatoes, black olives, ham and pepperoni."

"Smells good," she admitted grudgingly. Good? It smelled fantastic.

He pulled a bottle of wine from one of the bags. "And red wine, a nice Merlot." He presented it with a flourish. "A very good year, I believe."

She tried not to smile. "Okay. And what's in there?"

"Ah. Our entertainment for the evening."

"A movie?"

"Absolutely."

"Bogart?"

284

"Who else is there?"

"I hope it isn't *Casablanca*."

"You don't like *Casablanca*?" He clapped his hand to his head. "I don't believe it. It's the greatest movie love story ever."

"Oh, I like it." She crossed her arms over her chest. "But it's a little obvious, don't you think?"

"There's nothing better for a date."

"This isn't a date."

"No." He smiled sheepishly. "This is an apology. For this morning."

"What makes you think I won't throw you out right now?"

"Boundless optimism. And"—he waved at the pizza—"deep dish, tomatoes, black olives, ham and pepperoni."

She shook her head in surrender. This was probably a big mistake. "I give up. You can stay. For the pizza and the wine and the movie but that's it. Understood?"

"Absolutely." He traced an *X* over his heart. "I promise."

"Okay. I'm going to change. There are dishes in that cabinet. I'll be right back." She walked into her bedroom, Sam and Cindy Lou right behind. Faintly, she heard Greg whistling in the kitchen. One after another the dogs jumped on the bed and settled down.

"This is not a smart thing to do. I can't be around this guy. Even though I do seem to want to be around him. One of those moth-to-the-flame or lemmings-to-the-seas kind of things." Sam stared silently. "It's probably all your fault, you know. If it hadn't been for that tumble in the park I wouldn't have known what this guy does to me." Quickly she found a pair of jeans and a sweatshirt and changed out of her suit.

Morgan walked into the kitchen. Two glasses brimming with wine sat on the counter next to two plates with big slices of pizza. She grabbed a plate and a glass. "Get your movie. Let's go into the living room."

"I'll follow you anywhere."

She slanted him a sharp glance but his expression was innocent. She sank down on the sofa and Greg headed to a chair.

Sam bounded in front of him and leapt into the seat.

Greg laughed. "Sorry, Sam. Your spot I guess."

Sam's tail wagged in response.

"I'll take the other one, then." He stepped to the matching chair but Cindy Lou was there before him. "Not here either, huh? Well, I guess that just leaves the sofa."

Morgan rolled her eyes toward the ceiling. Great. The last thing she wanted was him sitting right next to her. On the other hand, this was as good a time as any to see if they could really be together without passion rearing its irresistible head. After all, they were going to work together. "Sit down."

He settled a good three feet away from her. At once both dogs planted themselves on the floor between them, eager for any accident that might mean pizza pickings for grabs.

"This is great." She sighed.

"Yep."

They shared a companionable silence for a few minutes. The tension within her from the moment she saw him eased in the enjoyment of the food and his easy, relaxed company.

"How did you manage to pick my favorite pizza and my favorite wine?"

"Lindy told me."

"I should have known." She took another bite and chewed thoughtfully. "Did she tell you anything else about me?"

"Yep."

"Like what?"

He shrugged. "Stuff. You know, the usual."

"The usual?"

"Yeah, she filled me in a little on the adventures of Morgan Phillips."

She grimaced. "Which adventures are those?"

"I think she mentioned hang gliding and dog sled expeditions and alpine skiing and—"

"Enough. I get it. You can stop now. Besides, I don't do that kind of thing anymore."

"And seven fiancés."

"Six. The It—"

"I know," he laughed, "the Italian doesn't count."

His laugh was contagious and she couldn't help joining him.

"So you know all about me but I don't know anything about you."

He pulled a sip of his wine. "Not much to tell, really. I come from Chicago originally. Typical mid-

287

western, all-American upbringing. Two sisters. No brothers. Started Casablanca Computers about ten years ago. Sold it to you for big bucks. That's about it."

"What are you going to do now?"

"I don't know." He pulled his dark brows together. "I've been talking to a lot of people, checking out some opportunities since I've been in town. For the immediate future, of course, I'll be with Phillips and Hughes. After that," he shrugged, "I guess I'll just wait and see."

"So, what movie did you bring?"

"*Sabrina.*"

She smiled with pleasure. "Good. I like that one."

He unfolded his long legs and got to his feet, plucking the tape from its box and sliding it into her VCR. "I do too. It's not too dark, not too intense. Just a nice, enjoyable love story. It's perfect for—"

She narrowed her eyes. "Not a date."

He tossed her his lopsided grin and her stomach fluttered. "A laid-back night like this."

He sat back beside her, picked up the remote control and hit PLAY. Within minutes they were caught up in the story of the stodgy businessman and the chauffeur's daughter.

Morgan relaxed and admitted privately this was turning into a nice evening. Greg was funny and sharp and she realized she liked being with him. No pressure, no stress, just a pleasant night shared by two people who could actually turn out to be friends.

Midway through the movie, Cindy Lou jumped

up beside Morgan on the sofa, circling around on the cushions and edging her closer to Greg. Not to be left out, Sam scrambled up beside Greg and nudged him toward her until their shoulders touched.

A current of electricity arced between them. All thoughts of mere friendship vanished. With every breath she took she was more and more aware of their close contact. She tried not to breathe at all and kept her gaze firmly on the TV. If she looked at him, she'd lose it. She couldn't possibly stay plastered against him like this. It was just asking for trouble. The best thing to do was ignore it. That's it. Just pretend he wasn't here.

The movie droned on but she couldn't keep her mind focused on the plot. All she could think about was that morning. The scene played over and over in her head. The heat of his body against hers. The aching need to crush her lips to his. The overwhelming desire to be in his arms.

"I think I need more wine." She leapt to her feet.

"Wait." He pulled her back down beside him. "I think we need to talk."

"Talk?" She shook her head. "I don't think we need to talk."

"I do." His voice was firm. "About this morning."

She pulled a deep breath and braced herself. "What about this morning?"

He raised a brow.

"Okay, okay. Talk."

He ran his fingers through his dark, silky hair. "Nothing like this has ever happened to me."

She laughed weakly. "You mean you've never had a passionate encounter in an office before?"

"Oh, sure, I've done that." His voice sobered. "I'm serious, Morgan, I've never felt this way before."

Her breath caught. "What way?"

His gaze met hers. "The way I feel about you."

She didn't want to hear this. "I don't think—"

"Morgan," he said sharply, "listen to me."

"Nope. No way." She sprang to her feet and crossed the room. "I don't want to listen. Listening to you, hell, even being in the same room with you is dangerous."

He stood but didn't approach her. "Why?"

"Why? You know why!" She aimed an accusing finger at him. "You do something to me."

He grinned. "Great. You do something to me too."

"No." She shook her head. "It's not great. It's . . . it's creepy. Weird."

He stepped toward her. "I don't think it's weird. I think it's kind of wonderful. In fact, I think—do you believe in love at first sight?"

She snorted. "After six engagements—"

"Seven if you count the Italian."

Eight if you count Win. "Whatever. After being in and out of love, I don't believe in it at all. Love's a fantasy. That's all. It's a fairy tale. A romance novel. A movie."

"Maybe you've just never found it."

"Maybe it doesn't exist. Not in real life anyway."

"Just in dreams?"

The reminder clenched her stomach. It was love

in her dreams. And sorrow. "I'm not falling for that one."

"What one?"

"The old 'you've dreamed about me so you must love me' line."

A smiled played across his lips. "Oh, have you heard that line before?"

She heaved a frustrated sigh. "Not until now."

"I think it is love. I think I'm in love with you. And further, I think you're in love with me."

"Hah! Get off it." She glared. "We barely know each other."

"So what?" He shook his head. "Have you ever tried to dial an on-line service during peak hours and gotten a busy signal?"

"Sure but—"

"And then tried to connect over and over again with no luck?"

"Yeah, so?"

"But then finally, you hear that click from the modem and even though it takes a few seconds more you know immediately that you're in." He blew a long breath. "That's how I feel about you."

She narrowed her eyes. "What am I, America Online?"

"No. Damn it, Morgan." His eyes flashed with annoyance. "What you are is fate. My fate."

"I don't believe in fate."

"I didn't either, until now. What I feel for you was immediate and unquestioned. There's not a doubt in my mind about this. And it doesn't matter that we don't know each other very well because, somehow, it sure feels like we've known each other forever. Besides, we have a lifetime to get to know each other."

Her eyes widened. "What do you mean?"

"I don't know exactly." He had that look of a man caught in a trap he wasn't prepared for. Good. That'll send him packing.

"Marriage?" She raised a brow.

"I don't . . ." He squared his shoulders. "Why not?"

"I can think of a million reasons why not and not one reason why." She shook her head. "You can't be serious about this."

"I've never been more serious in my life. I love you and you love—"

"I do not!"

"Yes, you do, and sooner or later you'll quit denying it." His eyes narrowed. "Fair warning here, Morgan, I don't intend to be number eight on your love 'em and leave 'em list."

"Seven."

"It doesn't matter! You can go through a hundred fiancés for all I care. I plan on being husband number one. And only."

An unreasonable sense of joy surged through her and she shoved it viciously out of her mind. She wouldn't risk the kind of heartbreak she felt in her dreams. The dreams of him. And regardless of whether she believed in dreams, she had no doubt whatsoever that getting together with this man would destroy them both.

"No, it won't work. Period. There can't ever be anything between us."

"That must make me a real idiot then!" He smacked his hand against his forehead. "I thought there already was!"

"Well, you were wrong!"

"Was I?" He stalked to the door and jerked it open. "I don't believe that. And furthermore, I don't think you believe it either!"

"Don't tell me what I believe!"

"I'll tell you anything I want! It's not my fault you're too scared to listen."

"I'm not scared." She scoffed. "I've never been scared of anything."

"You're scared of this. I'd say you're terrified. I can see it in those incredible green eyes of yours. I don't know why exactly. But I'm going to find out." He started through the doorway, then swiveled back. In two long strides he reached her and yanked her into his arms. His lips crushed hers in a kiss hard and fast and dangerous. He released her and headed back to the door.

"I'm not giving up on you, Morgan Phillips. Like it or not, I'm going to spend the rest of my life with you!"

"In your dreams, pal!"

"Yeah." Fire flared in his eyes. "There too." The door slammed shut behind him.

"Damn you, Greg Spencer!" She yelled at the door. "I don't like you! I don't love you! I don't want you! And I don't ever want to see you again!"

She stalked over to the TV and slapped the stop

button. Sam gazed at her with reproachful eyes.

"No. We're not watching the rest of it. I'm not in the mood."

Sam lumbered off the sofa, padded into the bedroom and returned, planting himself in front of her. He spit Greg's drivers license at her feet.

"Great. I still haven't given him his license." She picked it up and stared at the picture for a long moment.

"What have you done to me?" His image grinned back. "I've never been afraid of anything in my life. And I've never wanted anything as much as I want you."

She glanced at the dog. "What am I going to do, Sam?"

Sam stared silently.

"What in the hell am I going to do now?"

Chapter Fourteen

"You look awful." Lindy followed Morgan into her office.

"Happy Monday to you too." Morgan tossed her bag down and stalked to her desk. "I had a very bad weekend."

"Oh?" Lindy smiled her overly sweet and completely fake smile. "Spend time with the weasel, did we?"

"No!" Morgan collapsed in her chair. She pushed her hair away from her face. "First of all, I didn't get any sleep."

Lindy perched on the chair in front of the desk and narrowed her eyes. "That's getting to be a real problem for you, isn't it?"

"Yeah. And it's not the only one. I spent hours on the phone this weekend with my mother, who's going crazy getting ready for tomorrow night's party for Dad and trying to pull together a wedding."

Lindy raised a brow. "I thought you were doing it at your folks' house in the country and it was going to be small and intimate."

"Yeah, that's what I thought. It seems to be growing by leaps and bounds. Mom keeps saying I'm her only child and this is her only chance for a real wedding."

"Is she sure you'll go through with this one?"

Morgan bit her lip.

"Morgan?"

Morgan pulled a deep breath.

"Morgan?" Lindy studied her. A slow smile quirked her lips. "Thank God. Win's joined the Morgan Phillips' top ten dumped fiancé list, hasn't he?"

"Yeah, I think so," Morgan muttered.

"What a relief. I was really worried for a while there. What made you change your mind?"

"I don't know. Marrying Win seemed like such a good idea at the time." She rubbed her forehead and sighed. "It's what our parents have always wanted. It means we'd keep the company in the family."

"You and Win don't have to be married for that to happen."

"I suppose. And I've known him forever. There are no sur—"

"Yeah, yeah, no surprises. Right."

"And I could have children."

Lindy snorted. "I know a dozen guys who'd be more than happy—"

"Lindy!"

Lindy smirked.

"Anyway, I decided that of all the really risky things I've ever done, marrying Win might be the worst."

"So have you told him yet?"

"No." A queasy feeling settled in the pit of her stomach.

"Can I be there when you do?" Lindy leaned forward eagerly. "I'd kill to see his face when you tell him to get lost."

"I'm not exactly going to tell him to get lost. We still have a company to run."

"So when are you going to tell him?"

"I don't know for sure."

"Well, you'd better do it soon. Doesn't he want to announce it tomorrow night?"

"That's the plan." She pulled a steadying breath. "I'll tell him before that."

Lindy shook her head. "He's not going to be real happy about this."

"I think it's for the best."

"Well, duh." Lindy studied her for a moment. "So what are your plans?"

"Oh." Greg's smile flashed in her mind. "I don't know."

"What about the computer hunk?"

Morgan stared unseeing at the papers on her desk.

"Morgan? What about Greg Spencer?"

Morgan shook her head.

"Oh, damn, it's him isn't it? You like him don't

you?" Her eyes widened. "You more than like him."

"No, I don't." Morgan jerked her head up. "I don't like him at all. He drives me crazy. With his Bogart quotes and his pizza ambushes and his gray eyes and the way he kisses and—"

"You've kissed him?"

Morgan folded her arms on the desk and buried her face in them. "Yes. No. Actually the first time was an accident. The second time *he* kissed *me*. Then we attacked each other here."

"In the office?" Lindy's eyes' widened.

"Yeah, but that was mutual. But then he kissed me again at my place."

"At your place?"

Morgan raised her head and glared. "I blame you for that one."

"Hey, I just told him what kind of pizza you liked. That's it. So . . ." Lindy's voice was casual. "What are you going to do about him?"

"I don't know. It's a textbook case of mixed emotions." Morgan shook her head. "You remember that dream I used to have?"

"Dream? Oh, you mean the one where you're dancing with the love of your life? Sure, who could forget a recurring dream that hot?"

"Yeah, well." She groaned. "He's in it."

"Whoa." Lindy shuddered. "Isn't that kind of creepy?"

"No kidding."

"So that's why you can't sleep." Lindy narrowed her eyes. "Do you think somebody's trying to tell you something?"

"I think this is a disaster waiting to happen."

"Why?"

Because when I wake up I have such a sense of loss I can barely stand it. "Instinct. Gut reaction. I'm not sure." She blew out a long breath. "I just have a really bad feeling about this."

"I've got to tell you, I'm kind of impressed." A smile of admiration quirked Lindy's lips.

"About what?"

"I've never known you to think before jumping into a new relationship before."

Morgan raised a brow.

"Hey, pal, I call 'em like I see 'em." Lindy rose and started toward the door. "And what I see is my best friend tied up in knots over a dream lover who turns out to be real."

"I'm not tied up in knots."

"Bull."

Morgan heaved a heavy sigh. There was no arguing with Lindy when she thought she was right.

"Don't forget, I'm taking off early tomorrow. We're supposed to have a little family dinner with the Hughes before Dad's party."

"It's already noted on the calendar." Lindy opened the door to leave.

"Will I finally get to meet your mystery man tomorrow?"

"Maybe."

"Do me a favor, would you?" Morgan said. "Make sure Spencer knows he's invited."

"Oh?"

"Strictly a business courtesy."

"Yeah, right."

"He might need a ride too. The country club's kind of hard to get to if you've never been there before."

"I'll take care of it."

"And ask him to review the Casablanca figures I was looking at. If there really is a problem there he should be able to spot it."

"Anything else I can tell him for you?"

"No," Morgan snapped.

Lindy paused by the door. "I just thought—"

"I know exactly what you thought."

"This is going to be fun." Lindy chuckled and walked out.

"Fun? Hah! I wouldn't call this fun!" Morgan yelled after her. "I'd call it a mess!"

"Why doesn't she ask me herself?" Greg glared at the stack of files and discs in Lindy's arms.

"Gosh, let me think." Lindy dropped her burden on his desk. "She's the boss. She doesn't have to ask you if she doesn't want to—that's what she has me for. But I'm betting that has nothing to do with it."

"No?"

"No." Lindy's voice was firm. "Let me tell you something about my dear friend Morgan. She has a gift for business. Some kind of natural instinct. She's clever and careful and totally together. It's come as kind of a shock to everyone who knows her well."

"How so?"

"Look, I've already filled you in on some of her

more adventurous escapades and the long line of engagements. When it comes to doing something completely crazy, stupid in fact, regardless of whether we're talking risk-taking or men, Morgan's middle name has always been impulsive. She's never thought twice about diving off a cliff or into a relationship." Lindy shook her head. "I don't know why I'm telling you all this."

"I appreciate it, though."

"I figured you would." Lindy rested her palms on Greg's desk and pinned him with a determined gaze. "What I'm trying to say is she's not doing that with you and it means something."

"What do you think it means?" he said slowly

Lindy narrowed her eyes and shook her head. "You're not as bright as you look, are you?"

He flashed her a grin. "Actually, I'm brighter."

Lindy laughed and headed for the door. "I was right, this is going to be fun."

"Thanks."

"No problem. I have a good feeling about you two." She winked and left the office.

Greg leaned back in his chair, his confidence renewed, his determination strengthened. He'd spent the weekend trying to work through his feelings about Morgan. Why not? He couldn't do anything but think about her anyway.

It was crazy, all of it. A week ago he hadn't even known her. Now, he not only wanted her, he loved her. He'd never been so certain of anything in his life. Certain enough that the idea of marriage didn't send him running for his life. No, he definitely wanted to marry the infuriating woman. Wanted her by his side always. Wanted to grow old with her. Wanted her to be the mother of his children. Hell, he'd never even thought about children before. What had she done to him?

And what had he done to her? It didn't take much to figure out why she was so scared. He should have realized it right away. If her dreams were the same as his, then she probably woke up with the same feelings he did: that deep, deep sense of tragedy and loss. He could see why she didn't want to risk experiencing that kind of devastation for real. He didn't particularly want to go through it either. Admittedly, it was scary, but nothing in his life had ever seemed so right. He was willing to take the chance. For her.

"I'll just have to wear you down, Ms. Phillips," he muttered. And he could start at her father's party. It would be perfect. A little champagne, a little dancing and a lot of moonlight. What more could he ask for? He laughed to himself. "You don't stand a chance, Morgan."

An hour later laughter was long forgotten. Morgan was right about Casablanca's figures. Something just didn't make sense. He wasn't exactly sure what but he'd work it out eventually. He may have sold Casablanca but it would always be his baby. A baby with big problems. He pulled his brows together and stared at the computer screen.

"What in the hell is going on here?"

* * *

"Win, we really need to talk."

"Later, Morgan." Win's gaze focused on the far side of the country club ballroom. "I see someone I should suck up to. Business, my dear. You understand, sweetheart." Win brushed her cheek with his lips in a vague, irritating parody of a lover's affection and strode across the floor.

"Oh, sure, no problem," Morgan said under her breath. "I just wanted to break our engagement. That's all."

She watched him make his way through the festive crowd of well wishers. Since she'd decided she wasn't going to marry him, she hadn't had a minute alone with him.

"He looks like he's taking it well." Lindy came up behind her.

"Where have you been?" Morgan flagged a waiter.

"Working. My boss took off early today." Lindy accepted a flute of champagne.

Morgan plucked her own glass off the offered tray and sipped it gratefully. "The woman's a witch all right."

"Uh-huh. But is she an engaged witch?"

"Look at that, Lindy. It's amazing." Morgan nodded at Win. "The man should be in politics. He definitely knows how to work a crowd."

"Weasels are good at that. I hear they've very social animals. But one thing this country doesn't need is another weasel in office." Lindy pulled her gaze from Win and glanced at Morgan's hand. "You're wearing the rock. You haven't told him, have you?"

"I was supposed to see him last night but he couldn't make it. And tonight at dinner, everyone went on and on about the wedding and the future and grandchildren. They're really pleased about this."

"You should have—"

"What did you expect me to do? Announce that I was backing out of one more marriage? It's not like I could slip it casually into the conversation. 'Why yes, Mom, Dad, Mr. and Mrs. Hughes, I do plan on having children but not with Win. He's a weasel.' " Morgan grimaced. "I just haven't had a chance to talk to him."

"Morgan!"

"What do you want from me?" Morgan glared. "I couldn't very well tell him over the phone or send him e-mail."

"Sure you could. You've done it before."

"Well, I couldn't do that to Win."

"Why not?"

"I've known him all my life. It would be really tacky not to break up in person. Rude even. Downright dishonorable."

"Dishonorable?" Lindy snorted. "Win is the last person in the world who would even recognize the word *honorable*. He deserves everything he gets."

Morgan stared. "You really hate him, don't you?"

"Let's just say I see through him. I can't believe you don't."

"Win's okay. But I have to be diplomatic about this. Even if I'm not going to marry him I'll still be working with him. We have a company to run. I don't want to screw that up."

"Well, all I can say is you'd better tell him soon."

Morgan's gaze remained on Win. "I will. The moment I get him alone. Maybe it'll be easier here anyway. With this crowd it's not like we can have a big emotional confrontation."

"Safety in numbers. Works for me." Lindy drained the rest of her champagne, her gaze sliding past Morgan. "And speaking of what works for me . . ."

"Good evening, ladies." Greg's voice sounded behind her and her pulse raced. Damned traitorous body. She breathed deeply and pasted a welcoming smile on her face.

"Morgan." He nodded politely.

"Greg." Whoa. She thought the man looked good in a business suit or running shorts, but he was positively spectacular in a tux. It was enough to weaken her knees.

"Lindy, did I remember to thank you and your friend for the ride out here tonight?"

Lindy shrugged. "No problem."

"Friend?" Morgan raised a brow. "What friend? Is this the mystery date?"

"There's no mystery." Lindy laughed. "You just haven't met him, that's all. He's around somewhere. I'll track him down and haul him over here."

Morgan tilted her head toward Greg. "She's been dating this guy for months and is very secretive about him."

"I am not!"

"Don't listen to her, Greg. She tells me everything but I don't even know his name."

Lindy grit her teeth. "It's D. B., okay? D. B. Farley."

"Initials? You're giving me initials?" Morgan teased.

"Everybody calls him D. B. He's not wild about his full name."

"What is it? Come on, I won't tell." Morgan glanced at Greg. "You can keep a secret, right?"

Greg nodded in a mock serious manner. "My lips are sealed."

Morgan's gaze drifted to his lips, his wonderful, talented, skillful lips, then rose to his eyes. Amusement lingered there as if he knew exactly what she was thinking.

"Okay, I give up." Lindy sighed with exasperation. "It's Dunston. Dunston Bartholomew Farley. Now, are you happy?"

"Ecstatic." Morgan and Greg traded glances and she stifled a giggle.

"I can see why he goes by D. B." Greg pulled his brows together and nodded toward the orchestra. "Are they playing a waltz?"

"Yeah." A waltz? Just what she needed. "My mother loves them. She says it's a shame waltzing ever went out of style."

"She might be right. In fact, recently, I've grown to appreciate the waltz. Would you like to dance?" His gaze caught Morgan's and she knew he was asking for far more than a mere old-fashioned dance.

"Oh, I don't waltz," she said quickly.

"Excuse me?" Lindy snorted. "What about all those years of ballroom dance lessons your mother forced you to take? Didn't they include the waltz?"

"Lindy." Morgan threw her a threatening glance. "It's been such a long time. I don't think I remember the first thing about waltzing."

"Really?" Greg murmured. "Lately, it feels like I've been waltzing every night."

"For goodness' sake, Morgan, dance with the man." Lindy scanned the ballroom. "I'm going to get more champagne and find D. B. See ya later."

"Later," Morgan echoed.

"Morgan." Greg plucked her glass from her fingers and handed it to a passing waiter. "Shall we?"

"This isn't a good idea."

"Why not?"

"You know why not."

"No, I really don't"

She stared up at him and shook her head. "Why do I get the feeling it's pointless to argue with you?"

"Because it is."

She placed one palm on his shoulder and her other hand in his. "I should just surrender right now."

"Yes, you should." His fingers pressed lightly just above the small of her back, on the bare skin exposed by the low drape of her silver dress.

"I'm starting to think all resistance is futile."

"Right again."

Heat spread through her body from his touch. She could barely breathe.

They swirled around the room with a natural

grace that owed little to hours of tedious lessons and everything to the way their bodies seemed to move as one. She followed his every step with an ease born of . . . what? Practice? Hardly. They'd never waltzed together. Not really. Only in her dreams. And his. But it was as if they'd danced with each other . . . forever.

"People are staring, you know." A smile tugged at the corners of his lips.

She raised a brow. "That's kind of egotistical isn't it? To think you're the center of attention?"

"Probably, if it wasn't true. Take a look."

Morgan had been too caught up in the feel of his arms around her to notice, but sure enough, the focus of the crowd was directly on them. On the two of them. Dancing as if they'd been made for each other. She wanted to bury her head in his shoulder and hide, but that would have made it clear that this was no idle turn around the dance floor. "Please say we're not the only ones dancing."

"Okay." He bit back a grin. "It would be a lie though."

She groaned. "I don't believe this."

"I thought you enjoyed being the center of attention."

"I just don't want everyone to know."

"Know what?"

"About us," she snapped.

"Too late," he murmured. "We might as well go for the big finish."

She sighed. "What the hell. Let's do it."

"Follow my lead."

"Do I have a choice?"

They danced to the edge of the floor, in flawless sync with the music. She moved in perfect counterpoint to his every step. If not for the hundreds of speculative stares, it would have been fun. He held her closer and swung her in a long, low dip that had nothing to do with any waltz step she'd ever learned, and ended with the final downbeat of the music.

Applause broke out and she relaxed. There wasn't anything to worry about here. These were all her parents' friends and business associates. And she was Morgan Phillips. This group always had, and probably always would, expect the unexpected from her. A ballroom dancing exhibition was minor compared to what she might have done just a year ago.

Morgan curtsied to the crowd but directed her comments to Greg. "You really know what you're doing."

Greg bowed. "Hey, even in Chicago we dabble in the social graces. Besides, yours wasn't the only mother to force her child to take dance lessons. Where do you think all those little boys you danced with came from?"

"I never thought much about them. They always looked so miserable." The orchestra struck up a new song and eager couples flooded the floor.

"They were. Come on." He grabbed her hand and led her laughing through the French doors and out onto the terrace. "Wait right here." He turned and disappeared into the club.

She sauntered to the edge of the terrace and leaned her forearms on the stone balustrade just beyond the light thrown from the ballroom windows. There were sconces out here but it was still early in the season and nobody had bothered to turn them on. Morgan stared up at the sky and watched stars wink out behind encroaching clouds. A hint of rain wafted in the air. The light breeze held the threat of a storm. A dangerous night, in more ways than one. A chill shivered down her spine.

"I thought maybe you could use this." Greg handed her a fresh glass of champagne.

"Thank you." The last thing she needed was to be alone with Greg. Why was it the only thing she wanted?

He returned her smile. "I gather you've forgiven me."

She laughed uneasily. "There was nothing to forgive."

"That's what I thought." He wandered idly along the edge of the terrace to the steps leading to the wide lawn and the tennis courts.

She trailed after him. "How so?"

"I mean I didn't do anything Friday night but tell you the truth." He shrugged. "And you couldn't take it."

"I can take it. I just don't buy it." She brushed a strand of hair away from her face. "It's all a bunch of nonsense. All that fate and destiny crap."

"How do you explain it then?" he said quietly. "We have the same dreams. We have the same strong attraction to each other. We feel like we've known each other always. And this sense of déjà vu that surrounds us gets stronger every time we're together. Can you deny any of that?"

"Of course I . . ." She sighed. "No, I can't."

"In that case, Morgan." He stepped closer and tilted her chin up. His eyes glittered in the faint light from the ballroom. "Accept it."

His lips met hers in a touch as gentle as the breeze. She sighed with the inevitability of the kiss and everything that went with it. He was all she wanted. Maybe all she'd ever wanted.

He wrapped his arms around her and drew her close against him. Why did they fit together as if they were halves of the same whole? As if she'd been waiting all her life—no, longer—for him and only him. Was he really her destiny?

He drew back and stared into her eyes. "Accept it, Morgan."

In his eyes she could read love and longing, passion and promise. A wave of sorrow as intense as anything she felt when she woke from her dreams swept through her. She stepped out of his embrace and shook her head. "I can't." Panic filled her. "I wish I could make you understand. I don't understand myself, but I can't."

She had to get away from these feelings. She had to get away from him. He spelled disaster and she knew it as surely as she knew she didn't want to live without him, as surely as she knew she had to. She turned to flee but he grabbed her arm and jerked her back.

"Why, Morgan? Why won't you at least talk about this?" Anger furrowed his forehead.

"Talking to you about this, talking to you at all, even being around you, is dangerous. And I can't handle it. I don't want to handle it." She wrenched out of his grasp. "I have to go. Now."

"I have to talk to you!"

"No!" She nearly ran back into the ballroom.

Calm, Morgan. Stay calm. She drew a few deep breaths. The music had stopped and all eyes were on the stage. Her father, flanked by Hughes the third and Win, was speaking. Hell. She was missing his retirement speech. She pushed her way through the crowd.

". . . but we leave the company in good hands. The hands we always wanted it in. The hands of our children."

She reached the stage, forced a lighthearted smile to her face and walked up the few steps to join her father. He put his arm around her and addressed the guests.

"My friends, this may be the end of one era but it's the beginning of another in a family business that will be even stronger in the future." Win stepped up beside her. "I am very pleased tonight to announce—" *Oh no!* Her stomach clenched. "—the definitive joining of Phillips and Hughes as a family—" *Not now!* Her heart stopped. "—and the upcoming marriage of my daughter, Morgan, to Winston Hughes the fourth."

Damn.

Chapter Fifteen

The words reverberated in Morgan's head.

"... *the upcoming marriage of my daughter, Morgan, to Winston Hughes the fourth.*"

Surprised murmurs broke out followed immediately by enthusiastic applause. Win took her hand and brought it to his lips. She smiled feebly. A nauseous sensation settled in her stomach. Why hadn't she told him?

"And you're all invited to the wedding. It's going to be soon, before she changes her mind." Laughter greeted his comment. Victor Phillips grinned at the gathering. "I promise you one hell of a celebration!" The crowd roared its approval.

In the back of the room, Greg's gaze caught hers. The shock on his face slapped her with an ache that stabbed straight into her heart. She had to get to

313

Victoria Alexander

him. She had to explain. Regardless of how much she thought any future with him was a tragic mistake, she couldn't let him believe this.

The orchestra launched into a romantic ballad and Win led her off the stage and onto the dance floor.

"We have to talk, Win," she said under her breath keeping her public smile firmly in place.

He pulled her into his arms. "Not now, Morgan, we'll have all the time in the world to talk."

"No, we need to talk n—"

"Congratulations." A vaguely familiar couple broke in and the opportunity was lost.

The rest of the evening sped by in an endless blur of best wishes and frustration. No matter how hard she tried, she couldn't get Win alone. And she hadn't even been close to Greg. He was obviously avoiding her. Once she spotted Greg and Lindy in an animated conversation. Maybe Lindy was telling him the truth about her so-called engagement. Hope fluttered and died. There was no way Lindy would save her from this one.

On the other hand, maybe it was better if Greg didn't know she was calling the wedding off. Sure, he'd find out eventually. But if he thought she was getting married he might just give up on his ridiculous idea of marrying her himself. He might leave her alone. Exactly what she wanted. Wasn't it?

The band played its last song and Morgan breathed a sigh of relief. It's about time this fiasco ended. Now maybe she could talk to Win.

"Win." She joined him and said good-bye to a few

lingering guests. "Why don't you drive me home and we can finally talk? It's important."

"I'm sure it is, Morgan," Win said smoothly. "But didn't you drive your own car?"

"I'll leave it and have Dad pick it up later." She took a deep breath. "Come on, Win. It's over an hour back to the city and I don't want to drive it by myself. And it will give us a chance to be alone."

"Morgan, you surprise me." Win chuckled and leaned closer. "I'm just as eager as you are to be alone but we'll have the rest of our lives for that."

"That's not what—"

"Besides, I promised my parents I'd stay at their house tonight to discuss the changes in the company and the wedding. Now, that's really important. I'm sure whatever you want to talk about can wait." He shrugged. "Sorry.

"I hope we're interrupting?" Lindy stepped up beside Morgan.

"Not at all." Win smirked. "How did you like the party?"

"Oh, it was interesting." Lindy's smile was as phony as Win's. "Definitely interesting."

"I found it kind of enlightening." Greg's voice sounded behind her and she groaned to herself.

"Enlightening?" Win frowned.

"Yeah. You just never know when you're going to hear something that makes all the little puzzle pieces fall into place." Was she the only one who heard the grim note beneath Greg's nonchalant comment?

"As much as I'd like to stay and chat, I have a hot date waiting," Lindy said.

"I never did get to meet him." Morgan frowned.

"You were busy getting engaged, pal." Lindy's pointed glance told Morgan exactly what her friend thought of the announcement. Not that she wanted a reminder. "Anyway, I need a favor. Could one of you give Greg a drive back to the city? D. B. and I have other plans and we're not going back right away."

"I'm not driving back tonight. But Morgan is."

No way! "But I—"

Win raised a questioning brow. "Sweetheart, you just finished saying you don't want to drive back by yourself. This is perfect. Is that okay with you, Greg?"

"If Morgan doesn't mind."

"Of course she doesn't mind."

"No, it's perfect," Morgan muttered. "Just perfect."

"Great. Works for me." Lindy smiled sweetly. "I'll see you tomorrow."

"I'll see you tomorrow too." Win leaned forward and brushed her cheek with his lips. A hot blush washed up her face. "Take care of her, Spencer. She's very important to me."

"I can imagine," Greg said under his breath.

Win strode off and Morgan and Greg walked out to the parking lot in silence. Why didn't he say anything? She was afraid to even look at him. She had no desire to meet his eyes and read the questions and accusation she was pretty sure she'd see there.

Thunder cracked. Lightning lit the night sky.

"The perfect end to a perfect night." Morgan jammed the key viciously into the lock of her beat-up Jeep and slid into the seat. She leaned over and unlocked his door.

He settled in and stared out the window. Apparently he didn't want to talk to her either. They pulled out of the lot. Rain plunked against the windshield.

"This isn't exactly what I expected a jet-setting heiress to drive."

"It's a classic. Besides, I was never a jet-setting heiress," she snapped. "I was . . . I don't know, an adventure hunter maybe. It doesn't matter. Those days are long gone. And I love this car. It's got character."

He snorted but didn't say a word. And why not? Was he trying to say she didn't have any character? He had a lot of nerve. Just because she wasn't willing to trust her future, her life, to some stupid dream. She shifted into a higher gear and punched the gas.

Within minutes rain pounded the car.

"It's raining pretty hard." His tone was indifferent. "Maybe you'd better slow down."

"I've driven these roads most of my life. My parents live just a few miles from the country club. I grew up around here." Her words were clipped. "I know what I'm doing."

"Could have fooled me."

"Do you want to drive?" She glared out the windshield. Damn. The wipers were going full blast but

317

it was still tough to see through the water sheeting off the glass.

"I would but I can't seem to find my license."

"Oh." She winced to herself. She had to remember to give the chewed mess of a license back to him.

Morgan squinted and struggled to keep her focus on the road. It wasn't easy. The storm's fury increased and so did the level of tension in the car. She didn't mind fighting the weather. It was battling her own tumultuous emotions that was getting to her. Why in the hell did she have to own a car with such a small front seat? The Jeep had always taken her anywhere she wanted to go but her hand on the stick shift was way too close to his knee for comfort. The warmth of his body was way too near to ignore, his solid presence way too compelling to forget.

"Morgan, I really think you should slow down," he said mildly. Maybe it was the tone in his voice and the condescending nature of his words. Maybe it was the strain of fighting the rain. Or maybe it was the stress building inside her since the moment the engagement was announced. Whatever it was, Morgan Phillips had had quite enough.

"Do you want to walk?" she said through gritted teeth. "I can stop right now and let you out."

"I don't want to walk."

"Then get off my back and let me drive!"

"I've been letting you drive and I've risked both our lives in the process." A sharp note sounded in his words.

"I'll have you know I've never had a serious accident."

"Define serious."

Wind buffeted the car and she fought to keep it on the road. She eased off slightly on the gas. A precaution, nothing more. There was no way in hell she'd admit that he was right and her driving this evening was a bit more reckless than usual.

"Pull over."

"Why?"

"License or no license, I'm going to drive."

"Fine. See if you can do better." She slammed on the brakes. The Jeep fishtailed on the wet pavement. All her energy focused on reining in the out-of-control vehicle. She tried to steer out of the skid but only succeeded in slowing their spin. A split second before they left the road she realized she couldn't pull a rabbit out of a hat this time and braced herself. The Jeep slid with an almost careful precision off the pavement and into a ditch, lurching at a nasty angle and shuddering to a stop.

Morgan gripped the steering wheel and rested her head on her hands, willing the sudden trembling that shook her body to go away. She'd called on the deep reserves of calm and confidence she'd always been able to count on whenever she was in a tight spot. And they'd never failed her. But they always left her weak and shaky.

"Are you okay?" Concern colored Greg's voice.

"Yeah." She blew out a long breath. "You?"

"Yeah. We'd better get out of here before this thing rolls over." His side of the car was higher than hers. He pushed the door open and pulled himself up and out. "Okay," he called. "Pull yourself to the door then grab my hands."

"Easier said than done," she muttered.

"What?"

"Nothing. Wait." She groped around under her seat and found a flashlight. "Here, take this." She flicked it on and handed it up to him.

"Got it," he yelled. "Now you."

She scrambled to reach his door. "You try climbing out of a Jeep in an evening gown." She reached up to grasp his arms and he hauled her out of the car and onto the pavement.

Lightning flashed and illuminated the sorry scene. The Jeep rested on the driver's side at a forty-five-degree angle; two wheels sunk deep in mud.

"Damn." Her poor car would never be the same.

"It's really not that bad." Greg studied the vehicle. "I don't think it'll take much to pull it out."

"The perfect end to the perfect evening continues," she said under her breath. "Come on. Let's go."

"Where?"

"There's a motel just up ahead, around that curve. One of those places with an office and a bunch of tiny quasi-cottages." Morgan started off. "We can call for help."

"Don't you have a cell phone?" Greg fell in step beside her.

"Not tonight. It didn't go with my dress."

"Whoa! Sarcasm from the adventure hunter." She could hear the laughter in his voice.

She turned toward him and planted her hands on her hips. "What's so funny?"

"You." His gaze traveled from her sodden hair, past the ruined dress that even dry clung to her like a second skin—now probably revealing any secret she ever had—to her wrecked high heels. One thin silver strap had slipped down over her shoulder and she self-consciously pulled it back into place. She felt positively naked. "A self-respecting cell phone wouldn't go near that dress right now. You look like a drowned rat. And you're going to freeze. Didn't you even bring a jacket?"

"Poor planning on my part, I know." She gave him her haughtiest look and then sneezed.

"We have to get you out of this rain." He shook his head, stepped toward her and pulled her close.

She gasped. "What are you doing?"

"What do you think I'm doing?" He scooped her up and carried her in his arms. "You won't get ten feet on this road in this mud with those shoes."

"I can walk! You don't have to carry me." She crossed her arms.

He strode forward, ignoring his irritated burden. His warmth surrounded her and all she really wanted to do was snuggle against him. Her voice wasn't nearly as firm as she'd intended. "Put me down."

"Nope." He shifted her weight. "Has anyone ever told you you're heavier than you look?"

"In case you haven't noticed, it's raining."

"Oh, I noticed all right."

"Well, I'm wet. That adds weight. If I'm too much for you, you can put me down. I—"

"Shut up, Morgan," he growled.

"Nobody tells me to shut up." She glared.

"I do. I'm the man of your dreams, remember."

"Man of my dreams! I'll tell you where you can put that man-of-my-dreams crap!"

He stopped and heaved a heavy sigh. "I can't take it. All this weight and that mouth too." He shifted her again and before she realized what he was up to, tossed her over his shoulder in a fireman's carry. "There, that's much better."

"Greg, put me down!"

"Sorry, Morgan, my love, I can't hear you from back there." He patted her butt. "So shut up and enjoy the ride."

"Enjoy the ride? Hah! And don't touch me again!"

"Sorry. Can't hear you."

He probably could hear her, the annoying man just enjoyed pretending not to. She grabbed on to his jacket and held tight. "Enjoy the ride, right."

With every step she bounced against him. Uncomfortable, but not without its merits. The view from this angle wasn't bad. The rain had done just as much damage to his tux as it had to her dress. His pants were plastered against him and with every stride she noticed the long, lean muscles of his legs. Not bad. Not bad at all. Of course, all the blood was rushing to her head.

She lost track of time but it couldn't have been more than a few minutes. The storm died as quickly

as it had sprung up and the moon peeked from behind the clouds.

Greg stopped. "Morgan?"

"Yeah?"

"I think we have a problem."

"You're just now realizing that?"

He swung her to her feet and aimed the flashlight
at a sign. "Is this the motel you were talking about?"

The feeble flashlight cast a minimal amount of
illumination. "Yep. This is it. The Riverview Motel.
I think the office is to the left of the sign."

Greg pulled his brows together. "Morgan, there
aren't any lights on."

"That's okay." She marched up to the office door.
"The electricity is probably out." She knocked right
beneath the faded, wooden Welcome sign. "Hello.
Anybody home? Customers. Right here. Paying
customers. Freezing customers."

"Morgan."

She turned from the door and narrowed her eyes.
"What is it now?"

"The sign, Morgan. Read the sign." He pointed
with the flashlight.

She sighed. "Fine. Okay, it says . . . 'closed for the
season. See you . . . next year.' " Her heart sank. All
at once every devastating moment of this entire disastrous evening crashed in on her. She sat down on
the front stoop of the office with all the grace of a
deflated hot air balloon. "I give up. That's it. The
final straw. I'm cold and I'm wet and I look like
pond scum—"

"Drowned rat."

323

"Whatever." She choked back a sob. "This has been absolutely the worst night of my entire life."

"It hasn't been my favorite either." He raised her chin up until her gaze met his. "Hey, are you crying?"

"No." She sniffed. "It's rain."

"The rain has stopped." He smiled his lopsided grin and her stomach flipped over. "You're beautiful when you're wet."

"Well, then I must be gorgeous."

He laughed. "You are."

"Don't say that!"

"Why?"

"Don't say nice things to me! Not when I'm mad and cold and wet. I just can't deal with it right now. Or you. My resistance is way too low." She pulled herself to her feet, stomped to the closest and largest cabin and tugged at the doorknob.

"If they're gone for the season, it's probably locked."

She folded her arms over her chest for warmth and nodded at the door. "Then break it down."

"Break it down?"

"Yeah, you know. You put your shoulder against it and push."

Disbelief rang in his voice. "You're not serious?"

"Of course I'm serious. They do it on TV all the time."

"That's TV. This is real life."

She scoffed. "It doesn't look very hard."

"Of course it doesn't look hard. They have stunt

men and special effects and computer-enhanced graphics and—"

"I don't think it takes a computer to break down a pathetic little door." She sighed. "But if you can't handle it . . ."

"Here." He thrust the flashlight at her. "Hold this."

She grinned and pointed the light at the door. He peeled off his sopping jacket. "What are you taking that off for?"

"Because," he said with the measured tones of a man losing his patience. "That's how they do it on TV."

He took a deep breath, wedged his shoulder against the door and pushed.

Nothing happened. He tried again.

The door didn't budge.

"You know what else they have on TV, Morgan?"

"What?"

"Doors that look real but are made of balsa wood. A child could break them. But since this is real life and not TV, this door"—he pounded his fist on the door—"is solid wood. You know, the stuff trees are made out of."

Morgan studied the door. "Maybe this time you should take a running start at it."

Greg practically sputtered. "A running start?"

"Couldn't hurt."

"A running start?"

"You said that."

"Yeah, but I still don't believe it. A running start?"

"I'm just trying to be helpful."

"Don't be so helpful."

Morgan shivered. "Come on, Greg, I'm freezing."

"This is stupid." He stalked off. "If I kill myself—"

"Oh, buck up. You're not going to kill yourself. A dislocated shoulder, tops." She waved him off. "But I think you're too close. Back up a little more."

"Back up a little more?"

"Yeah, that's good." She pointed the flashlight at him.

"Hey!" He jerked up his hand against the light. "I'm not going to be much good with a dislocated shoulder and blind, you know."

"Whoops. Sorry." She aimed the light at the door. "Okay, go for it."

He muttered something under his breath and took off. He pounded past her, crashed into the door and bounced backward.

The door didn't budge.

"Wow." Morgan shook her head. "Tough door."

Greg groaned. "You think so?"

"Yeah, they don't make 'em like that anymore. So," she said brightly, "ready to try again?"

"Morgan, does it strike you that this is not entirely legal? Technically, I think it's breaking and entering. Or at the very least trespassing."

"It's only a crime if we get caught. Besides, I'll send them a check for the door and anything we use. Okay. Now." She pointed the flashlight at the sturdy door. "Try it again."

"No, Morgan, I'm not trying again. I'm not putting my shoulder on the door and pushing. I'm not running up and launching myself at it like a cartoon character. This is how normal people, people who are not on TV, usually get doors open. They knock. See." He pounded on the door. "But nobody's home." He pounded again. "So we—"

"We what? Freeze to death out here?" Morgan pulled her brows together. "Greg, I really don't—"

"Hand me the flashlight." He held out his hand.

"Why?" Suspicion sounded in her voice.

"Just give it to me." He snatched it from her hand, bent down and aimed it at the grass.

"What are you looking for?" She crouched beside him.

"I saw something fall from the top of the door frame. Something shiny." He pawed through the grass. "It might be a key."

"A key? Who would be that stupid?"

"Hah! Look." A key glinted in the light. His fingers closed around it. "Apparently the owners of this place are that stupid."

She got to her feet, took the flashlight and trained the beam on the lock. "What are you waiting for? Open the door."

He stood and tried the key in the lock. It turned and the door creaked open.

"Great." Morgan said, and tried to push past him.

"Hold it a minute."

"What for?"

"Are you really going to marry that creep?"

"He's not a creep," Morgan said with more conviction than she felt. "Now, let's go in."

"I don't think so." Greg blocked the door. "Not

327

until you answer my question. Are you going to marry him?"

"It's really none of your business."

"Of course it's my business." Anger exploded in his voice. "It's been my business since the moment your crazy dog tied his leash around us. It's been my business since the first night you invaded my dreams. And it's been my business since the second I realized I can't live without you!"

"Well, you're going to have to, aren't you?" She shoved past him into the cabin and flashed the light across the room. "Where's the damn light switch?"

"You haven't answered my question." He was one step behind her.

"The electricity probably isn't even on," she muttered.

"Quit stalling, Morgan." He grabbed her and yanked her into his arms. "Tell me if you're really going to marry Hughes."

"I'm engaged to him, aren't I?"

Greg snorted with disdain. "That's never seemed to make a difference to you before."

"You don't know anything about me!"

"I know all I need to know. I know I love you and I know you love me."

"Hah, you don't know that!"

"Yes, I do. You can deny it all you want but I know as surely as I've ever known anything in my life, you love me." He gripped her tighter. "You can't love me and marry someone else. If you marry Hughes you'll regret it."

"Oh yeah?" She glared at him, his face silhouetted

by the moonlight from the door. "Maybe not today, maybe not tomorrow, but soon, and for the rest of my life?"

"Stop it, Morgan!" He shook her. "This isn't a movie. I'm not Bogie and you're not Bergman. This is real life. You can't marry Hughes."

"I know that." She drew a deep breath. "Marrying Win would be the second biggest mistake I could ever make."

"The second?"

"Yeah, the biggest would be marrying you!"

"But I love you!"

"Well, I love you too!" She jerked out of his grasp. "So what? I love you. Big deal!"

She could hear the smug grin in his voice. "I knew you loved me."

"Congratulations," she snapped. "You love me. I love you. And while I hate to end this terribly heart-warming moment, we're both going to catch pneumonia and die if you don't do something to warm up the rest of us." He stepped toward her. She shoved her hand flat against his chest. "Not that."

"I just wanted the flashlight." He took it from her. "And you do know you've changed the subject again."

"Yeah, I know."

"I'll let you get away with it for now. But tonight we are going to talk."

"Like there's anything else to do here." Immediately, she regretted her words. *Right, Morgan, what else could you and the computer hunk, literally the man of your dreams, do in an lonely cabin all night but talk?*

Greg didn't seem to notice. He skimmed the light around the rustic room, illuminating various pieces of sheet-covered furniture and a small corner kitchenette. "This place is bigger than it looks. But I thought I saw chimneys on these cabins." The beam lit a stone fireplace, logs already laid for a fire. "There you go, Morgan, there's your heat. They might be stupid about their keys but they're smart enough to have a fire already laid for their first guests, kindling and everything."

A tall box of matches stood on the hearth. Greg lit one and touched it to the dry wood. It caught quickly and within minutes the fire was blazing.

Morgan held out her hands to the flame. "Do you see any blankets around here?"

"No, and I'll bet they're packed away somewhere." He tugged at a sheet and pulled it off to reveal a plump, overstuffed sofa. "These will have to do."

"Yuck." Morgan grimaced. "They're all dusty."

Greg raised a brow. "Take it or leave it."

"I'll take it." She snatched the sheet from his hands.

He tugged another one off a quaint brass bed. "Well, this looks cozy."

"Don't get any ideas. Now turn around."

"Why?"

"I want to get out of this dress."

"Great."

"No, it's not great. I want to take this off so it can

dry and that's it." She heaved an exasperated sigh. "I'd better make myself clear right now. We're obviously stuck together here until morning, because I, for one, am not trudging down the highway in the dark, but nothing is going to happen between us."

"If that's what you want." He turned his back to her.

"Not especially, but that's how it has to be." She turned away from him and peeled off the damp, clinging gown.

"Why?"

"You've been wanting to talk so let's talk. About us. And dreams and fate, okay?"

"Fire away."

She wrapped the sheet around her and stood staring at the fire, trying to pull her thoughts together. "Let's start with the dream. We already know we have the same dream."

"Right." She heard furniture dragging across the floor. "Here, sit." She turned. He'd pulled the sofa right behind her, facing the fireplace. "We might as well be comfortable."

He faced her wearing a sheet of his own, *looking for all the world like a classic Greek statue.*

An image of him popped into her head as if they had played out this scene before. A sense of déjà vu swirled around her with such force she caught her breath.

"What's the matter, Morgan?"

"Nothing." She shook her head to clear the disturbing sensation, clutched her sheet tighter and sat on the far end of the sofa. She nodded at the other end. "You can sit over there."

"Keeping my distance, huh?" He settled into the spot she indicated.

"You got it. Okay, let's take this one step at a time." She chose her words thoughtfully. "We have the same dream."

"Right. We've established that." His voice softened. "And a wonderful dream it is, too."

She ignored him. "And you think it means we were meant to be together? That somehow we're connected to each other?"

"I think it's fate," he said firmly.

"I don't get it." She studied him for a moment. "Here you are, some kind of computer whiz, dealing with high-tech, solid, down-to-earth facts every day, but you believe in something as far-fetched as fate."

"I never did before now."

"So why now?"

"The dreams, I guess." He shrugged. "The fact that we share them. That's the biggest thing. You have to admit, it's pretty strong evidence."

She nodded. "Go on."

"There's also the way I feel about you, as if we've known each other forever. And there's that intense sensation that somehow, we've been through this before. Being with you seems so right." He shook his head. "It doesn't make much sense when you look at it rationally and I've always been a very rational person, but there you have it."

She plucked nervously at the edge of her sheet.

"And when you wake up?" She glanced at him. "How do you feel when you wake up?"

He rested his head on the back of the sofa and stared at the ceiling. Long moments passed. Finally, he blew a reluctant sigh. "Devastated."

He reached his hand out along the sofa cushion.

"Me too," she whispered, and slipped her hand into his.

"So what are we going to do?"

"I don't know. I don't know about fate or destiny or any of that stuff. I do know I feel the same way you do." He squeezed her hand. "But . . . I also feel that if we accept that whatever is going on here has some kind of cosmic significance, we have to accept all of it."

"What do you mean?"

"I mean if we go along with this whole thing: the idea that we're destined for each other, that we share some great eternal love, we also have to realize that it's going to end in tragedy."

"I don't—"

"No, Greg, listen to me." She trapped his gaze with hers. "Don't you see? We can't have one without the other. We can't have the joy without the sadness. If the feelings that we have for each other, the feelings that haunt our dreams, are real, so is the heartbreak. And you have to agree it's a killer. I wake up weeping with a deep, deep sorrow that I never even suspected could exist before." She shivered. "Right now, it's only a dream. But if we get together . . . Love. Sex. Marriage. Whatever. The dream becomes real and so does the nightmare. I just couldn't face that."

He lifted her hand to his lips and kissed it gently. "I love you, Morgan. I'm willing to take the risk."

"I'm not." She pulled her hand away. "I can't."

Greg stared at her, the firelight reflected in his eyes. "I think the two of us can face anything. Together."

"Fate? Destiny? Hah!" She struggled to her feet, clutching her sheet to her, and paced before the fire. "That's like standing outside in a storm and shaking your fist at the heavens."

He stood and faced her. "Isn't that what you're already doing by denying what we feel for each other?"

The truth of his statement hit her with a physical force. She groaned and sank down on the sofa, burying her face in her hands. "Damn, I didn't think of that. Any way you look at it, we're doomed."

He sat next to her and wrapped his arm around her. "Look at the bright side."

She glanced up. "What bright side?"

"We're doomed together." He pulled her closer.

She snorted. "That is a comforting thought."

"And with luck, we'll have a few good times before the end of the world as we know it."

She pulled back and glared at him. "Don't make fun of me. I'm serious about this. We're in big trouble here."

"So." He pulled her back and in spite of herself, she nestled against him. "You're a believer now?"

"Like I have a choice." Damn, it was good to be

this close to him. She leaned against the hard, solid warmth of his body. The vague, spicy scent of his cologne wafted around her. His sheet had slipped and her head rested on the sprinkling of hair on his chest. She could hear his heartbeat. "This is nice."

"Isn't it?" His fingers trailed along her shoulders and drew lazy circles on her back.

She turned her head and kissed his chest. His muscles tensed beneath her touch.

"Morgan?"

"Hmmm?" She traced the circle of his nipple and watched it harden.

"What are you doing?"

What am I doing? "Nothing."

"Nothing?" He dipped his head and nibbled on her earlobe. Shivers of delight coursed through her.

"Not a thing," she said, a breathless catch in her voice. *I should stop this right now.*

His lips followed the curve of her neck in a slow route of exploration. She moaned and her head fell back. *Or maybe in just a minute.* His tongue dipped into the hollow at the base of her throat and lower. He pushed aside her sheet and cupped a breast in his hand, drawing a nipple into his mouth. Pure pleasure flooded through her. She gasped and her nails dug into his arm.

"Oh, Greg, oh, please."

"Please, what?" he murmured against her skin. His voice echoed in her head.

"I am not hurting you am I, my love? There is still time to stop."

335

Chapter Sixteen

She froze.

A chill rushed down her spine. "What the hell was that?"

"What?"

"Oh, jeez! Yuck! Get off me!" She pushed him away and tumbled from the sofa.

He scrambled to his feet, his sheet dropping, forgotten, to the floor. "What?" His head swiveled from side to side. "What is it? Is somebody here?"

"Yes! No!" Fight or flight kicked in and Morgan couldn't move fast enough. She bolted across the room. Her sheet caught and pulled free. "Yow!" She tried to cover herself with her hands. "Give me that, you—"

"What?" Helplessness rang in his voice.

"You're naked!

"So are you."

"I know, but that's your fault!"

"How is it my fault?"

"Look!" She gritted her teeth and pointed. He glanced down. Her sheet was firmly beneath his foot.

"Oh." An impish grin quirked his lips. "Sorry."

"You aren't sorry at all. Give it to me right now!"

"This?" He plucked it off the floor and waved it at her like a red flag before a matador. "Is this what you want?"

"Yes!"

"I don't know." He dangled the linen at arm's length. "Are you sure?"

"Yes, damn it, give it to me!"

"Well, if you insist." His voice was low and suggestive.

"Not that! I want the sheet! Right now!" She reached out, snatched it from his hand and gathered it around her. "There." She looked up. He still stood in the center of the room. His skin glowed in the light of the fire and he looked for all the world like a bronze statue. A well-sculpted bronze stature. She took it all in with one quick assessing glance. A very, very well-sculpted statue. She groaned. "Put your sheet on."

"I don't see why." He shrugged and the movement did interesting things to the rest of him. "I kind of figured we were headed in this general direction anyway."

"Well, we're not." She scooped up his sheet and tossed it at him. "Here."

"We're not?" His brows pulled together in frustration. "Why not? I thought—"

"I know exactly what you thought!"

"I know you did." His voice sharpened. "You were thinking pretty much the same thing."

"Well, I came to my senses."

"Wonderful. I have the woman I love melting in my arms and she comes to her senses. Aside from everything else, it's not terribly flattering." He wound the sheet around him. "And what do I have to thank for this sudden, and I do mean sudden, change of heart?"

She clenched her fists. The voice—his voice—the memory, or whatever it was, still rang in her ears. "It's that 'been there done that' feeling. I can't take it. This is way too creepy."

"Morgan." He started toward her.

She thrust out her hand. "Just stay away from me."

"Great." He plopped onto the sofa. "So we're back at square one."

"Right. Square one. Where you love me and I love you but we're doomed if we get together."

"Doomed is starting to look pretty damned good," he said under his breath.

"There's only one thing to do." She steeled herself against his response. "We'll just have to be friends."

"Friends? I don't want to be your friend!"

I don't want to be your friend either. "This will work. Think about it."

"I don't want to think about it." He crossed his arms over his chest.

"Oh, come on, Greg." She perched on the edge of the sofa and patted his knee. He glared back at her. "We still have to work together, you know. It would be nice if we could do it without all this passion and all this angst."

He glared.

"I didn't say it would be easy." *It'll be the hardest thing I've ever done.*

"Morgan, the last thing I want is to be your friend. What I want is to be your love, your lover and your husband."

Me too. "Nope." She shook her head. "That's the road to ruin. Doom. Tragedy. Disaster. No love, no sex, no marriage."

He clenched his jaw. "I can't stop loving you."

Neither can I. "You'll just have to work on it.

"I'm not giving up, Morgan. We belong together and we will be together. But for now, okay, I'll be your friend."

"Good." It was good, wasn't it? If they didn't commit to each other, or to love, then they would avoid whatever dire catastrophe fate had in store for them. It made sense. So why was she just the least bit disappointed? And a tad annoyed that he'd given in so easily?

"Besides, you're going to need a friend."

"Why?" She narrowed her eyes.

"I told you we needed to talk."

"I think we've done more than enough talking for one night."

"Not about us, about business. About your company."

"Oh." Relief washed through her. Business was a nice, safe subject. "What about the company?"

He hesitated, as if he didn't quite know how to begin. "You asked me to take a look at Casablanca's files."

"I thought there was something weird there but I couldn't figure it out.

"Well, I did."

"And?"

"And the books are all screwed up." Greg shook his head. "I'm still working on it; it's very subtle and very clever. But figures change or disappear all together, then reappear. It looks like someone's funneling money out, then putting it back in."

"What?" Shock raised her voice. "I don't believe it!"

"You'd better believe it. There's more."

"More?"

"From what I've been able to figure out so far, it looks like it all points back to your fiancé."

"Win?" She gasped. "You think Win is stealing from Casablanca?"

"Yeah." He pulled a deep breath. "That's not all. You only gave me the records for Casablanca but I found something else, again very, very subtle, that leads me to believe this isn't the only division where figures are being juggled."

"And?"

"And I think Hughes is behind that too."

"You're talking about embezzlement."

"Or money laundering." Greg shrugged. "I just don't know right now."

"Damn it." Morgan leapt to her feet and strode back and forth across the room. "The son of a bitch. He's stealing from the company. From his father! From my father! From me! I'll kill him. I'll personally wrap my hands around his neck and squeeze. What a . . . a . . . weasel!"

"Morgan, you'd better sit back down."

"Why?"

"You're not going to like this part."

"What part?"

"Sit down."

"Wait a minute." She stared suspiciously. "I know I should never have trusted him but how do I know I can trust you?"

"I don't know. You have to trust somebody." He paused for a moment. "Besides, I don't have anything to gain so it might as well be me. Now, sit."

She sat. "Okay, I'm ready. I can take it."

He raised a brow. "I hope so. First, what do you know about your father's partnership agreement with Hughes' father?"

She furrowed her brows thoughtfully. "Well, Phillips and Hughes is a private company. Dad and Mr. Hughes each own fifty percent. They've always wanted to keep the business family owned. So on the day they retire, I get forty percent, Win gets forty percent and our fathers retain ten percent each. It's really pretty straightforward."

"Not exactly." Greg racked his hand through his hair. "Apparently several years ago, when you were off adventure-hunting or whatever you call it, there was a new clause put into the agreement."

"What kind of clause?" she said slowly.

"If you weren't married, or were married to someone your father didn't approve of at the point of his retirement, your forty percent would not go to you but would be sold publicly. You'd get the money, of course, but you'd be completely out of the company."

"I don't—"

He held up his hand. "Wait, I'm not done. If, however, you were married to Win by the time of their retirement, you'd keep your ownership but all control would go to Win. You'd essentially be a silent partner with absolutely no power."

"That's ridiculous." She crossed her arms. "My father would never do that to me."

"Think about it for a minute, Morgan. Would you put the company you'd built from nothing in the hands of a daughter who wandered around the world spending your money in one dangerous escapade after another?"

A heavy weight settled in her stomach. "No."

"Don't be too mad at your father about this. After you took an active role in the business, and did well, he told Win to remove the clause. He signed all the papers and assumed it was taken care of. From what I understand, Win simply didn't follow through."

She shook her head. "How do you know all this?"

"Lindy told me."

"How did Lindy find out?"

"She just said something about evil ways."

"She's good at that." Morgan paused. "Why didn't she tell me?"

"I don't know. You'll have to ask her. She only told me after your dad announced your wedding plans."

"My wedding plans? That's a laugh." She scoffed. "But a lot of stuff makes sense now. That's why Win wanted to get married so fast. You know it's set for the day Dad officially retires."

"The day he turns over ownership to you."

"Yeah. Aside from a meager twenty percent, Win would have complete and total power."

"And if he didn't marry you, the company would go public. There would be audits, accounting and everything that goes along with it. His juggling of the books would be exposed. And—"

"He'd rot in jail for the rest of his hopefully very long and miserable life." She clenched her teeth. "First thing tomorrow, he's dead meat. I'll tell my dad the wedding's off. I'll contact the police. I'll talk to—"

"I think you'd better hold up on that."

"Why?"

"Look, I don't have any real evidence. Not yet. He's been really clever in all this. I'm going to have to have access to company records beyond Casablanca."

"No sweat. I'm still a player in this game. You can have whatever you need."

"It's going to take some time."

"I have confidence in you." She nodded firmly. "You're a computer whiz. You can do it."

He sighed. "I hope so."

"I am calling off the wedding, though. I was going to do that anyway."

He shook his head slowly. "I don't think that's wise. Not yet."

"Why not?"

"If you call off the wedding, Win will realize the company will go public and he won't be able to hide what he's done. There's every chance he'll bolt. I'd bet he's got whatever money he's siphoned off in an account somewhere out of reach. Until we can prove all this, I don't think you want to make him nervous."

"So what are you saying?" Her voice rose.

"I'm saying you'd should go along with the wedding plans like nothing has happened."

"The wedding's next week. What if we don't find what we need by then?"

"You don't have to say 'I do'." A glimmer of amusement twinkled in his eye. "From what I've heard you've made it to the altar before and backed out at the last minute."

"Three times, that's all. I try not to make it a habit."

"Hey." He grabbed her hand. The emerald flashed in the firelight. "I won't let you marry him. I couldn't do that to anyone. Let alone . . . a friend."

"What a mess." She groaned.

"Come here." He patted the cushion beside him. She narrowed her eyes. "Don't look at me like that. I just thought one friend could put a comforting arm around another friend."

"Okay, why not?" She slid over next to him and he put his arm around her.

They sat quietly and watched the fire slowly die. Morgan struggled to accept everything Greg had told her. She leaned her head on his shoulder and her eyes drifted closed. Being in his arms was where she belonged. Where she'd always belonged. If she wasn't so certain it would lead to tragedy this was where she'd want to stay. Forever. She sighed and snuggled closer.

"That's it." Greg pushed her away and got to his feet.

"What?" Her mind was groggy. She must have dozed. "What's going on?"

"You. You're what's going on." He stalked around the sofa muttering to himself.

"What did you say?"

"Nothing," he snapped.

"What are you doing?"

"I'm putting my clothes on."

"Why?"

"Why? I'll tell you why." She heard the zip of a zipper then he stomped back into view, carrying his still-damp shirt. "It's this friend business. I can't sit here all night with you in my arms and not want to make mad, passionate love to you. It's above and beyond the call of duty." He shrugged on his shirt and fumbled with the buttons. "I'm getting out of here. I'd rather be walking the road in the dark than sit here wanting you. It's driving me crazy."

"Really?" She couldn't help a pleased smile.

"Really."

"Wait a minute. You're not going to leave me, are you?"

"That's entirely up to you. If you stay, I'll come back with a tow truck. If you want to come, fine."

"I'm not staying here alone." She scrambled off the sofa and grabbed her gown. "Damn."

"What now?"

"Look at this." She held it up.

"Looks dry."

"Well of course it's dry, there's hardly anything to it."

"I noticed that earlier tonight. In fact, I'd bet every man at the party noticed."

She ignored him. "Don't you see a problem?"

"Not one I didn't see before."

"Earlier tonight this was floor length."

He frowned. "It doesn't look that long."

"It isn't now. It's shrunk. It'll barely cover my butt."

He bit back a smile. "That is a problem."

"And I can't very well go hiking in a sheet."

"I wouldn't think so."

"So, you're just going to have to stay with me."

"No way." He shook his head. "Sorry, Morgan, old friend. You either come along or stay by yourself. I'm getting out of here while I still can."

She glared. "You know, sometimes you're really annoying."

He narrowed his eyes. "And if anyone would recognize annoying, you would."

"Fine. Obviously, I have no choice." She flung the end of her sheet over her shoulder, lifted her chin in as regal as manner as she could muster and marched to the door. "I'm ready. Let's go."

He opened the door and muttered. "How did I get myself into this?"

"How did *we* get *ourselves* into this?"

"I don't know about you, but I met a crazy dog with a mind of his own."

She smothered a smile. Good old Sam. She stepped outside and swiveled back to him. "Do you think we can pull this off?"

"I hope so. But it means we're going to have to spend a lot of time together."

"I know."

"Probably day and night. Definitely nights."

She swallowed hard at the thought. "Okay. Greg?"

"Yeah?"

"We will be able to beat Win won't we?"

"Sure we will." His voice softened. "I told you: I think we can do anything together."

"I just want to put Win where he belongs: behind bars."

"I don't think he'll fit too well, though. You remember what Bogie said in *We're No Angels*?"

She shook her head. "What?"

" 'Well, I'll say one thing for prison.' " He laughed and pulled the door closed. " 'It's a better class of people.' "

"Where have you been?" Greg glanced up from the computer in the small office in Morgan's apartment. Sam and Cindy Lou lay at his feet.

Morgan peered at the screen over his shoulder. "Rehearsal dinner, remember? This damned wedding is tomorrow in case you've forgotten."

"I wish I could." Greg heaved a sigh and leaned back in his chair. He'd become a fixture here, a rather pleasant fixture. He even had his own key. Morgan argued to herself it was a necessity if they were going to get the goods on Win. It was impossible to try and uncover Win's treachery at the office. Every night since the party Greg had been at her place, tapping into Phillips and Hughes' records. "Has Lindy come up with anything?"

"No. Nothing solid and nothing on the embezzled funds." Morgan shook her head. "And she's pretty sure Win destroyed the revised agreement."

"Covering his tracks?"

"Yeah, the weasel. If this was a Bogart film the bad guy would have kept the incriminating evidence around for the hero to find at the last minute."

"Too bad this isn't a movie."

"It's getting pretty close to the last minute though."

Greg laced his fingers behind his head and groaned. "I feel like I've been sitting here forever."

"You have." She smiled. "Come on. I'll rub your neck." He raised a brow. "Just your neck." He dropped his head forward and she massaged the tight muscles. "Wow, you are really stiff."

"Yeah, I know." Morgan kneaded the hard flesh for a few minutes, with only an occasional sigh or grunt to let her know her efforts were appreciated.

He certainly did have nice shoulders. "Did Lindy ever explain why she didn't tell you any of this?" he asked after a few moments.

"Not really." Morgan pulled her brows together. "She was pretty vague about it, which isn't like Lindy at all. Normally, she spills her guts. She's up to something. But I've been way too busy this week to press her about it." Her hands stilled. "Have you found anything at all?"

"Not yet. I know there's something here, I just can't seem to pinpoint it."

"We're running out of time."

"I know that." Sharpness edged his words. "I'm doing the best I can."

"Hey, don't snap at me. I'm the one with everything on the line here."

"I'm not snapping." He drew a deep breath. "I'm just frustrated. And you're not the only one with everything on the line, you know." He grabbed her hands and pulled them down flat against his chest until her cheek touched his. She should stand back or at the very least protest, but it was so good to be with her arms around him like this. In spite of spending all her spare time with Greg it seemed like forever since he'd touched her. The annoying man had lived up to their agreement: he'd been a perfect gentleman, the sadist. And nothing more than a friend. "Don't worry. There's no way I'd ever let you actually marry him."

"I'm not worried about that. I don't plan on going through with it either. I just don't want to get all the way to the altar before I call it off."

"I hope we don't cut it that close." He turned his head and his lips grazed her cheek. He hadn't kissed her all week. "Mmmm. This is nice."

"What are you doing?" She really should move.

"Kissing you."

"That's what I thought." Not that she wanted to move. "Um . . . do you think you should?"

His lips wandered to a wonderfully sensitive spot just below her ear. "Probably not."

Shivers coursed through her and weakened her knees. "Is this what a friend would do?"

"Probably not."

A breathless note sounded in her voice. "But we're just supposed to be friends, remember? We agreed."

"Probably . . ." He swiveled in the chair and pulled her on to his lap. ". . . not."

"Greg, we—"

"Did I ever tell you how much I like you in low-cut dresses like this?" His mouth murmured against her skin and trailed a long, hot path down her throat and lower.

"I don't think you mentioned it." She gasped. "This isn't a good idea."

"No, it's definitely not a good idea." He dipped his tongue in the cleavage between her breasts. "It's a great idea."

She closed her eyes and moaned. "This isn't how a friend behaves."

"No? I think it's very friendly." He slipped his hand into her dress to cup her breast and free it from the silky fabric. He bent and drew her nipple into his mouth.

She arched her back and moaned. "This is a horrible mistake."

"Maybe. Do you want me to stop?"

She twined her fingers in his hair and pulled his head to hers. "No."

"Good." His lips crushed hers with an eagerness she relished and shared. Without warning the desire she'd struggled to ignore, or at least control, burst free, and she was lost in the burning need to touch him and taste him and join her body with his. For this moment nothing else mattered.

She struggled to sit upright and face him. He caught the hem of her dress and tugged it up her thighs and she shifted to straddle him on the chair. The hard evidence of his arousal pressed through the fabric separating them and her excitement spiraled. If this was the road to doom and destruction, if this was the highway to whatever devastation fate had in store for them, the least they could do was make it one heck of a ride.

She tunneled her hands up under his shirt and yanked it over his head. The heat of his skin burned through her fingers and into her soul. He wrapped his arms tighter around her as if he couldn't get her close enough. Her tongue met and thrust and parried with his in a preview of what she knew was to come and wanted as she had never wanted anything before. Somewhere in the back of her mind she realized this wasn't sex. It was love, and she'd never really known the difference before now.

She threw her arms around his neck and he drew her tight against him in a frenzy of surrender and need and desire. The chair toppled over backward and spilled them onto the floor. He didn't seem to notice. She didn't really care.

Dimly she heard an indignant yelp and ignored it. They rolled as one away from the upended chair. She thrust her leg between his. He ran his hand up her hip to the waistband of her pantyhose and yanked it down. A low growl punctuated their labors. Her hands trembled and she fumbled with his belt buckle. He slid his palm down the curve of her stomach, then lower to mold his hand hard to her. She struggled to unzip his pants, his erection straining against her efforts. His fingers slipped inside her, and his thumb traced circles on flesh at once singed and thrilled at his touch. She cried out. A growl sounded again. He thrust his tongue into her mouth in rhythm with his fingers.

A bark rang out. They ignored it. A second followed and a third until Morgan's haze-fogged mind registered the interruption. She turned her head toward the persistent dog.

Sam stood towering over them.

Greg gasped. "Go away, Sam."

Morgan sighed. "Go away, Sam."

Sam growled.

"Come on, Sam," Morgan said. "Be a good dog and go away." She trailed her tongue along Greg's jaw.

He didn't seem to notice. "What ya got, boy?"

"Greg!" Frustration grit her teeth. "Focus here. I'm yours. Now. This is it. I'm ready to challenge the gods. Let's go for it. Don't worry about the dog. He'll be fine. I, on the other hand—"

"Right." He smiled and pulled her tight to him. "What was I thinking?"

Sam barked.

Morgan groaned. "I give up."

Greg flashed her a wicked grin. "Don't go away." He propped himself up on one elbow and studied Sam. "Okay, pal. You've got our complete attention. What's up?"

Sam spit out a chewed, misshapen, laminated license.

Greg's license.

Greg pulled his brows together in disgust. "What is that?"

Morgan flinched. "That's what's left of your driver's license."

"My license? Great. So you had it all along."

"Not me." She nodded at the dog. "He had it. Blame him. But now that you have it back . . ." The tips of her fingers drifted along his back.

Greg stared at the license.

She nibbled on his shoulder. "Greg?"

He shook his head.

"Greg? Come on. If we're going to thumb our noses at fate I'm ready. I'm willing." She nipped a little harder. "And I don't want to be friends anymore."

"That may be just it, Morgan." Greg scrambled to his feet and stumbled to the computer.

"Where are you going?" Morgan stared. "What might be it?"

"Get me the chair, would you?" His gaze fixed on the screen; his fingers flashed across the keyboard.

" 'Get me the chair?' " His mind was obviously no longer with her. "Sure, no problem." Morgan heaved an indignant sigh, got to her feet and righted the chair. "I'm just willing to risk the end of the world for you and all you want to do is play with that stupid computer." She slid the chair up behind him and he sat without looking. "Do you want to tell me what's so important you can't even keep your mind on, well, what we were about to do?"

"Damn, I am such an idiot."

"No argument from me on that one." Morgan picked up her pantyhose, balled them up and tossed them on a chair, then struggled to rearrange her dress. "But aside from the obvious, what are you talking about?"

"It's the one area I really haven't looked in." He turned toward her, his eyes glowing with excitement. "Licenses, licensing agreements, anything to do with authorizations, sanctions, et cetera. I don't know why it slipped my mind. The who, what and wherefores of licenses tend to be so convoluted it would be the easiest place in the world to hide what you don't want anybody to find."

"Okay." She brushed her hair away from her face. "You think this might be it?"

"I don't know. But I sure haven't found what we're looking for anywhere else." He shrugged and turned back to the screen. "It's going to be a long night, Morgan. Why don't you make some coffee?"

"Coffee." She held her hands out in front of her. They shook with repressed passion. She drew a long, steadying breath. "Coffee, right."

"And don't forget to thank Sam. He gave me this idea."

She glanced down at the Beardie. Sam grinned up at her. She returned it ruefully. "I don't quite know how to thank you, boy."

He thunked his tail on the floor. She bent down and wrapped her arms around him. "Good job, Sam," she whispered in his ear. "Bad timing but good job."

Morgan straightened and started toward the door. Greg reached out and grabbed her hand. "Hey, have you ever seen *In a Lonely Place*?"

"It sounds vaguely familiar but," she shook her head, "I can't seem to recall it."

"And you call yourself a fan."

"No, I call him," she said, nodding at the dog, "a fan." She thought for a moment. "Wasn't it about a screenwriter and a murder?"

"That's it. It's got a great couple of lines in it."

"Just what I need right now: a slick Bogart character comment on life." She sighed. "I'll bite. Let me have it."

He studied her for a moment, his manner serious, his gaze intense. " 'I was born when you kissed me. I died when you left me.' " He brought her hand to his lips. " 'I lived a few days while you loved me.' "

Her heart stilled. Her breath caught.

Play It Again, Sam

"I told you once I was born when I kissed you. I never had the chance to tell you I died when I thought you'd left me."

"And I . . . I lived only the days when you loved me."

Morgan closed her eyes against the rush of emotion that threatened to overwhelm her. She'd heard the words before or words just like them. But not in the movies. No. She'd said them or he'd said them. Somewhere. Somehow.

"Morgan." Greg got to his feet and gathered her into his arms. "Are you okay?"

"No." She relaxed against him. "Yeah, I'm okay."

"What happened? What's the matter?"

She pulled away and stared into his wonderful storm-colored eyes. She'd seen them before. She'd seen them always. In her dreams. In her life. In her future. She reached up and pushed his hair away from his forehead. "Fate. Destiny. Whatever. It's kind of like fighting city hall isn't it?"

"You mean we can't win?"

"No, I mean you just have to understand the rules of the game."

"And do you understand the rules?"

She shook her head and sighed. "I have this awful feeling that we won't really know how to play until the game's almost over.

"And then it just might be too late."

Chapter Seventeen

"I've never seen you nervous before." Lindy leaned against the four-poster bed and eyed Morgan. "It's kind of creepy."

"Creepy pretty much describes it." Morgan paced the length of her girlhood bedroom, clasping and unclasping her hands. "Have you talked to Greg?"

Lindy glanced at her watch. "Not in the last ten minutes."

"And?"

"And he said he was making progress. Tell me again why you wanted to cut this so close."

"I didn't want to. It just worked out that way." Morgan blew a long breath. "If Win caught wind of any of this he'd be long gone by now. As long as there's the prospect of marriage to me, and everything else that goes along with it, he'll stick around.

If Greg had just managed to get the evidence we need before today . . ." She twisted the emerald on her finger. "We should have called this off a long time ago."

Lindy shrugged. "Yeah, but it sounds like you would have blown your chance to get Win."

Anger narrowed Morgan's eyes. "The weasel." She stalked across the room and back. "Where did you say you put Greg?"

Lindy sighed. "For the third time, Morgan, Greg's in the library. He has his laptop and he's dialed into the company. He'll come up with something. So would you please relax?"

"Relax? That's easy for you to say. Have you seen this?" Morgan strode to the window and gestured at the scene outside. "Look at this. A disaster waiting to happen."

Lindy joined her. "Looks like a traditional Morgan Phillips ceremony to me. Let's see. Folding chairs that can be stacked quickly in case of rain or cancellation. A bar with hard liquor to not only supplement the champagne but provide relief to a jilted groom or an exasperated father. And aren't those silk flowers? I mean the real ones don't really last from wedding to wedding."

Morgan grit her teeth. "Lindy."

"I'd say it looks pretty much like every other wedding you've almost gone through with."

"This is different," Morgan snapped.

"Oh, yeah?"

"Yeah, with every other wedding, and keep in mind here my engagements outnumber the near-miss weddings, at this point I was still planning on going through with it."

"I remember."

"Damn. Just look at that. This was supposed to be a small, intimate, family affair. Who are all those people?" Morgan slumped on to the window seat and groaned. "It's bad enough that I'm going to call off one more wedding. But all of my parents and their friends and everybody I know or have ever known in the world is out there."

"So what?" Lindy raised a curious brow. "Most of them have been through this with you before."

"It's just different this time, that's all."

Lindy stared at her for a long moment. "I don't—" Her eyes widened. "I get it. It's because of him. The computer hunk." She laughed. "You're in love. You're really in love this time."

"Yes, I'm in love. Really." Morgan glared. "And I'm really not that wild about it." She rose to her feet and paced again. "It drives me crazy. He drives me crazy. Everything drives me crazy."

"You still have that dream?"

"Yeah." *And really strange memories or visions or whatever even when I'm awake.* She turned on her heel and headed toward the door. "I'm going downstairs to see how he's doing."

"Wearing that?"

"What's wrong with this?" Morgan stepped to a full-length mirror and studied her image. "I like it."

"It's not exactly a typical bridal gown."

"You don't think so?" Morgan turned and considered her reflection over her shoulder. "It's got a train."

"It's not a train. It's a big, net bow tacked right above your butt." Lindy shook her head. "The dress barely reaches your knees. It's strapless and cut so low half the guests will be wondering how in the hell you keep it up and the other half will be hoping you can't. And to top it off, it's sequined."

"Yeah but it's white." Morgan grinned at her reflection. "Besides, I have a hat that goes with it. It'll be great. I'm going to see Greg."

"You're cutting it a little close, aren't you?"

Morgan glanced at the clock on the dresser. "It's only three-thirty. The wedding isn't until four. I'll be back before you know it."

"Well, just make sure Win doesn't see you. It's bad luck for the groom to see the bride before the wedding."

"He's not going to be a groom." Morgan stuck her head out the door and glanced up and down the hallway. "Besides, he deserves all the bad luck he can get."

"I wasn't worried about him." Lindy shook her head. "I was worried about you."

"Yeah, well, aren't we all." She stepped into the hall. "See ya later." The coast was clear. Morgan headed to the stairs and furtively crept down to the first floor. This was ridiculous. Sneaking around her parents' house like a thief in the night. Jeez. She hadn't done this since she was sixteen.

She slipped into the library and closed the door behind her. Greg didn't even notice. He sat behind her dad's desk, intently working on the laptop in front of him. Sam and Cindy Lou lay on a leather sofa. Both dogs raised their heads in welcome.

Morgan leaned against the door and watched Greg for a minute. His suit jacket was tossed on a chair. His tie hung loose around the neck of his off-white shirt. The man knew how to dress all right. He looked as good in a suit as he did in a sheet. Every now and then he'd jot something down on a notebook. She'd never seen anybody so intense on a job. Her heart swelled. He was doing it for her. He could have just backed Casablanca out of the deal, accused Win of impropriety. Instead, he was doing it to save her half of the company, her heritage. What a guy. A guy well worth risking the end of the world for. And wouldn't a short time with him be better than a lifetime without him?

Greg sighed but didn't look up. "No, Lindy, you can go back and tell Morgan I haven't found anything yet."

"We're almost out of time."

He looked up in surprise. "Morgan! What are you—" he narrowed his eyes. "What in the hell are you wearing?"

She twirled around. "Like it?"

"Yeah, I like it." Desire simmered in his voice. "What's it supposed to be anyway?"

"My wedding dress."

He raised a brow. "There's not much to it, is there?"

"Nope. I got it a couple of years ago. There was no way I was going to lend credibility to this farce by buying something new so I had a dressmaker add the train."

"That's the big bow on your butt?"

"—and I bought a hat."

"That'll make all the difference in the world."

She sauntered over and perched on the edge of the desk. "So . . ."

"So." He sighed and looked up at her. "Nothing."

That heavy weight in the bottom of her stomach was back. "I hate it when you say things like that."

"Me too." He shook his head. "We might have to face some hard facts here. Win's very, very good. Whatever he's done he's done it well and I can't track it down. At least not yet. I need more time."

"You've got a half an hour," she said hopefully. "And maybe I can stall the wedding a bit."

"I'm not giving up." He shrugged, "But I can't guarantee anything." He hesitated. "You know, even if we expose Win, we still might not be able to save your share of the company. I mean, we've concentrated on finding out how he was siphoning off money. We haven't done anything about your dad's partnership agreement."

"I know." She shook her head, "I'd hate for any of the company to go public but if that's the price we have to pay to put Win away, I guess it's worth it."

He stood and pulled her into his arms. "I'll love you anyway, you know that, don't you?"

"Yeah." Her gaze searched his. "I still have that overwhelming feeling that we're headed for disaster but I don't seem to care anymore."

"Or maybe it's worth the risk?"

"Maybe." She laughed weakly. "I'll give you as much time as I can. But when we get to the 'I do's' I'm out of there."

"It's a deal." He kissed her firmly and released her. "Now get out of here before I rip that poor excuse for a wedding dress off you and play wedding night right here."

"Hold that thought." She stepped toward the door. "First we get Win, then we challenge fate." She tossed a halfhearted grin over her shoulder. "As Lindy would say, this is going to be fun."

The strains of the "Wedding March" drifted in through the open French doors and jerked Greg's attention from the computer.

The wedding was starting and he still had nothing. He was so close. With luck, just another few minutes was all he'd need. "Damn."

Sam stared from across the room.

"What am I going to do, boy?"

Sam looked as if he might actually answer. The dog slid off the sofa and leisurely stretched one leg after the other. Then he trotted out the open door.

Greg glanced at Cindy Lou. "Aren't you going with your friend?"

Cindy Lou obediently jumped off the sofa and sprinted after Sam. Greg smiled in spite of himself. They really were smart dogs. He could use a little more intelligence himself right now. And a whole lot of luck.

He'd only hinted at it to Morgan, but he wasn't at

all sure he could pull this off. Even if he could, he didn't know if there was anyway to bypass the partnership agreement. The deadline was the end of the business day: five-thirty as defined by the agreement.

Maybe she should have called off the wedding when he'd first told her about it. She could have gone to her father and he probably could have rescinded the clause. Now it was too late. She could lose her company and Win would probably get away with his treachery. Unless Greg could find something in the next few minutes.

He turned back to the computer with a desperate determination. She was depending on him. He couldn't let her down. But even if he couldn't save her company he could still save her future and his.

There was no way in hell he'd let her marry Hughes.

How many people had her mother invited anyway? A sea of faces greeted her. All expectant. All smiling. Not one recognizable.

Morgan carried a large bouquet of tulips cut from her mother's garden and walked down the grassy aisle on her father's arm. She struggled to keep whatever kind of blissful expression a happy bride would wear on her face and noted what a lovely picture they must have made: passing under the dozen or so bowers bedecked with her mother's spring flowers and the florist's finest blooms to create a churchlike atmosphere under the open, blue sky. Here and there huge baskets sat filled with tulips and gladiolus and lilies and daffodils.

When was the last time she was this nervous? Or had she ever been this nervous? Morgan hadn't done anything in her entire life from shooting rapids to jumping out of planes without total and complete confidence. Confidence that had deserted her today. Her father squeezed her arm as if he sensed her distress. He probably chalked it up to her finally going through with a wedding. Little did he know.

They reached the end of the aisle where Judge Hanley, an old friend of her dad's, stood waiting. As her maid of honor, Lindy stood off to one side. Morgan caught her gaze and Lindy shook her head slightly. Great. Greg still didn't have the answers. Victor Phillips lightly kissed her cheek and winked, stepping back to symbolically give her away to her soon-to-be-husband. Win stepped up beside her and took her hand in his, a triumphant smirk on his face.

She wanted to slap him.

She wanted to scream.

She wanted to turn and run.

Where was Greg?

"Dearly beloved . . ." Judge Hanley's voice boomed over the gathering.

She forced herself to stay calm. Until the "I do's," she didn't have to worry. Not really. She squared her shoulders. This was moving way too fast. She had to think of a way to stall.

A bark sounded in the distance. Then another and another. Morgan turned toward the far end of the aisle. Sam ran straight at her, Cindy Lou right behind. Both dogs barked hysterically as if they were chasing rabbits. Invisible rabbits. Just before he reached her, Sam swerved into the right-hand row of seats, Cindy Lou close on his tail. Guests jumped to their feet in a weird parody of a crowd at a ball game doing a wave.

"Get those damn dogs," Win roared.

Here and there a brave soul flung themselves at the speeding fur balls but most of the crowd was either too stunned or too slow to do much but stare with their mouths open.

Sam and Cindy Lou broke from the row of chairs that ran parallel to the seating and dashed into another row. Once again guests popped up like bread from a toaster. The beasts emerged from the end of the row and sprinted across the lawn toward freedom. Morgan would have thought it funny if she hadn't been so grateful. After all, wasn't it her duty as the bride to make sure everyone was settled before going on with the ceremony? Try as she might, it only took a few minutes to right upended chairs and ease the nerves of disgruntled guests.

"Morgan, sweetheart." Win smiled pleasantly but his eyes were cold "Let's go."

"Yeah. Okay." She took her place beside him. *Come on, Greg. Where are you?*

The judge picked up where he'd left off. Why was this moving so fast? Why hadn't she insisted on a church wedding? Or at least a judge who stuttered? Her bouquet hid her hands and nervously she twisted the emerald. She had to do something.

". . . if anyone knows any reason why these two

should not be joined together . . ." The ring slipped over her knuckle. ". . . Let them speak now or forever hold their peace."

A horrible howl, the wail of a hound from hell echoed over the lawn. The gathering turned as one toward the blood-curdling sound. Morgan yanked the ring off. Another howl sounded, substantially weaker than the first. Like a much smaller, younger dog trying to imitate a larger one. Like Cindy Lou trying to be like Sam.

Guests traded uneasy glances. Others nodded as if to say, "I told you so." If this had been a less civilized crowd, they'd be laying bets right now as to whether or not this wedding would take place. From the expression on their faces, Morgan would put the odds at fifty-fifty. She bit back a grin and casually tossed the emerald into the grass.

Win heaved an annoyed sigh. "Judge Hanley, I think we're ready." He slanted her an irritated glance. "Again."

"Not yet." Morgan shook her head.

"What now?" Win's brows drew together in an angry frown.

"My ring, Win. My emerald."

"What about it?"

She tried to look as contrite as she could. "I think I dropped it."

"You dropped it? You dropped it?" Win's face turned a distinct shade of wild cherry cough drop red. "That ring's worth a small fortune. Where did you drop it?"

Morgan waved vaguely at the ground. "Down there somewhere. Maybe."

Win dropped to his knees. Several others joined him and within minutes everyone in the front row was combing through the grass searching for an emerald that blended in quite nicely with the turf. It took fifteen minutes before a friend of her father's located the gem snuggled up beside a floral arrangement. The crowd breathed a collective sigh of relief. Say what you would, this was a group that knew good jewelry when they saw it.

Judge Hanley leaned toward them. "Want to try it again or shall we call it a day?"

"Again." Win's jaw clenched. He drew a deep breath and his expression softened. Morgan didn't trust him for a minute. "We definitely want to finish this. Today. Don't we, Morgan?"

"We definitely want to finish it."

He narrowed his eyes. She smiled sweetly in return.

"Very well." The judge glanced at the book in his hand. "Do you, Winston Hughes the fourth, take this woman to be . . ."

Oh, no. The 'I do's.' This is it. If Greg wasn't out here in the next minute she'd have to call it off herself. There was no way she'd take this fiasco any further.

Out of the corner of her eye she saw Sam and Cindy Lou lope up and sit just off to one side of the judge. What were they up to now? With any luck it would be a wonderful distraction.

". . . Morgan Phillips, take this man to be you—"

"Nope. She doesn't." Greg strode up the aisle. Relief coursed through her.

"Sorry, Judge. He's right." She glared at Win. "I do not. I don't. I won't. I wouldn't. Ever."

Win's mouth dropped open. His eyes widened. He was obviously shocked. "Morgan, what—"

"Don't what me, you—"

Greg reached her side and grabbed her hand. "Come on, Morgan."

She lunged toward Win but Greg yanked her back. "Don't stop me. He deserves a good belt. And I'm just the one—"

"Shut up, Morgan." Greg tried to pull her down the aisle.

"You weasel! No. You're lower than a weasel. You're weasel sh—" Horrified and very proper gazes fastened on her. "—poop. You're a pile of thieving weasel poop."

Win's expression hardened as if a lightbulb had come on over his head, and he understood exactly what she was talking about. For the first time she realized he could be dangerous. Very dangerous. "We have to get out of here. Now." Greg hurried back down the aisle dragging her behind him.

"But I want to tell—"

He stopped, grabbed her and stared into her eyes. "If you want to have anything to tell, we need to get back to the laptop in the library. Now. Do you understand what I'm saying?"

Abruptly she realized any evidence he'd found would still be accessed through the portable computer. Exposed and vulnerable to anyone who walked in the room. "Damn. Let's go."

They sprinted toward the house, slowed by the height of her shoes and the dogs leaping at their heels. Confusion created mild chaos among the guests. She heard her parents call her name but she ignored them. First, she had to see what Greg had found. Then she'd tell her folks everything.

They pushed open the French doors to the library and stepped to the desk. Sam and Cindy Lou slipped through the doors behind them. "Okay, Greg, what did you find?"

"Actually, it's not that simple."

Unease trickled through her. "What do you mean, 'not that simple'?" She peered at the screen on the laptop.

He flicked off the power.

"Hey. What did you do that for?"

"Morgan, you have to keep in mind, he's been really clever. He's hidden—"

"Come on, Greg," she said impatiently. "Now, you're stalling. Just tell me what you came up with."

The door from the hallway swung open and Win stepped inside, closing the door behind him. "Yes, indeed, Spencer, I'd love to see what you came up with as well."

"How did you get here so fast?" Morgan glared. "You're not even winded."

Win shrugged. "I work out."

"You know full well what I found." Greg's voice was as hard as his eyes.

"Let's pretend for a minute that I don't." Win,

stepped toward her father's bar, a piece of masculine whimsy disguised as an antique world globe. "Do you mind if I have a drink, Morgan? Sweetheart?"

She gritted her teeth. "Don't call me sweetheart. I hate it when you call me sweetheart."

Win bent over the bar, straightened and aimed a small handgun directly at her.

"What do you think you're doing?" She crossed her arms over her chest. "And where did you get that?"

"Didn't you know about this?" Win shrugged. "This is your father's. He showed my father and I where he kept it once, oh, years ago, in a misbegotten moment of trust, I guess. Pretty clever, keeping it in a hidden drawer in the bottom of his bar. Most people would put it in a desk."

"My father doesn't like guns," she muttered.

"Yes, well, lucky for me he has this one." Win chuckled. "He said he bought it to protect his family. Don't you just love the irony of it all?"

"What are you going to do, Hughes?" Greg stepped in front of Morgan.

"What do you think I'm going to do?" Win rolled his eyes at the ceiling. "I'm going to shoot you. First I'll kill you, then her. Or maybe Morgan first, then you. I haven't decided for sure."

A tiny sliver of fear slid down her spine. She ignored it. "Oh, come on. You don't expect me to believe you're really going to kill us, do you?"

"Yeah." Win laughed with genuine amusement. "I do expect you to believe it. It's true."

"You won't get away with this," Greg said.

"Whoa. That was original. Where'd you get that from? An old movie?" Win smiled a nasty smirk. "Of course I'll get away with it. Everybody saw you drag my blushing bride away from me right there at the altar. The poor woman was fighting you every inch. All that kicking and screaming."

"Hey! I was screaming at you. I was trying to kick you."

"You know that and I know that but do you really think that's how it looked to all those guests?" Win shook his head. "I don't think so. Especially when I, as the distraught grieving groom, tell them how Spencer here was wildly jealous and wanted you all for himself. You, of course, would have nothing to do with him. So he kidnapped you from your own wedding and by the time I broke in here, he had killed you and turned the gun on himself."

"Greg," she said out of the side of her mouth, "that's a pretty workable scenario, isn't it?"

"Yep." Greg's gaze fastened on Win. She sure as hell hoped behind those steely gray eyes he was thinking of something. Something clever and quick.

"Are we screwed here, Greg?"

"It's okay, Morgan." Greg's voice was flat and even, and hope flickered within her. "It'll be fine."

"Correction. I'll be fine. You'll be dead." Win gestured with the gun and her stomach lurched. "Now, you two move away from the desk and from each other."

They stepped sideways along the wall to stand about a foot apart.

"More." Win said sharply. "Call me crazy, but I don't trust the two of you together." They inched away until a good yard separated them. "That's better. Now, as much as I hate to rush things, as soon as the furor dies down at the wedding site, lovely job your mother did by the way—"

"Thanks. What part did you like best?" she said brightly. "I know I really liked how she mixed the garden flowers—"

"Shut up, Morgan." Win sighed. "As I was saying, people, parents, whoever, will be coming up here to find out what's going on so I'm kind of pressed for time. Who wants to go first?"

"I will," Greg said coolly. Her gaze caught his and she knew exactly what he was doing. If Win shot him first she just might have a chance to escape.

"Hey, I don't want a sacrifice here, I want a rescue."

"Don't count on it." Win pointed the gun at Greg. "Okay, say goodbye."

"Wait!" Morgan's voice squeaked. "You can't shoot him!"

"Of course I can shoot him."

"Oh sure you *can*. Duh. Any idiot can see that."

Greg raised a brow. "Thanks."

"Buck up, Greg, he's got a gun—we've got nothing. The fact that he can shoot you isn't even in question."

Greg stared. "I'm glad you're not letting emotion cloud the issue here."

"What's the point?" She shrugged. "He's going to shoot us. We're going to die or at least be horribly maimed which means he'll kill us eventually because he wants to shut us up and doesn't want to have us lingering in a hospital where some bright but impoverished intern will hear our drug-induced mutterings and put two and two—"

"Morgan," Greg snapped. "You're babbling."

"Yeah," she said under her breath, "but you're still alive to hear it."

"And you're both bickering. I—" Win's eyes widened and he shook his head. "I don't believe this. How could I have missed it?"

"Missed what?" Morgan said innocently.

"The two of you. Together." He waved the gun at Greg. "You've been boffing her haven't you?"

Morgan lifted her chin. "I resent that."

"No." Greg's manner was icy. "I have not."

"Too bad. I was really looking forward to the wedding night myself." Win leered and Greg's fists clenched and unclenched by his side. "You've obviously got something going. After all, he's willing to go first. It's really kind of sweet. Touching almost."

"Touching. Really, quite, quite touching. If you two can pull yourselves away from one another, I know it has not been an hour yet, but I am ready if you are, St. Gregory."

"St. Gregory?" Morgan whispered, and shook her head. The strongest sense of déjà vu yet crashed through her with a power that knocked the wind out of her and left her gasping for air. Odd images of Greg and Win and herself swirled through her mind like a bad print of an old movie.

"Morgan?" Greg's brows furrowed and he stepped toward her.

"Stay where you are." Win gestured with the gun. "I think I've had enough of all this."

"No, wait, Win." Morgan's gaze meshed and locked with his but her eyes wouldn't quite focus. Win's figure seemed to fade in and out. Almost as if the image of another man was superimposed over his. Jeez, had she cracked under the stress of her impending doom? She shook her head again and her vision cleared. "At least tell us why you did all this."

"Why?" He snorted. "That's pretty trite, Morgan. Just like your boyfriend's comment. It's straight out of the movies, but okay, I'll go for it. We bad guys can't resist a bit of bragging and I guess I'm definitely in the bad guy category now."

His eyes gleamed and he looked every bit as wicked as any villain Sam Spade or Philip Marlowe ever faced. "I worked for the company from the day I got out of school. Less than a year ago you waltz right in and you can do no wrong. I could live with your share being public, Morgan. I'd still have most of the power. But I couldn't, no, I refuse, to share it with you. So I took what I could get out of it. Marrying you would have made it that much easier." His expression hardened. "It's my company,

Morgan, it was always supposed to be mine. It belongs to me."

"Because you are mine. You were always supposed to be mine. And now, legally, you are. St. Gregory is the interloper here. You belong to me."

Her breath caught at the venom in Win's voice and the matching echo in her head. Win's image wavered in front of her like a surreal music video. She reached out to grab something, anything, to steady the dizziness that gripped her.

"Morgan!" Greg's voice carried a note of concern and she jerked her gaze to his.

His gaze burned into hers and she knew for all the rest of her life she would remember the pain in his eyes and how very much she loved him.

Greg looked like a frame of film out of sync with the soundtrack. Like a cheap foreign horror flick. Was she drunk? Drugged? Why did it seem that events were heading relentlessly toward a climax she could do nothing to prevent? A helplessness she'd never known held her in its grasp.

"Morgan." Greg sounded as though he were a great distance away.

"Don't move!" Win's voice was stretched and distorted.

Every action, every reaction, was sluggish, torpid, as though they were stuck in slow motion. She turned her attention to Win. Behind him, the library door swung open and smacked with an almost careful ease into his back. He jerked forward like a boneless puppet.

He will kill him! It's what he planned all along! How could I have been so blind? This is my doing! All of it.

"No!" Morgan threw herself toward Greg. She couldn't let him die!

Morgan's scream rang through the room. "Greg!"

I cannot let him die!

The gun fired.

No! Not again! . . .

. . . It's not supposed to happen this way! Not this time!

They're supposed to be together. Forever. That's my job.

My mission. It's the reason I'm here. The only reason I'm here!

I can't let him kill her!

I can't let them lose each other!

I can't let history repeat itself!

I gotta do something!

I gotta stop this!

Now!

Chapter Eighteen

The edge of her vision caught a gray-and-white blur that crashed into her and knocked her to the floor.

"Sam!" The dog lay crumpled beside her.

Greg dove to tackle Win. Lindy burst through the open doorway with a stranger. Victor Phillips and a crowd of others jammed the hallway behind them.

Greg got to his feet, gun in hand. "Get up, Hughes. Lindy, call the police."

"Sam." Morgan sobbed, and cradled the dog's head in her lap. There was only a small streak of blood but she was certain the dog was dying. "No, Lindy, call a vet." She glared at Win through her tears. "You shot my dog, you bastard."

"Big deal." Win shrugged. "Spoiled, flea-ridden bag of fur."

"Give me the gun, Greg." She held her hand out. "I want to shoot him."

Greg shook his head. "As much as I'd like to let you, you can't shoot him."

"I'd be happy to shoot him for you," Lindy said.

"Nobody's shooting anybody." Morgan's father took the gun and handed it to the man beside Lindy. "Mark?" Morgan's family doctor slipped through the crowd into the library. "Take a look at the dog, would you?"

Greg raised a curious brow.

Victor chuckled. "We always have Mark, Dr. Mills, on hand for Morgan's weddings. Just in case. It always seemed a wise precaution. This is the first time we've needed him though."

The doctor knelt beside Sam and gave him a quick once-over. He wasn't a vet, Morgan sniffed, but if he was good enough for her family he'd probably do for her dog. "How is he? Is he going to make it?"

Dr. Mills leaned back and shook his head. Fresh tears sprang to Morgan's eyes. "I don't know quite how to say this."

Greg put his hand on her shoulder and squeezed. "I can take it. Go ahead."

"Well—" He drew a deep breath. "It looks like the bullet just grazed him. There's no entry wound. No significant blood. Nothing much more than a scratch."

"But," Morgan said as she gazed down at the limp animal, "he's unconscious."

Dr. Mills shrugged. "I think he fainted. You'll

want to put some antiseptic on that scrape but otherwise he should be fine as soon as he comes around."

"Fainted," Win said with disgust. "What a worthless excuse for a dog."

"And you would know worthless, wouldn't you?" Morgan narrowed her eyes. "Has somebody called the police?"

"I'll take care of it, Ms. Phillips." The stranger beside Lindy nodded.

"Morgan, this is D. B." Lindy grinned. "He's a security expert."

"Nice to meet you." D. B. nodded to her father and escorted Win out of the room.

"A security expert?" Morgan's gaze caught Greg's. He looked as confused as she felt. "What's going on?"

Lindy glanced at Victor. He nodded. "It's kind of hard to explain. First, Greg, what did you come up with?"

Greg grimaced. "Nothing."

"Nothing?" Morgan stared.

"Nope." Greg shook his head sheepishly. "Other than that weird business about money disappearing and appearing in Casablanca's accounts I couldn't quite get to anything else."

"But you let Win think—"

"Well, I had to stop the wedding." He grinned. "Sorry."

"It's okay." Lindy laughed. "Win was really good. So good, in fact, that D. B. and I needed to stall him. When I found out about the partnership agreement

I—" Lindy winced. "Technically you could say I blackmailed him."

Morgan gasped. "Lindy!"

"So," Greg said slowly, "he took the money out of Casablanca to pay you and you put it back in."

"Right." Lindy smiled modestly. "Pretty clever huh?"

"But." Morgan shook her head. "I'm really confused here."

"Let me see if I can straighten it out." Lindy paused to gather her thoughts. "You know Win was funneling money out of the company. He put it all in an account in the Caribbean."

"Go on." Morgan nodded.

"But Win is really smart and D. B. and his computer nerds had as much trouble pinpointing it as Greg did." She glanced at Greg. "Sorry. They finally figured it out this week. Anyway, Win needed to marry you to gain control of the company and keep what he'd done secret."

"I get that. But how does blackmail fit into it?"

"If I blew the whistle on him, he'd have no chance with you. Keep in mind, this started long before you decided to marry him. Who knew you'd be that stupid?" Lindy shrugged.

"Thanks."

"The whole blackmail business was really a ploy to keep him distracted so D. B. could get evidence of his embezzlement. I drove him nuts." Lindy eyes snapped wickedly. "I've never had so much fun in my life."

"There's one thing I still don't get." Greg narrowed his eyes thoughtfully. "Who hired D. B. in the first place?"

"Guilty." Victor raised his hand. "A couple of months ago I started noticing little things that didn't quite make sense. I suspected either I had total idiots working for me or someone was ripping us off. I hired D. B. with the understanding that I didn't want to know what he suspected until he had solid proof. He gave it to me today. And Lindy explained everything else."

"I see," Morgan said quietly. A million thoughts raced through her mind. Morgan glanced down at Sam. His eyes were open and he gazed up at her. She hugged him. "Good dog. I can always count on you, can't I, boy?" Sam staggered to his feet and Morgan got to hers. She stared at her father. "You almost let me marry Win."

"I was just about to open my mouth to stop it when this young man charged in and rescued you." He nodded at Greg. "Good job, son."

"Thanks." A modest smile played across Greg's lips.

"Besides—" Her father pinned her with a pointed glance. "I never imagined you'd actually go through with it."

"Your confidence is overwhelming." Morgan sighed.

"Speaking of confidence, explain that nasty little clause you put in the partnership agreement."

"There's nothing to explain, Morgan." Victor's voice was firm. "Now that you've become involved in the business yourself, you tell me. Would you turn a big chunk of your company over to a daughter who skipped from one adventure to another? Who apparently had no regard for how much she spent or on what? Who went through fiancés like there was no tomorrow?"

Morgan gritted her teeth. "Probably not."

Victor's voice softened. "Don't forget, my darling daughter, after you proved you could handle the job, and you really seemed to care for the company, I thought I had eliminated the clause."

"Okay," she muttered, "I forgive you."

"Good." He laughed and kissed her forehead.

"Excuse me," Lindy said. "Isn't there still that pesky problem of being married to someone you approve of by five-thirty?" Lindy glanced at her watch. "It's five after five."

"That is a problem," Victor murmured.

"I'll marry her." Greg raised his hand.

Victor drew his brows together. "And if I don't approve?"

"A big part of your company goes public. So what." Greg squared his shoulders and looked her father right in the eye. "Look, sir, Phillips and Hughes is a great company. And I'd love to be a part of it. But all I really want is her. Period. She's the only thing that matters to me. So it doesn't matter whether you approve or not."

Victor studied him for a long moment. "Okay, you'll do."

"Hey!" Morgan glared.

Victor called to someone in the hall. "Tell Judge Hanley we're going to have a wedding after all."

"Wait just a minute." Morgan crossed her arms. "Don't I have some say in this?"

"We don't have a license, sir." Greg shook his head. "Will a marriage still be valid for purposes of the agreement without a license?"

"It's the spirit of the agreement, my boy." Victor nodded confidently. "Trust me on this one." He turned to Morgan. "Your mother's probably getting the guests back in their seats. Let's go or we'll never get you two married by five-thirty."

"Hold on!" Morgan stared from her father to Greg to Lindy and back to her father. "What makes you think I'm going to marry him?"

Lindy nudged Victor. "She loves him."

"And I love her." Greg's tone was unyielding.

"Excellent." Victor beamed. "Spencer, I'll give you five minutes to convince her. And if you can't, you have my permission to drag her back kicking and screaming the same way you hauled her up here." He ushered everyone out of the room, and Greg and Morgan were alone.

She drew a long breath. "This won't work."

"Why not?"

"You know why not."

"Morgan." His gaze caught and locked with hers. "I watched you during all this with Win."

Memories of the encounter with Win, the fear, the helplessness the sorrow rushed over her.

"You had that feeling, that sense that we'd done this before, didn't you?"

"Yes," she whispered.

"I think," he stepped toward her and took her

hands in his. His words were measured as if he was still working them out for himself. "I think that we made it."

"What?" Confusion washed through her.

"Don't you see? This is the tragedy you've been so afraid of. Win could have killed us both. Or worse for me"—his eyes held an intensity that caught at her heart and stole her soul—"he could have killed you. I couldn't have survived that. I can't live without you."

"I can't live without you either." Tears fogged her eyes.

"Then marry me, Morgan Phillips," he lifted her hands to his lips.

"Greg—"

"Marry me now."

"I guess I'd better." She sniffed. "I probably owe these people, especially my mother, a wedding. Any wedding. They've been waiting a long time."

"So have I, my love." He smiled. "So have I."

"Mr. Phillips, there's one thing I still don't understand." Lindy walked beside Victor back to the wedding site.

"And what's that, Lindy?"

"Well," she stopped and studied him. "This is a private company. Nothing is really written in stone. Why can't you and Mr. Hughes just do what you want? I mean why bother with this five-thirty deadline business?"

"No reason, really." Victor shrugged. "And you're absolutely right. We can do exactly what we want.

There's no reason in the world to push this wedding today. But Morgan doesn't have to know that."

"But—"

"Think about it, Lindy, if you had a daughter who'd been through seven engagements—"

Lindy raised a brow. "You count the Italian?"

Victor snorted. "I'm her father. I count them all. Anyway, when you have a daughter like that, who you love dearly by the way, and you meet a man who doesn't want her money, who's already risked his life for her and who looks at her like nothing else in the world exists except her—and, in case you didn't notice, she looks at him the same way—well, you just don't want to let that one get away. This couldn't have turned out better if I'd planned it all myself." Victor chuckled. "I figure it's part of a father's job to do what he can to make sure his little girl lives happily ever after. Besides, I'm getting too old to keep giving away a daughter who keeps bouncing back."

"Yeah, but at least she hasn't gone through marriages the same way she's gone through engagements."

"She's never been in jail either." Victor shook his head. "I'd hate to push my luck on either score."

She gazed into his eyes, dark as a stormy sky and filled with love and passion and the promise of eternity, and repeated the words after the judge. Words she'd never paid much attention to. Words with a whole new meaning.

"...to have and to hold from this day forward..."

For now and for always.

"...until death do us part..."

His lopsided smile clutched at her heart and she knew somewhere in the depths of her soul that even death would not end what they'd found with each other. He was right. It was fate. They were meant to be together as surely as the sun was meant to rise tomorrow. As surely as the stars were meant to wink and laugh over the heads of lovers who waltzed through nights filled with dreams.

And nights filled as well with one true love destined to last for all time. A love fated to pull their souls together again and again.

A love they would know not just once...

...but forever.

What ya think, kid? Pretty good, huh? . . .

Yeah, me too. I had a job to do and I did it. And a damned fine job if I do say so myself.

What? This? Nah. It's just a scratch. Only hurts when I laugh. Heh heh heh-ow! Just kidding.

Relax, kid. The tough part's over. The mission's at an end. Pippa and Spencer, I should say Morgan and Greg, are gonna spend their lives together the way it was always meant to be. It's swell.

Me? All I got left to do now is live out a long and happy life as a pampered pup. A little game of fetch here and there. A good movie now and then. It's gonna be great. Have you caught how they're treatin' me these days? Yeah. Like a real hero. I could get used to this.

Let's go check out the kitchen. See what kind of chow they got in there for us. Somethin' tasty I hope.

And I got a confession to make to ya, kid. I couldn't have pulled this one off without ya. You were a big help. And ya know, I've gotten used to ya. Yeah, I kind of like having ya around.

In fact, Louie, I think this is the beginning of a beautiful friendship.

Dear Readers,

This book gave me the unique opportunity to discover a new love and rekindle an old.

The old, of course, is the work of Humphrey Bogart. What a terrific actor and what great movies! And what a wonderful excuse to watch them. ("No, sweetie, Mom isn't watching movies. This is research.")

And I fell in love with Bearded Collies. Researching the breed convinced me this would be the perfect dog for my family. Thanks to a concentrated campaign (including taping pictures of the breed all over the house) we should have a Beardie by the time you read this. Naturally, we'll call him Sam.

By the way, I love to get mail. Write to me at:

P.O. Box 31544
Omaha, NE 68131

In the meantime: Here's looking at you, kid.
I've always wanted to say that.

Love,

Victoria

IT'S A DOG'S LIFE ROMANCE

Stray Hearts by Annie Kimberlin. A busy veterinarian, Melissa is comfortable around her patients—but when it comes to men, too often her instincts have her barking up the wrong tree. So she's understandably wary when Peter Winthrop, who accidentally hits a Shetland sheepdog with his car, shows more than just a friendly interest in her. But as their relationship grows more intimate she finds herself hoping that he has room for one more lost soul in his home.

___52221-7 $5.50 US/$6.50 CAN

Rosamunda's Revenge by Emma Craig. At first, Tacita Grantham thinks that Jedediah Hardcastle is a big brute of a man with no manners whatsoever. But when she sees he'll do anything to protect her—even rescue her beloved Rosamunda—she knows his bark is worse than his bite. And when she first feels his kiss—she knows he is the only man who'll ever touch her heart.

___52213-6 $5.50 US/$6.50 CAN

Dorchester Publishing Co., Inc.
P.O. Box 6640
Wayne, PA 19087-8640

Please add $1.75 for shipping and handling for the first book and $.50 for each book thereafter. NY, NYC, and PA residents, please add appropriate sales tax. No cash, stamps, or C.O.D.s. All orders shipped within 6 weeks via postal service book rate. Canadian orders require $2.00 extra postage and must be paid in U.S. dollars through a U.S. banking facility.

Name_____
Address_____
City_____ State_____ Zip_____
I have enclosed $_____ in payment for the checked book(s).
Payment <u>must</u> accompany all orders. ❑ Please send a free catalog.

DON'T MISS *LOVE SPELL'S* WAGGING TALES OF LOVE!

MIRIAM RAFTERY

Taylor James's wrinkled Shar-Pei, Apollo, is always getting into trouble. But the young beauty never expects her mischievous puppy to lead her on the romantic adventure of a lifetime—from a dusty old Victorian attic to the strong arms of Nathaniel Stuart and his turn-of-the-century charm. One minute Taylor and Apollo are in modern-day San Francisco, and the next thing Taylor knows, a shift in the earth's crust, a wrinkle in time, and the lovely historian finds herself facing the terror of California's most infamous earthquake—and a love so monumental it threatens to shake the foundations of her world.

_52084-2 $4.99 US/$6.99 CAN

Dorchester Publishing Co., Inc.
P.O. Box 6640
Wayne, PA 19087-8640

Please add $1.75 for shipping and handling for the first book and $.50 for each book thereafter. NY, NYC, and PA residents, please add appropriate sales tax. No cash, stamps, or C.O.D.s. All orders shipped within 6 weeks via postal service book rate. Canadian orders require $2.00 extra postage and must be paid in U.S. dollars through a U.S. banking facility.

Name_____
Address_____
City_____ State_____ Zip_____
I have enclosed $_____ in payment for the checked book(s).
Payment <u>must</u> accompany all orders. ☐ Please send a free catalog.

Christmas means more than just puppy love.

"SHAKESPEARE AND THE THREE KINGS"
Victoria Alexander
Requiring a trainer for his three inherited dogs, Oliver Stanhope meets D. K. Lawrence, and is in for the Christmas surprise—and love—of his life.

"ATHENA'S CHRISTMAS TAIL" Nina Coombs
Mercy wants her marriage to be a match of the heart—and with the help of her very determined dog, Athena, she finds just the right magic of the holiday season.

"AWAY IN A SHELTER" Annie Kimberlin
A dedicated volunteer, Camille Campbell still doesn't want to be stuck in an animal shelter on Christmas Eve—especially with a handsome helper whose touch leaves her starry-eyed.

"MR. WRIGHT'S CHRISTMAS ANGEL"
Miriam Raftery
When Joy's daughter asks Santa for a father, she knows she's in trouble—until a trip to Alaska takes them on a journey into the arms of Nicholas Wright and his amazing dog.

___52235-7 $5.99 US/$6.99 CAN

Dorchester Publishing Co., Inc.
P.O. Box 6640
Wayne, PA 19087-8640

Please add $1.75 for shipping and handling for the first book and $.50 for each book thereafter. NY, NYC, and PA residents, please add appropriate sales tax. No cash, stamps, or C.O.D.s. All orders shipped within 6 weeks via postal service book rate. Canadian orders require $2.00 extra postage and must be paid in U.S. dollars through a U.S. banking facility.

Name_____
Address_____
City_____ State_____ Zip_____
I have enclosed $_____ in payment for the checked book(s).
Payment <u>must</u> accompany all orders. ❑ Please send a free catalog.

A FAERIE TALE ROMANCE

VICTORIA ALEXANDER

Ophelia Kendrake has barely finished conning the coat off a cardsharp's back when she stumbles into Dead End, Wyoming. Mistaken for the Countess of Bridgewater, Ophelia sees no reason to reveal herself until she has stripped the hamlet of its fortunes and escaped into the sunset. But the free-spirited beauty almost swallows her script when she meets Tyler, the town's virile young mayor. When Tyler Matthews returns from an Ivy League college, he simply wants to settle down and enjoy the simplicity of ranching. But his aunt and uncle are set on making a silk purse out of Dead End, and Tyler is going to be the new mayor. It's a job he takes with little relish—until he catches a glimpse of the village's newest visitor.

_52159-8 $5.50 US/$6.50 CAN

Dorchester Publishing Co., Inc.
P.O. Box 6640
Wayne, PA 19087-8640